DRACO SANG BOOK 1

DRAGON BLOOD

MARY BEESLEY

MONSTER IVY
PUBLISHING

Volkar Lake
GRISTLECOVE
NANSUT
ELYSIU
Vhril River
Bahana River
MITEF
NE
BRANMAR
SICCUM
S
N
W
E
S

Dragon's Gate
Nogard's Pass
Azure Lake
Shi Castle
Danbe Canyon
Draco Sang Camp
Lion's Camp
Kiptos
Abaddon
PHA
High Sea
Scorpion Sea

*To Teancum. He laid down his life for his friends.
Greater love hath no man than this.*

ONE - DISGRACED
CAL

Cal needed to kill something. He needed to eat.

He prowled the desert as if he were king of the sand—a far cry from the truth. His sweaty palm tightened on his hunting knife, his prized possession. Steps quiet, he neared the Sahana River. No animals, no tracks, no life. The dead bank glistened in the heat, taunting him. He glowered back.

Cal followed the curves north to where a jumble of rocks crossed the river, making it more secluded than the open banks. Water splashed ahead. He crouched behind a boulder, stomach clenching in the hope that he'd found prey. His tongue rasped over chapped lips.

Peeking through the slabs, Cal spied a girl digging for fiddlers. He swallowed his spit and ground his teeth. She would have scared any larger prey far away. Unhappy fingers twitched on his knife.

The girl was young, maybe nine or ten. She knelt in the languid water, twisting her hands into the riverbed. With a grunt of pain, she yanked her arm free. A palm-sized crea-ture with a thorny shell and squiggly barbed legs clung to the flesh of her thumb. Teeth-tight, she levered a knife between the shells and pried them open, revealing one bite of meat.

Cal had zero skill at catching fiddlers. It took patience. Lots of patience.

She tossed the prickly brown shell onto the sand and held up a glossy muscle tinged pink with her blood. Instead of putting the morsel in her mouth, as Cal would have done, she set the meat in a basket on the far riverbank. The inside of the wicker shone with the gleam of dozens of fiddlers.

Cal stared; saliva coated his tongue. There were enough for a real dinner. Enough to satisfy the ache in his belly. Enough to take some home to his ma.

He swallowed. He needed to get across the river and within arm's reach of that basket.

He jerked behind the rock, squelching the thought of stealing. Cal wasn't a thief. He focused on a black bug burrowing in the sand—all crunch and goo, no meat. Images of fiddlers sprang back to his mind. Stealing was wrong. And yet, his hunger was wrong too.

He craned his neck, peeking over the boulder. The girl yanked another fiddler from the earth. It dangled in her fingers, taunting him. He should join her in the hunt, dig for his own fiddlers. He'd managed to catch a few before, but tonight, the thought of doing the tedious work repulsed him. His whole body hummed with impatience. He rolled to the balls of his feet as hunger took control.

He buried the tip of his hunting knife in the sand by his feet. His long tunic and leather sandals landed next to it. Wearing only his shorts, he stalked toward the water. Her back was to him, her focus on her work. He should turn around. Leave her alone. Stealing was severely punished by the Elders. He'd promised Ma he wouldn't get into more trouble. He told himself to stop, but the meal beckoned. Darkness rose in his breast, forcing him forward. As silent as a breeze, he waded across the slow water. His calloused palm shot forward and dug into the basket. Raw fiddlers squished in his grip.

The girl turned, her eyes wide. He was sixteen, much bigger and stronger than she. She shrank back as her focus flicked from his full fist to his bare chest to his hard-set jaw.

He told himself to give back her fiddlers, that this was wrong, but his body had come untethered from his mind. An invisible force seemed to control him as he brought the fiddlers to his mouth, but before the tenderness passed his lips, a rough palm gripped his shoulder and yanked him back.

Cal whirled. Fiddlers flew and disappeared under the brown surface of the water. "No!"

"What do you think you're doing?" The deep voice was hard.

Rage replaced Cal's hunger as he stared at the ripples in the water. A good meal, gone.

Hands on hips, a large man glared down at Cal. "I recognize you, Callidon Mirrason. It's not the first time you've broken the pact. Wait until the Elders hear about you stealing from my daughter."

Dread curled in Cal's belly. Not another tribunal. He refused to stand before the Elders again and be told how he was a disgrace. How he was *cursed.*

Apologize and promise restitution, that's what he needed to do, but the words wouldn't come. The violent force growing within him seemed to flex and crackle to life. Cal's fingers curled tight.

"I don't think even your ma can convince them you aren't cursed now."

Cal swung for the man's nose, but he ducked as if he'd been expecting it. He threw out a punch, slamming his fist into Cal's stomach. Cal stumbled and fell, crashing into the river. The girl's scream pierced the water as her father's foot pinned Cal to the muddy bottom. Rocks sliced his back. Hot panic swirled through his chest as he fought the urge to inhale. He shifted left, and the foot shoved harder. His back barked in pain. His lungs howled for breath, but his mind sharpened and calmed.

Water distorted the man's voice as he yelled down at Cal under the surface. "Are you done fighting?"

Cal was just getting started. Gripping a small rock, he rammed it into a hairy calf. The water slowed the thrust, but he twisted it into the muscles. Red swirls inked the murk. The foot recoiled, and Cal wrenched free. He plowed to the surface. Panting and dripping, Cal spun to face his foe. He adjusted his grip on the stone and raked wet hair out of his eyes. Anger throbbed, commanding him to strike.

"Stop!" the girl cried.

Cal's nerves hummed in anticipation. Initiating violence as he had done was forbidden in Siccum. For sixteen years, he'd tried to keep his head down, eating porridge and mining the burning sand for precious little gold to live by. Cal had been a servant of the greater good, weak and obedient. *Not anymore,* said a voice in his mind. A menacing growl issued from his belly.

The man swung, his fist aiming for Cal's face. Cal ducked. Following through with the rock, he smashed the man's elbow. The crack reverberated through Cal's wrist. The man staggered back. Blood dripped down his forearm, which dangled awkwardly at his side.

The painful angle of the arm, or perhaps the girl's symphony of screams, jarred Cal out of his one-track rage. The bloodthirsty filter fell from his eyes. He blinked, and the scene refocused. He saw the cowering girl and the bleeding man. A father protecting his daughter. One of the families from his village who suffered through the same searing Siccum summers as he did.

The urge that had driven him to cruelty abandoned him, leaving him hollow and ashamed. The rock slipped from his fingers and buried itself in the slow current.

"I'm sorry." Even his voice had lost its strength. What had he done?

He clambered up the rocks and snatched his belongings without pause. He ran north, away from his village. When sand burned his feet and sun scorched the scratches on his back, he put on his tunic and sandals. He trudged through barren desert, failing to find any prey, his mind preoccupied with the failures of the day. He knew stealing was wrong. And attacking that man was worse. How could he face Ma and Grandpapi now, especially after he'd lashed out at them at dinner? Loneliness and shame twisted like a knife. Bile rose in his throat, but his stomach had nothing to expel.

He returned to the river, abandoned of all but discarded fiddler shells. He stripped and slid under the water. Regret rolled over him. Scrubbing at his limbs, he tried to wash his wrongs away. But as he plodded home, they clung to him, as painfully as his shirt stuck to the cuts on his back.

Like a beacon far across the sand, the lights of Siccum called. As the night settled in, the heat of the day lifted. A breeze ran cool fingers through his wet hair. Come summer, he wouldn't have any relief. He seemed to struggle with the festering heat more than others.

He slunk around the north wall and entered the city gate near his two-bedroom home. Hunger gnawed. If only he'd been a second faster and gotten the fiddlers into his mouth…

He entered his small yard and locked the gate behind him, securing it against night predators. In front of the house, his ma and her father, Grandpapi, sat on rocking chairs in the sand. Unlit torches dotted the circular wall protecting their home. The family hen clucked and pecked at Cal's toes.

"Cal, you're home." Relief softened Ma's voice.

Grandpapi scowled in disappointed silence. Cal knelt before Ma's chair, forcing his knees to bend and his head to bow.

"I'm sorry about before. I'm sorry I said your dinner wasn't good enough. I'm sorry I spit on the table. I don't know what came over me." That was the truth. And Cal knew he'd better get control of his new impulses fast. People already thought him cursed. The curse of Prince Nogard, the Black Dragon, was a myth meant to scare people into submission. Despite the stories, naughty children did not grow into monsters. "I lost my temper. I'm grateful to have food, *any* food. Please, forgive me."

Night shaded Ma's expression, but he felt tenderness in her fingers when she lifted his chin. "I'm sorry we don't have more. I know how you go hungry."

"No," he lied. "You feed me well." It wasn't her fault porridge no longer satisfied. It wasn't her fault greed had possessed him like a crazed beast.

"Shh. Just a minute." Her thin robes, smelling of citrus and sage, rustled against his face as she stood. She slipped into the house and returned a moment later with a ceramic bowl. "It's cold now."

He took it with thanks, hunger snapping within him.

"She wouldn't let me eat it," Grandpapi said. Starlight reflected off white hair.

Cal wolfed down his meager porridge. "I'm sorry, Grandpapi. I acted terribly at dinner."

"You did." Grandpapi's tone cut like shards.

If only that were the only thing he had to confess. He sucked in a long breath and forced the next words out. "Something happened down at the river."

Ma and Grandpapi tensed as if expecting a blow.

"A girl was digging for fiddlers." Cal gulped. "And I sort of tried to take them." He stared at the flecks of gray sand to avoid their disappointed faces. "I didn't see her father at first."

Insects hissed and fluttered across the silence.

Head down, he whispered, "I attacked him when he stopped me from eating the fiddlers I'd taken." His voice cracked. "I hurt him. Badly." He roughly swiped at watery eyes as he waited for a response that didn't come. "I will be summoned to tribunal. Again." His previous offenses had been petty things, nothing like this. What would his punishment be? Working the giretorbie pits was the worst. The smell unbearable.

Eyes glittering with fear, Ma reached up and wrapped thin arms around his shoulders. "Everyone makes mistakes." Her voice lacked conviction.

He straightened his spine. "I'm going to apologize. Maybe I can talk them out of telling the Elders."

Grandpapi's raspy voice was hard. "Tomorrow you can see if that does any good. But it's time to put this day to bed. You must rise better. Your heart must be stronger than your flesh. Do not give in to dark desires." Grandpapi stretched out a wrinkled hand, and Cal lifted him easily from his seat.

"Too strong for your own good," Grandpapi mumbled as the boy helped him into the house.

Cal brought the rocking chairs inside. They would need them for breakfast.

"I'm sorry," Cal said, wishing he could erase the hurt he'd caused his family. Wishing he could start the day over and end up the conqueror instead of the accused.

"Good night, my love." Ma's voice was kind, but her eyes betrayed deep sadness. She looked so tired.

With regret wedging between his ribs, Cal slipped out the

door and sucked in the cooling air. The curious hen waddled over to his feet.

"I don't have food for you," Cal said. "You're supposed to have food for me. You look plump enough for a good meal."

He plucked the bird off the ground. Tying the rope around the hen's neck, while trying not to think about breaking it, he tethered her to the far wall. His family depended on the daily egg, and he had no right to kill his mother's hen. Last year he'd saved his spending money for months, foregoing food and a new tunic to buy that bird for Ma. That was a long time ago. A different Cal. A good one.

Cal flung out his thin rug and spread it on the flat sand. As he lay on his back and looked at the bright stars, hungry jaws snapped in his gut. Sleep. Tomorrow there would be porridge. He wrapped his arms around his belly, trying to squeeze out the sharp demands. It failed. Rolling to his feet, he paced, debating the fate of the chicken.

Near the house he heard their whispers.

The window rug was pulled back to let in the night air. The hush of Ma and Grandpapi's voices drifted through. Cal crouched below the window.

"Can't prevent it," Grandpapi said.

Ma's sigh was heavy with despair. "It's happening so quickly. I'm scared."

Cal's ears strained as his mind scrambled over the words.

"It's time to go north," Grandpapi said quietly.

Go north? Cal had begged to leave Siccum for years. He looked forward to the caravan's rare appearances, not just for the treats and trading, but to ask the travelers' questions about the wider world. Each time he built hope they could travel north with the caravan; each time Ma flatly refused.

"We can't do this on our own anymore," Grandpapi said. "It's time to find the Lion."

The hairs on Cal's arms rose at the weight of the whispered word, *Lion.* He risked a peek over the window sill. His family huddled at the table.

"Oh, Papi, I'd hoped we could have escaped it. Fifteen years in this forsaken sandpit and still …" her voice dissolved.

She hated it here too? The realization rocked Cal. She'd always been so cheerful. Annoyingly peppy. *Fake.*

Ma's head drooped in her hands as she sobbed. Her loose hair blanketed her arm, the golden hue so different from Cal's dark brown. A trait he assumed he inherited from his father. He knew so little of the man.

Grandpapi's withered fingers rubbed Ma's back with tenderness. "Don't despair for things you can't control. You did your best, my dear. But the boy is changing. His father's poisonous blood is ripening." Unfamiliar rancor hardened Grandpapi's voice.

Cal reeled, falling back on his heels. They were talking about *him.* His fingernails dug into the clay wall, anchoring him. The rare times Ma spoke of his father, she painted him a hero. A hardworking fisherman who died in the silver waters of the Scorpion Sea, aptly named for the sting in its waves. *She lied.*

Outrage spread through his skeleton. "I'm poisoned?" Cal's sharp accusation blasted across the room.

Ma and Grandpapi jerked their heads. Ma scrubbed at the salty streaks down her cheeks. "Cal. Honey. I thought you were asleep."

Cal vaulted through the window. Ma recoiled. His temper cooled at her fright. He perched on his chair and rested his clasped hands gently on the table. Slow breath. "What are we escaping? What's happening too fast? What about my father's blood? You talk like the Elders—like I'm cursed."

Ma cowered like the rats Cal trapped in his snares. He

counted in his head to keep from lashing out with impatience. *One. Two. Answer me. Three. Four.*

Ma swallowed. "Your father did some terrible things."

Grandpapi didn't refute it. He speared Cal with distrustful eyes.

Cal's jaw dropped. "You lied to me."

"Yes." Ma held his gaze, no longer quailing. "He's dead." Her voice was cold. Remorseless.

"You're glad." His world shifted. He sucked in a dizzy breath.

Ma ignored the comment. "And so, I painted a new picture of him. I remade him into the honorable man I wanted you to become."

And he'd failed. He couldn't hold Ma's stare. Or answer for the things he'd done. He'd caused her tears and pain.

And his father had been a bad man.

Apparently brown hair and broad shoulders weren't the only things he'd inherited from the stranger. And Ma and Grandpapi hated him for it.

Cal stood. They didn't move. "I'm sorry. I'll do better."

No reassuring replies. No words of encouragement.

He shuffled away. Forsaken silence followed him out the door. He crawled onto his mat. Questions bombarded. Who was his father really? What bad things had he done? Cal wanted the truth.

For hours he lay sleepless, searching the starry sky. No answers appeared there. When the moon slipped behind a lonely wisp of cloud, he rose and crept into the quiet house. As if he were a shadow, he stalked into Ma's bedroom. She kept her personal things in a tin box at the bottom of her trunk. He hesitated. He'd never dared invade her privacy before. It was wrong.

But, she'd disrespected him first. She lied to him. He undid the latch. She rolled over in her sleep. He shifted some cloth and lifted out a small box. Creeping from the room, he also stole one of their precious candles before drifting outside. Sitting on his mat, he opened the box. An amber ring glinted in the low light. How much food could this have bought them? Pushing that unhappy thought aside, he took out a stack of papers. He skimmed dozens of letters from his aunt Elssa. Nothing of interest he didn't already know. Cousins in Mitera. Gossip about strangers.

At the bottom was a stiffer piece of parchment. Block letters blazed across the page. He held the candle flame closer. The bottom of the note and the signature were gone, but he gobbled up the remaining words.

DEAREST MIRA,
I'LL BEG YOU FOR THE LAST TIME. PLEASE COME HOME.
I MISS YOU DESPERATELY. YOU'VE PROVED YOU WILL
SACRIFICE EVERYTHING TO PROTECT YOUR SON. BUT
YOU CAN'T PREVENT HIM FROM GROWING INTO A
DRACO SANG. IT WILL HAPPEN—EVEN IN SICCUM.

Cal rubbed his eyes. He squinted as he re-read the shocking words. What in the great skies?

YOU CAN'T PRETEND AWAY OR OUTRUN THE DRAGON'S
*BLOOD, MIRA—I **KNOW** THIS. PLEASE FACE THE FACTS.*
*PLEASE LET ME HELP YOU. I **CAN** HELP HIM.*
I FAILED TO PROTECT YOU ONCE. I CAN NEVER
FORGIVE MYSELF FOR YOUR SUFFERING. I WILL NOT
LET HARM COME TO YOU AGAIN. NO ONE WILL HURT
YOU. I SWEAR IT ON EIO. COME HOME. WE WILL
PROTECT YOU. I'VE DEVOTED—

The paper was torn at the end of the line. Cal wheezed out the breath he'd been holding.

I am Draco Sang.

Ma had taught him a little about the Draco Sang. Warlike, primitive, and vile, they constantly fought amongst themselves, the weak becoming slaves to the powerful. Ma had said their leader, Queen Mavras, had risen to power fourteen years ago by killing the king, her brother. Apparently, that was a common tradition in their land. The Draco Sang lived in Skotar, the country just north of his kingdom of Elysium. The raging Rugit River separated their worlds.

The Draco Sang were the enemy.

Cal stared at the paper; all inklings of fatigue blasted away by the words. He looked up at the stars, chest tight with anxiety as he remembered the common tale of the *cursed* Draco Sang.

Long ago, there lived a prince. Nogard, the second son by a year and a day, wanted to be king. He killed his father and moved to end his brother, but the crown prince, Enosh, discovered the plot. Soft-hearted Enosh could not bring the sword of justice down on his brother. Instead, he banished Nogard from the Kingdom of Skotar.

Nogard climbed the icy mountains where only beasts dare go. In the cave of a hibernating bear, he found his salvation. Nourished by the blood of the beast, he swore his revenge on Skotar. Wearing the bear's fur as his own, Nogard returned when summer kissed the kingdom. His brother's wife, Queen Ima, picnicked in the sun with her ladies. Only one man guarded the group. And he stood on the southern edge—a fool.

Nogard took pleasure in killing the guard. And the

women. Until only Queen Ima remained. She was beauty and grace. Lust ripened within him. She fought, but his soul had turned cold. When he'd finished with her, he held his spear above her heart. A fragment of her brightness struck him, and he could not kill her. "Tell my brother hello," he said with a voice harsh from disuse. He left Ima bleeding on the summer grass.

Enosh sent his soldiers to hunt his brother, but they did not return.

Inside the queen, a baby grew.

High in the mountains, through icy winters and frozen summers, Nogard's heart turned to stone, and his skin scaled over as he transformed into The Black Dragon. When his leathery wings were strong enough, Nogard took to the sky. He descended on Skotar, tearing apart the castle with talons and teeth until he found his dear brother and the queen. Nogard held them in his arms, high in the sky, where they could watch the destruction as he burned to the ground the kingdom that was his greatest desire. Only a few farmers in the fields survived.

Nogard set Enosh, Ima, and the small son in her arms down among the ashes. To suffer life without their precious castle and kingdom—Nogard's worst punishment. Little did he know the true punishment he'd given. The curse he'd created.

That little boy grew.

He grew into a dragon, too.

And if you follow Nogard down paths of hatred and greed, then, little child, you will become a monster, too.

People always included that last line when telling the story. It didn't feel so ridiculous now, not when Cal felt mean and angry inside. But, he didn't believe in any cursing. The Draco Sang were no more *monsters* than he was.

Blood thrashing, Cal tore through Ma's box for the rest of the letter, but it was fruitless. He slumped as he reread the short passage that changed everything. Who had written this? Who knew his father? Who knew about him?

Fingers trembling, he carefully replaced Ma's things and tiptoed the box back to her trunk. He wanted to scream at her, but he bit down on his tongue and swallowed coppery blood instead. Sleep veiled Ma with youth and peace. The worry lines around her eyes had disappeared.

The letter had said, *"You've proved you will sacrifice everything to protect your son."*

Despite her lies, she was his whole world. He loved her with all his wild heart. His frustration softened, but still he wondered what she was protecting him from. The same thing that had hurt her? He slipped out, replacing the candle and returning to his sleeping mat.

Stars rained down. He rubbed the water out of his eyes, and the lights reaffixed in the sky. Devastation mixed with fatigue. He was a Draco Sang pup. The enemy. And his mother had kept it from him—and his grandpapi hated him for it. Why?

Groggy and grumpy, Cal woke to a jaundiced sky. Last night's words replayed in his mind. Not the words about his failure. No. He buried that guilt. He thought of Ma and Grandpapi's covert conversation about him. He thought of the letter. He was Draco Sang.

Whatever that meant.

The hen across the yard pecked at the barren ground. A brown egg shone from her pile of straw. He marched to the spot, picked up the egg, and cracked it into his mouth. Slimy warmth slipped down his throat, washing over his hunger. He cocked his arm and hurled the shell over the wall. He peed in the fresh hole he'd dug behind the house. Ma's shuffling feet and the clang of her breakfast pan called him inside.

"Good morning, son." With a smile, she passed him a handful of kernels and scraps. He didn't smile back. "Please take these to the chicken and bring me the egg."

"There wasn't one. I already looked."

Ma frowned. "All right. Well. I guess we'll do without. I'm sorry, dear."

As Cal fed the chicken, remorse failed to hack its way through the ice forming on his heart, ice that Cal hardly noticed. Back inside, he sat at the table. Ma fiddled with the small oil burner. She established a flame and set a metal plate over the top.

"Cakes today?" Cal asked, delighted.

"I thought we'd do something special. They'd be better with an egg."

He wasn't sorry. She'd lied to him.

"But I'll mix in some porridge, and they'll be just fine. I've even got three oranges left. We can put one on top."

"I thought we were saving those for Drosday fest."

A shadow passed over her face, and she paused her mixing of the dense batter. "We're not. Please go wake your grandpapi for breakfast."

Patience fraying and questions buzzing in his mouth, Cal clamped down his retort and obeyed. He pulled back the sheet that hung in the doorway to Grandpapi's small room. Yellow light streamed onto the old man.

"Up, up. The Siccum sun awaits."

"The Siccum sun waits for no one." Grandpapi's eyes stayed closed.

"Ma's making cakes."

"I'm up." He lifted his head and unsuccessfully tried to sit.

Cal chuckled. He moved to the bed and hauled the elderly man to his feet.

"Not so fast." Grandpapi wobbled. He tugged on his thin tunic. Cal clamped down on his impatience with the old man as Grandpapi shuffled out of the bedroom and through the kitchen. "Morning, daughter," he said on his way outside to visit the hole.

Cal sat in one of their three chairs, thinking about the long miserable day ahead at the mines. And then he had a tribunal to dread. Ma dropped the first cake onto the hot plate. It sizzled and puffed in a drop of melted lard. She arranged orange segments overtop before setting it in front of Cal.

"Grandpapi first." He said it to show that he could be a good son. *Fool,* said the voice deep inside.

"Thank you, Callidon," Grandpapi said as he walked in and sat. He shoveled an enormous bite into his mouth.

After an eternal minute, Cal's was ready. Orange juice soaked the grainy cake, sweetened with flecks of date. There was nowhere near enough. Never enough. He licked his plate clean. "What's the occasion?"

Ma and Grandpapi shared a pointed look.

"We're leaving Siccum," Ma said. "We're going north."

A smile burst across Cal's face. The north had tugged at him, silently summoned him, every day of his life. And now he was finally going to follow the call of adventure.

"We're leaving," Ma said. "Tomorrow."

He blinked in surprise. "Cross the desert alone? Why not wait for the next caravan?"

"I think it's worth the risk."

"Why?"

She chewed on her lip. "You're changing. You need help controlling your emerging desire for power and dominance."

Cal balked, exposed and embarrassed. She'd cut through his shields and seen straight to his heart.

"There's a man I'd like you to meet. Titus. It would be

good for you to learn from him. He can teach you discipline and control." Ma stacked empty plates. "You used to speak about being a soldier—"

"And you always said no." They'd discouraged his dream of fighting, his interest in war and strategy. He'd learned all he could about battle, but Siccum had little to offer in that department.

"Well, I'm saying yes now."

"Why?" And why hadn't she told him his father was a Draco Sang?

"Because I see you have talents. Ones that are wasted mining the sand."

"What talents?"

Ma's mouth opened, but no words came.

Grandpapi watched Cal. His fingers drummed the table, and Cal clamped his hand down on the annoying beat. Grandpapi jolted back, pulling his hand to his chest as if Cal had burned him.

Cal's brow creased as he looked from Grandpapi to Ma. What else were they not telling him?

"After today at the mines." Ma's voice was an anxious rush. "Close out your wages and inform the chief. I'll settle matters around town. I'll see what I can get for the house and gather supplies. We'll leave tomorrow at dawn." Ma's amber eyes locked on Cal. "It's a long, hard trek out of the desert. You will have to pull Grandpapi and everything else."

"I can do it."

"I know you can. Never forget that you are strong enough. Good enough."

Cal wasn't so sure. An unfamiliar wild simmered beneath his skin.

"It's going to be a hard road ahead." Her voice caught as she spoke, as though she wasn't talking about the journey across the desert, but one far more serious—and difficult.

All roads in Siccum led to Siccum. Where would this new path lead? What kind of welcome would he receive in the north? Could he find his place with the Draco Sang? He anticipated the journey with eagerness. May it lead him *home*.

THREE - CROKATOR
CAL

At the mines, hunched-over figures searched for precious flecks in the endless sand. Cal hardly noticed the sun beating through his thin robes. People he'd lived with, played with, worked with all his life, silently turned on him. They glared their disapproval. News traveled fast. Opinions changed faster. He ignored their pointed looks. His fingers panned the sand without it registering with his brain.

When the pit chief berated him for messing up the line—he hadn't—Cal thought solely of going north, of leaving Siccum and finding *his* people.

At the close of the shift, Cal approached his chief. "Today's my last day."

The man grunted. "I was surprised when they told me what you did. Thought I heard the name wrong. I hate being wrong. Almost as much as I hate to lose a good miner. You fooled me. Just shows, you don't truly know any man's heart."

Cal clenched his jaw, biting back the violence awaking at the chief's words—even if they were true. "Please, can you pay my last wages now? I'm leaving at dawn."

The chief turned a leathered face to Cal and lifted an eyebrow. "Tomorrow? Where would you go?"

"North."

He snorted. "Oh, really? So you're not going to throw yourself into the sea?"

Cal wanted to send him to the waves. "Can I get my wages, please?"

"No. You can't. It's not payday. And do I look like I carry around coin?"

Cal choked back his rising temper. "Where can I go?"

"The account chief comes on payday. How long have you worked here?"

Cal's fingers curled into fists. "I can't wait until next week. Can you please help me?"

"You think you can cross the desert on your own? Without a caravan? You'll die halfway across, especially with that old man. It would be a waste of good coin anyway."

Cal's fist shot forward, connecting with the chief's jaw with a satisfying crunch. The man staggered back, clutching his face. His eyes bulged. Surrounding miners stared in shock. Cal bolted.

Panting and overheated by the time he got home, he slammed the gate. A handcart sat in the yard. Grandpapi rocked in a chair, and Ma bustled about, humming while she packed.

"Last day as a miner," Grandpapi said. "Congratulations."

"They refused to pay me because it isn't wages day."

Ma popped her head out of the house. "That isn't right."

"That's what I thought." Cal paused. "I might have punched the chief to let him know."

"That isn't right, either."

"They robbed me."

"Cal." Ma's voice sharpened.

"I'm sorry. But he deserved it for cheating me." Cal had to smash that smirk off the man's face.

Grandpapi shook his head.

Ma sighed. "I guess we'd better leave now. I'd convinced the Elders to let us go without further punishment if we never return, but we can't afford to stay here tonight and give the angry chief time to plan his retribution." Frustration flashed over her face.

Regret pressed down on Cal. "I'm sorry."

She looked away, jerking at the twine she was tying around a blanket. "I'm almost done packing. We got a decent price for the house, at least. We'll need the money when we get past the sand."

When their belongings were settled in the cart, Cal lifted Grandpapi on top, tucking a blanket around his legs. Ma set the chicken in her father's hands.

"Oh, bother," Grandpapi said as it clucked and flapped.

That sound was going to get annoying fast. "Can't we just eat it and be done with it?" Cal asked.

"We might have to," Ma said. "I hope it doesn't come to that."

Cal took his place at the front of the handcart, where two pieces of wood jutted out on either side. A third piece cut across the front, forming a rectangle frame around him. He put his hands on the front bar and pushed. Slowly, the cart moved through the sand. Ma closed the gate, and together they left the only home Cal had ever known.

A smattering of people watched in hostile puzzlement. Leaving Siccum was as rare as rain. Siccum was a tribe of close-knit families who'd lived here for centuries. Ma and Grandpapi had transplanted from the north fifteen years ago, and they'd struggled to set deep roots. Their pale skin and sharp accents set them apart, but now Cal wondered if there was more to their shunning than that.

They followed the river north, and Siccum disappeared from all but memory. Dusk fell. They stopped at the water's edge, and Grandpapi stretched his legs as they filled their canteens. Ma passed out bananas and cheese, both rare luxuries. Cal savored every bite, thinking that life was getting better and better.

"I know you've already spent a long day at the mines," Ma said. "But we need to keep moving. The farther from the village, the better chance of going unnoticed by night prowlers."

Cal's excitement cooled. There would be no wall to hide behind tonight. He touched the hunting knife that hung on his rope belt.

"If we keep a good pace," Ma said. "We should get to Branmar in seven nights."

Cal loaded Grandpapi back into the cart and started pulling. Stars sprinkled the sky, and the waxing moon guided them. Ma set the pace, and Cal trudged behind, determined to keep up. Left foot. Right. Left. Right. Eyelids drooped. Desert faded as his focus wavered.

As if through fog, the dreaded click of the crokator found Cal. Alarms rang through his nerves.

"Cal." Ma's whisper startled him with her closeness. "It might not know we're here. I'll push from behind, and let's try to outrun it."

What a waste of energy. Of course it had found them. With a jolt of adrenaline, he jogged. The clicks got louder. It came from behind. Where his ma was.

"Get in the cart, Ma." His voice came in huffs.

"Shh."

"Get in the cart!" His shout rolled over the dunes.

"It will slow us down too much."

The hissing accelerated.

"Get in, or I'll stop and throw you in." A fierce need to

protect her drove down his spine. Nothing would happen to her. The threat sharpened his mind and honed his senses.

The cart lagged as Ma's weight landed. Wheels groaned, and so did Grandpapi. Cal's body ached, and his lungs burned. He whirled the cart so it faced backward. The beast had to kill him to get to his family. He ducked out of the frame, pulling his knife free.

The hissing stopped.

If the moonlight hadn't cast a gleam on its eyes, he wouldn't have seen the slithering creature in the darkness. The shadow attacked. Large as the handcart, it reared its long neck and drove poisonous fangs at Cal's chest. He swung, knocking the creature off-course. The sharp scales on its face cut his hand as it struck again. He caught a fang on the edge of his knife. Venom slicked his blade. With a grunt, he heaved the beast back.

"Tail," Ma shouted.

Cal jumped, staggering against the cart as a barbed tail whipped in front of his nose. Frantic, he grabbed the chicken. The gaping mouth dove at him. He thrust the bird between razor teeth as he sliced at the crokator's short front leg. His knife barely penetrated the scaled skin.

With the chicken in its mouth, the animal retreated into darkness. A part of Cal wanted to hunt it down and kill it, but the other part, the part that settled deeply in his chest, the part that had instructed him in this fight, told him to run.

Heart pounding, bleeding hand on fire, Cal scrambled into the front frame of the cart and turned it north. He ran. He ran and he ran. Fear chased him even when the crokator did not.

FOUR - FED
CAL

*N*ight dissipated, and the cart stopped as Cal slid to the sand. Thin hands dragged his body across the dune. Cool water swirled over sweaty skin and pulled at his clothes.

"Drink," Ma said, her voice hoarse.

A trickle soothed his throat, then his blurry eyes sealed shut. When he pried them open, the sun shone high in the sky. He lay on the riverbank, feeling as parched and raw as the grit under his back. A blanket hung tented over him for shade. The strength and determination that championed him during the night had abandoned him. He felt hollow, weak, and hungry. So hungry. He shifted, but his body was unwilling to rise. Ma bolted to his side.

"Water." The word was a croak.

She knelt, cradling his head as if aiding a small child. He reached for the vessel with hands wrapped in linens. Murky thoughts shifted through haze. Ma held the water to his lips as he guzzled. Bit by bit, she fed him cheese, dates, and corn before giving him another stream of water. He sank to the sand, feeling her kiss his brow as his eyes closed.

The sun was greeting the western dunes when he woke. Memories of the crokator and endless running crystallized in his mind. Ma rolled up blankets while Grandpapi waded ankle-deep in the Sahana. Gingerly, Cal got to his feet. Everything ached. Ma unwrapped his hands. He gasped at the cuts, blisters, and blood. Deep gashes marred the back of his hand where the crokator had touched him.

"At least we finally put that chicken to good use," Cal said.

Ma's worried face cracked, revealing her white smile. "That was impressive back there. You figured out what needed to be done, and you did it. You saved us."

Her words spread healing warmth through his body. He'd done something right.

She squeezed his sore forearm. "I'm very proud of you."

His lips curved into a grateful grin.

Ma washed the linens and set them to dry. Cal waded past Grandpapi into the river. Though the water was too warm, it soothed the soreness pervading his body. After drinking his fill, Cal slipped under the waist-high current, letting the water lick the sweat and grime from his skin. When he shuffled back to the bank, Ma handed him a brimming bowl.

"Don't we need to save some of this?" Cal asked, looking down at the mound of porridge.

"You went twice as far as I thought humanly possible last night. Eat."

He did.

Ma studied him as if seeing him anew. "I couldn't get you to stop. You nearly ran yourself to death."

"I'm tired, not dead."

"But I couldn't reach you. I yelled, my throat raw. It's like you didn't even hear me."

"I don't think I did." He had heard only his heart, pumping him forward. Carrying his remaining family away from danger.

Shaking her head, she gathered the linens that had dried in the hot air. She smeared the last of their lard onto his cuts and blisters before wrapping his hands again. Muscles screamed as he lifted Grandpapi into the cart. They walked slowly. He didn't think he could have moved faster even if the crokator attacked again, yet a voice within him whispered, *yes, I could.*

The next day, Cal killed a snake that got curious about their camp, and they feasted on oily meat. As they walked, Ma told Cal more about the northern cities. She was from Kiptos, near the northern border. She talked about her sister in Mitera, the capital, where the king and his council of twelve rajas lived. She talked about the soldier friend she had grown up with named Titus. She said nothing about Cal's father. Nothing about the Draco Sang. They walked for miles. At the fire crossing, where melted earth burned endless holes in the sand, they had to slog through the middle of the river, fighting the current. Even still, a flying fragment of molten sand from a spitting hole burned Grandpapi's leg, nearly catching the cart on fire.

But they made it across the desert alive.

After the fifth night of traveling, as the sun began to illuminate the world, Cal saw green. It spread like a vibrant carpet before them. Bushes grew along the riverbanks. Tiny red and white flowers dotted the ground. The earth didn't give under his feet like the dunes. It held solid with dirt, minerals, and rock.

Ma clapped her hand to her chest. Her eyes sparkled like the yellow buds on the trees. Joy danced on her face. "Papi. Wake up. Wake up!"

"Morning already? Are we stopping?" came the muffled response.

"We've made it! Branmar is just over that rise."

Grandpapi sat up and laughed. Tears rolled over his wrinkles. "I didn't think I would see this side of the desert again. I didn't hope. I thought I would die with sand in my eyes."

Cal stopped the cart as Ma bounced over and kissed Grandpapi's wet cheek. Her forehead pressed against his.

Watching the awed joy on their faces, Cal's eagerness boiled anew. What would Aunt Elssa's house in Mitera be like? Would they welcome him? Would he get a glimpse of King Andras or one of the ruling rajas? Would Titus be willing to train him as a soldier, as Ma had said? He wanted to learn more about the Draco Sang and his father.

"Let's rest here for a bit before going to town," Ma said. "They won't thank us for arriving before the sun."

In the cool river, Cal took his time scrubbing away sand and stink—the past. He dropped near a skinny tree. He ran fingers along the bark, relishing the pleasure of velvety leaves. Blades of grass slipped through his fingers as he closed his eyes, but pinging thoughts kept sleep out. He'd rarely seen northerners. Once or twice a year, merchants came to Siccum with long caravans to trade goods for gold. At those times, the northerners adopted the cool robes and tunics worn in Siccum. He wanted to see the gowns and suits described in Ma's stories. He opened his eyes. Heads together, Ma and Grandpapi spoke in hushed voices.

"What's the plan?" he asked as he approached, annoyed to be left out. Again.

"Couldn't sleep? Shall we keep going?" Ma's voice betrayed her excitement.

"I had a great night's sleep," Grandpapi said. "I'm ready to see civilization. Sit down with a cup of tavo."

"Tavo?"

"Just you wait." Grandpapi scrambled to his feet as fast as he could, which wasn't fast at all. Giddy as a child, he marched north, past where the cart waited. "And I'm never getting in that wretched cage again."

Cal grunted in surprise and followed, pulling the lighter cart easily over the hardening ground. It was another mile before they saw the first house. Grandpapi's initial energy had worn off. He dragged along with his arm over Ma's shoulders, refusing to get into the cart. At this slow pace, Cal soaked up the details of the town, where they made houses out of precious wood, and each had its own garden. No gate or outer wall barred their entry. Two boys ran up and studied them as they entered town. Cal stared back.

Ma led them to a door with the words *The Oasis* cut into it. She knocked. The widest woman Cal had ever seen opened the door. His eyes bulged at her low bodice and large hips. No one in Siccum had the luxury of overeating.

"Happy morning to you." The woman dusted flour off her hands onto her dirty apron.

Yes, it is. Siccum lay behind. Fatness lay ahead.

"We're traveling through and looking for a room for the night," Ma said.

The woman looked them over, her gaze lingering on their faces and over the handcart. "From Siccum! Well, I'll be a pretty pig. I can hardly believe it."

Ma opened her mouth. No words came out. She shut it.

"Well, get your sunburned little bums in here. I'm Beal. Syrup buns will be out of the oven in five. Stars, this is exciting."

Cal's mouth watered at the smell. "Where may I leave my cart?"

"Aren't you a sugar! Those poor girls in Siccum must have cried their eyes out watching you leave. I see you've come to break all the hearts in Branmar too."

Blood flooded his cheeks. Grandpapi made it worse by saying, "He'd better not."

"Take it around back, dearie," Beal said.

Cal dragged the car behind the inn. A thin horse flared its

nostrils and shied away, his black eyes wide and distrustful. The feeling was mutual. In Cal's experience, all creatures were dangerous. Except chickens.

Inside the inn, Cal inhaled the sweet smell of food and comfort. He dug his nails into the skin inside his elbow. Yes, that hurt, and he wasn't dreaming. Grandpapi had settled into an enormous chair that had rests for the arms and went higher than his head in the back. He sighed into the fabric.

"Where's Ma?"

"She went upstairs to see the room."

Upstairs? Thumping drew Cal's attention to Ma and Beal walking down what he realized were stairs. He ground his teeth at his ignorance. He was a twit. And he'd had no idea. Why had they kept all this from him? Why had they refused to leave Siccum?

"How often does the post come?" Ma asked Beal.

"Every other day. Should be here within the hour."

The post came to Siccum only with the caravans.

"Can I buy some paper and send a letter?"

"'Course, dear. Help yourself at the desk."

While Ma wrote, Cal ate three eggs, a piece of sausage, and two of Beal's syrup buns. He'd never been so content in his life. Until the heavy food turned in his belly. He sat as a stone, determined not to lose the best meal of his life. Ma gave her letter to Beal and joined him at the table.

"Did you write to Titus?" Cal asked.

"No. My sister, Elssa." Ma picked up a sticky roll. "I hope she hasn't moved. I haven't had a letter from her in over a year. And I'm hoping she's been in better contact with Titus than I have."

That was a lot of hoping. "And hopefully she's okay with house guests," Cal said.

Ma's lips curled up. "Mitera is large and grand. Nothing like this tiny village. You will love it."

Even as excitement burbled up within him, Cal's heavy head inched closer to the table.

"I told her to write us in Neese. Six days' journey from here."

Sleep pulled at his eyes. Grandpapi snored lightly from the chair.

"Our room is the first door on the right up the stairs," Ma said. "Go to bed."

Cal walked up the stairs, a new experience for him. He padded softly, as if the floor might collapse with his weight. He ducked the low doorframe into the bedroom. His hair brushed the ceiling. Two small beds dominated the room. He knew he should sleep on the floor, but the impossibly fluffy bed beckoned. *You pulled the handcart.* He fell into the feather cloud and slept.

He woke at twilight to a stiff back. Grandpapi slept in the neighboring bed, but Ma was gone. He rubbed his kinked neck as he followed the sound of voices and the smell of roasting meat downstairs. People filled the two tables, and more stuffed the chairs. Cal joined Ma in front of a cold fireplace. She sat hunched over and barely lifted her gaze.

"You alright?" Cal asked.

"Fine, Cal." She managed a thin smile.

"Have you slept at all?"

"A little. Sleep didn't come easy. Lots on my mind. I had errands to run anyway."

Guilt punched. Ma wasn't used to sleeping on the floor. "I'm sorry I slept in your bed."

"I'm glad you did."

He wasn't. He had a sore spine, and now shame. *Stop listening to stupid thoughts.* "Will you go to bed now?"

She took his hand. Were her fingers thinner, or had he never noticed how thick his palms had become? New callouses graced his grip.

"Don't leave the inn," Ma said.

"I won't."

Her stare didn't break.

"I promise." He could do this one thing right.

"Goodnight, son." She kissed his cheek.

A sharp whistle cut the air. Cal looked up in surprise. The entire room was focused on him and his ma.

"Atta boy! He's here for two minutes and already snagged the prettiest girl."

Cal stared in confusion. Ma's grip tightened on his fingers, as if holding him back. *Oh.*

"Kiss her right and proper," a man yelled.

Heat rushed up Cal's neck. That was his ma! He dropped her hand and rose to his feet, planning, and looking forward to, connecting his fist with the man's nose.

Beal sauntered into the room. Her hips swayed against shoulders as she wormed between the tables. "Dinner," she sang as she set down steaming plates.

A girl scurried over and handed Cal a warm bowl. Fragrant garlic and roasted fat dissolved his ire. Food trumped fighting—for now. "Thank you."

She squeaked. Pink dusted her cheeks. She fled. He had the urge to give chase, discover what her lips tasted like. His blood heated, encouraging him. He forced the thoughts away and sat back down at the hearth.

"Spring lamb." Ma's voice was soft with fondness as she scooped the stew.

Sensations slammed into Cal as he ate. Meat melted between his teeth, tender and juicy and filling. The raucous crowd laughed and yelled over one another. Colored clothing revealed calves, shoulders, and necklines.

But the way Ma devoured her meal—he gaped. She finished hers before he did. She'd taken such small portions for years.

"That was amazing." She set her bowl aside, and her eyes glazed with satisfaction. "And now to bed." She sang the words in a low voice.

He chuckled at this new version of Ma, wondering again why she'd insisted they stay in Siccum so long. She already looked happier. She winked and slipped through the room. His jaw clenched at the admiring glances following Ma's thin figure up the stairs.

He rested against the mantel and studied the room, content to simply watch these people together. Not wealthy, but happy. Full of life. So different from Siccum. He yearned for this: good food, friends, laughter. They talked about neighbors, crops, and weather. When two men discussed the Rugit River, he tilted his ear to hear.

"The delta is at its lowest. They say it will be passable within a year. You'll be able to walk across it."

"That's just a rumor. The Rugit is impossible to ford. I've seen it with my own eyes. You'd drown before making it halfway to Skotar."

"Not at the delta, where it meets the High Sea. The Draco Sang are moving south. They will cross and kill us all."

Cal stopped breathing as he leaned closer. The Draco Sang must be powerful. The thought thrilled him.

"Stop it. You're ruining my appetite. We can handle a few uncivilized brutes anyway." But the man's tense face undermined his words.

They were scared of the Draco Sang.

Their conversation turned, and shortly after, Cal climbed the stairs. He spread out on the floor by the door, almost daring those men to try and get past him to Ma. He'd show them what a Draco Sang could do.

CAL

The landscape colored as they paced north. Each day gifted them fresh vistas and sweet scents. They traveled on roads thick with travelers and farm wagons.

Neese dwarfed Branmar. Ma left the men at an inn while she checked the town for a letter from her sister. Cal ate his second helping of goat pie and what Grandpapi had called tavo, a blissfully creamy cinnamon drink.

Ma burst into the inn, clutching a paper to her chest. "Thank the stars." She flung herself down on the bench next to Cal. "Happy day." She opened the letter from Elssa and cleared her throat to read.

"Sweet Mira,
I can hardly breathe knowing you are now north of the desert. I wish to demand that you come here directly, stopping only to sleep. I want to see this son of yours. I'm trying to hope that since you've left Siccum, things are going well for him. But since your letter was so sparse, you've left me with nothing but worry."

Ma's brows creased together. "Sorry, Elssa. I was in a hurry to get the note off."

"And all is not going well." Grandpapi glanced at Cal.

"What does that mean?" Cal asked.

Ma waved at them to be quiet and kept reading.

"Tell Father he has another granddaughter. That's now four grand-sons and two granddaughters he needs to meet."

Ma clasped Grandpapi's shaking hand. Cousins. Cal had *six* cousins. Ma's voice cut through the overwhelming thought.

"Oh, sister! I long to hold you. See your golden eyes. They are the pieces of you I remember most."

Ma's voice turned raspy.

"But, my dear, I must instruct you to remain in Neese—I have sought out Captain Titus."

Ma gasped and whispered in awed disbelief, "She found him. And he's a captain."

"He's been stationed here at the capital for the past four years. He comes by often. He always asks about you. He's expected to take his troops to Kiptos this summer. The Rugit River delta is drier than ever before."

Ma clutched her chest as she read.

"He made it clear that you are not to come any more north than Neese. He insists. He left here in an agitated rush after I let him

read your SHORT letter, but I believe that he will write to you in Neese.
I look forward to the day when I see you, Father, and Callidon.
Love, Elssa."

Tears dribbled down Ma's cheeks as she re-read the words in silence. It was only the second time Cal had seen his mother cry. He felt helpless and small. And for some reason, to blame. He slid his cup of tavo in front of her. Her tender eyes shone. She reached out and gripped their hands, her father in one and her son in the other.

"So, we will stay here?" Cal asked.

"Until we hear from Titus. We can afford to stay at this inn a few days before we need to find work and more permanent lodging."

Cal didn't like that plan at all. They were still too far south for any real answers about the Draco Sang. And Neese didn't have an army he could join.

"He will write," Grandpapi said.

Ma nodded, but her eyelids sagged.

Over the next four days, Cal explored Neese. They'd bought local clothes the first day. At least now people's focus didn't snag on his long robes. Now they stared at his face.

The vibrant city pulsed. Watching locals shop at market thrilled and intrigued him. He discovered that if he offered to help shoppers carry their wares, they were bound to give him something in return—an avocado, a bun, a handful of sweet peas. One woman gave him a spiced cookie, kissed his cheek, and told him to return to help her again. He intended to.

He flung himself into their shared room at the inn. "Any news?"

"Not yet." Disappointment slid underneath Ma's words.

"I'm sure Captain Titus is a very busy man now, and with his command to maintain, he can't be expected to write so soon." She lifted her shoulders, perking up. "He will. But if we don't hear from him by tomorrow, I've found a vacant barn outside of town we can rent, and I've inquired about work."

"We cannot stay here," Cal said.

"We must," Ma said.

"Why?" Cal's patience was gone. "It doesn't make any sense. There is nothing here for us. We should go to Elssa's as planned."

"Titus told us not to," Ma said.

"Why?" The word was a demand.

Grandpapi leaned forward in his chair as if better to hear Ma's answer.

"I've known Titus since I was ten. He's six years older than I am, but we grew up together in Kiptos. I trust him."

Cal's brows lowered. Her answer was weak, and she knew it. He was sick of her lies and evasion. The journey had kept his impatience distracted, but not anymore. "How did we really end up in Siccum?" Her old excuse of seeking the sun for a former sickness no longer held weight.

Ma didn't answer. Grandpapi didn't answer. She opened her mouth. Closed it.

"What is it?" The words burst forth. "What are you hiding? Frustration grew in his chest. Anger infected his mind as he contemplated his ignorant childhood. They had kept him in the dark. On purpose. He turned fiery eyes at them, jaw clenched, fists balled.

"Calm down, Cal." Grandpapi rose from his chair.

"Don't tell me to calm down." His voice rose with each word. "Tell me the truth."

"Control yourself, boy. You do not talk to your mother like that."

Vexation flowered in his chest, and Cal let out a guttural growl between gritted teeth.

The whites of Ma's eyes gleamed.

"Get. Out," Grandpapi said.

"No."

Grandpapi flushed with fear.

Cal straightened his spine and cracked his head on the low ceiling beam, fueling his fury. *Ow.* "Tell me I'm Draco Sang!" His voice rang like a bell and echoed through the stunned silence.

Ma's voice was a whisper, but each word was an oath. "You. Are. My. Son."

He lowered his voice. "But you fear me because I am also my father's son. I am Draco Sang."

Her shoulders slumped in defeat.

"When were you going to tell me?"

"I'm sorry," Ma said.

"That I'm Draco Sang or that you lied?"

"I took you to Siccum to get away from Skotar. To raise you far away from your Draco Sang heritage."

"Who is my father?"

"You're my son." As if saying it again made it more true. Her mouth set in a tense line on her paper-white face. She would not answer his question.

"I am the son of your enemy." Pain flared inside him as their faces reflected the truth of his words. Confirmed his worst fear. His body hummed with tension. "You hate me for it."

Grandpapi didn't speak, his lips thin.

"No." Ma's voice shook, but Cal wasn't sure what emotion caused it. It tasted like fear and regret. "I love you." She reached for him, but he stepped back.

His thoughts a twisting storm, Cal tore out of the room.

He sprinted through Neese as if he could outrun the truth. But knowing in this, too, he would fail.

His family, the one thing he treasured in the world, hated him. Hated him because he was growing into a savage like his father.

SIX - ABANDONED
CAL

The Sahana River flowed through Neese in all her glory, a far cry from the sluggish Siccum stream far to the south. Cal's blood foamed through his veins, churning like the river. His ma refused to tell him about his father. Why? What was so terrible that she turned pale at the mention of him? Pain flared in his chest. They hated the Draco Sang. How long would it be until he no longer had a home with them? How long until the violence blossoming in his chest cost him everything? He dropped to the banks. Leaning against a tree trunk, he threw sticks into the current.

He twisted at the sound of footsteps. The woman smiled when she saw him, then veered his way. He'd helped her carry milk and potatoes home yesterday. She had a pleasing smile and slim ankles.

"Lovely day to sit by the river." She settled at his side.

He stared at her pale fingers in the grass, close enough that she nearly touched his thigh. His thoughts changed course as his body warmed. "How old are you?"

"Twenty-two."

"Where's your husband?"

She bristled. "I haven't got one."

He threw a rock. It skipped once.

"Are you mad?" She looked up at him through her lashes. "You seem like you could use some cheering up."

One side of his mouth curved. "Are *you* going to cheer me up?"

Her gaze traveled over his body, lingering on his lips. Her cheeks colored.

His blood lit on fire.

"You could tell me about it," she said. "It always helps me to—"

Leaning forward, Cal wrapped his fingers around her neck and silenced her with his mouth. He pressed against warm lips, exploring deeper. Her hands found his chest, but not in a caress. She shoved. He didn't budge. Her weakness stroked his arrogance. His feral heart pounded in his ears. A tiny voice inside whispered, *stop*. With effort, he jerked back, releasing her. His blood bleated in protest.

Flaming eyes flashed above her scowl. "That's not what I had in mind."

He didn't look at her, afraid if he focused on her lips, now swollen and red, he would not be able to stop a second time. Hands hot and unsteady, he selected another rock. "Yes, it was."

She inhaled, as if preparing to unleash a cutting lecture.

"You should go." His words were a cold warning. He threw the stone into the river as she fled. *Yes, go. Stay far away from me.* Guilt replaced his lust. Maybe it was the river that was doing it to him. He'd also been at the Sahana when he'd stolen fiddlers and attacked that girl's father. He dug his fingernails into the dirt. The river wasn't the problem. It was no wonder his mother despised him.

Hours later, when the sun greeted the horizon, he

returned to the inn. Patrons trickled into the main room, hunting for a meal. A man sat at a corner table, a wide-brimmed hat shading his features. The man irked Cal, tugged at his attention. He felt searching eyes underneath that hat. Denying the sudden urge to fight the newcomer, he quickened his pace to the hall. He entered their rented room; Ma jumped to her feet in relief, but Cal did not go to her. He waited by the door. Grandpapi frowned.

Ma broke the tense silence. "I know I kept things from you. Things for you to learn as you became a man. I wanted to protect you from harsh truths."

"I can handle them."

"That doesn't make it any easier for me." She hadn't exactly agreed with him.

"My father didn't die at sea, did he?"

She flinched as if slapped.

"Is he even dead?"

She hunched over, sadness staining her features. Grandpapi shuffled forward and put an arm around her shoulders. He speared Cal with a warning glare.

"I don't know. I'm afraid maybe not." Ma's voice was shattered and small.

"He hurt you." Realization slashed like a serrated knife to his heart. "He's the one that hurt you." Cal thought back to the suffering mentioned in that old letter. "He forced you."

Ma's gaze shot up in surprise, and Cal saw all the pain and truth she'd hidden deep inside. He thought of the woman today at the river. He'd forced that kiss. What would he grow into? He shuddered at his own vileness. Just like his father. *No.* He would never become his father. He would never again be the cause of such anguish in a woman's eyes. Ice cut down his veins at the tears watering her cheeks.

"He gave me you," she whispered.

His voice was low and lethal. "I will kill him." A tremor ran up his back, strengthening his vow.

Ma's eyes popped, like twin suns. "No, Cal. You will forget him as I have. He does not rule our future. Don't give him another thought. He gave me you. My son. My star. And for that, I am forever grateful." Her love pierced his core, calmed his pain. She stepped close. Thin arms encircled his chest.

"I love you, Ma." But Cal *would* kill the savage who attacked her. He was no father of Cal's.

After Ma had a long drink of water, and they'd cleaned their hands and faces, Cal opened the door to usher them to supper. Ma stopped in front of him and touched a chunk of hair falling over his eye.

"How did this get so long?" Tenderly, she brushed the strand to the side.

Looking at her shining face, he determined to be better.

"Mira, we'll catch up," Grandpapi said. "I want a minute with Cal."

Ma nodded and ducked out. Dreading one of Grandpapi's biting lectures on his many failures, Cal slunk forward to sit on the bed.

Frown wrinkles went all the way down Grandpapi's chin. "Your mother has given her life for you, and you've repaid her with selfish outbursts and dishonor. Again."

Despite his commitment to control his demons, Cal's nerves flamed. He fisted the blankets at his sides, holding back his temper.

Ma flung through the door, panting and clutching her heart. "He's here. Oh, help me. He's here!"

"Who's here?" Cal leapt away from Grandpapi.

"Titus. Titus is here. Just sitting out there."

"This is great news, isn't it?" Cal asked.

"Wonderful." Her hands fluttered like birds.

"Well, did he see you?" Grandpapi asked with a crooked smile.

"I don't know. I saw him. I know I did. I wouldn't mistake that man for anyone. And then … I ran away." She barked out a short laugh. "He probably saw me. Oh dear."

Cal's eyes widened at her mumbling and fussing.

"Shall we go out there, my darling?" Grandpapi's usually stern voice was now light and teasing.

"I've got a new dress." Ma rifled through their chest of belongings and pulled out a yellow garment. The men turned their backs as she changed out of her loose pants and tunic. She crossed the room. Cal watched in surprise as she untied her braid and ran a brush through her long, tawny hair. As she stood before them, the timid cast of her shoulders reminded him that she was only sixteen years older than he. Thirty-two.

"My beautiful girl," Grandpapi said.

And she *was* beautiful. Had he never noticed before? Cal held the door open. Her vibrancy lightened his worries, but he wasn't sure how he felt about meeting the man whose arrival had made his mother dance. Cal thought he and Grandpapi were the only important men in her life, and he'd liked it that way. Deep down, he knew that wasn't fair to her. He did want her to be happy. He determined to greet Titus with a warm welcome. But when Ma waltzed up to the stranger in the hat he'd noticed earlier, Cal's stomach twisted into a knot.

"Mira." Titus said her name reverently. The deep voice was like a metal rasp down Cal's skin. Titus took off his hat and held out his arms to greet her. His hair grayed around the temples and through his trimmed beard. Two shining scars split his face, like a wild beast had clawed him. The longer gash cut across a bright blue eye, which, judging by the sharpness of his gaze, remained undamaged.

Ma took hold of both of Titus's hands as she stepped close. "Hello, Titus. *Captain* Titus."

"Titus will do."

They kept a pair of hands together as Ma turned and motioned behind her. *Let go of her,* Cal's inner voice threatened.

"Good to see you, Captain." Grandpapi held out a hand. "Thank you for meeting us. I imagine it wasn't easy to leave your duties."

Titus let go of Ma. He took Grandpapi's hand and wrapped an arm around his back. "Closford, it's been far too long, old friend."

"And this is my son, Callidon," Ma said.

Increasingly wary, Cal accepted Titus's outstretched palm. The grip was steel. The contact zinged through Cal's blood, wakening the shadows that crept ever closer to the surface. Who was this man? Titus's polite smile seemed to veil iron underneath. They stood the same height, but Cal felt the captain's searching stare grind him down to nothing.

"I'm pleased to meet you, captain," Cal lied. He tugged his hand free.

"I've been waiting a long time to meet you."

They clustered around a private table as the kitchen staff served dinner. Cal's stomach had adjusted to the rich food and large portions. With vigor, he attacked the roast pheasant, bitter greens, and boiled potatoes.

"How did you find us?" Ma asked. "Have you been searching Neese long?" She'd hardly touched her meal.

"No. I followed my nose and came straight here," Titus said, his tone flat.

Ma's face sharpened as she looked at him. No one laughed at the joke.

"You came all the way here. For us," Ma said. "I'm sorry that we are a distraction from your duties."

"Not at all. I have leave for any special assignments I find need my attention." The way he said "special assignments" snagged in Cal's mind. "Tell me about your journey," Titus said.

As Ma began her retelling, Cal fought with the angst rising within him. He felt like doing something rash and violent. It would be fun to throw the table back; maybe Titus's meal would land on his face. Cal shoved away the impulse and scowled at his empty plate. He refused to look at Titus or his swooning mother. Grandpapi kicked Cal's shin under the table—a warning to behave. Cal bit his tongue and shifted his attention to the people coming through the door. If anyone entering caught his menacing eye, they looked away first. He savored the petty victories.

Ma told Titus how Cal had fought off the crokator and run through the night.

"Impressive for any man, especially a boy of sixteen," Titus said.

"What do you say to the compliment, Callidon?" Grandpapi's voice was a rasp, drawing Cal's focus back to the table.

Titus scrutinized Cal, his blue eyes narrowed.

"Thank you, sir." Cal flicked his gaze away. He knew he was being childish, but his opinion of Titus didn't improve.

"What made you decide to leave Siccum now?" Titus asked.

It was none of his business.

"It was time to come home," Ma said. "And Cal has shown an interest in the army. We heard rumors that more soldiers are needed."

That was hardly the truth. Cal looked to his mother, but she and Titus had locked stares, as if they were having a silent conversation.

Ma spoke again, her voice low as if the words were heavy. "We had hoped you would *help* him."

Nope. Cal would find another army to join. Not Titus's.

"I left command with my commander," Titus said. "He has his orders."

Cal's jaw hardened as Ma reached forward and clasped the man's wiry forearm. Hope danced on her face.

Titus took her fingers in his hands. "Of course I will do everything I can for your son. Even after all these years, how could you doubt that?" His voice was a gentle caress.

Cal felt like an intruder on a private affair.

"Thank you," Grandpapi said.

Cal chewed on his tongue as Ma and Grandpapi looked at him. Waiting for his gratitude. There was only one thing he could say. "Thank you, captain. I would be happy to join your army. I don't want any special treatment. I'll work hard."

Titus had an annoying little smile on his face. "Fine words."

Cal bristled.

"I'd like to put them to the test," Titus said. "Before we head to Mitera."

"What do you intend?" Ma asked.

Titus looked at Ma when he answered. "You and Closford go on ahead to Elssa's. I'd like to take Cal out to the Spickle Woods for a little training. See what his skills are. We'll be safe enough there."

Ma's eyes welled with tears as she nodded. Cal hated the idea of testing and training with Titus before being allowed entrance into the army, but his ire softened at Ma's tenderness. They had never been separated before. He had not expected her to care so much. She loved him, despite his flaws and his monstrous father. And so he would go with Titus—for her.

Titus touched her hand again, drawing her gaze back up to his face. "We will meet you in Mitera before long. I'm sure."

Ma looked like she wasn't so confident. Cal would do all he could to keep his time with Titus short.

Titus's voice was barely audible as he pressed his words towards Ma. "It's not too late. I'm here now. It's going to be fine."

"What's going to be fine?" Cal asked, his voice overly loud.

Ma turned watery eyes on her son. "Titus will teach you everything you need to know to become the man, the soldier, you want to be. Listen to him. Trust him. And we will be together again soon."

Why did it feel like he was going off to war instead of a few days of training in the woods? "I'll do my best," Cal said, his brow tight with uncertainty.

Ma smiled. "That's all I'm asking."

"We'll leave after breakfast," Titus said.

"Thank you." Ma's voice was low with sincerity.

Cal didn't say anything. He was finally joining the army, becoming a soldier like he'd dreamed, so why did it feel like a nightmare?

SEVEN - BEAST
CAL

After breakfast, Cal looked around in dismay behind the inn for the missing handcart. Titus set a coin purse in Ma's hand.

She tested the weight. "Someone must have been desperate for an old, worn handcart."

"Very desperate."

"Thank you."

"Commander Asvig will call on you at Elssa's. If you need or want anything, he has strict orders to see to it."

She threw her arm around his square shoulders, and Titus's hands, nicked with scars, wrapped her waist. When they *finally* let go, Titus whistled, and his horse trotted forward. Grandpapi laid a hand on the saddle as if he knew what he was doing, as if he'd ridden a horse before.

There was so much Cal didn't know.

"Help me up, son," Grandpapi said.

Cal darted forward. Grandpapi gripped his shoulder. His voice was a low hiss. "You listen to Titus. You do what he says. Or you don't come back."

Cal jolted. "What?"

Bony hands tightened on Cal's neck before his grandpapi flung himself onto the horse. "Prove me wrong." Grandpapi's lips disappeared into a thin line.

Cal's mind whirled in confused thoughts. He barely registered Ma's hug. She only came to his jaw now. He mumbled his love when she did. She cupped her hands on his cheeks, looking him over as if memorizing his face. As if she might never see him again. What was going on?

Ma led the horse with Grandpapi hunched on its back. And his family, his whole world, walked away.

"Let's go," Titus said.

Cal slung his pack over his back, glad for Titus's hard tone, the emotionless command. The good-bye with his family had left him drained and anxious. Grandpapi always thought the worst of him. Or maybe the old man was the only one who saw him clearly.

They stopped at the shops. The boots cost more money than Cal made in a year mining. At first, he refused to let Titus buy them, but with the supple leather wrapped around his feet and at Titus's insistence, he relented and gladly threw away his well-worn sandals. He did not accept the offer of a new hat. He didn't want to look like Titus. He would have accepted a sword, like the one hanging from Titus's belt, but the captain didn't offer. Together, they headed east and out of town.

"What's in the forest?" Cal asked after they'd walked for an hour in silence.

"Beasts."

Cal shot a look at Titus.

"They will help mask your own animal smell."

"What does that mean?" Annoyance brought out thoughts of violence.

"It means you stink."

Cal huffed, speechless and insulted.

The scars on Titus's face wrinkled as he laughed. It was deep and rich, and it chafed against Cal.

So, he thought he was funny. This was going to be rough. Cal stayed quiet for a long time after that—hating Titus. He determined to learn quickly. The sooner he was done with this testing and away from Titus, the better.

They ate a small lunch in silence. Titus ignored him, which at first Cal enjoyed, but by evening, Cal was clawing at the walls of his mind, bouncing between curiosity and hostility. So many questions. How big was the army? Where were they stationed? Were the Draco Sang really moving south? What were they like? What kind of strategy did they plan for a potential attack? What weapons did they have? Had Titus been in any battles? Had he killed anyone? How did he get those scars on his face? What was his history with Ma? What would happen if Titus found out Cal was Draco Sang?

The sullen pride and coldness in Titus's eyes kept Cal quiet. After miles staring at Titus's back, he was no closer to understanding why they needed to go to the forest before he could join the army.

As the sun kissed the horizon, the Spickle Woods came into view. They'd traveled all day through flat land, walking between pastures of goats and sheep and farms. As they crested a small rise, deep green loomed in the distance, mysterious and grand.

The Blade River flowed down the middle of the Spickle Woods, pumping life into the ancient roots. Steep mountains on the east halted rainclouds while they spilled their contents on the vegetation. The forest cut a giant swath running north and south along the cliffs.

Cal had studied maps of Elysium. Despite her lies and omissions, Ma had taught him geography and interesting things about the world outside Siccum.

"We need to make it to the forest before we camp," Titus said.

Cal grunted his acknowledgment and swung his pack off his back.

"It isn't wise to stop here," Titus said, looking around the grasslands with distrust. "We need to keep moving."

Cal was hungry now, had been for hours. The pig-belly sandwich in his pack had been on his mind all day. He glared at Titus as he pulled out the sandwich. He pointedly shouldered his pack and started ripping into the bread as he walked. Still obeying. Still moving.

Titus's face stayed calm, but his blue eyes iced.

Three bites in, Cal stopped. An invisible alarm rang through his pulse in warning. Titus cursed. Cal blinked, and a sword glistened in Titus's hand.

"Get down," Titus yelled. "Hide."

Where? They stood in an open field, completely exposed. A figure sprang from the dry grass directly in front of Cal. He dropped his sandwich and groped for his hunting knife. His eyes sent images that his mind rejected.

The waning sun illuminated a mutant beast. A mongrel with the face of a man. Intelligent eyes above canine teeth. The attacker stood on two legs as tall as Cal. The thing held a club in one furry hand and a sword in the other. *This isn't real.*

Adrenaline cracked through Cal's paralysis, and he blocked a very real club aimed at his head. The impact on his forearm reverberated through his body. His blood roared.

A sword slashed at Titus. Metal clanged as Titus blocked the fatal blow.

"Where's your kitty?"

It speaks!

Titus answered the man-beast with a rapid slash of his sword.

"Where do you think you're going with my underling? My *prize*." The savage's high voice rasped like sand over rocks.

Titus slashed with his sword. Cal inched forward. He might not like Titus, but he didn't want Titus to die and leave him at the mercy of this nightmare.

"Get back," Titus yelled.

"I can help," Cal said.

"Not with that. Stay out of the way." A command.

Cal balked at the painful truth. The knife in his hand felt like a child's toy compared to the weapon Titus wielded with speed and skill.

Red stained a blur of silver as Titus sliced the attacker open. The humanoid dog fell. Titus sliced his blade across a fur-covered throat. He mopped a sleeve down his sweaty face and bent over his knees, panting. His bloody sword glistened.

Teach me. Teach me to fight. To do that. Cal ached to be powerful and deadly.

Titus checked the corpse's pockets, leaving everything but a bone-handled knife with a blade that was more silver than gray, with overlapping ripples in the steel like melted scales.

"What is it?" The mutant body, mangled and horrible, branded itself into Cal's mind. Could humans mate with dogs? He stared in disgusted fascination.

"Dracosteel." Titus balanced the knife on his hand. It was perfectly weighted. "Light, sharp, and unbreakable."

"No," Cal said. "*That.*"

Titus followed Cal's gaze to the body. "That." Titus's eyes were sad, almost tender as he looked at Cal. "Is a Draco Sang."

Cal's mind overloaded. His blood burned.

Nogard's curse was real.

And Cal would become a monster, too.

Ferth ran a whetstone down the length of his blade. The edge was already sharp enough to slide through bone, but the grating noise made Thirro twitch, so Ferth kept doing it. A slow rhythmic whine.

Dara lounged on Ferth's bed, a pallet of woven trisle stems. She looked a little too comfortable there, her legs splayed and her shaved head nestled against his feather pillow. Her nostrils flared slightly, as if to draw in more of his scent.

Ferth ignored the flirty gaze she sent his way. He already knew she wanted him. And that gave him power. Maybe one day he'd use it to his advantage.

Thirro glared at Dara, his beady eyes full of jealousy. The wings sprouting from his back ruffled, unfolding slightly despite the cramped bedroom. Ferth raised an eyebrow at Thirro's sudden aggression. Thirro scowled below his beaked nose, crossing his lean arms over his chest. Dark brown feathers rustled as he retucked his wings in tight against his back.

Thirro had transformed earlier this year, but it would be

a few more months before his new wings were strong enough for flight. Thirro was the only one of the three who had transformed, matured into his Draco Sang heritage.

Ferth was still an untransformed underling. He'd failed to honor his dragon blood. And his father never let him forget it. Ferth had thus far proven himself little better than a human slave. His father had transformed into his beast at age twelve. At sixteen and still human, Ferth was a disgrace. His whetstone sang along metal.

"Now you're just stalling," Thirro said. "Afraid of losing?"

Dara laughed, a high mocking sound.

Thirro's jaw rippled.

Ferth sat in his only chair, requiring his two friends to sit on the floor or the bed. Thirro remained standing.

Ferth's voice was low, conversational. "I'll let you two hunt as a team. Make this a little more interesting." Ferth stood before Thirro and Dara could answer and pretend they didn't want to accept the advantage. "Let's go."

They padded out of the room and through the low hall of the barracks. Ferth held the outer door open for Pearl, a pale-skinned, silver-haired slave. He tried to glimpse her face, catch her round gray eyes, but she lowered her head behind the high stack of linens she carried. She skittered past, but not fast enough to avoid Thirro's reaching hand grabbing at her backside.

Annoyance flared within Ferth. He clenched his fist, but kept his face placid, a practiced move to hide his shameful weaknesses, his concern for her. Humans were feeble. They existed to serve the mighty Draco Sang. And Thirro, a full-fledged Draco, had earned the right to treat the lesser humans as he pleased.

Ferth, Thirro, and Dara strode across the courtyard of Shi Castle, below the massive copper statue of the great Black Dragon, and through the main gates. Spring had ushered in warmer weather, and Ferth wore short sleeves. His hunting knife hung at his side, the only weapon allowed in this *friendly* game. They passed slaves tending the queen's fields and ducked into the shady forest.

"Do your worst," Ferth said.

Thirro rolled his eyes and walked away, his knife poised in his palm. Dara flashed Ferth seductive eyes before darting after the eagle Draco. Dappled sunlight drew spots on her dark head.

Ferth waited minutes, making certain he would not be followed. Boots soft, he slunk through the trees in the opposite direction. Magu were easy prey—once they were caught. He tracked his path effortlessly, curving deeper into the shadows. He paused at the edge of the clearing, peering through leaves. A mature magu watched her two babies gnaw and lick at the sap-crusted box Ferth had left there as bait. He grinned. He'd be the first to bring a baby magu to his father. Again. Dara and Thirro didn't stand a chance.

Ferth cocked his knife, training his aim on the smaller of the two knobby-kneed deer. He'd still have to carry it back, and Laconius would never know his son had chosen to bring him the *lesser* prey. The animal's big ears perked up. Ferth stilled at that; they didn't usually notice his presence until it was too late. Then the mother magu screamed and bucked at something on the other side of the clearing. Ferth's blade flung forward, embedding itself in the neck of the smallest animal. He froze as a spearhead hit his prey inches below where his knife quivered. He whirled.

A man hid in the trees—a slave, judging by the long hair, thin brown tunic and sandals. Eyes white, the man stared at the two weapons. He turned and ran. Ferth gave chase. The slave was big, taller, and broader than Ferth, but the man fled as if hunted by wolves. A long braid flung behind him. Ferth danced between the trees, gaining. What would he do when he caught up? He was duty-bound to bring him in for punishment. Ferth slowed, letting the man go.

The slave tripped. With a yelp, he pitched against a trunk and dropped to the ground, lumpy with roots and rocks. Ferth yanked to a stop.

The slave rolled to his back, hands up in surrender. Blood welled on his forehead. He glanced at Ferth's freshly shorn scalp, the mark of an underling, a future Draco Sang.

Ferth stood above him. "What's your name?"

"Kenji."

"What were you doing?" Ferth's voice was hard, the voice of a master, even though the slave looked at least five years older than he. He waited to see what Kenji would say. If the slave would lie.

He did not. Eyes so dark they were almost black held Ferth's gaze. His deep voice held steady. "I was hunting. Meat for the slave house. Many are hungry."

Compassion bloomed. Ferth was hungry too. He hadn't been allowed food since yesterday morning. Preparation for the upcoming hunger trial. He tilted his chin in thought. He knew what he should do. He was expected to drag this slave back for his whipping, or worse. If Queen Mavras was in a mood, Kenji could be killed for hunting in her forest without permission. Ferth poked around his mind, prodding at the beast that napped in his chest. His blood lay dormant, utterly uninterested in violence. Not even an ember of bloodlust to fan.

The cut on Kenji's brow went deep. Red streamed off his face and into his hair, but the man did not move to touch it. The slave's shirt was threadbare and filthy. Hating himself, Ferth peeled his shirt off and folded it into a neat band. Scowling, he motioned Kenji to lift his head off the dirt. Suspicious eyes watched Ferth as he wrapped the slave's wound, tying it tight.

"Get up." Ferth's voice was sharp but not at the slave. He hissed at his own piss-poor performance.

Kenji folded forward and lurched to his feet.

Ferth walked away. This was the slave's chance to run. He was giving him a wide-open shot, but Kenji did not flee. He followed Ferth.

Through tight teeth, Ferth exhaled annoyance.

As Ferth entered the clearing, the whining mother deer and her living child, after a beady-eyed glare his way, fled the scene. And now he'd lost the other fawn. Ferth knelt next to the dead magu. He pulled out his knife and wiped the blade in the grass. Ferth's scowl deepened at the looming presence of the slave. Kenji stood meekly at the edge of the clearing, waiting for Ferth's sentence.

He should leave him. Go win the hunt. Honor his father and his dragon blood. But Ferth knew the feeling of hunger. And wanting. He hated it. Ferth yanked the spear free, tearing out a chunk of flesh with it. He cleaned off the tip. A weapon stolen from the queen's armory. Another crime. Ferth dropped it in the dirt. With a grunt, he hauled the dead animal into his arms. He strode to the slave and thrust dinner into Kenji's surprised hands.

"Others are hunting to the west," Ferth said.

Kenji didn't move, his face a mask of confusion and fear.

Ferth picked up the knife and spear from the grass. "Well, don't make a thing about it." He stalked away, shirtless and without his prey.

Shame surged with each step he took. He'd given in to the weakness of his human heart. Again. The heritage his mother had given him. And his father despised him for.

He'd never met her. Didn't know her name. She lived in Elysium. If she still lived. Was her hair brown like his? Or her eyes amber? Did his straight nose come from her? He yearned for her—another weakness of his. Would she smile if she saw him? Embrace him? *No.* She would view him with hatred and disgust, like the rest of the humans. He was the enemy.

He dispelled his daydreams as a snapping twig drew him back to the hunt. He crept closer to the sound and crouched behind a thick tree. Dara and Thirro circled a young magu. Ferth calculated. They hadn't made the kill yet. The prey could still be his. He cocked his arm, but before he got a clear shot to throw, Dara lunged. Teeth bared, she tackled the thin-legged magu. It landed hard on its side, thrashing and bleating. Dara straddled it, her knee pinning its neck. Only then did Dara draw her hunting knife. She grinned as she jerked an ear back, and with sadistic pleasure, she carved its throat, and the fawn went still.

Ferth jolted as Dara's pained roar rent the air.

Her head snapped back as a tremor rippled through her spine. Orange fur spread over her scalp. Her ears lengthened, the tips going a deeper charcoal. Her lips darkened. Black outlined her large yellow eyes.

A fox Draco Sang.

She howled in triumph at her transformation, then lurched forward over the carcass as if dizzy. Thirro was at her side, bracing her as he tugged her to her feet.

"It'll pass," Thirro said, running a hand down her back.

Dara leaned into him, looking in awe at her thick palms, the sharp claws where her fingernails had been.

"Fur looks good on you."

"Feels good," Dara said. She purred and licked her canines.

Ferth sank against a tree trunk, heedless of the bark scraping his bare back. Dara had done it. They'd both beaten him in the only competition that ever really mattered. They'd been worthy of their blood. They were Draco Sang. Thirro an eagle. Dara a fox. Both strong beasts, tributes of prowess.

He was still a weak underling, farther from earning any fangs or feathers than when he awoke this morning. If he had whipped Kenji himself, would that have been enough? Ferth sat there long after Thirro and Dara had carried their winning kill away. It was near dark when he found the energy to return to the stronghold. And face his father's wrath.

NINE - PUNISHMENT
FERTH

Shi Castle and its surrounding buildings perched on the top of a wide plateau surrounded on three sides by sheer cliffs. The east side dropped to the frothing High Sea. A wall protected the west side, the single way in or out, unless one had wings. Ferth did not.

The lifelike copper dragon standing guard at the gates, green with air and age, glared his menacing greeting as Ferth approached.

Dara found him first. She sidled up as he marched down the hall of the barracks. Her giddy excitement itched against his skin. He ignored her as he pushed open his bedroom door. He went to close it, but she shoved her way inside. He propped the stolen spear against the wall. She eyed it, but didn't ask; she had other things on her mind.

"How do I look?"

Ferth faced her. Her round eyes dilated as he made a show of raking his assessing gaze over her body. She was short, but strong. Her leather vest and training tights bore witness that her feminine curves were still intact. The fur on her head and arms didn't cover her cheeks and chin yet, a pleasing feature. But she was still a Draco. And Ferth didn't find any of them attractive. She'd looked better this morning. "Congratulations."

Maroon-colored lips pouted as she stepped closer and put her paw on his chest. Her claws tickled slightly as she dragged them down. "What happened to you?"

Ferth's fingers clamped around her wrist. She gasped as he twisted her hand off his skin. "You'd better go collect your winnings. Laconius doesn't like to be kept waiting."

"We already left. He gave me and Thirro each our own bottle of barley wine for beating you."

"And you drank the entire thing already?" The question didn't need answering.

She grinned and slunk closer. She ignored his grip clamping her wrist as she pressed her chest against his ribs. "Should I have saved some for you?"

"Yes," Ferth said, pretending to care. "I'm hungry."

She licked her lip. She could eat as much as she wanted now that she'd transformed.

He stepped back, releasing her arm. He lifted a shirt from his trunk and dragged it over his head.

Dara watched with half-lidded, sullen eyes. "Laconius sent for you."

Ferth stilled.

"And you know how he doesn't like to be kept waiting." With that last jab, she bounced out of the room.

Ferth shuffled toward his father's quarters, but Laconius intercepted him in the middle of the massive courtyard. Ferth cringed. Tonight's shaming would be public.

Laconius towered seven feet tall. Wide buffalo horns curled over the sides of his head, above a mane of curly black hair. His leathery snout flared below flaming black eyes. He stomped up to his son and clamped a massive hand on his shoulder. He didn't yell. The quiet voice was worse.

"Dara, that ridiculous girl, a Draco before my own son?"

Guilt slid down his throat. He was now the last of his class of underlings to remain human.

Laconius turned at the sound of approaching feet. Ferth's empty stomach burned like vinegar as two Draco Sang dragged the slave, Kenji, forward, his arms tied behind his back. Ferth's shirt still wrapped the slave's head, the cloth stained red. They shoved Kenji to his knees at Laconius's feet.

"He was caught this afternoon outside the gates without permission." Laconius spoke to his son, but everyone in the courtyard could hear.

A small crowd had gathered, mostly underlings and Draco Sang. A few slaves watched from the edges, heads down but shoulders tight. Thankfully he didn't see Keturah. He didn't want the closest thing he had to a mother seeing whatever would come next. But Pearl, the slave he always looked for when he went to visit Keturah in the laundry, slipped out of the slave house. She hovered in the doorway, her eyes trained on Kenji. Ferth cringed at her lovely face, now contorted in fear. He snapped his gaze away, disgusted at his concern for her, for any of them.

"What was he doing?" Ferth's voice was hard as he studied Kenji.

The dark eyes were blank, glazed.

Laconius's brows furrowed in displeasure. "Does it matter?"

At least Kenji hadn't been caught with the magu. Or the spear.

"What happened to your head?" Laconius asked.

Kenji didn't even look at Ferth, not one condemning glance. "I dropped a box at the granary this morning," Kenji said.

Laconius's fat lips curled in disgust. "Six blows."

Ferth knew the law for a minor infraction. Six punches, anywhere on the body, *unless* the slave lost consciousness. Then it was over.

"I'll deliver the blows," Ferth said.

Kenji's cheek twitched, his only reaction.

"Why should you?" Laconius spat in the dirt as if his son were nothing but a glob of mucus. He motioned to Dara, who watched nearby. "I suppose it's only fair I give the privilege to her. She made us all proud today."

Dara swelled. She flexed her fingers, but before she could approach Kenji, Ferth spoke. "Then I'll request only the first blow. Dara can enjoy the honor of the other five."

Arms folded, Laconius looked down at his son, his only child, and an ember of hope for Ferth's future flickered back to life in his eyes. "Granted."

Ferth didn't allow himself to check if Pearl still watched, didn't linger on the strong body kneeling before him, now taut as a bowstring. Ferth stepped forward and swung. His fist connected with the soft spot on Kenji's face, just above his ear. The slave's head snapped to the side, and he dropped. Out cold. It was the only mercy Ferth could show the slave.

Dara's hiss broke the wave of silence.

"Get the body inside," Laconius said. He turned away, but not before Ferth caught the puff of pride on his father's face.

The smile Ferth turned on a pissed-off Dara was wide and genuine. He didn't look back as he strode out of the courtyard. Didn't help move the body. That was beneath him —at least it had to look that way.

Night blanketed the land by the time they reached the edge of the trees. Titus finally called a halt after they'd hacked their way inside the protection of the thick foliage. In the murky night, the shadows glowered and gleamed like ghosts. Leaves rustled and insects buzzed, scratching at Cal's overtired anxiety. Mutant maws gaped through his mind.

Titus spread his sleeping mat between massive ribbons of raised roots at the base of a gnarled tree. He pulled his pork sandwich from his pack while Cal laid his mat in nearby moss. Cal's sandwich was now food for the worms in the field. His mouth watered, and his stomach tightened.

"In Siccum, there is a myth about a fallen Prince Nogard," Cal said. "He turned into a dragon. He cursed the land that any who are violent, greedy, lustful, or disobedient would grow into monsters too. I thought that was just a parenting tool."

Titus's white teeth flashed in the dim light. "Oh, that is. The truth is worse. And better born in the sunshine of day. Tomorrow I will explain it all. Sleep now."

Cal's nerves hummed with tension. His body sang with unspent emotions. "Please tell me more."

"I will. When light conquers darkness." Titus lay on his mat.

Crickets chattered. Shadows loomed and crept closer. Panic rose. "Do we need to take watches in case there are more of those *things?*"

"No need. We have a lion guard."

Cal bolted up to a sitting. *The Lion.* Ma had spoken of the lion in hushed tones. After today, he wondered if it were more than figurative. He squinted at Titus, a black lump among the roots.

"Good night, boy."

Cal's heart pounded unevenly. He lowered to the floor. A sliver of stars shone between towering treetops, so different from the wide expanse of Siccum sky, where moonlight lit up the vast dunes. No walls protected him tonight. The forest sucked away all light and sleep, leaving only darkness and dread. Cal's breathing shortened and shallowed while Titus's breathing lengthened and deepened.

The curse was real. The Draco Sang weren't human.

What about me?

Tense thoughts of lions, monsters, and death kept Cal company long into the night.

Cal woke chilled and exhausted. Disoriented, he sat up in the pouring rain. The misty forest and his groggy head obscured all sense of time.

Dry and eating an orange, Titus crouched under a canvas that stretched from branch to branch overhead.

Cal searched for his pack, dreading he would find it ruined.

"It's over here." Titus pointed to the dry pack next to him. "Come eat."

In his wet clothes, Cal inched a sliver inside the overhang. "Roof. Smart."

Titus grinned. He tossed Cal some dried goat, a lump of cheese, and a bowl of rainwater.

"Thank you."

"Welcome to spring in the Spickle."

"It's better than summer in Siccum."

Titus raised an eyebrow as if surprised something pleasant could come from the grumpy youth. "I can imagine. Since you're already wet, how about a morning walk in the rain?"

"Lovely." But his tone was ugly.

Titus expertly wrapped Cal's pack in a watertight canvas before taking down his roof and wearing it as a cloak. Titus's wide-brimmed hat kept his head and face dry, while Cal spent the morning wiping rain out of his eyes and shaking water from his hair.

They turned this way and that until Cal had completely lost his place on the map. The exercise warmed his limbs, and the rain was pleasantly cool, a rare feeling, which Cal tried to enjoy despite his sticky clothes, soggy boots, and burning questions. The beautiful forest spoke to his soul, coaxing him out of his gloom. Plants of various shapes, sizes, and colors twisted and curled into the air. Mist caressed his feet, and birds sang above him. It felt right in a way the desert never had.

Titus finally stopped in a small glade. Giant trees with ribbon-like roots encircled the spongy ground. A thick pavilion of leaves and vines covered their heads, keeping the space almost dry. Off to one side, boulders clustered together like toys set aside by a massive child.

"Welcome home." Titus dropped his pack and shook out the canvas. "Help me secure this."

After they'd pulled the canvas tight across half the clearing, Cal spread his wet boots and clothes on a rock underneath the makeshift roof to dry and gratefully put on his spare set of clothes. He lounged on his sleeping mat, listening to the rain, and *waiting*. Titus picked through his pack, setting out a cooking pot and spoon before refolding his clothes. It wasn't long before impatience had Cal blurting out, "It's not exactly sunny, but it *is* day. Tell me about that *thing*. Tell me about the Draco Sang."

Titus sighed, looking suddenly older as he set his pack aside. He sat on a piece of canvas an arm's length away and rubbed at his manicured beard. "I promise you, Callidon, I will tell you the truth."

Cal shifted, unsettled by the piercing blue eyes and heavy tone.

"And you can stop pretending I don't know your father is a Draco Sang. That *you* are Draco Sang."

Cal's mouth flopped open, then closed. "I don't know what you're talking about."

"I said I'd be honest with you. But I can't make you be honest with yourself."

Cal's teeth clamped together.

Titus glanced out at the dripping trees. "You mentioned the myth of Nogard. As you saw yesterday, it's not entirely fiction. But I don't think you've heard the ending." Titus leaned back against a boulder. "Nogard did turn into a dragon and did burn much of Skotar. King Enosh and Queen Ima picked up the pieces of their kingdom, rising from the ashes of Nogard's fires with their small band of farmers. They wore with pride the scars the dragon had given them. They had survived, and they would grow strong again. The queen had borne Nogard's son. Named him Attor. King Enosh loved the boy and raised him as his own. But, when Attor was thirteen, he began to change. He grew violent, wild, angry, jealous, and prideful. I'm sure you can relate."

Cal bristled against the insulting truth.

"Attor's body began to change soon after. He grew fangs and claws. Fur sprouted on his shoulders and back. The king and queen wept and worried as they watched Attor begin to transform into a wolf."

The words resonated through Cal's bones. His mind filled with dread while his blood sang with hope.

"The dragon returned, over a decade after he had destroyed Skotar with his flames. It was a beautiful summer day, and the royal family, including Attor, surveyed the fields outside the castle walls. Nogard landed in their midst. He had grown bigger, blacker, stronger. He had come to claim his son. Nogard reached a clawed hand forward, securing Attor in his clutches, but before he could take to the air, the queen, brave Queen Ima, threw herself at the dragon, wailing for her son. She pulled futilely at the dragon's claws, yelling, 'take me instead. Let him go!' The dragon flung her away. Attor screamed as his father burned his mother to ash before she even hit the ground."

Unexpected tears welled in Cal's eyes. Embarrassed, he brushed them away.

"Nogard flew off with Attor, and the kingdom believed the prince lost forever. But a few weeks later, Prince Attor returned. He arrived at the white castle gate nearly dead from cold, hunger, and injury. They nursed him back to health, and as he recovered, they realized that he had not changed since the day his mother had died. He remained, from that day forward, half-man, half-beast. He walked and talked like a man, but he had the strength and wildness of a wolf. From him, all Draco Sang are born. They are born with the blood of the dragon. Attor's daughter, who matured into a lynx Draco Sang, took the throne after she killed her grandpapi, King Enosh, and her father, Attor. The Draco Sang have ruled Skotar ever since."

Cal exhaled into the silence. He couldn't process what he had heard. His vision blurred as he blurted his first question. "Why didn't Attor completely become a wolf?"

"That question has been debated for the last three hundred years. But I believe it to be the sacrifice of his mother. Draco Sang are fathered by hate, but mothered by love."

"Fathered by hate. Mothered by love." Cal pondered the tragic tale. "So the Draco Sang are truly half-monster, and have multiplied in Skotar over the last three hundred years."

Titus nodded. "As Draco Sang mature, they transform. Every one I've seen has clear humanoid features. You would not mistake one for an animal. Or a man. They have hands with fingers and a thumb, even if those also have claws or talons, or have webbing between them. They can walk upright, except the fish ones who live in the waters. They speak with cunning and intelligence. The Draco Sang rule Skotar. Humans are no longer viewed as equals—humans are slaves."

"And my father was like that thing yesterday."

"Your father is much, much worse than that little pup."

Is. Not was. Cal opened his mouth to laugh, but a wheezing gasp escaped. His father was alive. And he was a monster.

"And unless you conquer your blood, you will soon show physical signs of an animal as you mature into a Draco Sang."

Barbs in his chest clutched at Titus's words, holding them tight, validating them. Cal shook his head, as if he could erase the image of the abomination that had attacked them yesterday. He was not that. That was disgusting. "No." The word was a plea. He crouched low to the ground, groping for the trees at his back, seeking support and finding none. Yet he knew Titus spoke truth. His insides shattered as the beast inside unfurled its wings and howled through his blood. He wanted to tear Titus's eyes out.

Titus no longer leaned against the rocks; he poised in a crouch, his hand on the knife that hung on his belt, eyeing Cal warily.

"So, you're here to kill me?" That's why his mother had cried when she left. That's why Grandpapi had told him never to return. They knew what he would become. They'd sent Titus to get rid of him. It felt as if a blunt blade had been buried in his heart. "Why didn't you let the Draco Sang do it yesterday? Save you the trouble." Cal's mind whirled with possible attack and defense moves. He'd seen Titus's skill. Cal was dead.

"The Draco didn't want you dead, and neither do I. We're here to *prevent* your transformation. But you need to calm down."

Cal roared. Blood boiled in his ears.

"You're Draco Sang. But you don't have to let the beast control you. You can overcome your blood. Take control of your inner dragon."

Nerves flamed and Cal growled. Titus's words skittered over the storm in his mind. What was he talking about?

"Breathe. Calm your heart."

"I can't." Cal exploded into the trees, Titus's shouts barely reaching his ears.

Mud squished between his bare toes. Branches whipped his face and scratched at his arms, adding to his torment. He stopped. Heat steamed off his skin. His heart reveled in the power of the blood pounding through his limbs.

Leaves rustled nearby. He slipped through the wet foliage to the source. A pig rooted in the groundcover with her snout.

Kill it.

Quietly he found a fist-sized rock and crept forward. The

pig lifted her eyes, and Cal gave in to the song of his soul. The pig shrieked as Cal landed on her back. He drove the stone into her skull again and again. The crunch echoed through his bones. It was too easy to end her life.

As he sat next to his kill, splattered with blood and brains, the pulsing energy in his chest died, leaving him hollow and sad. The truth of what he was settled heavily on his ribs. He'd done exactly what his inner dragon had asked, like a pawn in its hands. He should have been stronger. Shame speared him with stark truth.

The Draco Sang were real, and he was one of them. He looked at his hands, calloused and thick, but still the hands of a man. How long before they become clawed and savage? Despair choked him as blood and death attacked his nose.

He was a monster.

ELEVEN - HUNGRY
FERTH

*A*rms folded over his grumbling stomach, Ferth leaned his shaved head against the wall of the shallow mining pit, waiting for the hunger trial to begin. *Let's get this over with.*

He eyed the other half-starved underlings in the pit. Like the rest, he'd stripped to his undershorts—no sneaking weapons.

Ferth was the last of his class to transform. The other trainees his age were now taunting spectators just above his head. Humiliation heated his spine. He was competing in the pit for the twenty-third time. He thought it must be a record. And not the good kind.

On the ground above the shallow pit, Mavras, the scorpion queen, perched on her throne of bones. Slaves brought her royal chair outside four times a year so she could sit in splendor as she watched the underlings fight for food. Her poisonous tail slashed back and forth in a display of sadistic eagerness.

"Time to feed the underlings," Queen Mavras said. The queen's hissing voice sliced at Ferth's ears.

Laconius stood at his place of rank at the queen's right. Arms crossed and dark eyes threatening, he glared at his son. Ferth flicked his gaze away. Fangs, feathers, and fur danced above his head as excited Draco Sang peered over the edge of the pit. In the muggy afternoon, the Dracos wore more jewelry and weapons than fabric. A swan woman with downy white cleavage caught Ferth's eye as she craned her long neck forward. She ruffled her chest and blew him a kiss. He didn't react.

The smell of roasted meat and fresh bread rolled across the quarry. Taunting Dracos dangled food over the edge of the pit. A squirrely woman took exaggerated bites. Chicken fat greased her fuzzy chin. Ferth appreciated her efforts to diminish his appetite.

"Oy, Ferth, watch out for that killer," Thirro said, pointing his downy arm at a trembling girl.

Ferth strangled the urge to reach out and yank Thirro into the pit. Ferth stood tall enough that he could easily touch the feet of the Draco Sang crowded around the edges. He tuned out the jeering and shouting as he inched closer to the girl. Brow furrowed, her violet gaze darted over the pit. Her freshly shaved scalp shone stark against her olive face, marking her as one of the newest underlings—a ten-year-old hatchling, just starting her training at the castle. Her first hunger trial. Ferth studied her. The overwhelmed gleam in her eyes matched the cluster of ten-year-olds cowering off to the side, but she was not with them. She did not look like a hatchling. Small breasts, square shoulders, and long legs marked her as older. Underlings jostled her as they elbowed each other for a good position. She didn't seem to notice, her mouth ajar as her gaze raked over the riot of surrounding Dracos. It was foolish, and rare, for a hatchling to try and join the center fray. She would earn an injury for her efforts, not food.

Ferth shoved his way to her side. "Stay right behind me," he whispered in the girl's ear, his lip accidentally brushing her skin. She shivered, and he gave her more space as he said, "I'll help you."

She stared at him, purple eyes eating him up like she'd never seen a boy before. He started to repeat his instructions, but Mavras threw in a handful of onion buns, and the frenzy began. The underlings at Shi Castle hadn't eaten in two days. It showed. Nails clawed. Fists flew. Elbows jabbed.

Ferth had always been good at the hunger trial. Instinctively he'd calculate where food would land, and he'd often be there to snatch it from the air. The problem was fighting off the ravenous underlings once he had the food. He'd learned years ago how to fight while chewing.

A chicken leg sailed into his palm. He handed it to the girl cowering behind him. Eagerly she grabbed it and brought it to her lips. Ferth twisted to block a fist directed at her head, and nails raked down his back. His elbow connected with cartilage as he whirled. His attacker bent forward, blood gushing from her nose. Ferth shoved her to the side. He ripped a corncob from a particularly annoying underling. The boy turned to fight. Ferth snarled, and the boy backed away. After reaching the corn back to the hatchling, Ferth snatched a flying potato. Why he had decided to help her, he didn't know. It made the trial more interesting, more bearable, at least. It was the kind of shameful behavior his father severely discouraged.

The spectators cheered his name several times, but he didn't look up. He took what he wanted out of hungry hands, throwing punches whenever someone opposed him. Most didn't, and he was glad. And he knew he shouldn't be. He should enjoy this violent dance and embrace the opportunity to display his prowess. He tried to give up control to the beast inside, and it fueled him with power and speed, but he failed to feel the passionate pleasure in this rampage that his people thrived on.

A roaring chant rolled across the crowd.

Molded and made up after his blood.
An heir of the Dragon has risen from the mud.

Someone's beast had begun to emerge. Someone was worthy of their dragon inheritance. Ferth glanced at his bare chest and hands. Still hairless and free of any talons. As always.

The hunger trial aimed to create an atmosphere where the underlings could yield to their blood and prove themselves worthy of their heritage. It seemed to Ferth more of a sick game for the court's entertainment, but it sometimes did work at exposing a Draco Sang. Just never for him.

The food disappeared; there wasn't nearly enough. The trial ended, at least for the Draco onlookers. The underlings wouldn't be allowed back into the dining hall for another two days. Bruises bloomed on Ferth's shoulders. Scratches striped his arms and back. But the other underlings were a bloody mess. Flecks of iron ore colored the dirt orange around motionless bodies. The girl leaned against a side wall. A red slash marked her neck and blood painted her hands. Ferth handed her the small potato.

She took it, careless of the gore dripping down her fingernails. "Thanks."

His lips curved up in amusement. "I see you snuck in weapons." He touched the tip of an overgrown fingernail, filed to a sharp point. Mistaking her wide eyes and delicate face for innocence would be a mistake. "What's this from?" He pointed to the red drip.

"That brute took my corn." Her gaze flashed to a stocky fourteen-year-old.

"And you took his flesh in return?"

Her rosebud mouth morphed into a wicked curve.

"What's your name?" She looked familiar, but he couldn't place her. He didn't see the nursery children often. They were housed on the far side of the stronghold, away from the citadel and the training grounds.

"Jade."

"Ferth."

She batted her eyes, puffed out her chest, and slunk forward a step.

"Don't do that."

Confusion furrowed her young face.

"You're a hatchling?"

Something flashed in her eyes. "No. I'm twelve. I just came to the castle." She looked down, then back up. "As tribute from my family. I'm from a band of lawless ones."

Plenty of Dracos lived in the wild, outside the strongholds and civility. They were encouraged to send their oldest children to the crown in exchange for the queen generally ignoring them.

"Why didn't you come here two years ago?"

Jade opened her mouth, but Mavras's high whine interrupted them. "Oh, my little ones. That was fun. I expect great things." The last words were a threatening command. She stood, her low tunic shifting to reveal scars above her heart in the shape of the royal brand. "One of you has made your ma very proud."

She pointed a skeletal hand toward the girl in the middle of the pit who'd sprouted a mane of hair down the back of her head. Her face bones and ears had elongated. The girl dipped in a heavy bow to the queen.

"A horse," Mavras pronounced. "Come and join my court."

Beto, a ram Draco, hefted the girl out of the pit and gave her a blue cloak. She preened under the attention.

Queen Mavras rolled large insect eyes over her court. "That's made me hungry." She motioned to the horde, the pincers on her shoulders snapping. "Come feast, my friends." Twin rhinoceros guards followed close behind as she strutted away.

A wad of spit landed on Ferth's bare shoulder, making his blood sing more powerfully than the hunger trial had. Thirro peered down, his eagle eyes glossy. "You're pathetic, Ferth."

Ferth grabbed one of Thirro's thin ankles and jerked. Thirro fell hard on his young wings. Ferth laughed as Thirro scrambled to his feet, cursing and swearing revenge. A storm of hate festered on his feathery face.

"Up and out, all of you." Beto's deep voice boomed over the quarry. Beto was the underling's head trainer. Ferth knew that voice even in his sleep.

Ferth discreetly nudged the prone figures on the floor with his foot as he walked past. It wouldn't be pleasant to wake up and realize you'd been left at the mining pit. He skipped the line for the rope ladder and swung nimbly out of the trench. He stalked off, alone.

He opened the door to his small room and gritted his teeth to stifle his groan.

Laconius, the mighty cape buffalo, the queen's sword, hammer, and strength, could barely fit into Ferth's low barrack. Flat horns curled over the crown of his head and ended in sharp points. Curly hair flowed over muscled shoulders. At any moment, Ferth expected steam to roll out of his leathery snout.

"Shouldn't you be feasting?" Ferth asked. He reached for his boots, but a steel grip caught his shoulder.

"Do you feel no shame? You, the only one in your class

still in the pit, and you waste your talent helping a hatchling?"

"Just trying something new to see if it would work." The excuse sounded weak, even to him.

Laconius's black eyes narrowed. Square fingernails dug painfully into Ferth's skin. "You want to try something new? Let's do it."

Dread coiled in Ferth's gut as his father dragged him out of the room before he could put on clothes or shoes. Slaves and underlings scrambled to get out of the way as Laconius marched him down the hall. When they emerged into the massive castle courtyard, Laconius let Ferth go with a shove. Ferth squared his shoulders and followed his father out of the gate and down the steep slopes to the valley. The short summer months were the only warm days in Skotar, and Ferth was soon sweating in the sun as he jumped over thorns, bushes, and rocks, trying to protect his bare feet.

"The beast will leave a man if he is too weak to honor his blood. It's a shame to lose your gift. A mutilation and an abomination," Laconius reminded him for the thousandth time.

"Yes, Father."

They wound up the thin trails of the neighboring mountain and stopped at Azure Lake, an endlessly deep pool of icy clear water.

"Climb with me." Laconius motioned to the rocky slope that jetted out over the lake. "They say some may see their future reflecting off these waters. Look with me."

Ferth wanted to ask who said that, but instead he dutifully scrambled up the rocks after his father. Crouching, he peered over the ledge into the blue deep. Sunshine reflected a brilliant array on the glassy surface. Ferth could only hope his future would be so serene and beautiful. But what lurked in the shadows below?

Strong hands rammed his back. He lurched forward. Wheeling his arms, he leapt back, away from the drop. Laconius shoved again, and Ferth fell off the rock.

He had not seen that coming.

Ferth cut through the air, sucking in a breath as he hit the surface and was buried in the frigid waters. Ice crawled over his bald head and danced across his face. Anger roared to life, waking the beast slumbering in his chest. He thrashed to the surface and howled at his father.

"Are you at least a water Draco?" Laconius yelled. "That would be less shameful than nothing."

Ferth slipped under, stifling his father's bark. He was a poor swimmer, and his limbs had nearly lost function. Flipping onto his back, he kicked toward the edge. Sinking, he rolled to his stomach. And froze.

Bright eyes blinked below him. Adrenaline spiked his heart, and fear sped his flight. He clambered toward the banks. The eyes drew closer, framed by a gilled face. Fins flanked white breasts and long arms. The Draco's lips curved up below eyes as cold and dead as a nightmare.

Ferth lifted his head and gulped down air. Land taunted him, scarcely a few feet away. His blood screamed with urgency. As his fingers touched the pebbly banks, a silky hand wrapped around his ankle. Ferth lurched forward and grabbed the branch of a tree overhanging the lake. With shocking force, she jerked him back into the choking cold.

His arms flew above his head as he clung to the tree. His hands burned as they slid down the bark. The roots caught, and he jolted to a halt. Ferth kicked at the creature, but she darted clear of the sluggish attack. Her face appeared inches from his. Wrapping her arms around his chest, she rubbed her slippery body against him. Fins scratched along his skin. Her clammy fingers danced possessively over his ribs and waist. He snarled, bubbles streaming out of his mouth. She smiled, showing four rows of needle teeth.

Blood thundered, and with renewed strength, he yanked hard on the branch. Gasping, he broke the surface. The Draco's scream pierced the water. She latched onto his legs, tugging him down. The tree cracked. It slipped forward, weakening its grip on land.

Laconius watched from the shore, his face stone. Ferth didn't waste his breath calling for help. Hand over hand, he inched up the branch. Blood dripped down his palms. Teeth sank into his calf. He sucked down a scream. His free foot connected with her face, and she released her jaws. Ferth scrambled up the rocky bank and into the long grass. Pink-skinned and shaking, he ignored the disgust on his father's face. Blood trickled down his legs and feet as he wobbled by. He didn't look back.

He'd listened to the roar of his blood, fought for his life and lived, but never had he felt so human.

TWELVE - HEWAN
CAL

The rain weakened as Cal wallowed by his kill. Bright blue eyes on a massive golden face appeared between tree branches. Cal startled. He squinted, but it vanished. Merely a vision on the mist. With a grunt, he shouldered the pig. The forest fought his every step as he faltered under his heavy burdens. He broke into camp, dropped the body at Titus's feet, and crumpled to the ground.

"Are we eating this raw, or do you know how to make fire from wet wood?" Titus asked.

The question cut through the self-pitying fog in Cal's brain. "There's probably dry wood near the forest's edge. Near the flat lands on the way to Neese."

"So you *can* still use your head after that thoughtless episode."

Cal rolled to a seat. Mud added to the filth on his clothes. "I'm sorry."

"Don't be sorry. Be better. This is serious. You must overcome the dragon, or you will become a beast."

Cal couldn't meet the man's gaze.

"Unless that's what you want."

"No. It's not what I want." As he said the words, he realized how true they were. "I don't want to be like this."

"Then you had better be ready to work. Your blood is strong."

"I'm ready."

Titus nodded. He didn't take his eyes off Cal as a golden lion padded into the clearing.

Cal leapt to his feet, his blood flaring. He jumped in front of Titus, his arms up as meager protection. Every fiber of his being wanted to fight this mighty beast, kill it, and wear its mane as his own. He scanned the clearing; his knife sat on a boulder to his right. Slowly, he realized the lion hadn't moved from his stance by the entrance. Titus remained calm and studious. Everything felt wrong. Cal shivered against the creeping cold down his spine.

"You want to protect me. That's good," Titus said. "You haven't attacked yet. Although you clearly want to, and I thought you would. So, that's something."

"What is it? What's wrong with it?" Cal asked through gritted teeth, still poised to fight.

"There's nothing wrong with him. Meet Eio. My hewan. And you can relax. He won't hurt you," Titus said. "For now."

Eio dipped his head in greeting. As if he understood Titus's words.

Irked, Cal shuffled back. He groped for his knife, risking cutting his fingers rather than taking his eye off the unnatural creature. "What's a hewan?"

"I am Draco Sang," Titus said. "Or was. They wouldn't claim me now."

Cal's knees weakened, and he leaned against a boulder.

"And I am living proof that the beast can be overcome. When I mastered my blood, and it wasn't easy, Eio left my body."

"I don't …" Cal couldn't form words.

Titus strode to Eio and stroked the great lion's mane. "You can have this too. Don't let the beast take over your body and mind. Conquer it and be free."

Cal coughed out an overwhelmed laugh. "And a lion will leave my body?"

"Probably not a lion." Titus's smile held a touch of arrogance. "A lion is very rare. But there *is* a beast inside of you. And it *will* emerge. It's up to you whether that form is at your side or in your skin."

"I can't believe it, but I do." Titus was Draco Sang. Cal was not alone. He rolled to his feet. "May I touch him?"

"He says yes."

Cal halted. "He says?"

"There is a connection between us. A channel from mind to mind."

Cal supposed he'd have to believe that too. He marched forward and touched the wet fur on a muscly shoulder. His hand recoiled as if shocked. He jumped back, disgusted. Eio was an abomination. Hatred welled, for both Titus and Eio.

"Fight it," Titus said, his voice gentle. "Your blood revolts against me and my hewan. Don't trust it. Its motives are completely selfish. Either you or your beast will become master. Not both."

Cal nodded but moved away another step.

"Which way is north?" Titus asked.

Cal frowned. "I'm disoriented in here, and with the clouds, I can't see the sun."

"Close your eyes, and tell me if you can sense it."

Cal made sure to give Titus a skeptical look before complying. As he quieted his thoughts and relaxed his limbs, he felt it—a gentle pull, like a silky current, urging him to the left. Calling him home, he realized with a start. The betrayal chilled him. His lifelong desire to leave Siccum had been the dragon controlling him. Tricking him. Again. He held a shaking hand and pointed. He cracked his eyes open, hoping he was wrong.

"Due north," Titus said. "I don't feel it this far south, but Eio always knows. Many heirs of the dragon don't ever feel it, and certainly not this far away."

"Far away from what?"

Titus shrugged. "The dragon."

"Prince Nogard?" Cal's voice was incredulous.

"His grave. His cave. Dead or sleeping, I don't know. They're just theories."

"He can't be alive after three hundred years."

Titus's brows rose. "Now you're the expert on what's possible?"

Cal closed his mouth, wisely dropping the subject of his ignorance. His mind rolled over his past, haunted by the heritage he barely understood. "My mother …" His voice disappeared.

"She took you to Siccum when you were a baby to protect you. She went as far south and away from Skotar as she could go. Your blood smells. Eio scented you long before we got to Neese. We are in the Spickle Woods in the hopes that the animals here will mask your scent long enough. Draco Sang hunt Elysium for their own. Be grateful they didn't bother to cross the desert, or they would have found you and taken you back to Skotar, where they would have raised you to become one of them."

"She's known all along. She sacrificed her life for me." He said it with reverence, his heart aching for her. How could he ever repay that debt? All of the terrible things he'd done, all the mean words he'd spat at her, flashed through his mind. Stones piled on his chest.

"She loves you more than life."

Her love strengthened him, hardening his resolve to overcome. *Mothered by love.* He would succeed. Her sacrifice would not be in vain.

Titus put a hand on Cal's shoulder and opened his mouth, but Cal blurted the next dumb thought that came charging in. "Are you my father?"

Titus folded like he'd been punched in the gut. His hand tightened on Cal's shoulder as he looked the young man in the eyes. "No, I am not."

The disappointment that hit surprised Cal. Grief flickered across Titus's face, and Cal saw how deeply the captain loved his ma. Titus had suffered as well. Cal's vow for revenge renewed. He would find his father. And he would kill him. Not just for himself, not just for his ma, but for the man before him painted in sorrow and regret.

Titus rubbed his hands together, shaking off the heaviness. "Let's see to this pig."

They were not so deep in the forest as Cal thought, and they soon had hauled enough dry wood for a steady fire. While Cal dug a hole, Titus prepared the pig. He hacked off a hind leg and threw it at Eio. Cal's blood reacted.

"Hey!" Cal jumped out of the hole. "That's mine."

Titus frowned. "And are you the only one who's going to eat it?"

"He's a lion. Can't he hunt for himself?"

"He can."

Eio tore off a chunk of meat. One of his front canines was missing.

Inexplicably angry, Cal's arm rolled back, aiming to launch his rock at the hewan.

"Control it," Titus said, now standing.

Cal hurled the rock against a tree and roared in frustration. Eio lunged to his feet, muscles rolling beneath yellow fur. A moment later, he lay back down, his focus entirely on dinner.

Coward. Spineless chicken.

"That's not good enough," Titus said. "The beast will win if you only resort to distraction and redirection. You must willfully control it."

"It's getting stronger, louder."

"It will come quite forcefully now. You must be stronger, Cal."

Discouraged and subdued, he finished digging the pit. Titus started a fire at the bottom. The light brightened camp and dried out their belongings. Cal changed out of his blood-splattered clothes. When the flames subsided, they laid the pig in her ashy grave and covered her with a blanket of sticks and leaves.

A little boy a long way from home, Cal curled up under the canvas for a long night of stormy dreams. He longed for Ma and Grandpapi, the familiar faces to talk through his fears. The smell of roasting meat wafted through the air, drawing hungry visitors. Eio prowled the perimeter of camp, guarding him and his breakfast.

He might have been wrong about Eio.

*L*ong summer days cast the evening in sunshine. Ferth stopped at the farms. With one eye on the lazy sentry, he picked two apples, devouring them before he noticed they weren't ripe. The zucchini tasted sweet and fresh, and he stuck extra in his shorts. A slave tending the field watched him do it but said nothing. Instead, the man shuffled over and handed him a bunch of strawberries.

Ferth glanced at his tattered shorts and bloodied limbs. Pathetic enough for a slave's pity.

Strawberries were not served in the underlings' kitchen. He'd had them only twice: from his father the day before he became an underling, and when he won the tri-stake tournament at only fourteen.

Warmth spread over Ferth's chest as he accepted the gift. He hesitated to leave the man and the healing human contact, but the slave shooed him away. A guard walked toward that end of the fields, and Ferth couldn't linger.

Ferth picked at strawberry seeds and stems in his teeth as he crossed the castle courtyard. Back in the barracks, in the privacy of his single room, the edge of his hunger blunted, he peeled off his shorts. Dried blood caked his hands and feet and the teeth marks down his shins. He tugged on fresh clothes. He was expected to get treatment with the underlings' healer, but instead he went to find Keturah.

Few Dracos graced the halls as the feasting, drinking, and revelry in the citadel would continue for hours. He crossed over the courtyard and into the slave houses. The humans pointedly ignored him, busying about with their duties as if that made them invisible. He took the twisting stone stairs down.

Fires lit the murky basement. He scrunched his nose at the smell of urine and lye. Keturah bent over a laundry bath. Her thin face flushed in the heat, and her eyes pinched as she worked through the steam. A gray braid trailed her spine. She looked up, and her scowl melted into a smile. She wiped wrinkled red hands on her apron before motioning him over. He bent down several inches so she could plant a kiss on each cheek. Laconius didn't approve of their relationship. He thought a man shouldn't visit his nurse after the age of ten, but Ferth ached for the comfort of Keturah's gentle kindness.

"How did the hunger trial go?"

"Same as always. I'm still here."

The other laundry workers had slowed their work and cocked their heads to listen, surely hoping to add interest to their day with gossip.

"Come." Keturah led him to her small office. She managed the laundry and had the tiny corner room for her duties. She shared a bunk on the fourth floor, but Ferth hadn't seen it. Her office basement was her one private space.

With Ferth's rigorous training schedule, he hadn't been down to see her in weeks. As Keturah closed the door on the outside world, he sighed in relief. She motioned to the single chair, but Ferth shook his head, insisting the tired woman sit. He sank to the floor and rolled up his pant legs. Keturah jumped from her chair to the medicine box. It was commissioned for laundry accidents, but she used it frequently for Ferth.

"You haven't had this much trouble at the trial in years." She dabbed witch hazel over the gashes.

"These are from a lovely lake lady in Azure."

Keturah raised pale eyebrows.

"Father thought a swim would do me good. Maybe bring out a water Draco. Or he was trying to kill me."

"I'm sorry." She laid a hand over his. Her skin felt dry and papery, but the warm touch comforted.

"Don't be. It's my own fault I remain human. Too weak. Too soft."

A shadow passed over her face. "There were many babies before you and some after. But of all those assigned to me, I think you are the only one who knows my name. You are not weak. Or soft." She poked the dense muscle of his forearm. "There was strength in you even as a suckling baby. You are powerful, Ferth. You will make a great Draco Sang one day." Her voice quivered on the last words, as if they tasted foul.

"One day isn't good enough. My father is losing patience."

"He's a fool."

Ferth laughed, and the bands around his chest loosened. No one dared speak ill of Laconius, the fearsome army chief, except Keturah, who commonly tore him apart in the privacy of her tiny basement cell.

She smeared her special salve into his cuts. She made the green-tinged cream from painstakingly gathering healing herbs, then preparing them with loodia pulp. "You still have more of this?"

He refused to admit how often he dipped into the small tin she'd refilled just last month. "Yes."

They sat in comfortable silence as Keturah worked his wounds. How could he want to transform when he knew it would cost him this? How could he give up control to the beast when it meant giving up this sliver of home—even if this thing that he clung to was only stolen snatches of love in the shadows? Melancholy settled over his slumped shoulders.

"You know the plumloch flower?"

He nodded.

"It waits until the ground is near covered in frost, and in the moment before it would be frozen forever as a mere bud, it throws open its petals and blossoms into the jewel of the north. A more beautiful bloom, you will never find. But you must wait for it."

"Thanks, Keturah. But if you're right, you will soon fear me and hate me."

"No matter what, Ferth, I will love you."

She didn't mention her fear, the fear that all the slaves shared of the Draco Sang. When he was a child, and they were alone, there were times she scolded him for losing his temper and becoming violent. But never did she say a word when others were present. In company, she would applaud his strength, passion, and pride. Her pale eyes betrayed her heartbreak.

"Eat with me," she said, brightening. She unwrapped a small sandwich and held out the larger half to Ferth.

The shadows in his chest reminded him of his aching hunger. His mouth watered. *Take it. She's just a slave. She's even offering it.* Ferth denied his blood. He knew of his failure even as he forced the beast back, but he could not bring himself to take her meager meal. "No, thanks." He would feast soon enough, and she would continually go hungry. He hoped Kenji had shared his magu with her.

"You're practically starving." She held the fragrant cheese closer.

Ferth found the small zucchini he'd brought for her and set it on the table. "Thanks for fixing me up. Again." He waved goodbye and left before he ripped all her food right out of her thin hands and shoved it down his throat.

FOURTEEN - SUBMISSION
CAL

The day broke sunny and dry. The pig was tender and juicy.

"You can take those to the river." Titus nodded to Cal's heap of clothes, covered in grime and guts. "And yourself." He handed over a bar of soap tied inside a thin sack and an empty water skin. "It's due east one mile."

Cal crept past the sleeping lion and into the forest, keeping the pull north always on his left. The Blade River twisted and churned, the froth grabbing at vines and branches. Cal climbed down the slippery rocks to the water. Braced against a boulder, cold water slammed his bare legs. He shivered as he scrubbed filth from his skin and clothes. A shade lighter than before, he dried in a patch of sunlight, feeling a ray of optimism.

"I will conquer this. Ma will see my hewan by the end of summer." He wondered what it might be. Nothing was as majestic as a lion; he just hoped it wasn't a weasel. He stood and shouldered the heavy water.

Back at camp, Titus took the water and poured the entire

jug over his dirty clothes. Cal's nostrils flared. Titus handed him two empty water skins. "Fill these up again."

Nasty words coated Cal's tongue. His arms refused to obey. He closed his eyes. *Do what he says.* Pretending he was fetching water for his mother, Cal snatched the empty jugs and left. It was a long, distracted walk back.

At the river, he hurled one of the vessels into the rapids. It caught on a branch downriver. *That was stupid.* His pride cooled as he climbed over rocks and roots and worked through chest-high currents to retrieve it. He returned to camp tired, hungry, and frustrated at his own weakness. He gently set the gourds at Titus's feet.

Titus didn't even look up from where he carved the bark off a branch. "Fetch an armful of firewood, and we'll warm up some meat and bread for lunch."

"Cold is fine."

Titus's blue eyes flashed up. "Go."

Cal howled. Titus raised an eyebrow, and Cal cut off the sound. Embarrassed, he dragged leaden legs out for more firewood.

After lunch, Titus held up the two whittled sticks he'd cut from the trees. Practice swords.

Excitement bubbled in Cal, quickly to be washed away by the tedious exercises Titus walked him through. Balance. Body awareness. Core activation. Coordination. Fluidity.

"Learn to hold your spine properly," Titus said. "Then we'll see about kissing swords."

The exercises demanded focus, and Cal thrust his mind and energy into the task, into the distraction. Time passed more kindly than it had in months. Three hours later, Cal's limbs trembling with fatigue, Titus called a halt. Cal handed the untested sword back to Titus.

"You held yourself well, body and mind," Titus said. "Preparation is the key to success."

Cal gulped from the water skin. "Tell me about the army. What are you doing to prepare? What is the training routine? How many soldiers? Are there more like us? What weapons do you have? What about the Draco Sang?"

Approval spread over Titus's face at the burst of questions Cal let loose. He brushed through Eio's fur as he talked, sharing stories of battle. Cal pressed for details as Titus taught him about strategy and combat. He told Cal of his role as a collector of Draco Sang children in Elysium. There was an army unit with others like Titus, men and women with their hewans. Titus had gathered them, although not all the Draco humans joined his army; most were living among the humans, keeping their hewans secret. Optimism spread through Cal as he listened to Titus paint a bright future.

Weeks passed. Every afternoon, Titus taught Cal weaponry. Every night, they talked of war. But every morning, Titus set Cal to doing chores. Cal complied with a mix of success.

Submissiveness shamed his blood.

"Self-discipline is the key," Titus would remind him in a voice that chafed like wet sand.

Cal didn't want to wash Titus's clothes. He wanted to piss all over them, which he did—twice. Other times, Cal returned the clothes dirtier than he found them. Titus would clench his jaw in disappointment but say nothing. Cal thought him a coward.

Cal learned to distinguish between the forces fighting for his control, but following only his human thoughts was extremely hard. When he was tired or hungry, it got harder. He often failed, giving in to the violence, rage, and passion of the dragon.

But, each morning, he woke with the same goal. "I will conquer this."

At each meal, Titus made Cal wait.

Cal sat cross-legged in front of his plate of wild greens and roki hen. Mouth wet, he watched Titus slowly eat his portion.

"What is this helping again?" Cal asked, tormented by the smell of roasted meat.

"Building self-control. Building it like a muscle. That was five minutes." Titus added an egg to Cal's plate as reward.

"I feel like a dog."

"Dogs are wonderful creatures."

Cal gritted his teeth. *Fifteen minutes. Not long at all. Just wait.* Hunger roared. His arm reached out for a piece of roki hanging off the side. Before Cal computed his intentions, he turned his fist from his food and smashed his knuckles into his temple. He pitched sideways. He closed his eyes and let the pain drown out the world.

"You can stop beating yourself up and eat," Titus said.

Cal's eyes throbbed as he rolled forward and snatched the plate.

"Not the prettiest effort, but I commend your determination. Tomorrow, keep control inside." Titus touched his skull.

Cal grunted. "Just like that."

"Just like that." Titus thumped him on the shoulder and went to get the practice swords.

Cal, much to his gratification, learned rapidly. They'd started sparring last week. Cal's blood sang with pleasure as he danced through the warm-up routines. Titus faced Cal, and keeping the tempo slow, they engaged. Titus adjusted Cal's technique as they worked.

"Harness your power. Use it, but don't give up your will to it."

"My blood," Cal said as they caught their breath between sets. "It helps me fight. I feel as if I have an internal guide directing my strokes, protecting me, helping me."

"That doesn't go away. It's hard to know what people feel

without dragon blood, but I have always had an extra sense when fighting. My instincts are strong. My reactions are fast. Those like me, like us, are the best warriors we can find. We are stronger, faster, more natural fighters than other men and women."

Cal jumped to his feet. He would conquer this. He would join the unit of soldiers with hewans in Titus's army, and maybe, someday, lead them. "Let's go again."

Titus looked almost bored as Cal fought as hard and fast as he could. Cal knew that any moment the captain could beat him. And in a flash, Titus slipped his sword past Cal's guard and smacked him on the side. Anger flooded Cal's veins, and he lashed forward. Titus knocked the wild blow away and slashed Cal's arms. The beast surged below the surface.

"Control it," Titus said.

Cal took a deep breath, but his heart continued its charge. *One. Two. Three.* Their swords clapped. *Four. Five.*

Titus's weapon jabbed in a series of lightning-fast strikes. Cal's sword flew into the trees.

Cal's vision tinted red.

With a roar, he leapt at Titus. He ignored the blow of the blunt sword as he charged inside the range of the stick. Cal's fists connected with stomach, jaw, ribs. A massive paw clamped Cal's shoulder and ripped him away. Rage pounded in his ears. He turned on the lion and tackled him to the ground. Tangled, they rolled in the ferns.

"Stop, Callidon! You can stop! Control this!"

The lion's jaw engulfed Cal's shoulder. Teeth scratched along skin, but Eio didn't bite, releasing him instead. The lion was a coward. Cal punched against the thick chest. Eio threw him across the clearing. Cal thudded on his back. Before he could get up, a heavy paw closed around his throat. Eio's blue eyes looked down at him. The world went black.

Cal woke to a painful headache and bruised throat. Shame wracked his body. He had failed. Had to be knocked out. He rolled on his mat. Titus leaned against Eio's flank. They both watched him with the same sad sapphire eyes. Eio wasn't lazy or cowardly. He was incredibly powerful, but *controlled.*

The opposite of me.

Head rolling, Cal crawled to Titus. The captain's beard, now growing down his neck, failed to hide the bruising. Cal tried to speak; a hoarse keening sound eked out. Titus tilted his head toward the water.

After a long drink, Cal said, "I'm sorry." His voice was raspy sand. "If the beast wins." Cal swallowed, his gut fighting against the next words. "You'll kill it." *Me.*

Titus didn't say anything. Didn't have to. Heartbreak and turmoil melted his features. Titus would kill him when he failed. A small part of Cal pitied the man having to execute such a job. What would he tell Ma after killing her son? Is that what Ma expected? Had she meant her goodbye to be forever? Grandpapi certainly had.

His thoughts shifted, and a new scheme came to life. Maybe he could escape Titus's blade. Flee north. Find the Draco Sang. A life in exile was better than death.

"You're stronger than the dragon blood," Titus said. "I know you can overcome this, son."

Son. Cal's head jerked up. Brine slipped down his cheeks.

"It's not over. Take control."

A trickle of hope returned. "Yes, sir." The tears were easier to wipe away than the despair. *I will conquer this.*

Titus faced north, an increasingly common habit.

"Your troops. Do they know you're Draco Sang?"

"The army does. They also know about the other nine Draco Sang descendants, our best fighters. They form a special unit. You will join them."

Cal could scarcely dream.

"But the rest of the world has not yet learned that every Draco Sang is not the enemy. That the curse can become a gift. The mentality needs to change, and I hope someday the people of Elysium will accept us."

"When does the army leave for the border?"

"King Andras is a good man," Titus said, his tone flat. "But he's a fool. He's too far south. The Rugit River was our greatest protection. Now the canals are draining the river faster than I imagined possible."

"Maybe Skotar won't attack," Cal said, trying to wipe the gloom off Titus's face.

"Listen to your blood. With the fertile Kiptos valley on the other side of the river with its lush fields, abundant resources, and weak human protection, do you think there is a chance the Draco Sang won't attack as soon as they have a clear path through the delta?"

No chance.

"My troops have orders to leave Mitera in two weeks. I would like to be the one to lead them to the battlefront."

"Go to them. I know what I must do."

"We will go together. When we have met your hewan."

Or after Titus killed him.

Not if he escaped first.

Ferth wiped a dribble of sweat off his brow. Sun seared his scalp. A slave, wrinkled and hunched, retrieved the arrows sticking from the target downrange.

"That was just a warmup," Thirro said, defending his piss-poor performance. He poured a stream of water over his downy head. The liquid beaded on his feathers and soaked into his shorts, the only clothing Thirro had worn since his transformation. His taloned feet did not do well in boots.

The slave handed Ferth his ten arrows and Thirro his.

Thirro thrust the empty water jug at the man. "Fill this up."

He nodded and trudged away from the narrow range on the far side of the training yard. Few Draco ventured there. Ferth and Thirro were the only ones in sight. Archery took discipline and finely-honed skill. Not like hacking with an axe. Flyers and perimeter guards were the only ones required to study archery.

Ferth checked his arrows' fletching and steel tips for dings or bends. "How much longer do you need to warm up?"

Thirro glared. "First one to get three arrows in the center ring wins."

"Go ahead."

Thirro straightened up. His arrow whistled through the air before sinking into the target, just a sliver outside of the center ring. He was one of the best archers—but not as good as Ferth.

Ferth's first arrow punctured the painted wood just a fraction inside Thirro's. Bull's-eye. That would tick him off.

Thirro exhaled through his huge nose. His next arrow hit the center ring. "One-one."

Ferth fired. "Two-one."

Thirro's third arrow was an entire finger-length wide. His square teeth ground together in frustration. Ferth didn't give him a chance to hope. His third arrow sank into the bull's-eye.

"Feast tonight in the citadel," Thirro said.

Ferth was not allowed in the citadel. No underlings were worthy. He kept his face cold. Thirro would not see that arrow hit its mark.

"I'd better go." Thirro stormed away, intercepting the returning slave on his way and shoving his bow and quiver into the man's hands.

The slave, now laden with weapons and water, walked up to Ferth.

Ferth took the heavy jug and drank. "Thank you."

The slave waited, slack-faced.

"I'll be a little while longer. You may go. I'll take care of my own weapon."

The man left without a flicker of emotion.

Trees whispered in the distance. A breeze kissed his neck. Birds sang. A rare perfect day in Skotar. Yet, rejection and loneliness darkened Ferth's vision. Shaking off the frustration, he strode downrange and retrieved the arrows. He returned to find a girl standing at his place. He halted in surprise.

"Thirro's a poor loser," Jade said.

A fraction of a smile cracked Ferth's gloom. "How long have you been spying?" He glanced around at the open space. "Where were you?"

She pointed to a rock at the bottom of a scrawny little tree. "Helps to be from the forest sometimes."

"Sneaky." And impressive. Ferth's mouth curved in amusement.

"How are you so good at this?"

"Practice," Ferth said. "Patience. Discipline." And he liked the relative solitude of the archery range. It had been a reliable escape these last few years.

"Do you think you'll be a flyer?"

Ferth shrugged, not trusting himself to speak for fear of admitting he might not become anything more than a slave.

She tilted her fine-featured face up to Ferth. "Will you teach me?"

His brows shot up, and he frowned, but she didn't back down. Sunlight lit the pale purples of her eyes, revealing hidden strength and cunning. "Don't you know that cowards fight with a bow and arrow?" That's what Laconius always said. Real Dracos faced their enemies within knife range. "And flyers." Ferth said those last words with a mocking grin. Flyers weren't disrespected like bug or water Dracos, but they tended to be considered *soft.*

Jade didn't laugh. "So, you won't teach me?"

"I didn't say that."

"I want to learn. I want to learn everything I can. Only a fool goes to battle unprepared."

Ferth stared at the girl who spoke his own thoughts. "How old are you really?"

He meant it as a joke, a compliment, but her cheeks

flushed, and her eyes darted. "Twelve." She spat out the word too harshly. Defensively.

Ferth twisted his bow in his hands, curiosity flaming. "You're lying."

Her jaw rippled, and her fists flew to an attack position.

"Oh," Ferth said, not so much as flinching. "Would you like to learn to fight hand to hand as well?"

Jade swallowed and dropped her hands.

Ferth waited.

"I'm not telling you anything," Jade said.

"Okay. You'd better run along to your nurse then."

Her eyes narrowed into slits. She hissed.

Ferth turned away. He plucked an arrow from his quiver and sent it pinging into the bull's-eye.

"Will you promise to teach me?" Jade asked. Ferth faced her again. "And keep my secret?"

"Yes."

"I'm fifteen, not twelve. But I'm small enough to pass."

Ferth laughed. This girl who didn't reach his shoulder was not one year younger than he. "Now you're really lying."

"I am not lying."

"Show me your brand."

She gritted her teeth and pulled back the collar of her shirt, revealing the scars marring the skin above her small left breast. *IJ06289.*

"289. That's twelve."

Jade lifted her chin in defiance. "The brand is the lie. I'm telling the truth."

"Brands don't lie."

"Mine does."

Ferth supposed it would be *possible* to sneak a baby a different brand. "And why, then? Why go to all the trouble to tell the world you're three years younger than you are?"

"You haven't earned that story yet."

Ferth rolled his eyes. She didn't look like a fifteen-year-old, but she had the snark of one. "Come. Stand here."

He picked up her petite hand. She glanced at her palm cradled in his and then up at his face. He flinched at the desire sprouting there.

"You're still twelve in my mind. That's too young for me." He said it as kindly as he knew how, but still, she bristled.

He placed her grip on the handle as he explained the mechanics of the bow. He curled her two fingers around the bowstring. "Elbow up. Pull back the string. Draw it across your chest."

Jade tugged. She strained and cursed. But the string would not respond. When it looked like the vein on her neck would explode, Ferth wrapped his hands over hers and forced her to relax.

"I'll see if I can find an easier bow," Ferth said. "This one is far too long for you anyway."

"I'll get stronger," Jade said. "And bigger."

Ferth wondered if she wasn't talking only about archery anymore. Again she seemed poised to fight, but Ferth had made no threats. He plucked an arrow and sent it downrange.

"Show-off."

He shot her a sideways grin. She took the bow out of his hands. Her arrow dove into the ground halfway to the target.

"Again," Jade said.

She exhausted Ferth's quiver stock of arrows, never once hitting the target.

"I'll get better," Jade said.

"I've no doubt." Ferth picked up arrows off the ground.

But would he?

SIXTEEN - TEMPTATION
CAL

In the weeks they'd spent in the Spickle Woods, Cal had grown like a weed on the food they hunted and foraged. Clumps of hair sprouted on his face. His shoulders and back thickened, and his muscles bulged. He tamed his long hair by tying it back with a leather thong.

The summer sun was weaker here than in Siccum, and Cal barely noticed the heat on his back as he hacked apart dead trees at the forest's edge.

A woman's song rose on the wind and speared his ears. The clear sound lured him in. Not caring he was shirtless, sweat dripping down his skin, he dropped Titus's axe and followed the clarion call.

Peeking from behind branches, he saw her under the shade of a nearby tree at the edge of the forest, overlooking the flatlands. She sat on a patchwork quilt, her shoes kicked off to the side. Her tattered dress clumped around her thighs, revealing creamy legs. In the distance, workers hunched over their crops. Her sweet song ended, leaving a void in Cal's chest.

Every fiber of his being urged him forward. He tore his

gaze away, but her image burned across his vision. Desire flamed.

He needed to get back to work. He sprinted to his wood-pile. He hacked and hacked and hacked until he reduced the logs to splinters, but still, his blood thundered for the woman. Without thought, he was back in the forest, watching her. Lust hazed his mind. He took a step toward her. And another. His thoughts clamored, *STOP.* He'd left Titus's axe. He needed to go get it. Teeth locked in an aching grimace, he dragged himself away. Back at his worksite, he hefted the axe. His heart swung like a feral blade. He'd been away from people too long. His body yearned to test its prowess. Such an easy target; she practically lay in wait for him.

On the brink of becoming his father, he darted into the forest until he found a tree thick with hanging vines. He attacked the living cords. He tied up his ankles, focusing solely on this one task. He cut more and moved up his body. His pulse pounded in protest. Vine after vine cinched his body until he was up to his nipples in green rope. He flung the axe away before he could slice free. He tied knots until, no matter how much thrashing he did, there was no escape.

And then he thrashed.

The ropes cut into his skin, but still he fought to break free. Finally, mercifully, exhaustion won out. His pulse slowed, and the beast slumbered. Daylight faded.

He was trapped.

His manmade cocoon slipped to the ground. Dried blood caked his skin. He closed his eyes and his mind. Minutes passed. An hour. Darkness claimed the forest. Cal imagined himself a cloud floating away on the breeze. A rustle of leaves snapped him from his stupor. He was a defenseless fool. The axe blade gleamed in the moonlight, out of reach.

Soft footsteps drew closer. Cal nearly peed in fright. He cried out in relief when Eio stepped into sight.

The big animal looked him over, then plopped to the ground with a heavy sigh. Cal's feet had lost feeling by the time Titus appeared. Wordlessly, Titus pulled out his knife and began cutting away vines. The silver light of the moon guided his work.

"I resorted to distraction." Cal shook his sore arms free. "There was a woman near the forest. I didn't know how else to stop myself. The want was so strong." His face burned at his admission.

Titus's eyes softened. "You did well, son."

"I should have done better. I should have been able to simply walk away. I should have been able to do nothing at all, ignore her."

"A beautiful woman is hard for any man to ignore."

Cal peeled himself off the dirt. His feet prickled. Muscles warmed as feeling returned. He picked up the axe, and together they returned to get the firewood. Yet there was none; instead, splinters and shredded trees decorated the site. Cal retrieved his shirt while Titus surveyed the wreckage.

"You had quite a fight." Titus put a hand on Cal's shoulder but said nothing more.

Over the next few days, a torrent of emotions and passions raged within Cal. Clear thinking was difficult. Sleep eluded him. A confused cocktail of commotion wracked his soul.

One morning, Cal killed a young magu, and they ate a hot meal of fresh meat and wild mushrooms. After cutting up the remains, he set them out to cool. Titus left to wash in the river, while Cal dozed against a tree.

The boy was quiet as he slipped into their small clearing, but Cal's blood buzzed, on full alert. His eyes popped open as the boy grabbed a handful of deer meat. He turned to run, but Cal lunged. In a breath, he'd wedged the boy beneath his knee and pinned scrawny arms above the boy's head.

"I shouldn'ta done it, mister."

Cal took pleasure in the boy's weakness. His hand wrapped around a thin throat. So soft. So easily crushed. A call for violence rang through Cal. In dismay, Cal thought of a myriad of ways to kill the thief under his palms.

"No," Cal growled, and the boy flinched. "No!" He jerked back and got to his feet. Gently, he helped the boy stand. "We have enough to share." He grabbed another handful of meat, delighting in the feeling of ownership over his actions. "Hold out your shirt."

Arms shaking, the boy tugged out the front of a threadbare tunic. Cal filled it with cooked deer.

"Thank you, sir." The boy spun to leave.

"Hold on."

The boy froze. His eyes darted. Cal pulled off his shirt. The boy stared in horror at the scabs and bruises peppering Cal's chest. Cal wrapped the meat in his shirt and handed the bundle back. His blood raged and slammed against the action.

"Good luck to you."

"My sis says thanks to ya too."

Cal nodded. The boy bolted. That's when Cal noticed the familiar figure watching from the shadows. Titus's grin split his bearded face wide open. Cal smiled back. The dragon skittered away, retreating deep within Cal.

That night, he slept deeply in his dreams. He stood at the top of a high pinnacle on a mountain hewn from diamond. The sunlight reflecting off the facets burned his eyes. The world far below the peak lay charred and barren. An altar of white stone stood before him.

"Callidon." The voice cut him to the quick. He saw no

one. "You gave the boy your meat, but would you give him your life?" The voice penetrated Cal's deepest crevices.

He wanted to run from the sound, the invisible presence. His crimes crawled over his skin. He wanted to bury them, cover his naked soul, but there was nowhere to hide on the translucent stone.

"I require a sacrifice. One life." An unbendable command.

The starving boy appeared on top of the altar. An ivory knife gleamed in Cal's hand, the hilt cold against his callouses. The boy's eyes widened, pleading and fearful.

You are worth more than he. The thought sprouted from deep inside Cal. *A simple task for a real man.* The blade trembled as he raised it. He imagined the boy's blood seeping over the white stone, running over his hands, staining the world.

He laid a palm on the boy's shaking shoulder. Two pulses pounded through the connection. The knife lowered a fraction. A shuddering breath escaped Cal as he turned the blade and thrust it squarely into his own heart.

The boy vanished. Pain wracked Cal. Agony spread over his limbs, and still, he did not fall. His heart continued to beat.

"Well done, my son." The voice gushed with pure love. How had it ever seemed otherwise?

Red tendrils curled from the throbbing wound in Cal's chest. They pooled over the altar, swirling into a crimson beast with golden eyes.

The vision hung vibrant in his mind as he woke and opened his eyes. White fur filled his view. Adrenaline spiked his limbs, sending him shooting to his feet. Panting, he peered at the sleeping mass. Amber eyes opened as a large wolf picked up his head. Cal lunged for his hunting knife. The wolf lurched to his feet and padded forward. With shaking fingers, Cal held out the blade, a weak defense.

Laughter filled Cal's head. He clutched a hand to his ear as he tilted, off-balance.

"Hello, Callidon Mirasson." The wolf spoke to his mind. And the voice was Cal's.

He rooted to the spot, staring bug-eyed at his hewan. The wolf was whiter than Siccum sand. Long-legged and broad of shoulder, its head came to Cal's ribs. The wolf's laughter crackled through Cal's mind. The beast bolted into the forest, right past a wide-eyed Titus and a crouching Eio.

"Son of Attor." Titus's voice was awed. His hand clutched his chest. "A wolf." He stared, unblinking, at the spot where the wolf had disappeared. Finally, he turned to Cal. "You did it, son."

Cal threw his head back and let out a whoop of joy. Pride bubbled through him. He jumped, exuberant and free. His thoughts were his own. His mind churned active and clear. The darkness had gone. The warm wholeness in his chest oozed strength. He danced over and, wrapping his arms around Titus's back, picked the captain off the ground. His blood did not revolt. Instead, a wave of belonging rolled through him. Home.

Titus barked a gruff laugh. "I'm proud of you. You have done what few people can—you have overcome the beast. An impressive beast."

Cal beamed.

"Now, the next step."

"Which is the victory celebration."

Titus turned somber. "You just let a wolf loose in the woods."

Cal's enthusiasm waned as earlier lessons came flooding back. He had to control his hewan. Master him.

"Where is he now?"

"I don't know."

"Find him."

Cal picked up his boots.

"No." Titus tapped his skull. "Use your connection."

Closing his eyes and quieting his thoughts, Cal searched his mind for the wolf. A tether reached out to vague images and emotions of a wolf on the hunt. Cal was sure he could follow the chain to his hewan's physical location. "He's hunting about a half-mile northeast."

"Call him back."

He tried to send thoughts down the tether. He didn't get a flicker of response from the wolf. He sent the command with more intention. Annoyed refusal returned to Cal's mind. The wolf kept hunting.

"He won't come," Cal said.

Titus motioned for Cal to help him prepare breakfast. "Another good reason we're in the Spickle Woods." He lit the fire. "The first thing Eio did? He ate my horse." Titus chuckled at the memory. "It was terrifying. I watched him kill it, heard his thoughts as he did. I did nothing to stop him. He revolted me. I was angry that this creature was my blood, my creation. Then, I did the stupidest thing I've ever done." Titus got a strange faraway look. "I tried to kill him."

The water Cal poured into the pan sloshed over the sides as he jerked toward Titus in surprise.

Titus held two fingers to his face. "These scars are from Eio. I couldn't kill him. It was an internal battle as much as a physical one. In the end, he clawed my face and left me. It took me a long time to track him down and master him. And for us to learn to trust each other."

"Does he ever fight you now?" Cal looked at the beast lounging on the matted ferns.

"Not like that. We disagree sometimes, but I am master. I have seen one rare hewan whose master was so full of honor that his hewan never rebelled. And it's a good thing, because we were in the center of Mitera and a grizzly bear can do a lot of damage." Titus set the pot over the fire. "But for the rest of us, we have to learn control and respect. You are utterly and completely responsible for that animal. You must be stronger, always. He has the form of a wolf and will have many natural wolf traits, but he is not a wolf born in a den and raised in a pack. He is born of your blood and raised on your passions. He will not act like a regular wolf, any more than Eio behaves like a wild lion."

Overwhelmed, Cal reached out to his hewan again. The wolf had brought down a deer and begun to feast. *"Come back here."*

The wolf flicked the command away.

Cal forced his will on the beast's mind. He pushed until finally the animal responded. The snarl that reverberated along the connection tightened Cal's jaw.

"I'm eating."

The ire pulsing along the connection was raw and crude and familiar. Cal pained for all the people who'd suffered from his temper. *"You come when I tell you to come. You hunt with my permission."*

Mocking laughter filtered back as the wolf tore into the deer's neck.

Cal turned to Titus, who sat eating wild eggs. "I'll be back."

Titus saluted.

"Save me some breakfast."

Titus snorted as if Cal had no idea what awaited him in the forest. He held out a flat cake to Cal. Increasingly wary, Cal also picked up a small water skin before following the invisible tether to the wolf he'd birthed.

The long walk calmed Cal. When the wolf came into view, it was with pride that he studied the thick white fur, lean legs, and muscled torso. The wolf ignored Cal as he tore into the bloody carcass.

"Your name shall be Lyko."

The wolf didn't look up from his meal. *"I like it."*

Cal grinned. He gathered tinder and dry wood and built a fire. He pulled out his knife as he approached the deer. Lyko's head snapped up. His eyes, the same bright honey as Cal's, narrowed to slits.

"I want that haunch," Cal said.

"You can have the foreleg."

"No."

Lyko kept his sunlit stare on Cal as he sank razor teeth into the deer's haunch. Cal tried to ignore the claws and canines as he stalked forward. Lyko jumped to his feet and stood over his kill. Ears flat against his head and baring blood-covered fangs, Lyko snarled.

"I'll decide what happens with my kill," Lyko said, both in Cal's head and with Cal's voice.

Cal lunged, leveling his face with the wolf's narrow head. Lyko's howl burned across Cal's mind. Cal gritted his teeth and returned the complaint. He roared into Lyko's mind, long and loud. He threw his knife into the deer's glossy eye and attacked his hewan. Hands buried in furry shoulders, he threw the surprised wolf back, with Cal landing on top.

"You are mine, Lyko."

"No, human. I am stronger, smarter, swifter." Lyko snapped at the air, his lips brushing Cal's nose.

Cal wheeled back in fear, but as he did, he recognized that Lyko didn't miss by accident. Lyko wouldn't hurt him.

The connection was deeper than mind to mind. Their blood, hearts, and souls were knit together irrevocably. The power of it lashed across the clearing where human and wolf circled, panting and glaring.

Cal, it seemed, had still not completely conquered his dragon blood. He turned from Lyko and slicked his knife free of the eyeball. *"I'm eating."*

A headache formed at the base of Cal's skull at the stress and strain of Lyko's angry refusals throbbing through his mind. Cal hacked at the deer and held up the meaty thigh in triumph. Lyko barked and bolted into the trees. Cal sighed. He set the meat low over the flames and took a deep drink of water as he waited. He kept track of Lyko's wanderings as his meal cooked. It was well after noon by the time he feasted.

"Meat's good."

"Thief."

Cal didn't deign to reply. Is this what his ma felt after she'd fought so hard to give him life, then he turned around and repaid her with selfishness and pride? Yet she still loved him. He felt it like an ember deep inside his chest. Now, he understood. Despite the work ahead, he would never leave Lyko. The mere thought filled him with despair and loneliness. Even now, half his focus was on the wolf sniffing around the opening of a rabbit hole. His hewan was beautiful and strong and wild. And Cal was proud of him. He'd felt isolated and alone growing up. Not anymore. He had a brother.

Cal ripped off a piece of meat and chewed, his appetite waning. He stomped out the fire and went to find his wolf. Lyko led him northeast, toward the cliffs. Cal's pace slowed as he thought over what to do next. How could he engage his beast without another fight?

He stopped mid-step as fear and surprise lashed out from Lyko. His wolf was a mile away. Cal jerked into a run as horror burned over his chest.

Lyko was caught in a hunter's trap.

Ferth jerked awake as Dara waltzed into his room without knocking. He flipped upright, glad he'd left on his undershorts.

"Thirro is livid about this morning. You bruised his wing," Dara said.

Ferth grinned at Dara. Knocking Thirro onto his back during sword drills had been a particular pleasure. "Does he want me to kiss it better?"

"He certainly wants me to," Dara said with a cocky tilt of her chin.

"You won't find him here."

"He might have pointed out to Beto how long your hair's gotten."

Ferth rolled his eyes.

"Beto banned you from the dining hall until tomorrow night."

Ferth's nostrils flared in annoyance. "And you're his little messenger now?"

Dara ran a caressing hand over the half-inch growth on his head. "I came to offer my services. I'm good with a blade."

Her fingers trailed down his neck, sending a tingle down his spine.

"Get out." The last thing he needed was Dara in here, flaunting her Draco Sang-ness in his face while shaving him back down to size.

"Sure is soft," she whispered, lips on his ear. She fluffed his hair again and danced out, slamming the door behind her.

Ferth hissed out an unhappy breath. No dinner. And he refused to humiliate himself by going with the underlings to get sheared by Ivan, the sadistic slug. He sat at his table; propping his broken piece of reflective glass against the wall. His fractured reflection frowned back at him. He tried not to look too closely at the loneliness lurking in his golden eyes. Cautiously he tipped his head and brought his straight razor to his scalp. The front was easy. Chunks of brown scattered his arms and table as his blade slid over his crown. He folded an ear forward and worked the spot behind. Warm liquid rolled down his neck as he sliced the skin. He cursed and set down the red blade. Groping around his trunk for a cloth, he found a clean sock and held it to his partially shorn head. A soft knock distracted him from welling self-pity. No one could see him like this.

To his mortification, the door slid open. Pearl held a small stack of his folded clothes. She froze on the threshold when she saw him.

"Excuse me. I didn't think you were here." She turned to leave, then hesitated. Twisting back around, she stepped into his room and closed the door. She set his clothes on top of his trunk and straightened up. Pale gray eyes locked on his. "Would you like me to help you?" There was no pity in her voice.

His razor was sharp. Sharp enough to slit his throat clean open. "Yes."

A curt bob of her head, and she moved to stand behind him. He wiped his blade with his sock and handed it to the slave. Her hands were feather-light on his sensitive scalp. His core warmed with desire. What would those hands feel like over the rest of his skin? Hair rained over his back and shoulders. To his disappointment, she made no move to touch him or brush it off.

Pearl didn't so much as scratch him with the knife. When she finished, she set the weapon on the table and walked to the door. "I'll return with a broom."

"No," Ferth said. "I'll get it." It was as close as he would come to saying thank you.

After she left, he dug out the tin hidden in his trunk. Only a sheen of oily green remained in the bottom. He swiped his finger and spread the cool relief over the cut in his scalp. Would Keturah make him more? Was it unfair to add to her workload because of his recklessness?

EIGHTEEN - TRAPPED
CAL

A net of woven vines suspended an enraged Lyko three feet off the ground. Cal hid in the trees as two hunters circled their prey. Blues and greens painted their faces, while animal skins covered their bodies. One wore a beaver headdress, the other a fox.

"He's a beauty." The voice was female.

"He'll make a glorious biretta." The hunter with the fox skin was a woman as well.

"He's mine."

"He might have been yours if you'd been the one to bait the trap, but as you didn't, he's actually not. And you took home the skunk last week."

"Forget about the skunk," the hunter with the beaver-skin headpiece said. "Forget about anything we've ever trapped before. I've never seen anything so beautiful, and you're kidding yourself if you think I'll let you keep him."

Fox Woman spat at the ground. "A wolf won't make Mikilo take you back. He's far too happy in my cave."

Cal drew closer to the women as they argued.

"Sushwin pact. Whoever kills the wolf, keeps the wolf."

Cal's heart stopped.

"Sushwin swear it."

With the butt of her spear, Fox Woman drew a line in the dirt. They stepped behind it.

"Seems a little unfair," Cal said.

The hunters whirled as he stepped out of the bushes and into view. They leveled twin spears, and each pulled out a knife. Adrenaline exploded through his heart.

"He's ours."

"Undoubtedly," Cal said, keeping his voice casual though his nerves buzzed. "What would I do with him, anyway? I don't wear skins."

"Baby hunter, you are. You can't catch your own furs, but you can't take ours."

"If only they knew how close you were to wearing my fur," Lyko said.

Cal paused, listening to the distracting voice in his head. He wondered then if the women wore skins to look more like Draco Sang. Why would anyone want that? "Seems to me," he observed as he inched closer, "that you'll ruin his fur by shooting your spears through the netting. Such a pretty pelt to damage needlessly."

"He'll kill us."

"Not as dumb as she looks," Lyko said.

"Not mighty hunters like you," Cal said.

Beaver Woman snarled and jabbed her spear toward Cal. "Leave or we'll kill you, too."

"No."

Two hunters coiled to fight.

"The wolf!" Cal flicked a fearful gaze behind the women to the docile wolf in the net. Beaver Woman tilted her head in Lyko's direction. Cal lunged. He grabbed her spear shaft and yanked. She lurched forward. He knocked down her knife as he clamped her against his chest. Fox Woman sliced across his forearm with her spear tip, splitting his skin.

Cal leapt back with his hostage. He held his knife to Beaver Woman's throat. Blood dripped off his arm and down her bodice. He ripped off her hood, and coppery curls fell around her shoulders. She looked barely older than he. Her body trembled under his knife.

"Release the wolf," Cal said to the woman now poised to fight. "And I'll release your friend."

"You won't kill her," Fox Woman said, her tone mocking.

Cal hitched the knife higher. The girl gasped as he drew blood. "I will." His tone was flat, but his mind hiccupped. He couldn't kill her.

Fox Woman studied him from the shadows of her cowl. She stalked close to where Lyko hung.

"*I don't trust her,*" Lyko said.

Fox Woman lifted her knife as if to cut the ropes with her left hand. At the last moment, her right hand jerked the spear forward.

Cal dropped the girl in his arms. His knife left his fingers before his brain could object. The weapon buried itself hilt-deep in Fox Woman's back. Her spear stopped at the base of Lyko's neck.

He'd killed every hare he could find in the Siccum sand this way, but as the girl slumped to the ground, bile rose in Cal's throat. Horror, black as sludge and sticky as tar, coated his chest. He heaved ragged breaths as red spots clouded his vision. The world spun as he jolted forward, his eyes glued to the weeping knife wound. Blood seemed to drain out of him as it did the girl.

"*Get me out.*"

Cal eyed the second hunter, but she was shocked to stone. Her spear lay on the ground, her palms face-up and her gaze glassy.

He crawled forward and felt his victim's neck. No pulse. He gripped the knife handle with a sweaty palm. The stained blade came free with a sickening scrape. He doubled over and vomited in the dirt. Blood beaded on the blades of grass under his boots. Tears washed his face as he purged again. Stomach tight and vision blurry, he twisted and hacked at the net until Lyko fell to the bloody dirt with a heavy thud.

"I'm sorry," Cal said to them all. To the entire world. He put one foot in front of the other and walked away. Lyko followed, his tail limp, and his head hung low. Cal didn't look back.

He found the river, or the river found him. He submerged, letting the current whip him until his body was as numb as his soul. He washed the red mud from Lyko's fur. Cal's arm needed attention, but he didn't dare face Titus yet. Not after what he had done. Not after he'd killed a woman.

Staggering into the forest, he found a welcome tree and shriveled up in the fronds, careless of his cold, wet clothes. Dark dreams tormented him. Everything he touched died. And he could not get clean.

He woke to Lyko curled against his back, sending his warmth through Cal's icy body. Cal sat up. Lyko shifted and laid his muzzle on the ground. Gold eyes watched Cal. He reached out a hand and stroked the white head.

"Yes, Lyko, you are mine." And now he knew just how deep that truth ran. *"I will serve you and protect you."*

Lyko stuck his neck farther out along the dirt toward Cal's boots. *"And you are mine. I will serve you and protect you."*

Cal's heart warmed a degree. The killing would haunt him forever, but he knew he would do it again. The bond demanded it. He would fight for his blood. Even when it meant becoming a monster—a murderer. He would debase, humiliate, shame himself for Lyko, for his family, for Titus. To keep them safe.

He got to his feet. Lyko clung to his heels as they returned to camp.

Titus's head snapped up. Relief relaxed his face as Cal broke into the clearing.

"Just in time for breakfast," Cal said, his voice light.

Titus's sharp gaze traveled to Cal's bloody arm and sliced shirt. "What happened?" He came forward to inspect the wound, obviously cut with a blade.

"Just needs a couple stitches."

Titus opened his mouth. Closed it. Nodded. He turned to the wolf, face expectant.

"Captain Titus, meet Lyko." *"Can you also understand the words I speak aloud to others?"*

"I'm not deaf."

Cal frowned at his wolf's condescending tone.

"I'm happy to meet you … in the flesh." Titus bowed as if meeting one of the ruling rajas.

Lyko dipped his head.

"And this is Eio," Cal said.

"Ah yes, the spineless chicken," Lyko said.

Cal chuckled, but his hand went to his neck where he could almost still feel the crushing paw. How many memories did he and Lyko share? All of them? The thought wasn't entirely unpleasant, and a feeling of devotion coursed between man and wolf.

Titus ran a hand through his shaggy hair. Despite his unkempt beard, he looked younger than when they'd met just weeks earlier. He sighed as if a great burden had lifted. "If only I had the same hope for your brother."

Body systems faltering, Cal's legs wobbled. His voice was a hoarse whisper. "What did you say?"

Titus reeled back as if slapped. He pinched his eyes shut. "I meant it figuratively, as in all our Draco Sang brothers."

Cal's heart hammered. "No, you didn't."

Lyko growled.

Titus opened his eyes. He looked to Cal, then to Lyko, then back again.

"I have a brother?" Emotions clashed through Cal's body. Did he have a half-brother somewhere north? Ma couldn't have had another child without him knowing, could she? Frustration hardened his words. "Tell me."

Titus sighed, stress returning to his brow, aging him again. "Sit." He pointed to a boulder.

Cal perched on the edge, compliant but tense.

"I didn't mean to say anything, but I've been thinking so much about him these last weeks here with you. Mira and I both thought you were better off not knowing."

"Because I can't handle it?"

Titus's voice came out low. "She wanted to spare you pain."

"Pain isn't my enemy. Ignorance is."

Titus looked at Cal for a long moment before dropping his gaze to the dirt. He paced, his shoulders tight. He took off his well-worn hat and twisted it in his hands.

Lyko stood next to Cal, his muscles coiled. Cal had nearly bitten through his tongue by the time Titus spoke again.

"Mira and I grew up in Kiptos, on the northern border to Skotar. Back then, it was smaller. The canals had not been built, but it was still very beautiful." He seemed to see past Cal to another time, and his face softened. "She was one of the few people who knew I was born a Draco Sang. And though I'm seven years older, she loved me anyway. She was the reason I was able to control the dragon. We made plans to marry."

Cal's chest caved at the wistful misery on Titus's face, the man who should have been his father.

"Mira was only fifteen when it happened." Titus's gaze shifted along the ground. "I blame myself. The beast must have scented me. He hunted me, but instead, he found her. I led him to my greatest treasure. To perfect Mira." The words ripped out of Titus as if torn from the flesh of his heart. "He left her on the banks of the Rugit, bloody and barely breathing."

Lyko's warmth penetrated Cal's side. The touch did nothing to dull the horror. He'd known it had happened, but it seemed so much worse hearing Titus say it. His blood curdled as he imagined his ma left like litter on the edge of the river, water licking at her battered body.

Titus's heartbreak was nearly palpable as he said, "We let the town think that the child was mine. My father let us live in the cottage at the edge of his land. We planned to build a life there together, but Mira lived in terror. Nightmares tormented her. She couldn't escape her fear that the Draco would return for you."

I will find him, and I will kill him. Cal's oath renewed itself.

"The village had a healer, but Mira was afraid to go to him. She didn't want anyone to know the truth. When she went into labor, she came to me, refusing my pleas to go to the healer. We had prepared a small cave in the hills to keep it a secret. She had heard false rumors about Draco Sang births. That some babies were born with horns or beast marks or brands. We shouldn't have gone to that cave. Although, perhaps we saved the healer's life by staying away. You looked like any other healthy human baby." Titus tried to smile, but it sagged. His shoulder slumped forward as if he couldn't endure going on.

Cal's ribs tightened around his lungs. He couldn't bear to hear the rest, but he couldn't breathe until he did.

"While Mira labored, *he* came. We were merely children compared to him. He was a monster. A raving bull with curling horns over his head."

The hairs on Cal's neck rose. Lyko shifted as if chilled.

"Eio was our only protection, and he was no match for this Draco. We were untrained, unprepared, and afraid. Your father left Eio unconscious and missing his front canine. When he entered the cave, I held up the only weapons I had, my two knives. He laughed at me. 'Was that your abomination?' he asked. 'You're a disgrace to your blood, but I'll leave you alive because you will help this woman. She will live to breed for me again.' Mira cried out for my help, but instead, I lowered my knives." Titus hung his head in shame.

"He would have killed you," Cal said.

Titus nodded. "But I didn't even try to fight."

"It's not your fault. It's that Draco's fault."

Titus looked into the trees. "He watched, enraptured, as Mira gave birth to a plump screaming baby boy. He took the child from me as soon as he took his first breath. He licked the boy and cut the cord with his teeth. He raved about the boy's power and lineage and the mighty Nogard. He looked down at an ashen Mira. With a knife from his belt, he cut an *L* on her swollen breast. Branding her his. The Draco Sang brand all their babies at birth. They smell the infant for power; if the child is human, they get the mark of a slave on their forearm. If they are Dracos, they get a brand over their hearts. She was no Draco, but I think in his own twisted way, he was honoring her by marking his name over her heart, elevating her above other humans. 'Heal swiftly,' he said. 'For you shall bear me many more that reek with power.' Milky blood trickled down her chest."

Cal swallowed bile.

"Mira didn't say a word. Her face bleached to parchment. I've never seen pain like it was painted on her stricken face. With the baby in his arms, he disappeared into the night. I unfroze and jerked into action. I grabbed my two knives to go after him, to remedy my cowardice. I was halfway out the door when I heard her weak whimper. It was only then I realized there was another baby."

Blue eyes pierced Cal as he sank against Lyko. The truth punched him in the gut. "I have a brother." A full blood brother.

Titus nodded once, his eyes hooded. "Your ma fought to keep you inside, keep you a secret, save you from your brother's fate. It nearly killed her."

"Then she took me south. She left you to protect me." She sacrificed everything to save him.

"She would have given her life to protect you. Or your brother."

"I have a brother." Saying it didn't seem to help the truth sink in. *My brother.* Where was he now? What was he like?

Sadness blanketed Titus. "I failed her. In her greatest need, I could not save her son."

"Maybe it's not too late. Maybe he's healthy and well in Skotar. Maybe he's overcome his beast."

"It would not go well for him if he has. No. Do not mistake me. If he is alive, your twin is a Draco Sang of high rank. He is preparing to attack Elysium. You are his enemy."

"What kind of Draco do you think he is? A horrid bovine like your father?" Lyko asked.

"He's your father too."

Lyko's lips peeled back in disgust. Cal sorrowed for his ma, for the brother he'd lost before ever knowing him. Grief hung over the camp like a storm cloud. After a heavy silence, Titus placed his hat on his head. His spine straightened. "There is still joy to be had, son. Mira will rejoice when she sees you and Lyko."

Cal relinquished a smile. He'd finally bring a portion of happiness to his ma and grandpapi. He was returning. Alive and still human.

Titus pulled a cloth from his pack and unwrapped the

Draco knife. He handed it to Cal. "I want you to keep this and remember that not everything about your heritage is bad. You are still a Draco Sang. With that comes power. Wield it wisely."

Cal's palm wrapped the soft bone handle as he accepted the gift, marveling at the lightness and immediately cutting his finger as he *tested* the edge of the Draco-steel. "Thank you."

Titus cracked a grin. "And now, we go north."

"North." *Toward Skotar and my brother.*

Ferth opened his bedroom door to Laconius's unpleasant scowl.

"Good morning, Father."

Laconius grunted. "Six weeks. You bear the mark of the beast by the morning you turn seventeen, or you are no longer my son."

Ferth's jaw locked.

"I'm leaving to scout the Rugit. The time is ripening to attack. I'll be back to see you a Draco Sang, honor of your family. Or you will not be fit to be my slave." Laconius pivoted and stormed out of the barracks.

Ferth let out a long, slow breath. Then another.

Hollowed out and haunted, Ferth hiked to the training grounds, skipping the dining hall Beto had banned him from until supper. He joined his usual group, the only human his age.

Beto looked over Ferth's head.

"Smooth as a baby's butt," Ferth said.

"And hairless as your own," Dara said.

"Keep it shaved," Beto said before Ferth could snap at Dara. Beto tilted his chin away and yelled to the gathering trainees, "It's sprints this morning. Let's go."

Hunger weighed down Ferth's limbs. He slogged through the runs, barely able to keep up with the hungover Draco trainees. Beto set them in a line across the packed dirt field.

"Hungry?" Thirro asked from his station at Ferth's right.

"Bruised?" It had certainly looked painful when Thirro landed on his back yesterday, courtesy of Ferth.

Thirro hissed through his jumbo beak-shaped nose. "You can't even grow wings."

"No one wants to be a weak-boned bird."

Thirro dropped his practice sword. Sharp fingernails fanning out, he charged. Ferth kept his wooden sword and whacked it against Thirro's feathery arms and neck.

"Stop," Beto yelled. Thick ram horns curled around his face. His skull pendant shook against his chest as he glared. The wool on his back was shorn short, and thick muscles protruded from a leathery abdomen.

Thirro rubbed at his new bruises. He flung himself away, cursing. Ferth laughed, deep and maniacal. He mocked to cover his worry and failure. How could he satisfy the beast? What could he do before his father returned?

He would gladly don wings and wield his bow and arrow for Skotar. He'd gratefully exhibit anything, even a weak creature, like the moth girl from the class below. She'd left training immediately to go work as a scribe for Mavras. The full-fledged Dracos in his class with fighting ability continued to train together in hopes of joining the army preparing to invade Elysium.

As Ferth danced through his sword motions, he chanted the *Underling Supplication* in his head.

Have your own way, Beast!
Have your own way!
You art the Potter;
I am the clay.
Mold me and make me
After your will,
While I am waiting,
Yielded and still.

The others stopped for lunch. Beto handed Ferth an over-sized training mace. "Fifty lashes," Beto said.

"I'll eat an extra pie in your honor," Thirro said before the group left him alone in the fields.

Ferth gripped the chain in his hands and, with a giant twisting lunge, threw the boulder tied to the end across his body and downfield. Taking a breath, he turned and threw it back the other way. His muscles screamed, and his lungs burned. He zoned out the pain and let the strength and pride of his blood drive the boulder back and forth. His vision hazed. It wasn't until supper that night that the fog lifted and reality crashed back in.

Dara set her stew down across the table from Ferth.

His eyes flickered to the fox before returning to the tender goat headed to his mouth. "Why don't you eat in the citadel?" *And leave me alone.*

"Can't we visit our friend?" Thirro asked, joining the table. "It's not like you can come with us there."

And he loves reminding me.

"You gonna be a wash-out?" Dara asked.

"Never would have guessed it from Laconius's son," Thirro said.

"I heard Laconius would be leading the troops south if he didn't have to be here to babysit his runt," Dara said.

That was not even close to being true. Laconius wouldn't make that kind of sacrifice for his son. He hung around here to pull power from Queen Mavras. As an underling, Ferth was barred from court events, but he still saw signs of his father becoming a bigger threat to her power. Fourteen years ago, Mavras had killed her brother, King Icor, as well as Queen Sacor and their three children. Mavras killed until she was the single surviving member of the Regium bloodline. The last one bearing the royal brand.

Queen Mavras was sterile, a tragedy that more often befell females than males. Once, when Laconius's hopes for Ferth were higher, he'd confided in his son that he intended to become the queen's heir. Ferth would be next in line. Ferth tried not to care as that dream turned to ash. Tried not to dwell on how far he'd fallen, from a shot at the crown to facing slavery.

Mavras had yet to name an heir. If she chose poorly, it might be the last choice she made. Ferth thought the queen wise to dither on that subject.

"He's gone deaf," Dara said.

Ferth lifted his gaze. Lush auburn fur coated Dara's skull, but her cheeks and throat were smooth bronze. As far as Dracos went, she wasn't entirely hideous. His blood warmed, whispering that she was fertile. She would make his line strong. His lips curved up, showing a strip of teeth. He leaned forward with a predator's gaze. She flinched.

"Maybe you can help me," Ferth said.

"Why would I help you?"

"A dagger is still your weapon of choice? We can use those."

She squirmed in Ferth's trap, her cockiness gone. "If I hurt you, your father will kill me."

"You'd be doing him a favor at this point. As you said, I'm

no more than a runt." Ferth's muscles heated in anticipation. Dara was sly and fast. She would battle hard.

"Let's go, underling," Dara said.

Ferth stood, pushing his empty bowl aside. He swept an arm towards the door. "Dracos first."

She strutted out.

Ferth followed Dara into the courtyard, gilded by the warm glow of the waning sun. Thirro trailed behind. Ferth would slit his throat if he interfered.

The training grounds east of the castle faced the High Sea. A salt-kissed breeze blew across the plateau. After they selected their knives, Ferth led Dara to the farthest corner of the vacant fields. A low stone wall was inadequate protection from the sheer cliffs dropping to the rocky shore.

"What are the rules?" A touch of worry slid below Dara's scowl.

Guilt and pity flashed through Ferth, but he brushed them away. He blocked all thought, letting his body play. "Do your worst." A seductive grin curled over his face.

Dara blinked.

"And I shall do mine."

Her mouth dropped open.

"You'll be richly rewarded if you can pry my beast free." He tilted his shoulders, and her gaze traveled down the length of his body. He let her imagine her own prize. He turned his head, his voice devoid of any warmth or charm when he spoke to Thirro. "If you pass that tree, I'll kill you both."

"Big words for a runt." Thirro did not move forward.

"And now, my lady." Ferth's voice was a honeyed invitation. "Shall we dance?"

Cheeks flushed beneath Dara's slitted eyes. Letting out a yelp, she sprang forward. Ferth leapt to the side of her slashing blade. Her knife cut through the side of his shirt, exposing inches of abdomen.

"Trying to undress me so soon?"

She sprang again, feinting right and jabbing left. Ferth dodged. When she brought her arm up, he cupped her elbow and shoved her back. She staggered. He flicked his knife, slicing across her ear and shaving off a tuft of red fur. She shrieked and lunged. He grabbed her arm and knocked her knife loose. Wrapping his arm around her neck, he pulled her against his chest. The point of his blade pricked her ribs. Blood trickled down her ear and neck. Ferth smashed his lips against hers.

With a startled cry, she slammed her forehead into his. He released her, and she jumped back, panting. Ferth laughed, bellowing with the rhythm of his pounding heart and ignoring the throbbing in his skull. The beast in his chest was awake now, reveling in his power and manipulation.

She darted for her weapon, but he caught her heel and threw her foot up. She landed on her back in the dirt. He pounced, landing full on top of her. She grunted in pain as air rushed out of her lungs. He flattened her with his body, pinning her arms above her head. Through her vest, her heart knocked against him. She thrashed, her body wriggling. He could almost pretend she wasn't a Draco and enjoy the sensation. He licked her lower lip, and she froze. He brought his mouth down on hers, and she gave in immediately. He kissed her until her body softened beneath him. He drew back. Her yellow eyes burned with pure desire.

"Surrender." His voice was low.

Thirro was a statue mere yards away.

"I'm yours." Dara's open gaze drifted back to his lips.

Ferth smiled, satisfaction ringing through his soul. "Of course you are." He shifted, shoving her hard against the dirt as he lifted his weight off.

She hissed, a vicious threat. He didn't turn around. "Cold-blooded viper," she yelled at his back.

"I'm here for you, Dara," Thirro said.

"Go fly off the cliff," Dara said.

Ferth chuckled as their angry voices faded away. The dragon in his chest flexed its talons.

Cal fidgeted on the doorstep. He smoothed out his new shirt again.

Titus lifted a fist but looked over at Cal before knocking. "You ready?"

It had taken four days to get here. And although the grand streets, sprawling humanity, and great green castle of Mitera had awed him, this small house had held his attention every step of the way. He'd returned from the brink of turning into Ma's worst nightmare, and he had not come back alone. What would she think of him and his white wolf? Eio had stayed at Titus's estate outside the city gates, but Lyko stood at his side. Well, he was currently curled up in a cart, hiding and cursing Cal with every bumpy step. Wild wolves were not exactly welcome within the city, and Draco wolves even less so.

"Ready," Cal said with a nod.

Titus's fist connected with the wood.

A woman answered the door. She resembled his ma, but her hair was darker, her hips quite a bit wider, and her eyes not nearly as bright.

"Good evening, Elssa," Titus said.

"Captain." Her smile did wonders for her face. She shifted focus. "You must be my nephew."

"Cal." He held out a hand.

She made a *phsst* sound and attacked him with a warm hug. "Mira," she yelled over her shoulder before lowering her voice. "You couldn't have come sooner? She's been beside herself with worry."

They were spared having to answer by a woman's gasp. Ma appeared down the hall, frozen, eyes huge.

"I want to see her," Lyko said.

Cal smiled at his ma. Joy bubbled through his veins, spreading warmth over his body. He stepped over the threshold, arms up in welcome as she broke into a run. She jerked back with a scream as the white wolf jumped into the space between them.

"Lyko!" Cal scolded.

Ma's fingers dug into her chest as she tipped against the wall, her breath harsh staccatos.

"Sorry," Lyko whined and darted to hide behind Cal's legs. *"I was excited. I did not think how scary that would be."*

Cal couldn't stop his mouth turning up. Ma frowned, giving him a sideways slant of her eyes. She'd often sent him that glare when she wasn't a fan of his antics. His smile grew at the familiar face. *Her* face. There had been awful moments when he feared he would never see her again. He stepped forward and took her hand, drawing her away from the wall. He tucked her under his wing and held her shaking body tight against his broad chest.

"A wolf," Ma whispered into his shoulder. "You did it." Her hands clutched his back, as if feeling his humanness. When he finally stepped away, tears wet her face.

"His name is Lyko. And he's very sorry. His enthusiasm got the better of him."

"I know someone like that." She glanced at Cal, eyes full of love.

She knelt on the rug. Lyko lowered his head as he crept forward. She laid a hand on his nose.

"Hello, Ma."

"He says 'Hello, Ma.'"

Ma sobbed. "I feel you are mine, too." She threw her arms around Lyko's neck and buried her face in his fur. Delight rippled off Lyko and down the bond he shared with Cal.

Ma let go of Lyko, her glittering gaze fixed on the man standing at the door.

"I will leave you to your family," Titus said. "And return tomorrow."

She stood. "You belong here, too." Her fingers twisted the fabric of her pants. "If you will stay."

Titus stepped inside and closed the door. He looked suddenly shy, and about twelve years old.

"Thank you," Ma said, her eyes never leaving his face.

"Callidon did it. I am proud of him."

Ma didn't respond.

"But I wanted it more this time," Titus said, his voice quiet. "For you. I'd be lying if I didn't say I thought of you with every second. I still hope to one day earn your forgiveness."

The sound Ma made melted Cal's heart. "You never once needed it." She flew forward.

Titus picked her up in his arms. He set her down, and his lips parted, but before he could speak, Ma kissed him.

Elssa's hand flew to her own mouth, and her eyes glistened.

"Should we stop watching?" Cal asked as the kiss kept on going. And going.

"Probably, but it's kinda hard to look away," Lyko said.

"Gross."

"But after all their years apart ... It's just ..."

"Yes." Cal smiled as he turned his back. *Beautiful.* Lyko followed him into a small kitchen. Grandpapi napped on the couch.

Lyko stalked forward and licked the man's face.

"Getting into the kissing spirit?"

"I'm always in the mood."

Cal rolled his eyes.

Grandpapi wiped his face but didn't wake.

"Still lazy as ever," Cal said with a loud voice.

The old man jolted. His eyes popped open, and he yelped at the wolf face inches from his own.

"You need to stop doing that."

"He deserves it," Lyko said.

"Callidon." Grandpapi reached for him as he struggled to sit, and Cal helped him up. Grandpapi didn't let go of his hand. "I ..." Grandpapi's words died.

"I know you didn't expect to see me again."

The old man sighed. "I am very glad to be proven wrong. Forgive me."

"I do. And if you promise not to tell Ma, I'd admit that you were almost right about me. And I'm still far from perfect."

Grandpapi's wrinkled lips curved up, his hand tightening on Cal's. "I'm proud of you."

Cal didn't realize how much he'd wanted to hear those words until they sank deep into his soul. "I'm going to try to deserve that."

Ma, Titus, and Elssa entered the kitchen.

"Lyko's beautiful, isn't he?" Ma said.

Grandpapi nodded. "Very impressive."

"Are you hearing all this?" Lyko asked.

Six cousins and one uncle entered the kitchen, bearing crates of food.

"Just in time," Elssa said. "We've got more guests."

The evening was a blur of laughter, good food, and pure joy. Cal soaked up the feel of family and warmth. He knew he would need these memories in the coming months. It was deep into the night when Titus broke the news. He sat on the couch, Ma tucked under his arm. He tilted his head back so he could see her face.

"The army left for the border last week."

The bliss on Ma's face dissolved.

"I will leave in the morning to join them."

Ma looked to her son.

"And I will go with him," Cal said.

Ma nodded, though her chin wobbled. She turned to Lyko. "You will protect him."

It wasn't a question, but Lyko padded forward and laid his head on her lap in answer. She kissed him between the eyes. He licked her chin. She chuckled as she scratched behind his ears.

"I could get used to this," Lyko said with a rumble of pleasure.

"Don't." No, they couldn't get used to this. They were going to war.

TWENTY-ONE - ORPHAN
FERTH

Ferth paced his room. What more could he do? He'd manipulated and humiliated Dara. He'd even taken immense pleasure in it. But still, he remained furless and featherless. He snagged Keturah's tin of healing balm. Even if she didn't have more, it was an excuse to visit her.

One of Laconius's regular bodyguards, a pangolin Draco, sat on the steps outside the slave house, his scaly face tilted up to the sun. Ferth silently slipped past, running into Pearl and Kenji just inside the hall.

"Poxus is sitting outside the door," Ferth warned. "He looks bored."

Pearl's gray gaze washed over Ferth before the slaves turned and headed back the other way.

In three weeks, Ferth would join them here in the slave house. Would they even remember that slim kindness? No. The slaves would destroy him. Pushing away his doom, Ferth slunk down to the basement. He opened the door to Keturah's office and froze.

Jade sat in the only chair. Both women jumped at his appearance.

"What are you doing here?" Ferth asked.

Jade's gaze lingered on the tin in his hand. There was a matching one on the table. Ferth turned his palm, trying to hide his.

"I lost something in the laundry," Jade said. "This slave doesn't seem to want to return it."

Keturah stared, her gaze flickering between the two underlings crowding her small space. After a silent beat, she jolted and spoke. "Oh, yes. I am looking for it. I am sure I will find it. Please give me a little more time to look through the stacks."

Ferth frowned at Keturah's distracted tone. The woman's cheeks reddened, and her gaze seemed to land everywhere but on him.

Jade rose to her feet, her face hardening in anger.

"What is it you're missing?" Ferth asked, trying to draw Jade's attention from Keturah.

Jade ignored him. "Find it by morning."

Keturah nodded.

Jade reached for the tin on the table, then snapped her hand back before touching it. She turned to Ferth, her demeanor suddenly coy. "See you at training this afternoon."

Ferth nodded as Jade danced past and out the door.

"What does she want? I can help you find it or talk to Jade—"

Keturah held up a hand. "I'm sure it will be fine."

Ferth gave her a stern look.

"If I don't find it by dinner, I will ask for your help."

Ferth didn't believe her but nodded anyway.

"So, you're training her?"

"Hard to imagine any underling wanting more training."

"It's not hard to imagine a child wanting to be able to

defend herself." Keturah's voice was soft and her eyes far off. Ferth waited, but she didn't elaborate.

"I'll teach her what I can in the time I have left." He didn't admit that he enjoyed it. She was an adept student, and he'd grown fond of her flashing grin and cunning eyes. Even if he had to continually remind her that he was nothing more than a mentor.

Keturah's gaze snapped into focus.

"Three weeks until I join you in the slave house."

Her wrinkles crinkled. "No. You must never come here."

"Laconius will give me no more time. I've dishonored him enough already."

"If you wish it, I am sure you will have your claws by then."

Of course he wished it.

"You were always strong-willed."

Not strong enough. Ferth picked up the healing salve on the table. "I see you anticipated my visit." She held out chapped hands, and he dropped in the old tin. "Thank you for this."

"I will always do what I can to help my children."

Ferth flinched, the wound hidden in his heart pulling open. As much as he wanted to be, he was not her child. He was an orphan. His mother had left him at birth. His father was leaving him now. And no matter how much he wished it, Jade wasn't his little sister. Nor was she willing to be.

TWENTY-TWO - STRUCK
CAL

Once they passed the northern city of Kiptos, Eio and Lyko walked out in the open at their master's sides. They crested a low hill, and the Rugit River delta appeared in the distance. A fan of water poured out the narrow river channel and out into the glittering High Sea. And beyond it: *Skotar*. Cal's father's land. The land of the Dragon. His heritage. It looked like nothing more than a forested marsh. A half-mile south of the delta, tents were lined up in neat rows, with a few large ones dominating the center and to the side, training fields cut out of the grass. Cal breathed in the beautiful view. Titus put a hand on his shoulder before heading down the hill toward their new home.

A sentry hailed them. "Captain Titus." The woman saluted.

Titus greeted her, but his anxious feet did not slow. Commander Asvig lumbered alongside as they marched, debriefing his captain with rapid details. Word spread, and a large group met them at the command tent. Titus had told Cal of the other Draco descendants, but he was not prepared for the swelling in his heart as nine men and women, soldiers with animals in tow, approached. Belonging wrapped him like a blanket. He swelled at the thought that there were even more like him scattered throughout Elysium. Titus had sent dozens of letters out before they left Mitera, calling their Draco siblings to join the fight. And he'd sent a messenger with a personal plea to the "obstinate old woman in the mountain." Based on that title, Cal wasn't sure why they wanted her.

Cal looked over each face, each animal. The thought of his brother flashed through his hopes, but no. He was not here. There was a woman with a monkey on her shoulder, a grim-faced man with a massive python curled in the grass at his feet, a tall young man, barrel-chested and grinning at him, a tremendous grizzly bear standing by his side … Cal shared the brotherly grin before moving on to the next face, and his inventorying stopped. A young woman with skin the color of tavo and eyes like melted bronze, standing behind a black panther, stole his complete attention. Her fighting leathers were so tight over her sinewy frame, he nearly choked.

"Callidon and Lyko," Captain Titus said. "Meet your new unit." Titus introduced the nine Dracos and their hewans. Uriah was the one he wanted to be friends with, and Zemira was the one he wanted to be more than friends with.

"We have a tent set up for him as requested," Commander Asvig said. He was an older human with a belly that screamed wealth.

"I'll show him around," Uriah said.

Titus nodded in approval. "You and Zemira will take turns each morning, working with him before the unit's regular training. He has some catching up to do."

Zemira looked Cal over without a flicker of emotion. His innards steamed. He might have been more embarrassed by his inexperience if he weren't so looking forward to her *training*.

Titus scanned the others. "Bring your reports to me at command this afternoon. And all of you, meet me tomorrow after breakfast. Sergeant, show me the camp." With that, Titus turned and strode off.

Zemira stepped up. "Be at training field one tomorrow at dawn." Her panther glared at Lyko.

"Yes, ma'am."

She whirled, showing off a toned backside as she marched away.

"She'll warm up," Uriah said. "She's just shy with new people."

"Stone cold is the word I would have used," Lyko said. *"And her cat is worse."*

"What did she do to you?"

"She hissed. Actually flashed me a claw."

"Maybe she needs one of your face licks," Cal said.

"You're the one dreaming of kissing."

Cal stopped talking to Lyko, then followed Uriah and his bear, Poe, through camp until they reached a section with slightly larger tents.

"For the hewan unit," Uriah said. "And this is yours." He peeled open the canvas door. "Welcome home."

Those words had never felt so true. Gratitude rushed through like a warm river. He had a bed. For the first time in his life. His own bed. And a soft rug for Lyko. A trunk sat open against the wall, clothes stacked neatly inside. He even had a table and chairs. Parchment and a pitcher of water sat at the ready. It was so much. And all for him. He stepped outside, swallowing back his brimming emotions before he embarrassed himself before this self-confident, intimidating young man.

"Whose is that one?" Cal pointed to the largest tent two down from his.

Uriah cocked his wide jaw. "That's for the big boys."

"Let me know when we meet them," Cal said, his tone light.

Poe, the grizzly bear, stood on his hind legs, towering over them all. Fear burned down Cal's back, but when the bear growled, Cal thought it sounded a *little* like a laugh. Cal forced a rough chuckle.

"Well met," Cal said.

"Come on," Uriah said, eyes bright. "Next stop, mess tent."

Cal spent the rest of the day exploring camp with Uriah, feeling that he might finally have found a true friend, and wishing Uriah were his brother, too.

He'd turn seventeen tomorrow, and then Laconius would return and end him. In frustration, Ferth rubbed furiously at the relentless fuzz sprouting on his skull. He sat cross-legged on the floor and closed his eyes. Poking and prodding on his passions, he meditated on all the desires of his heart. He sought a path to honor his blood and welcome his beast. Images of Pearl's sad eyes popped up. Kenji's stoic submission. Keturah's concern for him. He shoved them all away with a growl. But another vision took their place. A woman appeared. One he'd constructed himself, over years of yearning. She was slim, with his same brown hair and amber eyes. She reached out to him, even now. Called to him. *I love you, my son. I will find you.* Tears leaked out. He opened his eyes, letting the image of cracking stone and dirty sheets replace his terrible dreams. They were all lies, anyway. Weakness.

Despite the sunshine, darkness festered over Ferth. He stormed through his training, breaking a younger under-ling's arm by accident. He was sorry, but being sorry was dangerous these days. He snuck onto the roof of the barracks. He splayed naked over the tiles, letting the sun's flames lick over his skin. He sweat for hours before he made his decision. He would run south. Escape Skotar. Tomorrow. Despite his failure, a measure of relief lightened his limbs as he dressed and climbed down the back wall.

A weak voice cried, "She's bleeding. Stop."

"She flinched." Thirro's mocking laugh echoed around the corner of the barracks. "It's her turn again." The sound of rock hitting stone rang out. Ferth's gut clenched as he stalked forward.

"Stop moving," Thirro said. "That's cowardly."

Ferth rounded the bend. "You're the coward."

Thirro's arm cocked back, a rock in his palm. He glanced at Ferth and let it fly. It sailed into a young girl's chest. A trail of blood already dripped along her shorn head. She crumpled against the wall with a tight moan. *Jade.* Ferth's blood flared. Three other hatchlings were lined up against the wall beside her. Stones scattered among their feet.

"Up against the bricks, Ferth," Thirro said. "You belong with them."

"Stop, Thirro." Ferth's voice was flint. His pulse soared, and his limbs steadied.

"Ferth is soft for the hatchlings." Thirro's tone was cold and mocking.

"You pick on them because you're too weak to fight someone your own size."

Thirro palmed another stone. He scratched it with a curled fingernail, as if thinking. In a flash, he threw it. It struck Jade's cheek. She brought a hand to her face. More blood oozed between her fingers.

Ferth boiled over. Steaming with rage, he attacked. He lunged, and the gates of his soul broke open as a volcano of violence washed over him. His fists connected with Thirro's jaw, his chest, his sides. Ferth was going to kill him. He wanted to feel the life drain beneath his fingers. Passion swelled, exploding through his limbs as he punched and jabbed. Thirro choked and groaned as his nose cracked under Ferth's knuckles. Thirro's part-eagle body felt hollow and light under his calloused grip. Blood beaded on brown feathers as Ferth's fingers wrapped around Thirro's throat. He squeezed.

Sharp pain shot along Ferth's nerves. He recoiled with a whine, loosening his grip. He staggered as knives sliced through his knuckles and shredded his back. He threw his head up and howled. The lament rang loud and bloodcurdling, more beastly than human. He sucked in a haggard breath and opened fiery eyes. The world spun. He blinked, and the scene crisped. Thirro's eyes veined with fear; grimy rocks painted with blood; sharp claws jetting out where Ferth's fingernails had been; gray fur over his thickened hands. He ran a long tongue over pointed canines before snapping his wide jaw.

Thirro shrank against the stone. He crawled backward, flapping his wings furiously, as if willing them to be strong enough to carry him away.

The shock blunted Ferth's fury. He growled, but took a step back, away from his prey.

"Congratulations." Thirro's voice quivered.

"If you touch her again, I will find you, and I *will* kill you." Ferth's voice was deep and gravelly.

Thirro didn't hesitate. "I won't."

"Go."

Thirro fled, bloody feathers floating to the ground in his wake.

The hatchlings and Jade stood as if statues, paralyzed against the wall.

"Go!"

The spell broke. Three scurried away like mice. Jade

stayed, studying him. She took a step forward, held her hand up as if to touch the fur peeking from his collar.

He stepped back, not wanting her touch in his feral state. Not trusting his new form. "There's healing cream in the tin from Keturah."

She jolted as if he'd struck her. Her eyes popped.

"She's the slave from the laundry. The salve is in my trunk. Apply it to your wounds."

He tore across the castle grounds, his new body limber and fast. He ducked into the armory and ripped off his too-tight shirt. His reflection flickered in a polished shield. Gray fur carpeted his scalp, shoulders, and upper back, but not yet his face or chest—that should come with time. He did not expect to look, or still feel, this human when the transformation was complete. His jaw cut a sharp line below jagged razor teeth. His ears had grown pointed and furry, but his eyes were the same shining gold as before.

"Well met," Ferth said, nodding to the wolf in the steel. "Took you long enough." He grinned, and it looked more alarming than happy.

There were Dracos to report to, celebrating to be done. Laconius was due back tomorrow, but right now there was something his new body craved. Slipping through the shadows, he snuck out the main gates. Tonight he hunted.

He loped easily through the mountains for miles until his keen nose picked up a trail leading him to a young mountain goat. He stalked in silence until he'd prowled close enough to lunge. Grabbing the horns, he jerked. The neck folded sideways with a popping *crack*. He slammed it to the ground and sliced its neck with his claws. When it was dead, Ferth pulled out his hunting knife. As he dismembered the animal, he realized, even with canines, he did not want to eat the meat raw.

Scrambling through the dirt and grass, he found a piece

of flint. After collecting a pile of dry leaves and sticks, he struck his claws along the flint until it sparked. He spiked the goat's hind legs and propped them over the flames. The last rays of daylight winked out.

Contentment filled his body as he sat in the cool summer evening and watched his meal ripen. He'd done it. He flexed his strong hands in triumph. He was truly a Draco Sang. His father would be proud. He'd join the army headed south. Conquer the human lands. A faded image of the mother he dreamed of flickered. He pushed her out of his mind. But he couldn't escape the feeling that he had not entirely given himself up to the dragon. He still felt the wrestle within him, man and blood vying for complete control.

When the smell of roasted meat had tormented him long enough, he sat in the weeds and tore long strips off the bone with his teeth. Rustling in the trees grew closer. He rolled to a crouch, muscles taut. A bear broke into view and stopped on the other side of the dying embers. He stood on hind legs, twice Ferth's height. Its roar rattled the trees.

No part of Ferth considered fighting the beast. His mind turned cold and calculating. He gripped the carcass and, with a giant heave, flung it. It bumped against the bear's paws. As the bear tilted its giant head to look down, Ferth bolted through the trees.

He ran until the fires of Shi Castle came into view. Out of breath, but exhilarated, he ambled up the steep slope toward the gates. A familiar whistle rent the air. Ferth dove to the ground as an arrow buried itself in the grass to his right.

"That be your only warning," a guard yelled. Nocturnal red eyes dotted the space above the high white wall.

"It's Ferth, son of Laconius. I'm returning late," he yelled.

"There be no wolf Draco at this castle."

Ferth cursed his stupidity. "My beast just emerged."

"He's obviously lying," a second voice said.

Ferth slowly got up, his hands out in surrender.

"Why are you outside the gates?"

"Come to the gate; you can verify my branding," Ferth said.

The two guards argued back and forth about it until Ferth grew impatient.

"I don't have a weapon." Hunting knives didn't count. "I haven't got a shirt, either. I'll keep my hands above my head, and you don't need to unlock the gate until you've verified who I am."

More muffled arguing. "That be fine. Permission granted to approach."

Slowly, Ferth climbed. He stood in front of the iron bars. Torches illuminated the brand across his left pectoral.

"LF09285," a mole Draco said, squinting at Ferth's scars.

"He's just a boy from up close," the flyer holding a bow said. "And his chest is hairless as a babe. Fearsome, though."

"You gave us a fright, boy."

"You shouldn't be out at night." They opened the gate. "Get in and get to bed before we decide to report you."

"Yes, sirs." Ferth slipped inside and ran.

"It's exciting to have a wolf."

TWENTY-FOUR - FOCUS
CAL

Cal's legs cried as he held them steady. His breath came in shallow puffs. Zemira, in those infuriatingly tight pants, inhaled slow and deep. She'd maintained the same split-leg crouch she made him hold, but she looked to all the world as if she were lounging, not lunging.

"Hold your arms higher," Zemira said, her voice mild. Her eyes remained closed, as if she didn't need to look to know that her weak student had faltered.

Cal grimaced as he forced his arms higher. The swords he held felt like solid lead. Every morning for three weeks he'd worked with Uriah or Zemira. Uriah taught him hand-to-hand combat. Zemira taught him *this.*

Much to his disappointment, there had been zero engagement with her slender frame. Instead, he'd been forced to hold still, only changing position when his knees buckled, as they did now. His legs shuddered. He huffed as he stumbled off-balance and righted himself, his muscles barking.

"You were distracted," Zemira said, gracefully lowering her arms and standing tall. The sun burst over the horizon, gilding her face and dancing over the empty training fields.

Opal, Zemira's panther, and Lyko lay watching, on opposite ends of the plot, as far from each other as they could get.

Cal's arms hung limp at his sides, the swords begging to fall out of his loose grip. "How about we take a little break from the mind games and work on knife skills?" He'd seen her practice, knew her speed and cunning.

"These are not games. Your mind is your greatest weapon. You must learn focus and control."

Yes. She told him so every other morning. "You scared I'll beat you?"

Her jaw twitched. Opal lifted her sleek black head. Lyko only chuckled at Cal's stupidity.

"Come with me."

Zemira strode to the training tent. A handful of early risers worked at various stations. She stopped at a thickly padded mat on the floor. She shrugged off her jacket; a sleeveless undershirt revealed toned arms. She dropped her sword belt on the floor and took off her thin boots. She set two hidden knives on the pile.

"How far is she going to go?" Lyko asked, mirroring Cal's thoughts.

"If you can pin me," Zemira said, stepping onto the mat and shaking out her arms. "Then I'll consider adding knife routines."

Cal's blood heated as he imagined her beneath him. He swallowed, hard.

"You're larger than I. This should be easy." Her thin smirk halted his fantasizing. "If you can't, then we continue training my way."

Face flushed, he peeled off his boots and weapons belt.

"Take your shirt off," Lyko said.

"Shut up." He hoped the wolf hadn't actually realized he'd considered it.

Cal faced Zemira, suddenly hesitant. He didn't want to

hurt her. Her wrists looked so small, her thighs thin and breakable.

He need not have worried.

She darted. Sliding across the floor, she snaked her legs around his ankles. He toppled, barely stopping his face-plant with his hands. She jumped onto his back. With a grunt, he rolled. She slashed to his front, sticking him to his back. His palms found her waist, tight and narrow, and he forgot for a moment what he supposed to be doing, pushing her away or pulling her close. His hands fell away as her knee ground into his sternum.

Dark eyes flashed as she loomed over his face. "Worse than I thought."

What? No. This wasn't over. Cal threw himself sideways, knocking her off. He scrambled to his feet. They circled. This time when she attacked, he was ready. She went for his legs, but he darted sideways, shoving her down. She danced back to her feet and leapt onto his back. He twisted, and she spun to his front. Close enough to kiss. He tried to block it out, the feel of her thighs tight on his waist, the warmth of her breath on his neck, his hands on her hips. *Focus.* She dropped a leg, wrapping it behind his knee. He stumbled, her body touching too much of his. He flung her away. *Focus.* He thought vaguely she might be right about his mind being weak and distracted.

He lunged, his shoulder ramming her thighs, but she didn't go down. She skipped sideways, her elbow connecting with his shoulder. He dropped to a knee. She rammed his side, and they both went down. This time when his shoulders hit the mat, it was her shin across his throat that kept him down.

Slow clapping drew her attention across the room. Beaming, she leapt off him. Cal coughed and sat up. Uriah stood near the mats with another man, a man even bigger than Uriah. Uriah walked toward Cal with a look of amused pity.

Zemira darted to the big man. She leapt into his arms, her legs going around his torso, almost the same hold she'd just had Cal in.

Uriah held out a hand, pulling Cal to his wobbly legs.

"You're late," Zemira said to the man she was wrapped around.

"I'll make it up to you." The voice was a quiet baritone.

She kissed the broad-chested man, and Cal's stomach dropped out of his body.

The kiss deepened, huge hands gripping narrow hips. Cal imagined his hands in that same place. He couldn't look away, even though every second was another punch to the gut. Today was his birthday. Seventeen. He'd been planning to celebrate by asking Zemira to have dinner with him. He was going to get to know her, draw her out of her shell, exchange more than one or two words. Clearly, she was not as shy as he'd thought.

"Who is that?" Cal whispered.

"Shem. Just arrived this morning with the supply wagon. He's one of the army blacksmiths," Uriah said. "And also, her husband."

Cal's focus snapped to his friend. He relaxed his face into indifference. "Oh."

"Yeah." Uriah gripped Cal's shoulder, as if he knew just what Cal was feeling.

Had he been so obvious?

"There's something about female Draco blood," Uriah said. "It's irresistible."

TWENTY-FIVE - DRACO
FERTH

Seventeen today. Ferth stared at the limestone ceiling of his bedroom. He'd always snuck in to see Keturah on his birthday. She would kiss him, sing him her silly celebration song, and give him a piece of hard sugar she'd saved. Now she would no longer welcome his visit. A dark cloud weighed down his ribs.

The breakfast bell rang, heralding the start of a new day. He dressed and headed out. Word had spread, and congratulations greeted him at every turn.

"Hey, late bloomer," Dara said, waltzing up to him as he picked out his sword for drills.

"Ready for a re-match?"

"I might not let you win this time." Her claws came up to touch his furry scalp, but he stepped out of reach.

He laughed. "So eager to get under me?"

She bristled.

Sword tip up, he stepped in line.

He'd looked forward to this day forever. Finally, he'd joined the ranks of the Draco Sang. He puffed with pride, but underneath, to his horror, he felt hollow.

I belong here. I belong here. As if repeating it made it true.

He swung his sword in sync with the Dracos surrounding him, *but* his movements were forced, stilted; that sense of belonging still evaded him. His camaraderie with the underlings vanished. They looked at him now with fear and awe. The other transforming Draco Sang in his class exhibited new respect, but he was now fiercer competition. He knew they had hoped he would fail to become a Draco. They had taken pleasure in his weakness. But now he was a wolf, a king of beasts, a true son of the legendary Prince Attor. It did not win him friends.

After supper, Ferth leaned against the outside castle wall, shaded by the great dragon's coppery wing. Laconius came into view, down in the valley. A Draco owl flew in front of the small company of scouts. Breathing heavy and coated in dust, Laconius was almost to the gate when Ferth leapt up.

"Father."

Laconius whirled, knife glinting in his hand. He stared at Ferth for several heartbeats before his wide mouth split open in a rare grin.

"My son!"

At his shout, the group all turned to look. They echoed praise before carrying their weary feet into the castle yard, following the call of hot food and home.

Laconius put meaty hands on Ferth's shoulders and studied him. "A wolf. I see it was worth the wait. You've transformed much already. Full fur on your face will come soon. And then we will do great things together. This was beyond my hope."

Pleasure pervaded Ferth's soul at the hard-won praise. He closed his eyes to soak it in. That was a mistake; he couldn't see his father's swelling pride on the back of his eyelids. Turning inward, the nagging feeling of wrongness in his heart amplified. Laconius's heavy arm wrapped Ferth's back.

Ferth forced a smile as he entered the courtyard at his father's side.

Queen Mavras waited at the steps of the citadel. "Welcome home, chief. What have you found on your travels? A gift for me?"

"My queen." Laconius bowed slightly. "I have come home to find my son a Draco Sang."

Mavras's gaze snapped to Ferth.

He bowed, much lower than his father. "I only showed signs last night, Your Majesty."

She studied him, her bug-eyes roving over his body. Her stinger lay curled around her scaly feet, docile for now, but a constant reminder she could kill them with a flick of her tail. "Fortune favors us with a rare beast. A tribute in part to you, Laconius."

Laconius straightened, his face bright.

Mavras motioned to Ferth. "I expect mighty things from you, son of Attor."

He bowed again. "Yes, my queen."

She favored him with one of her sharp smiles before turning to Laconius. "You bring me good news?"

"Very good."

"Come. We have much to discuss." She beckoned to the group of returned scouts. "Ferth, you will come, too."

Finally.

He trailed Laconius through the bronze doors of the castle. His first time in the main citadel. His eyes darted, taking in the grandeur. It was hewn from the same white limestone as the rest of the buildings, but the ceilings arched impossibly high, and under the grimy layer of grease and grit, the walls were smooth. To the left, Kenji scrubbed at the floor, but his strong arms seemed to make no noticeable improvement on the stained stone.

After passing through the entry hall, Mavras led them to a

meeting room. Plush chairs circled a marble table. Violent murals covered the walls, and beastly statues haunted the corners. Carved dark wood beams crisscrossed the ceiling.

Several officers already sat around the table. Mavras took position at the head seat, a throne decorated with skulls and scales. Ferth grinned as he nestled himself into a padded chair. Slaves laid out a feast. A silver goblet filled with rich wine stood next to his plate. Laconius drained his drink and grunted for more before the slave could move on.

Silence reigned as plates were piled high. Ferth's delight grew at the decadent dishes of roast meats, fragrant sauces, and soft breads. He kept an eye on an entire plate of strawberries a slave slowly carried around. His stomach bulged, and his head felt airy and light by the time the queen spoke.

"What news, chief?"

"The Rugit River delta is low," Laconius said. "Very low. It is passable now, but not well. I think, by this time next year, especially if it is another dry winter, it will be easy crossing. There is a ridge where I could stay hidden from view and see down to the delta. Elysium soldiers camp less than a mile south of the delta." He nodded to the owl who'd flown south with him. "Ore did nightly recon of the camp."

The scorpion queen turned to Ore.

"The camp is well-established," Ore said. "I counted three thousand soldiers and officers. That doesn't include the slaves." His words whistled through his strongly beaked face.

"They don't have slaves," Laconius said.

"They look and act likes slaves," Ore said.

"That is more than I feared," Mavras cut in. "Are they well trained?"

"I did not fly during the day. But they have two large training tents as well as four fields. They appear well-organized, well-stocked, and highly disciplined. They are commanded by …" Ore looked at Laconius.

"The Lion." Laconius spat the word with hatred.

"We've heard of this lion before?" Mavras asked.

"Yes," Laconius said. "His name is Titus. He had the blood of the dragon, but he was not worthy of it. His beast abandoned him. The lion now does his bidding, like a pitiable whelp."

"You know him?" Mavras asked.

She was cunning and discerning, Ferth realized, as he began to see how she controlled her court.

"I know him enough to wish him dead. I first met him in Elysium many years ago. I should have killed him then. I was distracted." Fire raged in Laconius's eyes when they flicked to Ferth, the charged connection so brief that Ferth thought he might have imagined it. "I underestimated his potential to annoy me. He's managed to hide a human who belongs to me." His wide nostrils flared. "Years later, when I picked up the scent of dragon spawn in the Seraf Mountains, he intercepted our chase. He killed my flyer and prevented us from taking the girl there. Her blood was strong. I went back for her later, but she'd already lost her heritage. She keeps her panther as a pet, a mockery."

"If she was too weak for her blood, you need not regret that you didn't bring her here. Although, I am never opposed to more slaves," Queen Mavras said.

If a Draco Sang lost their beast, they became a slave, and their pet was killed.

"How many Draco abominations in their camp?" Mavras asked Ore.

After a heavy pause, Ore said, "I have no clear numbers. One night I saw a grizzly bear walk right through camp. The soldiers did not react. He walked through unaffected, as if he belonged. That can only be the case of a man-controlled abomination, can it not? I suspect four other soldiers I've seen with animals, but have no proof they are abominations."

Slurping and swallowing and scraping of plates kept time as the queen thought. "Captain Jobu, when can you be ready to march south?"

"With a half company, three weeks' time, my queen," said the badger across the granite slab from Ferth.

"Good. Organize your half company. You may have your pick of the trainees. I will approve your officers. Make camp north of the delta by frostfall. You are to scout the river and details of the enemy camp. I expect sound battle plans by this spring. And." Her voice changed pitch, hardening. "You will hunt down and kill every Draco Sang abomination and pet in their midst. I wish to gift my chief the head of the lion by spring."

Violent lust flamed in Jobu's eyes. "Consider it done, my queen."

"Do not fail me in this." Her voice was a poisonous hiss. "Ore and Kurayha, you will go west with messages to the strongholds to send troops to aid my invasion in the spring. And to the lawless ones you can find, give them a promise of reward and position in Elysium when we have our victory if they join the fight. Laconius will lead the army to the border when the snow melts." A terrifying smile split her glossy face. "Feast! Next year we will be eating the ripe fruit of Elysium. We will suck the tender juice from that fertile land. We'll have dominion over the fair humans. We will build our empire!"

Ferth joined in the cheering and hollering, but inside he thought of Keturah, Kenji, and Pearl. Humans, just like the ones across the border, like his mother. Would she die in the invasion before he ever saw her? He recoiled at the thought of sticking his sword through human hearts. Who would protect them against the incoming pillage and plunder? He clenched his jaw against his cowardice. He was Draco Sang and needed to think like it.

But, why did he still not feel like one?

Fists pounded the table and feet shook the floor, rocking Ferth out of his worry. He shut off his thoughts and feasted, indulging with abandon. Others showed no inhibition as they ate like gluttons, burping and licking their fingers. Hours later, Ferth stumbled out, gut aching and head foggy. On the stone steps outside the barracks, he vomited.

He woke the next morning to his skull trying to squeeze out his brains. His belly whimpered and complained. He cursed his misery and had water and plain porridge in the underlings' hall for breakfast.

Captain Jobu was at the training yard when Ferth arrived. The badger watched the sessions in silence as the trainees worked hard to exhibit. Ferth fought through a splitting headache as he tested his Draco body's strength and skill. His new prowess helped hide the hangover, but still, it was not his best day.

At the end of the session, Beto called the Draco Sang trainees together. Jobu stood next to him, a head shorter, but stout. Black strips of fur slashed across Jobu's glossy eyes, and tusks lay over his bottom lip. A jagged knife hung from his belt below a worn leather breastplate.

"Get some rest," Beto said. "Tomorrow we'll start a friendly competition." He said the word with a laugh, as if it were possible to have anything be friendly in the training yard. "Esteemed Captain Jobu here is looking to fill a few spots in his half company. Any who impress him enough might be invited to go south with him."

A cheer rose.

"See you at dawn," Beto said, dismissing them.

Fists balled on his hips, Jobu's cutting stare watched them all leave.

They lacked a flyer. Eleven hewans in the army and not a single winged creature. Frustration swelled as Cal stood on the ridge facing north. Skotar was a mottled misshapen mass of black against the gray pre-dawn sky. A mystery. How could they prepare to fight an enemy they could not see or study?

Footsteps sounded behind him, heavier than Zemira's light steps. He whirled to find Shem approaching across the training field. Cal's gut coiled in dread. Did the man know of Cal's feelings for his wife? Was he coming to exercise territorial male dominance?

"Zemira sent me," Shem said. "She can't come this morning."

A mix of disappointment and relief clashed in Cal. "Why not?" His voice was sharper than he intended.

Shem was large as an ox, but his eyes held no malice or aggression. He was praised as the finest metalsmith in Elysium. He could make a sword nearly as strong as if it were made with Dracosteel. Cal might have wanted to be friends with him, if things had been different. If Zemira hadn't lodged in his heart.

"She's sick."

"Sick?" Cal didn't think Zemira would have allowed herself to be taken by something so common as a sickness. "Is she alright?"

"She'll be fine, nothing serious. She ate something that didn't agree with her."

"She's not so tough after all," Cal said with a half-grin.

Shem let out a deep chuckle. "I'll tell her you said that."

"Please don't."

"Go get some sleep," Shem said. "You deserve it. She wouldn't want me telling you, but you've impressed her."

Cal blinked in surprise. The compliment was dulled by the fact her husband delivered it, but still, he allowed the praise to penetrate. Since the morning she'd humiliated him on the wrestling mats, he'd been working hard, submitting without comment to every drill and exercise requested. *I've impressed her.* He resisted the urge to smile, scowling instead. *She. Is. Married.* He felt as if he were back in the Spickle Woods, fighting his worst enemy—himself. *I will conquer this.* Those words again became his mantra.

Cal turned his gaze toward the north. What lay beyond those banks, thick with trees? Was his brother there, lying in wait? Did he look south even now? Cal needed to find a way in. The makings of a plan began to form.

TWENTY-SEVEN - PEARL
FERTH

Heavy pounding on the door startled Ferth. He slipped the book he'd stolen from the queen's library under his thin mattress and opened the door on the slave steward, Herm. A slave trembled in the hog's leathery grip. Holding her by the elbow, Herm thrust her forward. Ferth recoiled.

"A gift from Laconius." His voice was gruff and slobbery.

Her snowy hair fell over her face and shoulders. She shivered beneath her thin shift. *Pearl?* Herm shook her, and she lifted her head.

Ferth's pulse soared. "Pearl," he whispered.

Watery pale eyes locked on his.

She warmed his blood. He wanted her. Now that he was a Draco, he could have her. An inner voice pressed hard to take her. How often had he thought of her lovely face, her slender body? But looking into her pleading eyes, he knew he would not. Calling on the full strength of his will, he kept his arms at his sides.

"She's a bit skinny," he said.

Herm snorted. "Not grown into your fur, and you're

already picky. I'll take this one to Jobu, then. He sits in his suite and judges us all unfit, but even *he* wouldn't turn away a pretty thing like this."

He turned to drag her away, but Pearl jerked. Ripping free, she flung her body against Ferth.

"Please." Her face pressed against his neck. Her heavy breath sent shivers down his spine. "Not Jobu."

The force of her trembling body shocked him. He wrapped his arms around her shoulders, holding her closer against him.

"Please." A whispered plea.

The word charged through him. He would protect her to his last breath. Lifting her easily off the ground, he spun inside and slammed the door on her enemies. Herm's cackles echoed off the stone hallway.

She shifted, her softness pressing against his chest as he held her locked in his arms. The scent of salt and female charged up his nose. The surge of emotions singing through his veins changed tune. She lifted her face to look at him, and desire hit like a flood. He could not stop his fingers from trailing up the smooth skin of her neck, her cheek, and digging into silky hair. The wolf inflamed him as he stepped forward and laid her gently on his bed. Hairy fingers traced her porcelain face as he kissed her jaw, her neck. She didn't react. He gripped her waist, his hand sliding over ribs, moving up. Sadness welled in her face as her eyelids fluttered closed. Her body turned limp, as if shutting down.

A word leaked from her lips. "Please."

He halted, the taste of her skin burning his lips. Laconius's repeated comments flickered over his mind. It is a human's privilege to serve the Dracos. They are little more than animals. Does the sun care what an ember thinks? Ferth looked over Pearl's face, calm and dignified, only a hint of pain. He thought of Kenji, strong and meek. They were not dumb animals. Keturah's voice came to his mind. *Never take a human by force. It is a terrible crime, my love. Small creatures do it to feel big.*

Ferth hissed out an annoyed breath and leaned back, taking his reluctant hands off Pearl.

Eyes like the moon blinked at him in surprise. He climbed off the bed, and she sat up.

"You will stay here all night." His voice was sharp, covering his cowardly behavior. "You will never mention this to anyone."

His body thrummed with want as he stormed out of his room. He needed to do something to make up for this. To defeat the shame wedged in his ribs. He stalked to Thirro's room. The bird was gone. Unfortunate. Ferth would have enjoyed the fight. Instead, he took Thirro's new bow, gifted to him for his increasing skill at archery. He spent half the night breaking it in.

When he returned, he threw the bow at Thirro's bed, hitting the sleeping form before slipping into his own room. Pearl slept curled up in his blanket. Refusing the demands of his lupine body, he lay on the floor.

She was gone when he woke. He ran a palm down his face to find that fur had claimed even more territory. The thick gray now covered nearly every inch of his pale skin; only two spots lacked fur. The entire left side of his face was smooth and human, as well as a palm-sized circle of bare skin above his heart. A little more time and those spots would fill in as well. Then he would look like a full-fledged Draco. He could only hope he'd feel like one by then. His sharpened hearing picked up the sound of Thirro cursing whoever had messed with his bow. Forcing confidence into his step, Ferth followed his raging hunger toward the smell of bacon.

After breakfast, he joined the gathering at the training yard. The first event of the competition was a speed drill.

Five hundred and four trainees ran the course. As Ferth waited his turn, he took notes. The dirt in front of the boulder crossing shined with slick mud. The beams hung awkwardly close together.

Beto blew his horn, and Ferth stepped up to the chalk mark along with twenty-one other Draco youth. Five officers, including Laconius, had joined Jobu to watch. At the horn blast, Ferth bolted. Heavy breathing and stomping feet chased him as the group raced across the yard and over the boulders. Thirro pulled ahead at the beams, his wings now strong enough to carry him over all the logs in a single leap. Dara, her face tight with determination, sprang over the first beam, and the second. A skunk-faced Draco fell, rolling into Ferth. Ferth scrambled out of the way, but it cost him. Thirro won by three seconds. Ferth came in fourth, a hair behind Dara. She beamed like she'd been handed the kingdom.

"At least now you know, next time we're in a fight, you should run away," Ferth said, wiping the smirk off her face.

Ferth didn't stand out in the power course either. The trainees hurled timbers and rolled boulders. He didn't come close to beating the ox, or the gorilla boy who was just starting to transform. The panel of watching officers ebbed and flowed over the hours, watching in stony silence. Ferth went to bed that night sore and humbled. Tomorrow he would shine, he determined. He would be in Jobu's half company heading south.

Hand to hand combat came the next day.

"Ferth, you're with Saxal," Beto said.

The afternoon sun lashed against his skin. He'd been fighting since dawn. His lips cracked, and his hands burned as exhaustion pulled at his limbs. Ferth was one of four trainees still holding a sword. Judges called out points for hits. The first to ten points or a killing hit claimed victory.

Ferth tilted a water skin and guzzled. Steam wafted off his fur as he sweat rivers.

"I'm hungry," Beto said. "Let's get this done."

Ferth stepped back into the ring. Saxal was a fully transformed vervet monkey. Despite his white beard, there was nothing elderly about the way he sprang and spun. Ferth lifted half-lidded eyes on the monkey who was flipping his wooden sword side to side.

The horn blew. Ferth attacked. Saxal jumped out of reach. Ferth turned and swung again. Another miss. After four dizzying minutes, Ferth hadn't landed a single blow.

Ferth inhaled a steadying breath and crouched. One step at a time, he moved in on Saxal, making no attack with his sword, exclusively blocking Saxal from escaping right or left. As Saxal retreated closer to the out-of-bounds rope, his dance turned frantic. In desperation, Saxal raised his sword a fraction too far above his head. Ferth lashed, slicing the monkey across the middle.

"Kill stroke," Beto said. "Victory, Ferth."

The crowd of trainees sent up a mix of cheering and booing. Saxal peeled back loose lips and squealed before spitting in Ferth's face. Ferth wiped slime off his cheek with his dirty shirt and lined up against a gorilla for the last fight.

Keal was strong, dwarfing Ferth in height and width. Ferth gulped down exhaustion. He would win this. And he would win it fast. Blood bubbled through his sore muscles. Ferth faked right and struck left, slapping Keal's long arm.

"Point, Ferth," Beto said.

The force of the responding blow nearly knocked Ferth off his feet as an iron fist slammed his shoulder.

"Point, Keal."

Another blow struck Ferth's hand.

"Point, Keal."

"Keeeaaal! Keeaaal!" a turtle-faced girl yelled. Keal tossed her a grin. The crowd cheered.

With a last jolt of strength, Ferth blocked a forward thrust and spun outside. Knocking Keal's long arm forward, he swung behind the gorilla. Keal turned to block the incoming strike, but he was too slow. Ferth's sword smacked the back of his neck.

"Kill stroke," Beto said, his voice emotionless. "Victory, Ferth."

The trainees roared in support. The watching officers clapped. Jobu's scowl remained above folded arms. Queen Mavras winked at Ferth from her station next to Captain Jobu. How long had she been watching?

"Well-fought." Keal held out a meaty palm.

Ferth accepted it, swallowing his surprise. No one else had offered a hand after their defeat.

"You, too."

"I'm starving," Keal said. "Let's eat."

"Yes, please."

They dropped off their sticks and headed toward the buildings together. Laconius appeared. Keal kept going, but Ferth stepped out of the trickle of traffic.

"You took too long with that monkey. You should have blocked Dara's knock at your knees. You gave her that hit. When fighting a flyer, you can't let them leave the ground."

"Yes, father."

"But you won. Jobu noticed. Let's celebrate."

Pride wormed through Ferth's chest as he walked next to his father. It was easy to enjoy his win when it felt like a game. What would it feel like when it wasn't a game anymore? When his sword was sharp and he wasn't collecting points, but lives?

Dinner was at the assembly hall in the main castle. Vaulted ceilings arched high over the large room. Giant fireplaces roared to life in each corner, but most of the light came from hanging chandeliers covered in dripping candles.

Ferth stopped walking, the murals on the walls demanding his full attention. Even with the smell of meat and wine beckoning, Ferth gawked. Each of the four walls had a different theme. Shining gold framed the gigantic paintings. The north wall depicted power and might as armor-clad Draco Sang stood victorious over their human kill. The east wall portrayed heritage. Prince Nogard, the Black Dragon, streaked across the sky, a small king, queen, and child clutched in his talons, as he torched the old castle. Ferth's stomach twisted at the display of pleasure on the south wall. Draco Sang fulfilled their lusts in ways Ferth hadn't even imagined. The west wall symbolized beauty and wealth. A fifteen-foot-tall portrait of Queen Mavras shone in exaggerated charm and splendor, gold lace draping her body and a crown of flame encircling her brow.

Light-headed and giddy from the engrossing art and the day's victory, Ferth stumbled to an open seat. He feasted.

"Well-fought today, trainees," Mavras said as she took her seat at the highest table. "There will be one more competition in two days' time, but tonight we celebrate our rising generation of warriors."

Feet pounded the dirty floor as musicians played a deep sweeping tune. It rolled through Ferth's body like waves on the High Sea. Fatigue fell away, and after much meat and more drink, he was up on his feet dancing. Familiar and unfamiliar bodies oscillated in and out of his vision and under his fingers.

He woke the next morning in the low branches of a tree far outside the castle gates. Harsh sunlight cut his eyes like razors. He had no recollection of how he'd gotten there. It bothered him. The last memory he had was rejecting Dara when she'd followed him out of the citadel. In vain, he searched his black memories from last night but found nothing to explain what had happened after that.

Next time he would keep his head. He would keep control. He was his own master.

Ferth dropped from the tree, his shorts tearing on a branch. He landed with a jolt that shot all the way to his throbbing skull. He breathed out of his mouth to escape his own filth. The castle courtyard was empty. He slunk to his room. He peeled off grimy clothes, sticky with spilled wine and old sweat. He reached for his towel, but it was gone along with the rest of his dirty laundry. The barrack was quiet, the Draco still sleeping off last night.

Clean clothes in hand, head on fire, Ferth staggered naked down the empty hall. A slave girl entered. Her eyes bulged. She whirled, hitting her shoulder on the door in her hasty retreat.

Flee, slave. He grunted at himself. Little did she know, behind his red eyes and wildness, she couldn't have found him more harmless than she did this morning. Rocks smashed around his head as he dragged down the path, feeling utterly un-Draco-ish. He ignored the sinking feeling that quite possibly he was acting *more* Draco Sang-like than ever before.

He dropped his fistful of clothes and fell into the mineral pools. Unrefreshingly warm water wrapped around him. *We are strong and cunning. We are fearless and brave.* In his head, Keturah's voice replied. *That doesn't make you good.*

He pinched away the thought of her. What did a human slave know about it? She hated the Dracos because of her own weakness.

Clean and dressed, he shuffled to the edge of the training yard. Dangling his feet over the edge of the cliff, he watched the turbulent sea froth and foam. The breeze tickled along the bare left side of his face, reminding him, and everyone else, that he was not fully a Draco Sang yet. He'd fought hard for his blood and embraced the wolf when it came. Now was his time to succeed.

And I will.

Keturah's soft admonition to follow a different path nagged at his chest, but he squashed it away more firmly this time. Deep inside, he wanted to go and see her, but now he could not. Now he was the monster she had never wanted him to become. He was a Draco Sang. A future king, he amended. She was nothing but a slave.

TWENTY-EIGHT - BLIND
CAL

Cal strode into Titus's tent, Lyko at his heels. "I'm going to Skotar."

"We're going."

"And Lyko."

Eio lifted a lazy head his direction. Titus dropped the paper on his desk as blue eyes snapped up.

"It's the only way," Cal said. "This must be done. We are sitting here blind. What of the rest of the border? What of their numbers and plans?"

Titus ran a hand over his neatly trimmed beard.

"It needs to be done." His voice was curt.

"Yes," Titus said.

Cal opened his mouth to protest, then realized what Titus had said.

"What do you propose?" The captain of the army motioned him to sit.

In the drizzle of a foggy gray morning, Ferth stood with the rest of the trainees in a semi-circle around Beto and Jobu. The training yard lay barren, no weapons or drills set up.

"Your test today is a rescue," Beto said. "Dara has been captured by the enemy."

Ferth's gut lurched in confusion and indignation. He glanced around the group. She was truly gone. *They* had just taken her. Did she agree, or did the officers force her? Was she hurt? He knew the officers well enough to know they would not hesitate to rip a weaker creature from its very bed if it served their purpose or desire. But Dara was a Draco Sang. She was one of them, not a slave. He forced his pulse to calm, but the thoughts festered. *Trust no Draco.*

"She's within a ten-mile radius of here. Find her and bring her safely back." Beto's face turned grave. "Do not kill. If you kill another trainee, don't bother coming back. You'll find a fate worse than death awaits you if you do." He swung an arm toward the gate. "I'll blow my horn three times when she's returned. Don't come back before then. Now get out of here."

A stampede of young Dracos ran toward the gate. Excitement and ambition fueled Ferth's muscles as he jogged outside the wall. He stopped as others fanned into the wild, disturbing any scent he might have found. Overhead, a dozen flyer officers soared over the citadel walls to watch the games.

He needed wings.

Thirro flew low to the east, and Ferth sprinted after him. Ferth yelled to Thirro when he got within range. The bald eagle peered down and slowly circled back. He perched on a thick branch above Ferth's head and shook water down on him.

"What's your plan?" Ferth asked, wiping drops from his brow.

Thirro guffawed. "I'd never tell you."

"Together we have a good chance of winning this. If we team up."

Thirro glided to the ground.

"I need your wings and eyes. You need my strength and skill."

"Fine." Thirro's face remained cold.

"I'll head east towards the High Sea. If either of us gets a hint, make this whistle." Ferth whistled.

Thirro echoed it. "I'm sure she'll be hidden from my view."

"Keep an eye on the officers. They might not be able to help themselves and fly over her very spot. Watch the other groups from above. If they find her first, we'll relieve them of their burden."

Thirro's lips curved up wickedly before he launched into the stormy sky. Ferth pounded after him, looking under trees and bushes and sniffing as he went.

Two hours later, Thirro circled back and landed where Ferth had bouldered down to the bottom of the eastern cliffs, near the water.

"I haven't seen anything," Thirro said. "There are a lot of trainees in the north. But look up."

Ferth tilted his head and squinted up the sheer rock face towering over him. Captain Jobu stood above, on the edge of the training yard, looking down the cliff at them.

"Hopefully that's a good sign," Ferth said. "With the brine and breeze, it's hard to smell anything but sea and rain, but maybe I'll pick up something farther ahead."

"Two are behind you, and seven are coming at the beach from the south side." Thirro took to the air. Within minutes, he returned. "I found her." His voice was a cocky preen. "She's on a high ledge of the cliff, bound hand and foot. She does not look happy."

How could she? Jobu didn't want to hide a box or object for them to find instead of Dara?

"Follow me." Thirro flew four feet above Ferth's head as he scrambled over large rocks to reach the base of the cliff. There, twenty feet above him, dangerously high, Dara poked her head over the small ledge. Thirro landed on the perch next to her. After a minute, he flapped down to Ferth.

"Are you strong enough to carry her to the top?" Ferth asked.

"Not yet." Embarrassment tinged Thirro's face.

"Help her off the edge. Slow her fall if you can. I'll catch her."

Thirro flew back up, taking his knife from his belt. A piece of rope fluttered away from the cliff and danced in the wind. Dara climbed over the ledge feet-first, dangling by her fingertips. Shouting issued up the coast as others spotted her.

Ferth braced his feet against cracks in the rocky ground

and held his hands up, fully aware this could go badly. Whose reckless idea was it to put her in such a precarious spot?

Thirro clutched Dara under the arms. When she let go, he flapped frantically, but still she plummeted. She slammed into Ferth's chest. Ferth groaned under the impact. His feet and calves pressed painfully into the slippery boulders as her sharp elbow speared his ribs. Anger flaring along with the pain, he flung her away. Her knees clanged against stone.

"Took you long enough," Dara said as she scrambled to her feet, coppery fur hanging matted and wet. Below blood-shot eyes, her nose dripped snot.

"You're welcome." How long had she been up there? Ferth resisted the urge to look up the cliff and glower at Jobu watching from above. Breathing hard, he turned to Thirro. "It's quicker going south. I'll follow where you fly. Keep us away from others."

"Stay close." Water dripped off dark wings as Thirro shook into flight.

Ferth gripped Dara's wrist, tugging her along.

"I can walk, thank you." She tried to twist out of his hand, but he tightened his hold.

"It's not every day you get the chance to hold my hand. Just enjoy it."

She hissed, but her arm went limp.

Thirro flew east toward the water, then turned south. He cried a warning as a hound Draco leapt in front of them. She pulled out a knife.

"Let me have her."

"Or what?" Ferth asked. "You'll kill me?"

"Maiming is allowed." The Draco's dark lips peeled back, revealing the small pointed canines that flanked her front teeth.

Ferth would have laughed if he hadn't sensed another trainee approaching. He didn't have time. Switching Dara to his left fist, he pulled out the knife he kept in his belt. When the hound attacked, Ferth had to let go of Dara to block a rapid series of stabs. The girl fought well, and it took Ferth too long to disable her. He kicked her in the chest, and she landed hard on the pebbles. By then, Dara was gone.

"Hurry," Thirro yelled. "She's over here."

Panting, Ferth sprinted along after her. He had to thank the trainee that had stopped Dara's escape, even if it meant more work breaking her free of her new captor. He left the unconscious snake Draco without a backward glance, but inside his chest tightened with pity.

"You can't tell me you'd rather he won than me," Ferth said. Dara was tight in his clutches as they rushed up the steep slopes. Blood soaked his forearm where the hyena had gotten a lucky strike.

"If I bring myself in, I win," Dara said.

"Not a chance."

They neared the gates when another trainee came into view. Ferth whirled Dara behind a tree and cupped a thick palm over her mouth. She squirmed and shrieked under his grip.

A cold blade touched her ear, still healing from their fight in the training yard. "Make another noise, and I'll cut it all the way off." Amber fur swayed under the puffs of his breath on her neck.

She turned to rock.

Thirro whistled. Dara glared as Ferth wiped her spit off his palm onto her furry neck. He grabbed her wrist and pulled her along toward the castle as fast as he could drag her. A handful of trainees chased them through the gates, but Dara remained in Ferth's tight grip when they stopped at the foot of the copper dragon. Thirro landed on Dara's other side.

"Victory, Ferth," Beto said.

"And Thirro," Ferth said. "We worked as a team."

Laconius and Jobu studied him in silence. His father's lips turned down a fraction.

Beto nodded once, his rare sign of approval. "Victory, Ferth and Thirro."

Dara ripped her arm free and rubbed at the chafes on her wrists as she scowled.

Beto blew the horn three times and spoke to the gathering crowd. "The competitions are over. Captain Jobu has seen your skills. His thoughts are his own." Beto's lips tweaked up at the joke. Jobu hadn't spoken a word to the trainees. "If he does not invite you to join his half company, then I'll see you tomorrow for basic training."

During a sullen supper, Dara glared daggers across the table at Ferth. He ignored it. He stabbed his stew, wondering if Jobu wasn't going to take a single trainee.

"Listen up," a rat-faced man said from the door of the mess hall. "If I call your name, you are to report to the citadel entrance immediately. Keal, Dara, Saxal, Thirro, Ferth …"

Ferth didn't hear anything after that. He vaulted over from the bench and knocked into the messenger's shoulder as he flew by.

A hundred trainees gathered in the square. Massive iron doors opened, and Jobu stepped out. He glanced over the group with a frown. "You will complete my half company and head south. You will refer to me as Captain."

"Yes, Captain." Ferth's voice rose with the others. *I made it.* He was leaving Shi Castle. He would be part of the force to take Elysium. There he would prove his power and worth. He would conquer his human heart as well as the human lands. Wild excitement hammered in his chest.

"Are you prepared to work hard? Fight fearlessly? Finish victorious?"

"Yes, Captain," they cried.

"I expect it from you. We leave in twelve days. We'll make camp at the delta before the ground freezes. Have your pack ready and your blades sharp. Armor, weapons, and supplies are commissioned to you. See to it that you get them and maintain them."

"Yes, Captain."

"You are unit five. Ferth is your unit commander." Jobu's black eyes locked on Ferth's stunned face. "As your leader, you will address him with your questions. And you will obey him."

Keal's voice rang out, "Yes, Captain," before the rest of the group trickled out their acceptance.

Ferth's body nearly floated as the realization hit. *Commander.* Dozens of eyes speared him with a mix of jealousy, resentment, resignation, and awe. He washed the eagerness from his face and steadied his features into what he hoped looked like respectful acceptance.

"Commander Ferth, join me inside." Jobu turned and retreated into the citadel. Ferth unfroze with a jerk, bounding up the stairs and slipping inside a hair before the heavy doors clanged shut behind him.

"You are young and inexperienced." Jobu marched down the hall. "However, it appears you are slightly less ignorant and weak than the rest of your unit. You are responsible for them. Discipline wins battles."

"Yes, Captain." Ferth's thoughts reeled and spun as he tried to swallow the overwhelming responsibility.

They entered a room where Laconius and four Dracos sat smoking thin pipes. The air plumed heavy and sickly. Smoke shot through Ferth's sensitive nose, straight to his brain. After a few breaths, his temples pulsed, and his fingers tingled. He barely stopped himself from covering his face with his shirt. *Show no weakness.* His senses surrendered.

"Ferth, meet the other unit commanders in my half

company. They've been with me for the last two seasons. Learn from them." Jobu accepted a pipe and sat in a pile of pillows.

Ferth lifted a hand to an ox man, a wolverine, a scaly green lizard, and a silky cheetah female who looked at him like he was lunch. He didn't allow fear one sliver of space in his heart.

"You five officers are the only soldiers I ever want to hear from," Jobu said. "Keep your units in check and well-functioning, and you will be rewarded."

Laconius motioned Ferth forward from where he still stood at the door. Ferth eased onto a low cushion. "Hello, Commander. Nice work." Laconius took a long pull on the pipe. "But you can't have this until that fur grows over your face." His father guffawed, a vibrating rumble. "Just remember to turn your left side to your friends and your right side to your enemies."

"I don't know," said the commander with the black-spotted fur. "That baby skin looks delicious." A feline tongue lapped over her canines.

"You're not allowed to eat him, Mina," Jobu said.

"Just try," Ferth said with a tight growl.

Mina laughed, and it sounded like a purr. "I like this one."

"There are benefits to being my commander," Jobu said. "Even if your face is an embarrassment."

Fortunately, Ferth's shirt covered the bare spot over his chest.

"Emil," Jobu said. "Give him a hit."

An arm like a tree trunk reached over. "Take it slow, boy."

Ferth winced under the watchful eyes. He didn't want to take it at all; he wanted to keep his thoughts sharp. But he could not appear the coward here. He tentatively brought the pipe to his lips. Smoke speared his blood and lit him on fire.

Laconius's mocking laugh rolled under the heavy waves of his consciousness.

Keep control. Stay alert.

Images of dancing slave men and women, an aggressive cheetah, and his father feasting flickered through his pulsing vision. The wolverine spoke to him, close by his ear, but what was she saying? With his mind clouded by the hallifer berry, he couldn't focus.

And then Pearl was there. Her gray eyes tethered him to this world, kept him from drowning. She settled on the pillows at his side, in the crook of his arm.

"Make her dance," Emil called to Ferth.

Pearl's narrow body tensed. She rolled forward. His eyes fluttered in faked pleasure as she buried her soft face in his neck, melting him.

"No." Ferth's voice was a low rasp as Pearl peppered his jaw with desperate kisses. He wrapped a protective arm around her waist, shifting her onto his lap, his entire body aware of her weight and the feel of her lips.

Emil snorted and waved a dismissive hand.

Pearl clung to him, remaining under the shield of his territorial touch. She fed him bites of meat and roasted apple and carrot. When the pipe passed his way, he didn't inhale. He laid his head back on the cushion, stroking her hair as she rested against his chest. If only this were real. If only she *wanted* to be here with him. The room blurred as he fought waves of exhaustion. When Jobu led a young slave from the room, Ferth unfolded to his feet. With Pearl tucked under his arm, her hands around his waist, he stumbled to his barrack. He stopped at the building entrance. If he took her to his room tonight, he wouldn't have the strength to say no. Not with his neck still tingling from her kisses. But why deny himself the pleasure? Cupping her chin, he tilted her face up. Above ashen lips, dark rings circled her eyes. Her narrow shoulders curved inward. Pity for her welled up as his desire was extinguished. With a supportive arm around her waist, Ferth changed course.

"Where's your room?"

Fear and confusion painted her pale face. She pointed a thin finger. He escorted her all the way to her tiny, shared room on the fifth floor of the slave house.

"Good night." He nudged her through the door.

"Thank you," she whispered as she stumbled over the threshold.

The slave house was silent as he walked out, as if the entire building held its breath against the predator walking its halls.

He cursed a sharp headache the next day. His shirt stank. He hurled it across the room, but he could not erase the sickly-sweet fumes on his fur. He sat up in bed and clawed at his scalp until his fur stuck straight up. Filthy. Old dirt and sweat from yesterday's games coated his body. Brown blood splattered his pants and crusted his forearm from his shallow wound, still untreated. He couldn't stand to smell himself. He turned itchy eyes toward the soft knock at the door. He growled, low and guttural, and mean.

Satisfying silence.

Then the knock came again.

Annoyed, he rammed himself to his feet and flung the door open, ready to tear the fool apart. "What?" His voice was deep and vicious, but his anger died the moment he saw her.

The slave flinched but didn't retreat. "Commander Ferth?"

Attraction slapped Ferth across the face. Her body, strong and curvy, pressed pleasingly against her homespun dress. Green eyes dazzled like emeralds. Rich brown hair tied back in a thick braid. He stared, paralyzed. His blood roared, screamed, begged for her. Her luscious fertility sang through his limbs like a homing call.

"Are you Commander Ferth?" Her voice sharpened.

"Yes." He cursed his voice for coming out weak and throaty.

"I am Shale. I've been assigned to assist you in the upcoming campaign."

"Assigned to me?" His lips curved up.

She frowned. Her tone carried ice and steel. "I am assigned to prepare your tent, attend your meals, wash your clothes. Things of that nature *only*."

Loud mocking laughter burst from Ferth. He clutched his bare chest as her absurd declaration rolled through him.

Shale's iron mask faltered, and fear flickered over her face.

She had no rights. No choice. She took a heavy risk simply by speaking to him like that. *Courageous. But very stupid.* His blood howled to take her. Teach her a lesson. He stepped forward and fingered a silky lock of hair, fallen loose of her braid.

"My slave." He said it as if tasting an especially nice brew.

Her square jaw rippled, and his hand moved to the spot. He stroked the line of soft skin with his dirty thumb. She'd turned to stone, but her plump lips yielded under his fingers. Her fear and anger burned like acid up his nostrils. He should show her his dominance right now. Slaves needed to be reminded of who held the power. His core warmed, and his fingers gripped her chin at the thought. Her burning eyes fell to the floor as her shoulders seemed to droop in defeat. He did not like seeing her like that, her brilliance dimmed.

Guilt, a sin among his kind, coiled in his gut, choking his lust. He dropped his hand and stepped back. His head throbbed. Let her have her victory today.

"How old are you?" he asked.

"Seventeen."

"Where are you from?"

"Here." Green eyes pierced him.

How had he never seen her all these years? Or was she lying?

She was tall for a slave, her crown level with his ear. Her gaze flicked between the bare circle of skin above his heart and the human left side of his face. Despite her serious scowl, her beauty speared him again. He found himself admiring the strength that emanated from her stance. So different from most of the slaves he saw. She reminded him a little of Keturah in that way. "You're bold," Ferth said. She lifted her chin a fraction and tightened her jaw as he studied her. "You're lucky that I like bold."

Her cheeks pinked as if she finally realized the foolish risk she'd taken with her brazenness.

Yes, she would do well for him. "How wonderful," Ferth said. "And, you've come just in time." He picked up his crumpled shirt and peeled off his pants. He tossed his rank clothes at her chest.

Red flamed over her face as she whirled.

"When you're done, come back and get the rest," he called to her retreating figure. He chuckled as he sprawled naked over his bed, feeling suddenly refreshed.

"*L*ead out, boss," Zemira said, her smile undermining her mocking tone. She tugged her pack higher onto her shoulder.

Cal sent her and Uriah what he hoped was a confident grin before lifting his chin and marching west, the rising sun a comforting warmth at his back as he headed toward an icy winter in the Seraf Mountains.

Boss. The word weighed heavier than the pack on his back. *Commander of this mission.* This was his idea. His responsibility. And Uriah and Zemira had *volunteered* to go with him. Titus had refused to let them cross at the dangerous delta, but he'd approved the plan to follow the river west into the mountains, survey the border, search for enemy infiltration, and find out if the narrow bridge near Volkar Lake was real or myth. If a bridge truly existed, they would cross into Skotar undetected.

Opal darted ahead, her steps light and unburdened by any added weight. She'd refused to be harnessed with a pack. Lyko had declined as well, but Cal had overruled him. Lyko, a pack of winter coats and extra potatoes strapped to his back, glared in resentment and envy at the prancing panther.

"You'll be glad for the supplies in a few weeks," Cal reminded his hewan.

"You'll be glad. I'm wearing my coat, and I hate potatoes."

They crossed the narrow bridge over the canals. Water pounded out of the river and south into Kiptos. The powerful river carried the promise of life to Elysium's land but seemed to seal their death on its course. Torrents of water rushed through the manmade ducts.

They stopped in a sunny clearing for lunch. Uriah passed around bowls of bean soup he'd snagged that morning from the army kitchen. Cal removed Lyko's pack. His wolf rolled in the grass in delight, rubbing his shoulders into the dirt.

"Not so tight," Lyko said when it came time to load up again.

"It'll fall off."

"No, it won't."

Cal loosened the straps on Lyko's shoulders before leading the way closer to the looming mountains. Lyko lagged behind as they wove through patches of forest. Now west of the canals, the Rugit River was a thundering, impenetrable storm to their right.

"I've got to visit that tree," Zemira said, motioning to a patch of vegetation. "I'll catch up."

As Cal wondered again how he was going to manage weeks of her presence, he and Uriah pressed forward along the faded trail toward the watchtower at the base of the mountains.

"Why is she barfing?" Lyko asked.

Cal halted mid-step, sending his confusion back to Lyko.

"Yeah. She's throwing her guts out behind those trees."

Cal dropped his pack. "Zemira," he said to Uriah before hustling back the way he'd come. He found Zemira on her knees, a pool of half-digested lunch glistening on the grass. He crouched at her side and laid a hand on her spine. Concern overcame his disgust. "We'll take you back."

She wiped her mouth with the back of her hand and scrambled to her feet. "No. I'm fine. It's nothing."

Uriah's deep voice cut in. "You're sick."

His grizzly, Poe, moaned in pity.

Zemira smiled at the bear before turning a stern face to Cal and Uriah. "I'm not diseased. I'm allergic to sunger beans."

Uriah raised a dark brow.

"I didn't realize they were in our lunch until too late," Zemira said, her voice hard. Her face was no longer tinted green; instead, her jaw set with defiance. "But I can still beat you to the watchtower." She hefted her pack and marched away, leaving Cal and Uriah flatfooted in her wake.

"What's a sunger bean?" Cal asked.

"No idea," Uriah said. "But they'll probably have something at the tower to help. I'm sure she'll be fine by morning. I've never known her to take sick."

As far as Cal had learned, the Draco Sang didn't generally take sick. Ever. But as he followed his friend, worry nagged. He didn't even notice until miles later that Lyko had "lost" his pack.

They borrowed coats from the supplies at the watchtower. No one asked Lyko to carry theirs. Zemira proved perky and alert the next morning when they started up the steep foothills of the Seraf Mountains.

The night before Jobu's half company left Shi Castle, Ferth picked under his clawed nails with a knife. Shale bustled around his tiny room, pointedly ignoring him as she packed his trunk. His gaze roved from her mouth, to her hips, to her hair. The song of her blood called to him in a steady toll. How could anyone find a Draco Sang attractive when there were humans like this in the world?

She picked up his short sword and, with a fluid sweep, pulled it free of its sheath. His pulse hitched as he jerked forward in his seat. Sly green eyes flicked to him.

Was she going to attack him? His limbs steadied, and his nerves flared in anticipation. He'd enjoy disarming her. The rebel would face swift retribution. His lips curved. She didn't engage his fantasy.

Her focus was on the sword; she checked its edge with an air of confidence before sheathing it and adding it to his pack. He slumped back, but his attention remained alert. He caught her discreetly testing the weight of a throwing knife before wrapping it in leathers.

So she knew of weapons. He had almost become a slave

who knew a whole lot about weapons. The question was, how did *she*? Had she worked in the armory before? Or maybe she'd been mistaken at birth for a Draco Sang. It happened sometimes when a scenting went wrong; a human infant was sent to the Draco nursery or vice versa. She could have trained for years before they realized she wasn't going to transform. It was rare, but she could have been a Draco Sang and lost her beast. They would have killed her abomination. He couldn't stand to watch it. He'd seen four abominations slaughtered, and each time the person acted like their heart was being dug out with a spoon, leaving them broken.

He watched her as he pondered her proficient handling of his weapons; she would have looked good in fighting tights, a sword hanging at her thigh. A thrill ran through him.

Dara appeared in the open doorway. "What's this?"

"*This* is Shale," Ferth said, not liking her tone.

Shale straightened up, rolling her shoulders back.

A touch of pride puffed Ferth's chest. "And she's mine."

"Send her over to help me pack when she's done," Dara said.

"No. And don't ever make the mistake of telling me what to do. Shale answers to me. Only."

Dara raked her yellow gaze over Shale, her eyes cold and calculating. Clawed fingers twitched at Dara's sides.

"That also means she falls under my protection." Dara's attention flicked to Ferth at the threatening chill in his tone.

"She's a slave."

"She's *mine,* and there will be consequences," Ferth said the word as if tasting torture on his tongue. "If she is so much as looked at in a way that displeases me."

Dara took a step back, but defiance or possibly envy flushed across her face.

Ferth hadn't shifted from his lounging seated position.

"You did well today in the drills. Your knife skills have surpassed even Keal, I think."

Dara's eyes softened with his praise, and her stance loosened.

"The other units are older and more experienced, but we're going to outshine them."

Dara grinned.

"Are you willing to outwork them? Outfight them? Are you willing to respect my leadership to do it?"

"Yes, commander."

Ferth threw a charming smile, and Dara leaned closer. "Go tell the rest of the unit what I said about Shale."

The desire on Dara's face washed away. She tipped sulky eyes toward the woman standing like a statue by the bed. "Fine."

"Yes, Commander Ferth."

Dara's lips curled. "Yes, Commander Ferth. Oh, and Chief Laconius wants to see you in his chambers."

"Thank you, Dara."

She whirled on her heels and stormed out.

Ferth stood. "Pick up a new whetstone from the supplies office," Ferth said to Shale as he walked past, close enough for his fur to brush her bare arm.

He had rarely gone into his father's chambers, even as a child. A pangolin Draco stood guard and opened the door at his approach. The room pressed in on him despite the high ceilings and open space. Weapons racked the walls, and parchments cluttered a thick desk. Laconius's horned head bent over a map before it turned.

"You ready?" Beady eyes found Ferth's.

There was always only one answer to that annoying question. "Yes, sir."

"Most of the warriors in your company are happy being warriors. That's all they will ever be. That's what they were made to do. You are not one of them. I expect more. You will rise to the top. The best in the half company. A king in the making."

"Yes, sir. I will make you proud." He would do it—no matter what he felt about it.

"Train hard. Keep your ears open. Watch Jobu and the other commanders. Study maps and parchments when you see them in command meetings. Know everything. A good leader is smart. A good warrior knows his friends as well as his enemies."

Ferth absorbed the instructions.

"Jobu will appoint a second when I bring in a full company in the spring. Make sure it's you." Laconius studied the left side of Ferth's face with a frown. "I won't miss that pup skin."

Heat rose to Ferth's cheeks, and he hated that he couldn't hide the flush as the thin skin revealed his shame.

"Must be from your weak mother."

Ferth leaned forward a fraction. *Tell me about her. Who is she? Does she still live? Where can I find her?* He ached to voice the questions, but they stayed trapped behind his heart.

"I'll look forward to a regal wolf greeting me when the snow melts."

"We will prepare the way for your army. We'll kill the lion. I swear it."

Laconius rose, then turned to his desk and picked up a long canine attached to a leather thong. "I took this tooth from the lion when I first meet him. I'll savor having the entire set." Wild hunger raged in his eyes.

"We'll hunt him down."

A heavy palm landed on Ferth's shoulder. "May the dragon keep you and bless you with victory."

Laconius crushed his son in a rare embrace. Ferth left, determined to win fame and victory. It was the only way forward he could see. He'd be the one to bring his father the head of Titus and his lion abomination. He would be Jobu's second.

A breeze whispering of colder weather shimmied through his shirt as he stepped outside.

Jade intercepted him in the courtyard. "You leave tomorrow."

"I'm sorry I can't take you with me." He wasn't sure if that was true. He'd come to care for her as he might have a younger sister, had he been so lucky. She was cunning and vicious, but he sensed a warmth beneath her sharp eyes that drew him in. She learned fast during their training sessions, and she worked hard. But he didn't want her near battle. She was safer here. "No twelve-year-old underlings in the army."

Pink lips pouted, but she didn't take the bait and again try to convince him she was fifteen. "One more training session?"

That he could give her. "Archery?" He'd found her a smaller bow, and although her range was still half the distance of his, she wielded the weapon with deadly accuracy.

"Let's see how well you do without a weapon," she said.

Ferth chuckled at her cocky swagger as he walked with her to the training halls. The building was empty this late in the evening. In the dim light, they faced each other across the mat.

"No biting," Ferth said; he still had a mark on his calf where she'd tried to rip out a chunk of his flesh.

Jade flashed a strip of white teeth and charged. He blocked her swinging fists—mostly. A smattering of stinging punches slipped through his half-hearted defenses.

"I hate it when you do this," she said.

"What?" His voice was airy and mocking—as if he didn't know.

She grunted and tried to bring a knee to his groin. He shoved it away with a laugh. She flared, peppering his blocking forearms with her fists. "Hit me."

Ferth didn't go on the offensive.

"Hit me."

He knocked away a swift kick to his knee, gripped her ankle, and flipped her back. "Better?" But it was his smile that sent her yelling.

"You're not even trying!"

"Yes, I am," Ferth said. "I'm definitely trying not to go home with another bruise."

She popped to her feet and snarled. She lunged. Ferth picked her off the ground, his grip pinning her arms. Her legs went around his waist. She tilted back, her face inches from his. The combat drained out of her as she studied his face.

"You're not like other Dracos," Jade said.

His face fell.

She looked sorry and spoke again in a rush. "Take me with you. I'm as good a fighter as half your unit."

"More than that," Ferth said, voicing the truth. "But you can't join. You're still an underling."

"I'll transform." She gritted her teeth, as if willing it to happen. He loosened his hold on her shoulders to set her down, but her thighs tightened on his waist. "I'll be marching with your father. I *will* join you this spring."

Before Ferth could tell her not to rush it, she leaned forward. Her hands gripped his neck, and she pressed soft lips to his. There was nothing unpleasant about her delicate mouth sliding over his. But he felt very wrong. He unfroze as her tongue slipped over his lip. He tilted back.

"Jade." Ferth's voice was gentle, but his stomach turned as her violet eyes darkened with the pain of rejection. She didn't fight when he loosened her legs and set her on her feet.

She craned her neck to look up at his face. "I know," she said. "Even though I'm fifteen, I'm not *big* enough. Yet." The last word dangled like a threat and a promise. She glared, her chin defiant.

Ferth put his arm around her shoulders. "Come on, I'll sneak you some peaches."

Jade's arm slipped around his waist as she let him lead her out.

The next morning, Jade was back at his side. The entirety of Shi Castle had gathered around the copper dragon. How she'd managed to sneak out of the mass of underlings and into the crush of Draco Sang without being noticed or sent back, he didn't know, but he wasn't surprised. She smirked as she slipped up to his elbow. Her eyes glowed when he sent her an impressed grin.

Queen Mavras stood below the gaping mouth of the statue, a glistening black crown perched on her sharp head. "For generations, we have lived trapped in these cold mountains. We smell the fragrance of the fertile Kiptos. We hear the tinkling wealth in Mitera. We see the abundance the weak humans enjoy. We, who are more powerful, more cunning, more deserving, have been without. We are the royal blood of the dragon. The time has come for us to take what is ours. Rule the weak. Bring pride to the Draco Sang."

The gathered crowd of Dracos erupted. Ferth pumped his fist and howled.

"The time has come to take Elysium," Mavras shouted over the cheering. After a moment, she raised her pinchers for silence. "Tonight we invoke the dragon's blessing on our journeys and battles."

Laconius stood next to the feet of the dragon. A shirtless slave boy of about fourteen years trembled at his side, his hands and feet bound with rope. Laconius lifted him and laid him across the stone base of the statue. Tears streamed down the boy's gray face, but he bravely stayed silent. Laconius bowed deeply to the dragon before stepping back, making way for the queen.

Queen Mavras placed a hand on the boy's head and spoke, her voice a sharp whine. "Oh Great and Powerful Dragon. Accept this, our sacrifice. Bless us with victory. Honor us with triumph. Deliver our enemies into our hands." Her tail sprang up. Venom glistened on the tip as it slowly came down over the slave's chest. The razor's point sliced into the skin on his sternum. Blood gushed. His bone-rattling scream rent the air.

Mavras lurched back as shimmering green scales rippled across the slave's skin. He shrieked, a long, forked tongue lashing the air. The wound on his chest clotted, but it was too late. The lizard-boy slumped against the pedestal as the venom did its work. Silence settled over the courtyard. Ferth forced his frozen lungs to contract. *That could have been me.*

Mavras's high voice broke the spell. "A miracle! An omen of victory. The Black Dragon has spoken. The Draco Sang will overtake the humans." She bared thin teeth as if daring anyone to dispute her interpretation.

Dracos shouted and surged forward, but Ferth stayed riveted to his spot. That slave was Draco Sang. Ferth knew that slave had never joined the underling training, never had a chance. He'd been a slave since birth. He should have been sorted with the Draco Sang, but he'd mistakenly been put with the humans. And then killed.

Slaves were supposed to be the undeserving, weak humans. Not true Draco Sang worthy of the blessing of the Dragon. It was meant to be as easy as that. How ignorant he had been. He should have known nothing was that simple.

Revulsion turned him away from the dead slave-who-was-actually-a-Draco. Along the back of the courtyard stood lines of slaves. Somber as stones. Keturah's attention bore into him, searing across the space. Her gaze cut him to the quick. A moment before he'd swelled with confidence and pride; now, he walked forward a child. He halted at arm's length and tilted his head so his human left side angled toward her.

"A wolf," Keturah said. "A regal animal. I can't think of a better choice."

He stored her praise.

"Laconius must be proud."

"Yes."

"And you?"

"Oh, yes. It is an honor to follow after our great father, Attor." He wondered why the declaration sounded hollow.

She smiled, but it didn't reach her eyes.

"I'm a commander in Jobu's half company." His pride in that accomplishment was genuine.

"It won't be long before you rise higher than that. You were made for greatness."

"You always say that, but I've got a lot to prove and a long way to go. It'll help when my fur grows over my face and chest." Why did he say that? She already viewed him as savage.

He flinched when her hand flew up. On instinct, he grabbed her wrist, holding it in the air. Fear spiked her face. He dropped her hand, ashamed. Slowly, she brought her palm back up and laid it over his human skin. Warmth penetrated beneath her touch.

"Never mistake humanness for weakness." The quiet of her voice only gave strength to the words. Deep wrinkles etched harsh lines, but her eyes burned soft and sad.

His training urged him to step back, break away from her impertinent touch. But he could not move. The closest he'd ever come to a mother, and somehow, she still looked at him with tenderness.

"And never mistake strength for goodness. You, my son, can be both. I wish I could meet your mother. I see her in your eyes—love and honor and courage. You have as much of her blood as your father's. More, I think."

He treasured her words even as he reeled back, his heart hammering. His eyes narrowed—to cover up the threat of tears. She had overstepped. Insulted him. His yearnings for his mother were his own. And not to be discovered. Thinking of his mother, wanting her, that was beneath him. He knew nothing of her, except that she was human—and that was enough to dismiss her. His spine straightened; his shoulders squared. Keturah didn't cower.

"Even when your fur grows over and your transformation is complete, you will always be my Ferth. And I will always love you. No matter what. I love you." She said it with ferocity, as if willing him to try and stop her, prevent it.

The words dismantled him. She'd spoken so openly, so freely. So improperly. As he stored her precious words deep within his heart, he glanced around, hoping no one had overheard.

Shale watched her master with the matron slave. Shale couldn't hear their words, but she hadn't taken her eyes off Ferth since he'd turned away from the dragon. The raving Dracos chanted and shouted in a chilling crush, but Ferth had turned his back and walked away from it. To a slave.

Shale stood to his left, the human side of his face fully visible to her. If she focused on that, on his eyes and expression, he looked almost gentle and human. He'd let Keturah touch his face. He'd bowed to her with respect in his stance.

Stop it. She wanted him to be human, but he wasn't. She *knew* what he was. And he frightened her straight through her skin. She'd nearly crumpled to the ground, she'd been shaking so fiercely after she'd left that first encounter in his barrack. He'd been deranged and violent, his eyes red and his stench unbearable. The feral delight in his face when he'd stood before her, naked and powerful, still sent ice skittering down her spine. The skin of her face and lips where he'd touched her still burned as if tickled by fire.

She didn't sleep last night thinking about what he'd said

to Dara. Did he realize the protection he'd given her? Deep down, she knew he would make good on his threats. The real nagging question was, why? She'd fought off past assailants who prowled after her—she'd get in close and knock them unconscious. But the well-trained fighters on this campaign weren't the drunken Draco around the castle. She wouldn't be able to hide in the kitchens anymore. The knife she kept sharp and strapped to her thigh was little protection or comfort. She would be punished severely for resisting a warrior. Ferth's words alone would shield her.

From anyone but him.

Shale had categories for the Draco Sang. She kept them ordered in her head: whom to avoid, whom to flatter, who was greedy but lazy, who was vicious but weak or strong but foolish. But Ferth had eluded her understanding. He was unpredictable, cunning, powerful, and mysterious. A dangerous master.

He terrified her more than all the rest.

As Ferth turned away from Keturah, the lupine side of his face angled toward Shale. And any delusions of his kindness vanished. She hoped she wasn't anywhere near him when the last of his humanity vanished.

They'd been in the mountains for weeks, traveling steadily west along the river towards Volkar Lake. No sign of the Draco Sang. No bridges or crossings into Skotar. Nothing but cold forest and Zemira's never-ending presence, reminding Cal what he would never have. They maintained their morning training sessions while breakfast cooked. It had been a particularly cold night—they'd all slept together in the one tent they had. Cal had not slept well. But the sun shone fiercely that morning, as if reminding the world of its dominance. After the first round of sword exercises, Cal and Uriah had taken off their coats, but despite the sheen of sweat on her brow, Zemira kept hers on.

"Both of you," Uriah said. "Come at me as a team." He looked to Cal. "Don't accidentally hit Zemira."

"Are we worried about that?" Cal asked with a laugh. "Am I that terrible?"

Uriah flashed large square teeth. "I wouldn't put it past Zemira. She's not one for sharing her kill."

Zemira rolled her eyes and attacked. Cal joined in. Uriah parried their strikes.

"Hit when I do," Zemira said. "Make him work."

Cal shifted his cadence. Uriah knocked the dull practice swords away with apparent ease. Cal strengthened his blows. With a feint to the knees, he brought his sword up at the same time Zemira swung from the back. Uriah's sword slammed into Cal's, and his left hand shot out, his open palm connecting with Zemira's belly and shoving her out of sword range. She gasped, dropped her weapon, and pitched over her knees. Cal and Uriah stared at her in surprise.

"Zemira?" Uriah's voice was strained and unsure.

She didn't answer, just hobbled over to the trees and vomited.

The boys didn't move. Wide-eyed, they watched in horror. Guilt spread over Uriah's bearded face. Zemira wiped her mouth and raked a hand through her short black hair.

"What's going on?" Uriah asked. "I've hit you a lot harder than that before without you so much as flinching. And don't tell us it's food poisoning or some fake allergy."

Zemira's eyes reddened, and her hand went to her belly, protectively.

Uriah gasped. "You're pregnant." His eyes held all the anger and betrayal Cal felt.

Cal's tongue glued itself to the roof of his mouth as Zemira unbuttoned her coat and pulled it open. She tightened her shirt over her stomach, revealing a bump. A shockingly large swell.

It was Cal's turn to fold over his knees, to hyperventilate. He couldn't think beyond one pulsing thought. "We have to go back."

"No," Zemira said. "That's why I didn't tell you. I'm not due for five months. We'll be home in three."

"You compromised the mission," Uriah said.

"There would be no mission without me," Zemira said.

"Titus certainly wouldn't have let you come," Uriah said. "What if something happens to you and the baby? What if we have to fight?" Uriah raked a hand through shaggy hair. "I hit you!"

"I'm fine." Zemira bristled. "And this is war. I'll do what I can so there is a safe world for my baby."

"We're turning back," Uriah said.

"No," she said. "We're scouting the border. We're not going back until we know if Dracos threaten from the west."

Uriah was four years older than Cal, Zemira seven years, but they both turned to him, commander of this mission. The deciding vote. Cal resisted the urge to cower under their heated gaze. Zemira's big brown eyes turned pleading. Irresistible.

They were supposedly halfway to Volkar Lake, but the terrain was increasingly difficult as they gained elevation. If they took her back, they wouldn't have enough time to return before spring, when Titus suspected the first attack would come. Cal would never forgive himself if Dracos crossed into Elysium, and he could have prevented it. He would never forgive himself if something happened to Zemira and her baby.

He certainly didn't *want* to turn back.

"She chose to come," Lyko said.

"There are still miles of unguarded border to scout," Cal said to his wolf.

"If she says she's fine, we keep going."

"She's got five months; we can be back in half that time," Cal agreed.

"If she's already that big." Lyko chuckled. *"I can't wait to see how huge she gets."*

Cal bit his curving lips and spoke to the others. "We'll

give ourselves three more weeks. Then we're returning, whether we find a bridge or make it to the lake or not."

Zemira sent him a grateful smile that melted his bones. Uriah's glare turned them back to stone.

"We'd better get moving," Cal said. "Clock's ticking."

Frost hit three days before they reached the campsite north of the river delta. Weary and stiff, Jobu's half company rolled to a stop at a barren clearing hidden from Elysium by a mile of dense forest.

Her new home.

Shale tightened her thin coat as she hauled trunks and boxes with the rest of the slaves. The massive communal tents went up first. Five hundred Dracos huddled inside the mess hall, thawing overheated mead and thin soup. Slaves rushed around, setting up, fighting the wind that threatened to tear their work down before they could secure the tents.

Kenji and Pearl found Shale struggling to set up Ferth's tent. Wordlessly they joined her.

"Pin down that pole," Kenji said as his thick shoulders strained to hold the canvas taut against the gale.

Shale's stiff fingers clutched at the wood while Pearl darted from corner to corner, hammering stakes into the solid ground.

"Last one," Pearl said.

Shale sagged in relief as a stake snapped from the ground.

Shale jerked for it, but missed. The iron head slammed into her elbow. She hissed, her teeth jarring, as pain seared through her old injury. A knob still bulged off her elbow where she'd been struck by the hilt of a sword three years earlier. She pulled her coat back, revealing a wicked scar, now red from the tent nail.

"I'm so sorry," Pearl said.

"It's fine," Shale said. "Didn't even break the skin. Looks worse than it feels." *Lie.*

Kenji recovered the stake and hammered it in, all the way to the head. After checking the other stakes, he crouched next to her. "Anything else I can help you with?"

"No. Thank you." She knew he'd be missed from the supply wagons before long.

"Do you want me to get you something for that?" Pearl asked. "A strong drink at least?"

Shale knew she would do it, too. Pearl would literally risk the skin on her back to sneak into the healer's tent if Shale asked. "Don't you dare," Shale said.

His back blocking his next action from any prying Draco eyes, Kenji leaned over and kissed Pearl's brow. "I'll see you at dinner." He stood.

"You better go, too," Shale said.

Pearl looked at the warped elbow once more before nodding with a resigned sigh.

"Thank you," Shale said.

Pearl left with Kenji, walking close enough to *just* not touch.

Shale ducked into Ferth's tent, grateful for the moment of reprieve. For an instant, the walls became her fortress, the wind her howling guards. Too soon, her peace disintegrated back to the hustle and work of an army camp. Two men brought Ferth's trunk, bed, table, and chairs. Shale ignored the throbbing pain in her elbow as she made up her master's quarters. She built a fire in the pit near the wall, under the flue that tunneled the smoke out to the sky. She sat, listening for approaching footsteps and hoping it would be a long time before *he* came.

She peeled off her coat, inching closer to the fire. Rolling up her sleeve, she cupped a cold, comforting palm on her elbow. She'd kept it hidden for years. She shouldn't have shown it to Pearl, added to her friend's worries. Shale leaned her head back and closed her eyes.

"Let me see that arm."

She jumped at the low voice. Her sleeve dropped down as she lurched to her feet. Ferth sat on his bed, watching her. He'd seen her rest by his fire. Horror slammed through her chest. What would the punishment be? How had she not heard him? "Excuse me, sir." Her voice waffled. "I'll go check the wells now. See how soon I can get you water for a bath."

"I said to show me your arm." He held out a hairy hand, his face as unyielding as his voice.

Her ribs tightened. "It's nothing. I'm fine. Won't hinder my work at all."

Ferth's jaw rippled in anger. Fangs flashed.

Shale lurched forward, baring her scarred elbow.

"Sit," Ferth said, pointing to the bed as he got up.

She sat.

He rummaged through his trunk and pulled out a metal tin. She stiffened as he sat close by her side, their knees nearly touching. He picked up her arm, the soft pads on his palm wrapping around her forearm.

"This is going to hurt."

Even though his voice was soft and low, fear stopped her breath. What was he going to do to her?

"It won't heal unless you break down the scar tissue." He opened the tin and scooped out a dollop of green goo. With his own strong fingers, he worked it into the buckle on her bone.

She bit her tongue and tasted blood as fire flared over the spot and zinged through her nerves. Ferth massaged harder, deep circles over her elbow. She sucked in a strained breath and let curses bang through her head. Against her will, her back arched at the pain. Ferth's gaze flickered up, but he didn't loosen the thumb now pressed into her elbow. The scar bled, but still he maintained the gruesome pressure, ignoring the red smear over his fur. Her hand went limp, dropping to rest on his thigh. His gaze snapped to the spot. She jerked her fingers off his warmth, her breath hitching.

Ferth thrust her arm into her lap, his golden eyes dark. "It will take time. I will help you again tomorrow." He stood and marched out of the tent before she could even begin to form a reply.

Wide-eyed and dizzy, she lifted her elbow. It ached, but the bump had diminished. It moved with greater ease and flexibility.

He'd helped her.

She had a list of things to do, but she sat dumbfounded and wary. Farther from understanding her master than before. First rule of war—or life: know your enemy. She did not. Her fear grew wings.

THIRTY-FIVE - ATTACK
CAL

Cal stood with Zemira and Uriah at the precipice. Icy mist hid the bottom of the gorge, but the booming churn of water pounding on rocks told him enough of what kind of death he'd find below. That sound had haunted him for the last two months since they'd left camp. Cal hurled a rock into the ravine. It was time to turn toward home. They were supposed to have started back last week, but they'd kept going. Just a little bit farther, he'd told himself each morning. And still the river ribboned out of sight to the west. No indication they were even close to reaching Volkar Lake, the lake so infested with water Dracos no boat dared cross it.

"At least we know no Skotar army can cross anywhere we've seen, except back at the river delta," Uriah said.

Cal sat on an icy boulder and absently stroked Lyko's head. What if the Draco Sang had attacked at the delta while they were wasting their time in these mountains? As much as he wanted to press on, it was time to head back. He admitted as much to the others. At dawn they would turn east.

"I'll scout a bit more tonight," Lyko said into Cal's mind. *"And I can hunt without you five scaring away the prey."*

Cal stood, snow crunching beneath his boot. "Lyko is going to run ahead while we make camp."

"Opal will go with him," Zemira said as her sleek panther padded toward Lyko.

"I could do without that." Disdain trickled along the connection.

"She can help you drag back my dinner."

"And dare get her paws dirty?"

Cal chuckled, but it strayed far from the truth. Opal was a hundred pounds of feline warrior. Well-trained, graceful, and deadly. Just like Zemira. But Lyko couldn't stand Opal. The opposite feelings Cal harbored for her human.

"Stay alert," Cal said.

Lyko bolted, trying to escape without Opal. His white fur blended into the winter forest. A black blur chased him into the trees.

"Stay together," Cal ordered.

The only response was the sensation of cold wind running pleasant fingers through Lyko's fur as he outpaced Opal up the slope.

Uriah's boots thumped the snow, heralding his approach. "There's a secluded spot with a bit of wind protection, south-west a hundred paces."

"Lead on," Cal said.

They stopped in the lee of a sharp rock jetty. Cal dropped his pack with a grateful groan. Zemira picked up Uriah's axe. Cal caught it by the handle, turning her around.

"Don't make me punish you for insubordination." He took the axe from her reluctant hands.

"I can help. Stop treating me like an invalid. Stop babying me."

He sent a pointed glance at her protruding belly, the coat no longer buttoning at the bottom. He'd seen pregnant women in Siccum, but he didn't remember their bellies being that large at six months along. Must be from Zemira's meat-heavy diet. Or maybe her Draco blood. Her husband was certainly large. Did Shem even know he would soon be a father?

Zemira failed to cover her growing bump with her thin arms. She rolled her eyes. "Poor choice of words."

"Rest," Cal said.

She sighed but didn't argue as she sat heavily on a fallen log. Her short black hair stuck up at odd angles, and her dark skin had lost its usual brightness. But even exhausted and travel-worn, her beauty was a knife in his ribs. She closed her rich eyes and leaned against a barren tree. Cal reprimanded himself *again*. She wasn't his. Would never be. Futilely he pounded away at his feelings, splintering the dry wood. Heart sore and muscles spent, he built a campfire and set on a pot of snow to boil. He'd scarcely sat down to rest by the warmth when he heard the call.

He jerked forward, eyes wide as Lyko's fear speared his head. Zemira lurched a moment later, her face ashen.

"Three Draco Sang." Lyko's thoughts jumbled as he sprinted through the trees. *"They're pursuing."*

Fear turned Cal's mind cold and sharp. *"Lead them here. We'll set a trap."* He turned to Zemira. "Tell Opal to follow Lyko here, and not to engage before she reaches us."

"Yes, sir."

Uriah stopped unfolding the tent and turned curious eyes on Cal.

"Three Dracos chasing Lyko and Opal," Cal told him. "They'll be here in minutes. You and Poe move into position there." Cal pointed to a clump of trees. "Zemira and I will take the left there. Lyko will halt here. We fall on the Dracos from behind. Let's try to at least keep one alive. But no unnecessary risks."

Uriah scrambled for his weapons. Within seconds he and

his grizzly bear ran northwest to wait.

Cal relayed instructions to Lyko and sent visual images. He checked his knives and unsheathed his rapier. "You stay out of the fight," he said to Zemira as they crouched in the bushes.

"Save your breath." She held twin short swords in front of her belly.

Cal's blood turned colder than the snow. How could he keep her from fighting now? She'd trained longer than he had. He cursed. They should have turned back a month ago.

Lyko and Opal barreled past, and a heartbeat later, three hideous, feral creatures followed. With a spike of adrenaline, Cal gave a shout and leapt out of the shadows. Lyko whirled, facing the enemy. Time slowed as a scaly man raised a curved sword over his wolf. Cal ripped his Dracosteel knife from his belt, ready to kill again to protect Lyko. Before he could throw it, Poe was there. The bear ripped the Draco's arm back while Lyko leapt for his neck.

Uriah engaged an enormous Draco with wide antlers branching out of a furry head. Opal ripped at its legs. Cal slashed his sword at a female with four bug-eyes and hard, iridescent skin.

Either Cal's memory was faulty or these Dracos were larger and more ferocious than the one that had come after him those months ago in Neese.

This is who he would have become. These were his people. His blood. Was one his brother? Or father? No one here had bullhorns. He forced the distracting thoughts away. It didn't matter. Not when he fought for his life. His pulse hammered an irregular beat as he slashed at misshapen noses and scaly limbs. He barely blocked a lightning-fast strike to his side. Bug eyes popped out as blood burbled out of a crooked mouth. The Draco slumped to the ground. Panting, Zemira pulled her bloody twin blades free of its back. She rolled her shoulders, her eyes grim and her jaw tight. Unhurt. Cal heaved out a relieved breath.

The crack of bone reverberated. Cal whirled to see Poe drop one limp Draco on the ground. Cal jumped to help Uriah with the last Draco, already feeling the pride and relief of victory.

Then, the flyer attacked.

Zemira wheezed. She thudded to the ground, an arrow protruding from her thigh. Opal leapt over Zemira. Stationing her body over her human, she roared at the bird hovering in the sky.

Cal dove as an arrow whistled past his ear. His own bow waited back at camp, unstrung and useless. He cocked a throwing knife and sent it careening toward the gray bird. The Draco swooped out of harm's way and cocked another arrow.

"Take cover." The words ripped from Cal's throat, strained and raw. His body turned to stone as the arrow sailed toward Uriah's exposed back. Poe shoved Uriah out of the way, and the arrow buried itself in the shoulder of the Draco Sang Uriah had been fighting. The Draco looked at the flyer with betrayal in his glossy black eyes before Lyko's claws slashed across its throat, ending its life.

Cal lost a second throwing knife hurling it at the bird, but the flyer had already turned and was flapping away to the north.

He needed to follow, chase the bird, find out how the Dracos had crossed the river. Could the flyer carry them over? Was there truly a bridge? Were there more? But when he turned to Zemira, his plans evaporated.

There would be no hunt.

Blood wept from her thigh, spilling over her pants in an expanding circle of doom. Opal lay next to Zemira, nuzzling her neck with a silken face. Biting air stuck in Cal's lungs. Blood painted Poe's fur. Uriah cradled his left arm; on his shoulder, red streaks leaked through his shirt.

One at a time. He pushed away the mountain of worries threatening to bury him as he knelt at Zemira's side. "I'm going to move you. We'll get this cleaned up. You're going to be fine."

Tears welled in her eyes as he heaved her into his arms. Tough, brave Zemira rested her face against his shoulder as brine rushed down her cheeks. "I'm so sorry."

Uriah moved gingerly as he added fuel to the weak fire and laid out blankets near the flickering warmth. Cal lowered Zemira. She hissed as her leg settled.

"Get her water and brace her shoulders," Cal told Uriah. "Pin her arms."

Uriah set his bulk behind Zemira and wrapped thick arms around her shaking frame, her arms tucked under his. She rested her head against his beard and closed her eyes. Cal set out the med kit. He cut a wide hole in her pants around the wound. Feeling completely inadequate, he examined the arrowhead. It was wedged into the muscle, but hadn't hit bone. He gripped the metal tip and looked Uriah in the eyes. Uriah gave an almost imperceptible nod and tightened his hold.

One. Two. Cal ripped the arrow free, feeling as though he'd torn it out of his own soul. Blood spurted, spreading sticky warmth over his hands. Zemira's body tensed, and a heart-rending whimper escaped her lips. Her face blanched as she slumped against Uriah, barely conscious. Opal pressed her head against Zemira's side, her beady eyes never leaving Cal.

Darkness fell as Cal cleaned and stitched the gaping wound. Uriah stroked Zemira's hair, whispering soft words. Cal wished he were the one holding her, comforting her, instead of the one digging around in her flesh, causing her to flinch and tremble. He spread healing salve over the wound and wrapped her thigh in linens. She shivered, her eyes barely opening. He forced bitter restorative tea between her wobbly lips. Uriah wrapped her in a blanket and laid her near the fire. Her arms hugged her belly. The pain in Cal's chest widened. Opal, blacker than the night, lay next to Zemira, supporting her side. Lyko took up Zemira's other flank.

"Thank you," Cal said to Lyko.

"I should have been more careful. I should have known their scent wasn't right. I shouldn't have led them here."

"I gave the order. You obeyed."

"I shouldn't have let them see me."

Two months without trouble, and they'd become complacent. And now they had paid a heavy price. His team had trusted him, and he'd failed them.

"I'll never make that mistake again," Lyko promised.

"No. We won't."

"We'll make them pay."

The violence in Lyko's thoughts stoked Cal's anger. *"Yes."* He added a log to the fire. *"Where did they come from? Did you see any bridges?"*

"No. I'll find out though."

"We'll see." They were in no position for another attack. And his heart had nearly stopped beating when he'd seen that blade swinging for Lyko. Could he risk sending Lyko out into danger again? Could he risk *not* sending him to scout? How long until that flyer returned? They needed to move camp. Zemira shivered under her blankets. He could give her a few minutes' rest.

"We need to know," Lyko's voice, sounding as Cal's own, cut through his thoughts.

"Do you think the bird was strong enough to carry them across the river?"

"Possibly. That was no regular bird."

Not even close. Cal had quickly gained a hefty respect for the Draco Sang. His heart pinched in horror at the thought of an entire army of those creatures attacking Elysium. The humans didn't stand a chance.

Cal cleaned the bloody water from the cooking pot and set more snow to boil. Body aching, he turned to Uriah. "You're up."

Uriah hesitated, then peeled off his coat and shirt. Bruises bloomed over his meaty chest. A long laceration cut his shoulder. Guilt attacked Cal's conscience. He'd come off unscathed, while his unit, his best friends, his family, lay wounded.

"I think my wrist is sprained." Uriah rolled his left hand around, but stopped to hiss as Cal brought a hot linen to the deep cut and began scrubbing. "He was so strong," Uriah said. "I've never seen that kind of power."

The thought chilled Cal. Uriah was one of the strongest soldiers in the entire army, and their best swordsman. "How's Poe?"

"He's fine. Nothing he couldn't lick clean." Uriah stuck a stick in his mouth and ground his teeth into the wood as Cal sewed his shoulder.

"This isn't going to be pretty. I can't see well, but even in daylight I'm not great." This was nothing like mending his robes in Siccum.

"Hopefully the ladies will like it," Uriah said.

Cal forced a smile. "I'm sure they'll love it. They'll be lining up for a look and to kiss you better." If they lived that long. He wrapped the wound and handed Uriah snow to hold on his wrist. "You should rest."

"That bird aimed to wound Zemira, not kill her." Uriah's voice was a whispered rumble. Flames reflected off brown eyes.

"I know." Cal's gaze flicked to the sleeping woman as he sat down next to Uriah. "By wounding her, he's taken us all out. We've got to assume he'll be back soon with reinforcements." How had it come to his? Yesterday he had complained their mission was futile, and they'd seen no sign of the Draco Sang. Now, he didn't know how he'd get them home alive.

Uriah swayed.

"Sleep for now. I'll wake you when it's time to move."

Uriah shuffled to the sleeping bear and lay next to the furry hill. Cal wished he could curl up with his crew and wake to a different reality. The heat of battle and the warmth of adrenaline had burned out, leaving a residue of cold fear. Forty yards away, the dead Draco Sang haunted him, pressing at his sanity. He made a torch from the fire. Creepy shadows followed him to the corpses. As he bent over the moose-man, movement made him jump. Sinister laughter echoed through his mind.

He clutched his chest as Lyko appeared. *"Not funny."*

"They're dead."

"Not the one that flew away."

"I'll scout." Lyko shifted away.

"Stop."

Lyko turned incredulous eyes on Cal.

He had to let the wolf go, take the risk. He took a deep breath and cleared away his frayed emotions. *"Walk me through every step of the way."*

Lyko pressed his snout against Cal's brow. Cal shuddered

as the white wolf disappeared like a ghost into the wintery night.

Feeling suddenly alone, he turned to the dead. He peered closer to their mutant faces, the melding of human and beast. *Is one of them my brother?* He jerked back. Traveling down that thread would drive him to madness. These Dracos had killed the sprout of hope he'd nourished. He'd never find his brother. His brother was Draco Sang. The enemy.

I don't have a brother.

The powerful reality of the Draco Sang shifted his perception of this war. Until today he hadn't fully understood what they fought against. Now he wondered how they could possibly prevail.

He stripped the corpses of weapons, all made from valuable Dracosteel. No parchments or maps hid in the armor. No food or packs. Their camp must be close. How many more were there? The chill in his bones had nothing to do with the cold.

Time to move.

The night was half-spent. Exhaustion rolled across his back as he took down camp. Wordlessly, Uriah got to his feet and helped. They left the fire burning, a weak distraction for pursuers. They didn't have time to build a sled for Zemira. Cal knelt at her side and tenderly brushed a lock of hair off her brow. He shouldn't have done it, but the spasm in his heart eroded his propriety. He wedged one hand under her narrow hip and the other under her shoulder. He scooped her into his arms, stifling a groan as his body protested the weight.

"I can walk," she mumbled before settling her head against Cal's chest and falling back asleep.

Uriah shouldered her pack and picked up Cal's too, now heavy with the Draco's weapons, before leading the way.

They hiked southwest along the mountain ridge, away from the river and into thicker forest.

Despite the stress and danger, Cal's body warmed at the feel of her in his arms. Each day, he tried to forget his feelings and every night his dreams betrayed him, sending him wild fantasies. Now in his reality, he held her as he never had before, and it was his nightmare.

After an hour of stumbling in the wan moonlight, Uriah said, "Poe found a shallow cave. One mile due south."

Cal's knees nearly buckled at the distance, but he answered with grim determination. "Lead on."

With each step, his mind waged battle with his muscles. Sweat greased his brow and itched down his spine. His arms numbed, and his legs turned to lead. Zemira mumbled and jostled in his arms, her sunken face reflecting dull silver moonlight. Uriah looked back over his shoulder increasingly often, his brow knitted. Finally, mercifully, they stumbled into the cave. Uriah threw down a blanket, and Cal nearly dropped Zemira onto it, his arms shaking and his legs twitching.

"Good work, Poe," Cal said.

The bear groaned softly before he lay down to guard the entrance.

Blood had soaked through Zemira's thin bandage. Before Cal closed his eyes to rest, he dug through his pack for his med kit. Chills racked her body as he unwrapped her thigh. Opal nestled closer against her back as blood oozed from the gash. He applied more salve and a clean bandage. He squinted in the low light at a dark spot spreading between her legs. His heart dropped as the fresh blood stained her pants. Cal laid a hand on her taut belly. He could do nothing for this bleeding. For her baby. *Please stay in there. Please be okay.*

Cal dropped next to Zemira and wrapped a thin blanket

over them both, hoping his heat might leach into her. If she struggled, it would wake him.

Lyko ran farther and farther away.

In the darkness, silent tears dripped down Cal's face. He didn't tell Uriah, didn't admit the fear to Lyko. The bird had aimed to kill both Cal and Uriah. He didn't kill Zemira because of her baby. The Dracos would be back for Zemira and the Draco Sang baby she carried. The blood on her groin flashed through his thoughts. If there was going to be a baby.

They'd have to kill him first. The thought didn't give him any consolation. He was sure that was exactly what the hunting Dracos planned to do.

"The bridge." Lyko's words pinged through his mind.

Cal blinked awake. Pale sunlight filtered across the shallow cave. He held Zemira, her body pressed against his. She sighed in her sleep as he shifted away, releasing her and recoiling. He turned his back to her, feeling rotten and woozy, but his heart protested, and his muscles screamed to hold her again. Uriah and Poe slept soundly at the cave entrance.

Stained with shame, Cal closed his eyes and focused on Lyko, now miles away. His wolf hid behind a boulder near the gorge. Lyko sent an image of a bridge, a natural formation, hewn from the mountain itself. The rock arched over the canyon, holding the two worlds together by a thin strip.

There it was, glistening and beautiful in the frozen mist. And Cal couldn't cross it.

"No sign of more Dracos on this side," Lyko said. *"If I cross I can search for a larger camp."*

"No."

Lyko didn't resist. Last night's encounter had humbled them both. A brief wish they could carry on the mission together flickered across the connection. Cal held the same disappointment.

"Hopefully those four made up the entire scouting party. Hopefully that flyer has a long way to go before he reaches his camp. Hopefully he won't return."

"That's a lot of hoping," Lyko said.

It was a lot of delusion. *"Where did they find you and Opal?"*

"Mile and a half southwest of here. I'll scout the area again." Lyko couldn't entirely conceal his fatigue from Cal as he lumbered away from the thin bridge.

"Quick recon. Then head here. Thank you, Lyko. Well done."

A heartbeat later, Cal slept again. He didn't wake until Lyko's tongue lapped his face. A portion of anxiety lifted, and Cal ruffled the furry white head. He crawled across the rocky cave, his body aching. He rummaged in his pack and tossed Lyko what little dried meat they had left.

"No Draco campsite on this side," Lyko said.

Cal's spine slumped. They must have camped in Skotar and crossed the river sometime yesterday. Did they use the bridge? Had they crossed because the flyer had spotted Cal's group? How many more were there? Why didn't they have more supplies and camping gear with them?

He would get no answers. He turned his focus toward his sleeping comrades. His only job now was to get them home safely. Without detours, he calculated the quickest they could get home was one month, once they were able to break camp, and that was only if Zemira could hold some of her own weight. Cal ground his teeth in frustration.

Lyko ate the dried meat without complaint. A first. He curled up and slept.

Cal grabbed his bow and arrows and slipped into the afternoon sun. Sore muscles loosened the more he jogged. After a short trek through the trees, he found a den of rabbits. Each of his arrows found its target between the eyes of a rabbit. Even the little ones—no sense leaving a baby without its family. He cleaned his arrows and slung the seven rabbits over his shoulder.

As he approached the cave, gleaming eyes peered at him from the shadows, hungry and sharp. Cal flung Opal a rabbit. With a flash of sleek ebony, she snatched it from the air.

"Don't even think about eating that in the cave."

Her face dripped with feline sulk as she slunk into the icy sunshine.

"You're welcome."

Two rabbits went to Poe, who joined Opal in the snow. The clang of Cal's axe hitting cold wood rang out, drawing a stumbling Uriah outside.

"I'm up," Uriah said. "I'm alive."

"How's the wrist?" Cal asked.

"It's good as new."

Liar. "Then make yourself useful. Can you hold a knife and skin a rabbit?"

"Don't patronize me."

Cal chuckled. He set aside the largest rabbit for Lyko. Uriah got to work on the rest. Cal lit the fire and took salt and an onion from Poe's pack. He set snow to boil and added bits of meat and onion. Uriah set out the leftover meat to smoke. Cal crawled into the cave and nudged Zemira awake.

"Time for breakfast."

She groaned to a sitting position, rubbing her face. "Where are we?"

"About a mile and a half southwest of our last camp. And only sixty miles to go." The joke fell flat.

"How did I get here?" The sharp focus of her gaze eased a bit of his worry over her health, but shadows hung beneath her eyes.

"I carried you."

She sucked on a trembling lip. "Thank you."

"Whatever it takes to get you home." He swallowed the

lump in his throat and held out a hand. He knew she hated being a burden more than the pain of the wound, but still she leaned heavily against him as he led her to a log by the fire.

"I need to pee," she said, her voice soft and very un-Zemira-like.

"Do you want my second pair of pants? They'll fit over the bandage."

"Yes, please. Can you get my clean underwear?"

Heat rushed to his cheeks as he nodded. He thought about fighting the crokator while he dug through her pack. He thought about rough desert sand as he picked up her delicate white underwear.

"Just help me over to that tree," Zemira said. "I'll be fine after that."

He left her leaning against a frozen oak, his pants and her underwear in hand, her wounded leg stiff and lame. Opal ran to her as he walked back to the fire to sit and wait with Uriah.

Anxiety nagged at his chest. What would she think when she saw the blood between her thighs? How much pain was she in? Should he tell Uriah? No, that would only add to his stress.

Zemira called to Cal. He raced back to the clump of trees. This time, despite her protests, he scooped her into his arms and carried her to the fire. Uriah handed her a bowl of stew.

"How do you feel?" Cal asked.

"My leg is on fire, but I'm fine. No fever. I'll make a crutch. Maybe now you'll be able to keep up with me."

He looked her straight in the eyes, and found only determination and defiance. Fine. If she didn't want to talk about the blood, he wouldn't push it. And there wasn't a thing he could do about it anyway.

"What do we know?" she asked.

He laid out the facts, leaving out that he thought they'd

spared her because she was pregnant, and that he'd bet his life they'd come back for her baby. "We need to stay hidden and move fast. We'll travel by day."

"I'll be ready to move in the morning." Her voice was iron.

"You'll set the pace." She opened her mouth, but he spoke again. "The goal is to get home alive. We don't do ourselves any favors if we get more injured or sick in the process." It was a reminder for himself as much as for her.

He started the guard rotation that night.

Ferth stretched out his legs and stared at the fraying stitches on the tent ceiling. This meeting had dragged on for two hours already. Captain Jobu and the other commanders talked in circles because there was nothing to do but sit and wait. Training progressed as scheduled. Scouts continued to report on the Lion's camp of Elysium troops with no remarkable changes. Winter clutched the half company, and each day the monotony dragged down morale. They itched to attack. Fight. Conquer.

Spring, when Laconius would bring the main body of troops, seemed impossibly far away.

Ferth's eyes drooped. The tent flap flung open. His head snapped up, and his fingers shot to his sword hilt as icy wind blasted the room. Jobu jumped to his feet as Talverson, a bearded vulture Draco, marched into the command tent, an agitated guard on his heels.

"Excuse me, captain," the guard said. "I told Talverson to wait. That you're not to be interrupted. He—"

"It's urgent," Talverson said. His wings hung limply, and

his head wobbled with exhaustion, but his eyes shone like lights.

Jobu shooed the guard away, and the tent door closed out the winter once again. "Sit. Report."

Talverson slumped onto a stool and gratefully accepted a warm mug of mead. He guzzled and guzzled, his knobby neck bobbing. Jobu cleared his throat. Finally, the raptor straightened his spine, setting down the drink.

"We found enemy spies near the bridge into Elysium. We engaged five days ago. I flew back as quickly as I could. Sisly, Rector, and Commander Trawp are dead."

Shock washed over the room, slamming Ferth against the back of his chair. Three Dracos dead.

Jobu voiced the thought in Ferth's head. "How many enemy?"

"Six, sir. If you include the animals."

"They're Draco Sang abominations!" Talverson flinched at the cutting anger in Jobu's outburst. After a heavy silence, Jobu continued with a slightly less hostile tone. "Did you manage to kill them at least?"

"No, Captain. The girl … she's with child."

Ferth's breath hitched. Jobu dropped to his seat, his mouth ajar. The other three commanders leaned forward, a greedy gleam in their eyes.

"A Draco Sang baby," Jobu said, his voice hungry. "Why would they send such a treasure into the mountains so ill-protected?" He rubbed his striped forehead. "Where are they now?"

"They were just east of the bridge when I last saw them, nearly a week ago. They can't have gone far. I shot the girl in the leg to disable her."

"That's an advantage as long as it doesn't hurt the baby. How large was she?"

"I didn't have long to study her, but I'd guess she's a few weeks from due."

"What of the others?"

"Two males. Skilled fighters. They do not appear to be injured."

"That's poorly done. Isn't it?"

"Yes, captain."

"I want that baby."

Ferth sat forward. This could be his chance to get out of camp. Earn success. "I'll lead the mission. I'll bring her back. That baby will be yours."

Jobu's beady badger eyes studied Ferth, lingering on the pale human skin still marring the left side of his face. Ferth cringed inwardly but hardened his gaze.

"No."

Heat wrapped Ferth's chest, and his fingers itched to brandish his blade.

"Although your willingness is noted," Jobu said. "And I trust you would do as you say, but you'll stay here. Your unit needs you. And you now have command of unit four since Trawp got himself killed. Tell the idiot, Shella, she's relieved of her duties."

Mina, the commander of unit three, twisted in her seat. Sharp eyes speared Ferth.

Noted. She is pissed.

Ferth sent a slow, smug smile across the table. Mina revealed sharp fangs before turning away.

"Talverson," Jobu said. "You'll lead the mission. How do you plan to take them?"

The vulture didn't look as eager as Ferth expected. Haunted exhaustion painted his wrinkly face. The enemy were weak-hearted abominations, not worthy of their blood.

"I'd suggest a quarter unit with as many flyers as you can spare," Talverson said.

Jobu choked on his mead. Foam sprayed over the table. "The girl is disabled, you say. You know where they are. You can fly. Yet you ask me for twenty-five warriors! Talverson, they didn't frighten you, did they?"

The flyer looked like a talking corpse. "No, Captain. I thought only of speed and limiting our casualties."

"Smaller units are faster. And there are only three of them, too weak to become Draco Sang." Jobu's raspy voice dripped with condescension. "Take Rumblin. Between the two of you, you can fly Phinx over the gorge. Cut them off before they leave the mountains. Kill everyone, including the pets, and bring me the girl."

A bat and a bulldog. Excellent warriors. So why did the whites of Talverson's eyes show? Could such a tiny taste of battle have ruined him already?

"Yes, Captain." The muscled vulture crumpled.

"Take one day's rest, then go. Do not fail me in this."

Talverson trudged out.

Jobu glanced at his four commanders. "Dismissed."

Ferth strode to the long, shared tents of units four and five. He yelled into each one. "Gather at the training fields. Five minutes. Units four and five."

Four and a half minutes later, the ninety-seven warriors left in unit four looked at Ferth with curiosity. His unit five stood off to the right.

"Line up," Ferth hollered. After a moment's hesitation while Ferth stared hard at the new unit, all one hundred and ninety-six warriors formed up.

Shella, a small and vicious cat Draco, stormed up to Ferth. "What is this about? Who gave you authority to tell my unit what to do?"

Ferth looked down at her scowling face. She didn't reach his shoulder. Trawp had left her with temporary command four weeks ago when he headed the scouting trip, but Jobu had disliked her so much, he hadn't let her take Trawp's place in command meetings. "You're relieved of your command. Get in line with the rest of the unit."

She blinked, her pupils shaped like long slits. Ferth didn't wait for her tantrum; he turned and yelled to the group.

"Unit four." His voice cut through the frozen dusk. "Commander Trawp is dead. Killed by the enemy while scouting west into the Seraf Mountains."

The warriors shifted their weight, eyes darting. Shella closed her mouth.

"Look around. This is your new unit. We are all unit four. *I* am your commander. We train on the east field thirty minutes after the breakfast horn. You might want to ask the veteran members of my command what happens if you're late. Or we can see who is stupid enough to find out." It was always entertaining to watch the humbling effect of having a Draco warrior shovel out the latrines. That was after they massaged his calloused feet. "Welcome to the family."

His oversized unit saluted.

"Dismissed."

Dara and Thirro raced to his side as he walked away.

"Is there an Elysium army coming from the west?" Thirro asked.

"I don't know."

"Did Trawp find an enemy camp in the Serafs?"

"I don't know."

"What do you know?" Dara spat the words.

Ferth stopped and spun. She crashed into his chest and stumbled back.

"Trawp is dead."

"Come on," Thirro said.

Ferth sighed, acting like he was doing them a huge favor, elevating them above the rest of the warriors. "There was a small Elysium scouting party, much like the one we sent out.

Trawp engaged the enemy in the mountains near Volkar Lake. Talverson is the only one who made it back alive. He flew in this afternoon."

"Will Jobu send more scouts west?"

"Talverson is going back with Rumblin and Phinx. They'll make sure the border is secure." Ferth wasn't going to be the one spreading rumors about a Draco Sang baby or traitorous warrior abominations. "See you in the morning."

Dara's eyes turned dewy. "I thought you and I could practice that spin move you showed us yesterday."

Not even a flicker of desire stirred in his gut as Dara leaned close. Her scent trickled up his nostrils—dirt compared to the way Shale lit up his senses. "Not tonight." Shale would be back in his tent, setting out his dinner. He had anticipated it all day.

Dara's face fell into a sneer.

"I'll teach it to you," Thirro said.

"Like you could." Dara sulked away.

Ferth laid a hand on Thirro's feathered shoulder. "I think you would have done a fine job."

Thirro walked away grinning.

Ferth strode to his tent. As a commander, he had his own. He hovered at the door, watching Shale's body move as she set out his plate and mug. Humans. He'd grown to want nothing else. And he balked at the realization no human would ever want him back.

He'd offered to let Shale sleep in the relative comfort of a pallet on his floor. She'd declined, preferring to sleep in the crowded slave tents. *Smart girl.*

It was times like this, when she hovered about his quarters, her hips swaying invitingly, that he wondered why he didn't take her to bed. She was his slave. It was his right. His privilege. But as much as he wanted to have her, he also wanted to protect her. Raging desire burned deeply, but an invisible force halted his haste and his hands. At least her elbow had healed, and he no longer had to touch her. That had been a unique kind of torture. Those times when lust struck strongest, Keturah's voice always called him back. He'd realized weeks ago that he cared for Shale far more than he ever intended. Far more than he cared to. He would conquer it. He was his own master. He almost welcomed the challenge. *Almost.*

"Evening, commander," Shale said. "It's deer tonight."

He unstrapped his weapons and dropped them into her waiting hands. She moved her fingers before they touched his skin.

"I noticed that Talverson is back, but not the others."

He tried to study her eyes, but her head tilted away, focused on his gear. "Always the observant slave."

Her fingers froze for a moment. "I'll sharpen these."

"Sit. Eat with me. You can do that after."

"I'll also get you another drink." She bowed as she backed away.

"Sit." His sharp tone stopped her steps.

Green eyes cut into him as she sat on the edge of the chair.

He settled across the tiny table. "Ah, lovely." He smiled, revealing sharp canines. "You can't tell me you already ate."

"I did."

"This."

Her lips sealed.

"That's what I thought." He speared a chunk of tender deer and held it an inch from her lips.

She inhaled but didn't open her mouth.

Oh, he loved her steel, that spark of fight in her eyes. "You've finally poisoned me, I see."

She jolted.

He chuckled and popped the meat in his mouth. "You're

too smart to do that. You don't want me dead."

Body rigid, her jaw clamped down on whatever argument popped to her tongue.

A nagging voice inside told him to stop teasing her. He ignored it. He held out another piece of meat on the tip of his knife. "I don't want you losing any of those delicious curves. Open up."

Her gaze turned to ice, but full lips parted.

His blade slipped between white teeth.

Spit coated his own tongue. His fingers itched to touch her. He forced his attention to his food. That's when he noticed the blossom on the table. Deep purple petals with golden veins. A plumloch. The late-blooming king of all blossoms. What Keturah had called him. How had such a delicate beauty found his stark table? Surely Shale would not have left such a thing. Not for *him*. He looked up at her smooth face, at glittering green eyes.

"You can go." His cold tone belied the heat of desire rolling through his veins. Not just the desire to kiss her lips, but the desire to hear her words spill over them. What was the story behind the flower? The elbow injury? The confidence in her weapon handling? Asking about human things was beneath a Draco Sang. His curiosity, and everything else, remained unsatisfied.

Her intoxicating smell of hazelnuts and juniper clung to his tent and hovered through camp. It washed over him in a tempting wind as she whirled away.

He wolfed down his meal and strode outside, toward the northern forest. He inhaled, inviting the air to chill his pulsing warmth. Evening painted the world a grayish-blue. A slave slipped out from behind the last row of tents. He squinted. Pearl. He ducked into the shadows as she glanced around. Moonlight lit her pale face, stoking the fire that had driven Ferth out tonight. She would be a pleasant distraction from the temptress in his tent. Help him remember that he was truly a Draco Sang.

Pearl disappeared into the trees to the north of camp. Ferth reeled in surprise. What was she doing? Escaping would be suicidal, although slaves had done stupider things. Silently he followed.

Encircled with flora, Pearl met another familiar slave. Kenji. His face lit up like noonday when he saw her. She leapt into his arms, silvery hair rolling down her back. His body seemed to swallow her up in his expansive embrace. She was the moon, and he was the inky sky. They melded together as if fulfilling their purpose.

"Kenji." Her voice was quiet music Ferth could barely hear. Music he wasn't meant to hear.

"Are you alright?" His voice was low and full of devotion.

"I always am."

Kenji gave her a look that said he'd heard that lie before. He cupped her cheek with a meaty palm, and then he kissed her, slow and hungry. His hands turned tender as he caressed her hair, her body.

Ferth felt as if a dull spoon hollowed out his ribs. Shoulders bent, he turned away, haunted by the power of their kiss, the humanness of it.

Jealous of slaves.

He would never taste a kiss that deep and beautiful. He would never be worthy of it. He tore away the traitorous tears that spilled from his eyes. He trudged back to his tent, empty and inexplicably sad.

The plumloch was gone.

Much later, he realized he should have punished them for severely breaking code. The thought hadn't even crossed his mind.

And that's why you haven't completed your transformation, you soft-bellied coward.

Fifteen days and no sign of the Draco Sang. They'd picked up their pace to nearly six miles a day. At this rate, they'd be out of the mountains and crossing the canals in a week. Cal breathed a little easier with each passing mile. They'd gone slightly south as they'd moved east, detouring to travel down easier slopes and put distance between them and Skotar. Every night Cal thanked the stars that Zemira's wound wasn't infected, that her baby still lived, and that the Dracos hadn't found them.

"I'll take the first watch tonight," Zemira said as they cleaned up dinner and covered the fire with leaves and snow.

"No." Cal shouldered his pack. They'd had this argument every night for a week.

"I'm strong enough. My leg is fine. Uriah got nearly as many stitches."

He wasn't worried about her leg. He was worried about what was a foot higher. "I trust him more than you."

The base of his head stung as her palm connected.

"I should punish you for that."

Uriah groaned and walked into the trees, out of range of the arguing.

"I'll sleep better after the first watch," Zemira said.

"No."

She adjusted her crutch, leaning heavily on it as they walked away from the scent of meat and fire. "Opal wants to take first watch then."

"Nice try." She'd wake Zemira the second Cal closed his eyes. "She'll stay at last watch."

They cut a half-mile through the forest and spread their bedrolls under thick branches, out of easy sight of the sky. Cal cringed at the full moon, its light illuminating the forest, and Uriah's upturned face as he sat watch, his back pressed against a tree. Through the bare branches, his pale skin gleamed. Cal still wouldn't ask Zemira to take watch. She needed the rest, and he needed the diversion of needling her. He considered asking Uriah to mask his face with dirt, but the nights had been quiet. The beard and uncut hair covered a good amount of Uriah's face, and Poe would take watch in a couple hours, Cal told himself as he squirmed under a low branch. Claustrophobia pressed on him as pine needles blocked out the world. He felt as if he'd barely closed his eyes when Uriah crawled in next to him. Uriah's beard scratched his forehead as the heavy man wormed close.

"What are—"

"Sh." Uriah's hot air steamed into Cal's ear. An elbow dug into his side. "I saw something."

Cal's body went rigid, his mind alert.

"I think it was a Draco flyer. It silhouetted against the moon for a blink. Man body with huge wings."

Cal brushed pieces of Uriah's shaggy hair off his face, wishing he could brush the fear away as easily. "How far away?"

"I'm guessing between one and three miles. I don't think it has spotted us."

Yet. "I'll have Lyko watch for now. Get some sleep. And keep hidden."

Uriah shifted an inch away.

"Your bedroll's far away."

"Yup."

Cal sighed and shifted his blanket over Uriah's broad shoulders. "Night."

"Try not to cuddle."

Cal forced a low chuckle; at the same time, he worried Uriah had seen him hold Zemira in his sleep. Too late to fret about it now. He had real problems. He hated to wake Lyko, but he needed those keen eyes. That deep trust.

Lyko only sent a minor complaining growl toward Cal as he rose and slunk like a white ghost over the snow.

"Wake me if you see anything larger than a squirrel, or smell anything besides the stink of our own camp."

"I do hope Uriah gets a good washing soon."

Cal smiled. *"You can trade places with me."*

"You make guard duty sound so good."

"Wake me in three hours."

Even after the jolt of adrenaline from Uriah's news, exhaustion pulled Cal under.

"Your turn, your highness." Lyko deepened his voice and sent it clanging through Cal's dreams.

Cal's teeth jammed as he jerked awake with a curse. *"Nothing?"*

"No. I saw the Draco bird. Same one that shot Zemira. It's making large patterned circles, sweeping from the northeast. Very thorough. It will find us soon."

Cold despair scratched along Cal's ribs. *"I said to wake me when you saw something."*

"I saw something. You're awake. You're welcome."

"How long did you watch?"

"About six hours."

Oh, Lyko. Cal's chest swelled. He loved that wolf and all his wild heart.

"He's heading west and south from the delta, moving to cut off our retreat."

"Now we've just got to figure out how to hide all six of us when it makes its pass overhead."

"Or how to kill it."

Trust Lyko to get to the root of the matter. *"Go to sleep."*

He didn't respond.

Cal squirmed out of the wedge between Uriah and the pine. As he sat, hood pulled low over his face, watching the sky, his mind whirled. No way that Draco had returned alone. Glimpses of shadowy wings blotted out the stars, but by dawn he'd lost all visual trace of the Draco Sang.

"Cold breakfast on the move," Cal said as the others emerged from the trees.

Zemira's thin brows shot up.

"The Draco flyer is back. He's patrolling the mountains from the east. Hunting us. Let's assume there are lots of others."

"Do you think he'll risk flying during the day?" Zemira bit her lip as she thought.

"Maybe. If he's trying to draw out an attack from us. And if he has a good number on the ground."

"What's the plan?" Uriah asked.

Nothing Cal had thought up the last few hours, or days, felt good. "We can head southwest, buy us a little more time before they'd find us, but we'd be back-tracking. We have a good chance to get to Nansut before they find us. I'm sure they have a healer; you could deliver your baby there. The locals might have to fight if the Dracos follow us there. I think that's the safest plan, for us and the baby at least." He studied their reactions. They didn't jump at the idea. "Or, we can take the most direct route to camp. Straight at the monsters. If we survive, we could be home in six or seven days. Or we could die."

Zemira's dark eyes flickered.

"We're going to decide this together. Think it over. Talk to Poe and Opal. Pack up and we'll vote."

"*I vote the attack route,*" Lyko said before Cal had finished talking.

"*Of course you do.*"

"*You do too.*"

"*Yes, I do.*" Hiding out the winter in a hut in Nansut while Dracos ranged over Elysium did not sit well with Cal.

Uriah passed around cold potatoes to the humans and smoked meat to the animals. When they stood ready to walk, Cal called in the votes.

"Poe and I vote to run straight at them. They're enemies invading our land. They don't get to come to our home and hunt us." Fire flared in Uriah's eyes.

Zemira cradled her melon-ball belly. "My ego got in the way. I was a fool to think that I could be the same fighter I was before this. I couldn't see how I might become a hindrance. I now have more to live for." Moisture crowded her eyes.

Cal held his breath. If Zemira wanted to go to Nansut, he would take her there.

"But Opal and I both know where our duty lies. We'll fight our way home."

Cal's heart nearly shattered. Guilt slapped across his chest. He should have taken her home a month ago. He was her commander. This was his fault. He nodded grimly. "Stay alert. Keep hidden. Let's go."

Lyko darted forward to scout ahead, Opal on his heels.

They were warriors. Some of Elysium's best. He would

cut down every Draco between here and camp. And he would get her home safely.

All that day, anxiety twisted knots in Cal's gut. No one spoke. His neck smarted after hours of craning toward the sky every couple heartbeats. They'd traveled eleven miles over rough terrain without a whiff of company when, without warning, Zemira dropped her crutch and slumped to the ground, her face peaky. Cal knelt beside her.

"I'm okay, just resting for a minute." Her face reddened as she gritted her teeth and clutched her belly. Opal licked Zemira's neck and cheeks.

"What's happening?" Urgency rang through Cal's voice, drawing Uriah down.

"Please don't have the baby right now." Uriah's tone echoed the same fear Cal felt.

"Baby's not coming for another month."

"Month," Cal said in dismay. "What happened to three months?"

She acted like she didn't hear him. Her eyes pinched closed as she curled on her side. "Not until we're home with a warm bed and Papi's there to greet her." Sweat beaded on Zemira's temples.

"Her, huh?" Uriah said. "It's like a girl to be difficult. Tell *her* if she comes out now, it won't be her father's face greeting her, it'll be Cal's ugly mug."

Cal was too strung out to laugh at the irony. He got Zemira the water skin and set up her bedroll. Two boulders shielded a tiny space bumped up against twin pines. He helped her over the rocks and down into her haven. She doubled over as another pain clutched her.

"I'm right over here if you need me."

She crumpled to the blanket. "Thank you, Cal."

His name on her tongue tickled his heart. "If they come

tonight, stay hidden. That is an order. You can't fight. No matter what you see or hear. Stay down."

To his dismay, she didn't argue, just laid her head down. He latticed branches for a roof and turned away, his chest tight. It felt as if death walked in the shadows around them. Cal and Uriah sharpened their weapons and ate cold, gristly meat. Poe took first watch, but Cal should have let the bear sleep since he certainly didn't. Zemira's stifled groans filtered across camp, and it wasn't until she'd finally gone quiet that Cal drifted to a jittery sleep.

In the darkness before the dawn, Uriah nudged Cal with his boot. "A flyer spotted us. Different bird than before. It took off in a dead dive to the northeast."

Cal rolled to a crouch, his pulse surging. "Poe, Opal, Lyko." In a breath, six glossy eyes drilled into him. "Pee over the boulders by Zemira to mask her scent. We'll move forty paces north, try to draw them away from her."

He threw on his leather vest, strung his short bow, and strapped on his knives before checking his rapier and taking a long drink of water. Uriah at his side, Cal marched north. He'd been brimming with a torrent of emotions for weeks. Now, his mind cleared, and his nerves steadied. He stopped at a small clearing, and his friends splayed around him, Uriah on his left and Lyko on his right. Dawn's gray prelude painted five grim faces. Cal wanted to say how much he loved them, but the words stuck in his throat. He cocked an arrow.

"*Flyer,*" Lyko said.

Cal had barely echoed the warning to the others before the beast dove into the clearing, slamming into Uriah's chest. Cal aimed an arrow at featherless wings of black membranes, but he couldn't get a clear shot without risk of hitting Uriah. Uriah threw the Draco off and raised his sword. Cal scanned away; tracking movement, he loosed his arrow at a Draco

Sang sprinting out of the trees. The massive dog dove, and the arrow sailed past. Cal pulled out his rapier.

The Draco slashed his own sword, holding Lyko and Opal at bay as his eyes darted, his nostrils flaring—*scenting*. The Draco dashed to the right, but Opal leapt in his path, slashing with her claws.

"Where is she?" the Draco yelled. His sword sliced into Opal's shoulder. Lyko bit the dog's hand, and the sword dropped to the dirt.

"Where's your other flyer?" Cal asked, raising his blade.

The Draco lunged toward where the bat battled Poe and Uriah. The bat fought in a series of diving bursts with lightning speed. Uriah slashed at membranes and tendons, but the bat danced out of range.

The dog Draco bolted, straight toward the abandoned campsite. Cal tore after him, his heart in his throat. The racing Draco whirled on Cal just as the vulture flyer landed on Zemira's boulders and threw back the branches.

"Hello, treasure," the flyer said as he peered into Zemira's hideout.

Metal flashed as Zemira thrust up, cutting through feathers.

"Naughty girl," he said as he jumped down on top of her.

Red rage rimmed Cal's vision. He slashed at the Draco dog, but could not break past. Zemira appeared in the bird's clutches. She thrashed as the vulture rose from the dirt, but he'd pinned her arms tightly. In agony, Cal jabbed at his Draco, cursing his lack of sword training. A deep roar rent the air as Poe pounded the earth and leapt high into the air. Giant claws sank into the bird's ankles, dragging him back to the earth. With a shriek, the Draco dropped Zemira.

Time stopped. Poe sprang, catching her. He cradled her in his arms as they tumbled to the earth. The flyer drew a blade. Circling Poe, he thrust his dagger deep into the grizzly's back. Blood plumed over russet fur. Poe's roar drowned out the matching one sent up by Uriah. Poe curled around Zemira, protecting her with his strength, his life.

Then Uriah was there, stabbing at the bird over and over in blind anguish.

Lyko snapped at the dog, giving Cal an opening. He burst through the Draco's defenses and slit his throat. Before the Draco hit the ground, Cal was at Poe's side. Zemira rolled out of the bear's limp arms. Poe fell on his face, motionless.

Uriah, face waxy and hair wild, pulled the serrated silvery blade from his hewan's back. Poe didn't move. Tears poured down Uriah's shaking face. Vaguely Cal noted a bat with bloody wings flap weakly out of the clearing and towards the dawn.

"Stay with me," Uriah cried, grabbing handfuls of fur.

Cal pressed cloth into the weeping wound and rolled the heavy bear to his back.

Uriah slammed his fists into the bear's chest. "Pump." He hammered again. And again. "Please live."

He threw his body at the bear, as if by his pure strength and determination he could get Poe's broken body to mend. Each hammer of Uriah's fist was a punch through Cal's own ribs. When it seemed that there was truly no existence beyond the rhythmic thumping of Uriah's grief, Cal laid his hands over Uriah's bloodstained fists.

"Let me take a turn," Cal said.

Uriah stopped. He crumpled, his body settling on top of Poe's. His brown eyes turned nearly as glossy as his hewan's.

Hot tears washed the gore and grime from Cal's face as he sat by his friend. Opal and Lyko laid their paws on the bear and looked at Uriah with shattered eyes. Zemira took one of Uriah's hands and held it in her lap, tucked close to her belly.

Not Poe. Poe had never rebelled against Uriah. Poe was honorable and courageous. And he was gone. It wasn't fair. It wasn't okay. Uriah knew they should have turned back weeks ago, and Cal hadn't listened. This was his fault. The silence stretched on. Unwelcome sunlight blazed across the scene and shifted over the sky. After what felt like hours of shocked agony, Zemira's voice permeated the fog. She sang The Warrior's Rite. Soft notes caressed Cal's pain and pierced his heart.

When we fall into the pit and darkness swallows us whole,
There we find that the Great Ones descend below.
They rise up and carry us on.
Though the road is grim and bleak,
They go before our feet.
Carry him home.
Raise me up.
If they leave us on the brink, for them we will not sink.
Let us carry the sacrifice on. Carry it on.
Grant us their mantle of honor that we might carry it ever onward.
Ever forever onward.

Uriah stirred. Zemira drew him into her arms. Leaving one hand firmly gripping Poe's fur, Uriah rested his head on her narrow shoulder. She sang while he soaked her coat with his tears.

After a heavy silence, Uriah stood, his tragic face hardening. He picked up their small shovel and cut it into the dirt. Cal found his axe and swung it into the frozen ground next to his friend. Zemira built a fire. She limped heavily and waddled as she walked.

The work numbed the torment of sorrow swirling through Cal's body. Too soon, and yet forever later, a gaping hole lay rent in the earth. It took every ounce of their strength to drag the mighty beast into the void. Poe rolled down with a heavy, final *thump.*

They covered their friend in dirt. Uriah designed a seven-pointed star with rocks over the grave, for honor and courage and love. Then he slumped on the ground next to the mound. Cal handed him a mug of warm broth. Uriah, hollow-eyed and gaunt, took it, as if out of habit.

Cal's chest crumpled as he surveyed his crew. Blood oozed from Opal's shoulder; she licked it constantly. Zemira's belly had dropped lower, and her face was set in a perpetual grimace. He and Uriah both had cuts that needed cleaning, at the very least. He wanted to just go to sleep and never wake up.

He brought out the med kit and wordlessly got to work. Opal and Zemira sat together by the low flames. He went to them first. Opal gave him a look like she wanted to tear his throat out as he sewed her shoulder, but when he finished, she pressed her nose to his hands in thanks. Zemira ran a hand over Opal's silky flank as she stared into the fire.

"Talk to me." His voice was quiet, as this place of reverence now demanded.

"I'm scared." The tragic honesty in her raw voice shook him to the quick.

He was a child, trapped in a nightmare. He held out war-stained arms, and the woman he loved in secret fell against his chest. Her strong, battle-trained body melted in his arms. "How soon is the baby coming?"

"Very soon. The pains are coming on. So far they've stopped, but one of these times, they aren't going to."

"It's fourteen miles home. Tomorrow we will carry you there." He meant it. With every sliver of strength he had left, he would get her and Uriah home. No more death. No more loss.

She didn't answer. Her breath had turned deep and slow against his neck.

Six feet away, Uriah stared at the sunset as if in a trance.

Lyko settled near his side, the man reached out and clutched a fistful of white fur. Silent tears coursed into his dark beard.

Cal shifted Zemira onto his bedroll and tucked his blanket around her. And then he got back to work. Collecting logs, weaving rope. Uriah watched but didn't see. It took hours, but even after the sled lay ready and Cal closed his eyes, sleep taunted him with death and pain. Cal rose again at dawn. Uriah lay at Lyko's side, his eyes closed, his hands clinging to Lyko's fur.

"Did you sleep?" Cal asked.

"A little," Lyko said.

"Him?"

"A little less."

The pain in Cal's chest was nearly overwhelming as he cooked the morning porridge. He pressed a warm bowl into Uriah's stiff fingers. Uriah had three bites before he forgot the bowl was there. Cal took it away, finishing the porridge. He would need the strength today. He packed food, water, weapons, and the med kit. Everything else went into the fire. He wasn't going to stop until they were home. Cal handed the lightened pack to Uriah, his best friend, his true brother. Ribs caving in, Cal laid a hand on Uriah's shoulder and turned him east.

Zemira didn't protest when Cal showed her the simple sled, made from branches and cushioned with a bedroll. Cal took up one rope around his shoulders, Lyko the other. Together they heaved Zemira along the packed snow. Opal limped alongside, her shoulder swollen and red. Cal stopped every mile to rest, give the ailing company water, and let a shuffling Uriah catch up.

Cal's leg ached and his back cried in pain, but still he dragged along. Lyko was too tired to even complain, but his steady steps set their pace. With every bump or dip, Zemira clutched her belly. The ropes frayed, and bits of sticks tore free off the sled. They were just coming out of the mountains, nearly to the canals, when they hit a sharp decline. Cal and Lyko marched with their heads down, their tongues dry. It was too late when they realized the danger and stopped. Cal lurched to slow the sled, but the branch he grabbed tore free. Zemira slid down the slope. She shrieked as she bumped over roots and rocks. She pitched off the sled just feet before it careened into a tree and crumpled to a pile of broken sticks. Reaching into a store of energy he didn't know he had, Cal sprinted down the hill. Opal raced to Zemira and licked her ashen face. Zemira didn't lift her limp arms to stroke her panther. Cal crouched at her side, fear a monster in his chest.

"Zemira. Zemira, look at me."

Her head wobbled up, her eyes red and sunken. "I'm okay."

His gaze darted over her body, looking for blood, broken bones. "I'm so sorry." He gave her water and a slice of smoked boar.

She refused the meat, her lips pursed. Her nails dug into his arm as she hauled herself to standing. Only six more miles. He would carry her. He would do it. Before Cal's shredded arms could pick her up, Uriah was there. He scooped her into his arms and marched on. Cal stumbled behind, his back hunched with injury. Frustration welled as they crossed the canal bridges. Even if the king and his rajas finally saw reason and gave permission to dam the canals, it seemed an impossible task now that the river had claimed them.

Uriah didn't stop once to rest until they were nearly to the first sentry. He set Zemira down. Color had returned to his face, and his eyes were focused on this world. Zemira held her belly as sweat dripped down her brow.

Uriah said his first words of the day. "You take her in. I can't."

Cal reached for Zemira, but she thrust out a hand, holding him back. Moisture seeped over her pants, spreading down her legs. "The baby's water." Her voice was raw and petrified.

"We're almost home. She's going to be okay, Zemira." Cal's voice carried as much false confidence as he could muster.

Uriah voiced no such encouragement. A well-loved bear had not returned with them. Nothing was going to be okay.

Cal heaved Zemira into his arms. She jostled against his chest. Bloody fluid soaked his arm. Pain laced his back, and his vision blotted. Yet he walked.

The first sentry called out when he recognized them, then ran forward.

"Go." Cal's voice was like Siccum sand. "We need the healer, and the blacksmith, Shem. Tell him it's Zemira. It's an emergency."

"Shem." Like a prayer, Zemira whispered his name into Cal's neck.

Cal agreed; he wanted her husband here more than anything in his life.

She hissed as her body seized up. Her fingers clamped on Cal's back. He grunted in pain as adrenaline carried him forward. They crested a ridge, and Cal's legs nearly buckled as camp came into view on the horizon. Warmth spread over his breast, and his eyes misted. "Look, Zemira."

Nothing could have been more beautiful. As the tents grew larger, a shadow broke off from camp and headed their way. Shem led the group, running faster than Cal thought possible for a man of his size. As he drew near, concerned eyes raked over Zemira. With intense relief, Cal shifted his trembling burden into her husband's arms. Shem kissed her sweaty brow, her teary cheeks, her chapped lips.

"The baby is coming now," Cal said in a broken voice.

Shem whirled, carrying her away with ease. She kissed his neck as they went. Opal limped along at his heels.

Relief and gratitude overwhelmed Cal, leaving no room for jealousy. He wilted, sinking into the mud. Firm hands wrapped his forearms, drawing him up, but when he looked into Titus's kind blue eyes, his legs gave out completely. Titus caught his weight, pulling Cal against his chest, holding him up.

"Oh, my son," Titus said.

The words spread like balm over Cal's heart, feeding him strength. He was home. May this embrace never end.

Cal forced his legs to straighten. Standing up, he looked for Uriah. Eio stood on his hind legs, his forepaws on Uriah's shoulders. Cal's broken brother nestled his face into the lion's golden mane, big hands clinging to silky fur like a child reaching for his mother. There they stood, silently, solemnly.

Tears soaked Cal's cheeks; his chest trembled. Lyko pressed against his thigh.

Soldiers and sentries gathered, gawking at the scene. Eio set his paws in the dirt, letting a grim-faced Titus put his arms around Uriah. Titus turned the tall man toward camp. Uriah kept a hand on Eio's mane as he shuffled along. Cal and Lyko fell in behind. The onlookers parted, eyes down, fists on their hearts as the worn warriors walked past.

The injured Draco dropped limply into camp. Wind whistled through his wings as he flopped grotesquely to his feet. Shale turned her eyes back to her work. Slaves were not interested in Draco Sang business. Slaves kept their heads down. She lowered her bucket into the well, marveling anew at the painless ease with which her elbow moved. All thanks to her terrifyingly mysterious master.

She peeked at the sliver of command tent visible down the path. Commander Mina and Dynacuss stepped in after the slumping flyer. He needed a healer. But, of course, that would come after he reported to Captain Jobu.

Ferth ran by while she worked the well. Golden eyes speared her as he whooshed past. She flinched beneath his stormy expression. He haunted her waking hours and invaded her dreams. Sometimes it was his human features that she saw, kind and smiling. Other times he was a wolf, pure raw Draco. She was a fool for even searching for more behind his mask. A dangerous, futile hope. She'd found a rare plumloch, protected in the warmth of a nest of undergrowth and ferns. A blossom that had defied the winter and found enough light and warmth to bloom into the most beautiful thing she'd ever seen. And she'd thought to show it to Ferth. Share her delight. What had she possibly expected by it? His face had turned stiff and cold when he'd seen it defiling his table. She determined to be wiser. She knew to tread carefully, keep her shields up.

Thinking Ferth would be in the command tent for a while, she took her time pulling water up from the well. As she hauled the heavy bucket towards Ferth's tent, stationed two down from Jobu's, a ray of welcome sunshine hit her back. She set her burden in the dirt and turned her face toward the rare winter warmth. Delightful heat speared her eyelids and tickled her lips.

Splashing water doused her moment of bliss. A Draco had dunked her face in Shale's bucket. The beaver rubbed at her filthy face and slurped at the fresh water.

"Excuse me." Shale was to keep her mouth shut. Be silent. Be invisible.

Black eyes glared up from the dirty water. A lip curled in amusement. "You're not speaking to *me*?"

"That water is for Commander Ferth. You've soiled it."

The Draco burped and knocked the bucket over. "I guess you'll have to get more."

Shale's heart clamored to fight, to lash out, to stand her ground—at the least. She bit her tongue, hard.

"No." A low, familiar voice said the word trapped behind Shale's teeth.

Her pulse soared. Would he punish her for obstinacy? Her gaze found his face. His left side, the fine human side, tilted toward her.

"*You'll* have to get more." Ferth's voice was sharp as he commanded the Draco. He turned, and the wolfish features appeared, dissolving any pretense of benevolence. Fire raged in his eyes.

Shale's insides folded over. What had happened at command? What had the flyer reported that had caused the violence festering beneath his fur?

"Your slave is a bit obstinate, commander. You should keep her in line."

What a fool.

In a flash, Ferth attacked. Shale blinked and the Draco's face was mashed into the mud, her arm twisted behind her back. Shale's breath snatched from her lungs as, knife in hand, Ferth shaved off chunks of the beaver's black fur.

"I'm sorry, sir." The Draco's eyes curled back to look at a tuft flaking into the wind.

"You'll fetch my water."

"Yes, sir."

Fur flew away as Ferth moved up the beaver's face. "Tell Shale you're sorry." He sounded lazy, almost bored.

"I'm sorry." She spat the words out.

Ferth kept shaving. "I'm sorry—"

"I'm sorry, Sh-shale."

"Yes. Up you go." Ferth lifted the warrior to her feet and brushed fur clumps off her shoulders. He picked up the bucket and thrust it into her chest. She grunted. His voice turned icy when he said, "Never speak to me like that again. And never come near my slave."

"Yes, commander." The Draco sprinted toward the well.

"I'm hungry," Ferth said lightly as he strolled past Shale.

Shale let out a pent-up wheeze and darted for the kitchens. *"What happened in command?"* She asked through the mental connection she shared with the hawk perched on top of the command tent. *Her* hawk.

"Two more Dracos, dead." Xandra was not sorry about it. *"Humans killed all but the bat Draco. The mother got away safely."*

"*Good.*"

"*Jobu nearly exploded.*"

"*I wish he had.*" The bruises that had peppered Pearl after a "visit" to Jobu made Shale's blood boil.

"*The baby was safely delivered at the Lion's camp.*"

"*Good.*"

"No," Xandra's voice in Shale's head turned low and pained. "*Ferth swore to steal the baby and kill the mother.*"

Ferth would do it. She did not doubt. Her insides turned to liquid.

"*I'm headed back to the woods. I left a rabbit for you at the spot.*"

"*Thank you.*" Shale longed to stroke Xandra's downy wings. Kiss her head. "*Stay safe. Stay hidden.*"

"*You need the warning more than I.*"

At the door of Ferth's tent, bread and pig belly in hand, Shale breathed in a heavy breath, steeling her nerves. Ferth paced the small space, running a hand over his furry skull. She set the food on the table and crept to the fire. She stoked the flames and set the water the beaver had delivered to boil. She dared a glance at Ferth. The wolf side of his face turned toward her, the picture of Draco pride. The penetrating amber eyes that pierced her dreams had turned arctic.

Her heart broke for that woman and her baby. A nightmare headed their way.

For two days, Cal hid behind the walls of his tent. No matter how much scrubbing he did with the bathwater, he couldn't wash away the pain and guilt in his heart. Pruned and pink and naked, he draped across his bed, his face buried in the blankets, searching for oblivion.

"Captain incoming." Lyko lay in a heap on the floor.

Cal didn't so much as lift his head as familiar footsteps drew closer.

"Ah," Titus said. "The fearsome warrior."

"Lyko says thank you." Bedding muffled his voice.

"One Callie is asking about her uncle."

Cal groaned, his head jerking up. "Why did they name her that? To torture me?"

"So full of yourself. Shem's grandmother's named Callandra."

"No, she's not." Cal glared at Titus, who chuckled at his own wit.

Titus's voice turned serious. "You saved that little girl's life. Her mother, too. They named her to honor you."

Cal's belly kinked. He didn't deserve any praise. "And we

lost Poe." He rolled off his bed and pulled on pants. His back barked in pain, still damaged from carrying Zemira. He took perverse pleasure in the injury, may it last forever, a reminder of the blood on his hands. His failure. How could he face Zemira? Stand in front of Uriah with Lyko at his side? How could he sit with the troops and laugh and inspire? How could he dishonor Poe by moving on from the grief and pain?

"Son."

Cal flinched. He was not Titus's son. More than ever he felt like the son of whatever hellish Draco had spawned him. The Draco Sang haunted his thoughts. In his nightmares, they came forward in turn, professing to be his father, his proud father, and laughing at his horror and shame.

Titus's deep voice rippled through his thoughts. "You can grieve for Poe. We all suffer his loss. But it is not your fault. You faced unexpected challenges, and you met them with courage. You gave all you had for your team. That's what true leaders do." He crossed the room and gripped Cal's shoulders, spearing him with clear eyes. "I am proud of you. Your mother is too."

"Never tell her."

"No. It is your story to share. All of it."

Maybe someday Cal could share his burden with her, knowing even now that she would help him carry it. And she would love him still. A trickle of warmth wormed into his frozen soul.

Poe had died to protect Zemira. Cal had not understood the full sacrifice this war might require, but he felt it now. The crushing weight. And he would pay the devasting price, and continue to pay it, until the war was won and his family, and every Elysium family, was safe from the Draco Sang.

"Alright." Cal sighed. "Let's meet the princess of the camp."

Titus's face lit up. Cal finished dressing, and together they stepped into the sunlight. As they wove through camp, soldiers and troops saluted, nodded, or tossed out friendly greetings. No one looked like they wanted to spit on him.

The hole in his chest shrank. Slightly.

Titus wore a pleased smile.

As they neared Zemira's tent, Titus lagged behind. "I've got some work to do."

Cal raised a brow but allowed the captain to abandon him. He spoke to the woman sitting outside the tent knitting tiny socks. "If Zemira is welcoming visitors, would you please tell her that Cal is here? I don't want to disturb her if she's resting."

The woman disappeared and, before Cal could do the same, she pulled the door open. "She says come right in."

"Oh. Okay. Thank you." He took an unsure step. The last time he'd seen Zemira, she'd been laboring in his arms, her blood, tears, sweat, and other unmentionable fluids greasing his skin.

On a large bed, Zemira perched like a queen. The lights of a blazing fire cast warm tones on her rich skin. She looked up from the tiny bundle in her arms and grinned, her eyes twinkling. Shem rose from his chair and held out a hand. Cal accepted it, and then the blacksmith wrapped an iron arm around his shoulders. Cal's back zinged in pain at the tight squeeze.

"Thank you for saving my girls," Shem said.

My girls. Some day Cal hoped to be worthy of a woman's love. That day seemed very far away. "I should have brought her home weeks ago."

"Even a man as strong as you can't control a force like Zemira." His honest face shone.

A smile cracked Cal's face. Shem was stronger than even Uriah. And he had let her go. Let her decide.

"What you did." Shem's throat bobbed. "Zemira told me of the trek home. I owe you not one life debt, but two."

Emotion clogged his throat. "You owe me nothing."

Shem motioned toward the bed. Zemira's beaming face lit up the world, chasing the grisly shadows from Cal's soul. She tugged back the baby's blanket. "Come and see Callie Poe."

"I'll get some dinner," Shem said. Pride oozed from the blacksmith as he ducked out.

Gingerly, Cal sat on the bed next to Zemira and peered at the new life. Big blue eyes blinked above a button nose. Her pink tongue slithered out of a wee mouth.

Happiness bubbled through the darkness. "She's so tiny."

"Hold her," Zemira said. She slipped Callie out of the thick blanket, leaving only a swaddling diaper.

"I've never. I don't—" Cal's protests fell away as Zemira set the infant in his arms. She felt lighter than air and more valuable than any treasure. "She's beautiful." His calloused hands contrasted her perfect golden skin. He ran a finger over a silky leg.

She was worth it.

This was what he fought for. What Poe gave his life to protect. Miniature fingers wrapped around his pinky, and his heart melted.

Zemira's hand touched his arm. He looked up at intense dark eyes. "Thank you, Cal."

He swallowed.

Tears glittered and fell down her cheeks. She wiped at them furiously. "This baby makes me weepy. Don't get used to it." She glared at him, trying to muster her usual ferocity.

"I wouldn't dare." He bit down on the smile tugging at his lips. Warmth spread over his arms. "Oh," he breathed and held the baby away from his side. Moisture seeped into his shirt.

Zemira giggled, then burst out laughing. "She must like you."

"I think it's the opposite."

"She was just so relaxed." Zemira took Callie. "I'm sorry. I'm still learning how to tie these properly." She replaced the soiled linen while Cal wiped at his shirt.

Shem came in with three steaming bowls.

"Callie's already marked her territory," Zemira said, pointing to Cal.

Hearty laughter echoed through the tent. "She's got good aim," Shem said.

Heat dusted Cal's cheeks at the praise he felt unworthy of.

Shem handed Zemira a bowl and picked up his daughter. Callie looked like a squirrel in his arms.

Cal took the chair near the bed; while he ate, the new life started to heal his soul. This softer side of Zemira suited her. She glowed. He dreamed of the day she could mother in peace, when the war wouldn't call her to fight.

When it was time for Callie's meal, Cal left, feeling renewed and strengthened. He would stop thinking of Zemira. At least, he would try.

FORTY - MISSION
CAL

Cal's arrow smacked the target with a satisfying *twang*.

"Nicely done," Commander Asvig said, hovering behind Cal. He was one of the six commanders under Captain Titus.

"It's a lot harder when it's a diving Draco."

"That's the truth." Asvig stroked his white beard. The man rarely picked up a weapon. His strengths were logistics, numbers, and, judging by his girth, eating. "We need to get those targets moving."

Cal glanced sidelong at the commander before letting another arrow fly. "Would you like me to look into it, sir?"

"No. Captain Titus has a mission for you."

Cal sent an arrow downrange, keeping his face passive. Two weeks at home and no movement across the border. He itched for action. But if this was anything like the last mission … He shuddered.

"Uriah hasn't left his tent," Asvig said.

Cal knew. It burned a hole in his gut. Acid ate across his ribs as he fired another arrow. It barely hit the target.

Asvig cocked an eyebrow.

Cal lowered his bow and faced the man. "Sir?"

"There is a woman of Draco Sang blood … name of Pelussa. Her hewan is a raven. She's a bit …" He paused. "Eccentric."

Oh, her. Cal had heard Pelussa called many things—grumpy, sly, blunt, crazy, cold, crafty. None of the labels made him particularly keen to meet her.

Asvig kept talking. "She's spent years in Skotar. She knows the Draco Sang, possibly better than anyone else in Elysium. She lives in Abaddon. It's not far away, but it's a difficult journey. You and Uriah are to go and convince her to come and help us."

Cal squinted into the drooping sun. A name like Abaddon was another bad omen for the trip. It was an obscure reference to destruction and hell from a story his mother had told him as a child. "She's turned away the other attempts, why send us?"

"She'll relate to you and Uriah. You'll be the ones to convince her." Asvig tucked thumbs into his bulging waistband. "Getting Uriah out of bed will be your first challenge."

"Great." His voice was flat.

"Be quick about it. We'd like you back well before snowmelt. We still believe the first attack will come in the spring."

"Yes, Commander."

Later that night, Cal and Lyko stopped at the kitchens to beg a couple of hot tavos and two dinner plates on their way to Uriah's tent. The soldiers with hewans each had their own tent. Uriah's was a fraction larger than the rest, room for Poe. Now the extra space gave it an unpleasantly hollow feeling. Stale air heavy with sweat and grief filled the space. The mound on the bed didn't move when they entered.

"What's the plan?" Lyko asked.

"Wake him up. Ask him to come."

Lyko scoffed.

"What's your idea?"

"Pretend to be assassins. That should get a rise out of him."

"Maybe not."

Lyko didn't have a rebuttal for that sad thought.

Cal crept closer to the stink. Uriah stared at the wall, unseeing. Deep shadows painted his empty face, and long, dirty hair matted his brow. Cal set Uriah's fragrant dinner near the man's nose. He sat on the nearby chair and put his feet up on the bed, same as he'd done every evening since meeting baby Callie.

"Mutton. It's okay," Cal said as he ate. "Cook still seems to have an aversion to salt. But the beets are delightful." He took a sip of tavo. "Oh, that goes down nice."

Uriah didn't blink.

Cal sighed. *"Try licking his feet."*

"Not going near them," Lyko said with an air of offense.

A moment later, attendants brought in the washing water Cal had asked for.

"Thank you," Cal said as they left. He finished his dinner, licked his fingers loudly, and stood. In one giant heave, he pulled Uriah to his feet.

Surprise flickered over his friend's face. Better than noth-ing. Cal started unbuttoning Uriah's shirt. After a moment, Uriah slapped his hand away.

"You are washing," Cal said.

Uriah gave in. "I can undress myself." His voice scratched, raw from disuse.

Good. Cal hadn't wanted to finish the job.

Naked, Uriah stared at the basin for a long time.

"Need me to bathe you?" Cal asked.

Uriah glared at him. Cal grinned. He could work with an angry Uriah. While Uriah turned his temper toward the soap,

Cal ripped the blankets from the bed and scooped up the rancid clothes. He set them outside to fester.

"Give us five more minutes," he said to the girl waiting by the door, taking clean sheets from her arms.

She wrinkled her nose at the mound Cal had thrown nearby.

Uriah dressed and went for the newly made bed, but Cal and Lyko blocked him.

"Sit in that chair," Cal said.

Uriah pushed him out of the way, but the shove was weak, his strength eaten away. Cal's chest cramped as he easily stood his ground. Uriah brought up a fist, but Lyko jumped and put his paws on Uriah's chest. Lyko pressed his nose against Uriah's brow.

Uriah slumped, but he sat where Cal pointed. He accepted the tavo. He didn't drink.

"Anniya," Cal called.

Hesitantly the young woman entered. With a reassuring nod from Cal, she smiled. Her glow radiated through the room, attacking the shadows. Uriah looked at her sidelong and sat a fraction straighter.

"Anniya, meet Uriah."

She curtseyed. "I'm honored."

Uriah grumbled something inaudible, and her smile faltered.

Cal stepped up and put a hand on her elbow, drawing her forward. Her body went rigid when she saw the wolf sitting on the floor behind Uriah.

"He won't bite," Cal said.

"I'm sorry." A hand flew to her chest. "He just startled me. He's so big close up."

Lyko puffed with pride. He stood and padded up close to her. Her eyes bulged. He practically loomed. Cal was about to call Lyko on his horrid manners when the wolf's lips peeled back, and he let out a bone-rattling growl.

Anniya screamed. The girl's arm trembled under Cal's fingers. Her pulse tripled.

Shock and anger flashed through Cal. "Lyko!"

Uriah jolted in his seat. Fire lit his eyes, and he swung a fist at Lyko. Lyko darted out of the way, as if expecting the strike. Uriah pointed to Lyko. "Get. Out."

A wolfine smile split his snowy face. *"And he's alive."*

Cal's fury dissipated, and he laughed at Lyko's ruthless effectiveness. Anniya looked at Cal like she'd walked into a mad house. Lyko pranced over to the bed and, with an air of arrogance, stretched across it.

Uriah snarled, but before he could reprimand Lyko, Cal cut in. "Anniya is giving you an overdue haircut and shave."

Uriah's face slackened, and he sank against the back of his chair as if cornered. Anniya pulled scissors from her apron, and after taking about twelve deep breaths, got to work. A bit of color returned to Uriah's cheeks as her hands flew over his head. Cal appreciated that she seemed to run her fingers through his hair and over his neck more than professionally necessary. She finished and pulled out a reflecting glass from a large pocket. She held it in front of Uriah.

"Such a handsome face I've unearthed."

Uriah's sad gaze moved from the glass to Anniya.

"I'm very sorry about Poe," she said. "It breaks my heart." She nestled her hand into the ample softness over her heart. "He's a true hero. And so are you." She leaned forward and kissed him on the lips.

Cal nearly fell over.

Uriah froze.

Her lips lingered. When she drew back, she sent him a shy smile before turning away. When she drifted toward Cal, he flinched.

"Coward," Lyko said.

Cal lifted his chin. "Thank you, Anniya … for the haircut." Heat danced across his face.

"Glad to help. Let me know when he needs another shave."

"Yes, ma'am."

She let herself out.

After a fat pause, Cal doubled over with laughter. He clutched at the table, howling. Lyko whistled.

"That was an unexpected benefit," he said, wiping tears from his cheeks.

Life showed in Uriah's eyes. Before the soldier could slip back into the abyss, Cal pulled him to his feet and dragged him outside. As they entered Zemira's tent, she bolted to her feet and rushed to Uriah. She threw her arms around him, holding him close. She fluttered around him, chatting and crooning, but what finally made Uriah's lips turn up was Callie Poe. He held her for a long time. So long that Cal nodded off as he waited in a nearby chair. When they finally left, the waxing moon lit their path.

"I'm hungry," Uriah said.

Thank the stars. Cal turned his brother toward the kitchens, Lyko at their heels. With a brimming bowl, Cal led Uriah to the edge of camp, where they settled on a boulder with a view down into the Kiptos valley.

"You ready to get out of here? Do something?" Cal asked.

Uriah shrugged and ripped into his bread.

"We're leaving tomorrow to go to Abaddon. Got to fetch Captain Titus a stubborn old woman and her raven."

"Fine."

Fine? Cal had speeches prepared.

"Must have been some kiss," Lyko said.

Cal smiled and watched the stars as Uriah ate his entire meal.

"You don't have to hold so tight." The wind whipped away Thirro's response, but Ferth still caught the edge of amusement in his tone.

He did not loosen his grip on Thirro's forearms. Fright clawed through his veins. High above the earth, the eagle held Ferth against his chest. He didn't fully trust Thirro not to *accidentally* send him careening to his death.

Far below, the Rugit River snaked through the land like a shadowy sash. Thirro was definitely flying higher than necessary out of pure sadistic pleasure. Ferth hated being in Thirro's control. Hated the brief shift in power. Hated that Thirro was milking the moment.

The fires at the Lion's camp spread a halo of light in the east. The closest Elysium town of Kiptos lay southwest by ten miles.

Thirro dropped. Ferth's guts shifted to his mouth. The ground rushed to greet them. Thirro hit a clearing in the trees and released his burden. Ferth sank to all fours. He grasped a handful of frozen dirt as he heaved in the chilly air, gathering back his wits.

Thirro shook out his arms, his wings folding against his back. "I must say, that was impressive flying. I wasn't sure we were going to make it. Hadn't realized how heavy your ego is."

"The baby won't be so durable. You've got to work on your landing."

Thirro squawked. "Next time I'll cradle you like a hatchling."

"There better not be a next time." Ferth stood and rolled out the tension from the flight. "Let's go."

It was a lot slower going on the ground, picking through bushes and climbing over rocks. Ferth didn't complain. They'd waited three weeks for a moonless night. Thirro wore a black hat to hide his white head. Ferth's pale gray fur rippled with the winter shadows. They came at the camp from the southwest. As they approached the first enemy sentry, Ferth held up a fist. He unstrapped the bow from Thirro's back. He did not allow himself to think as he sent an arrow at the lone guard. It struck home. The man slid down with a surprised grunt.

His first kill.

Icy fingers clamped Ferth's heart as he stared at the slumped human. Unexpected and unwelcome horror paralyzed him. It'd been so easy to kill the man, just a flick of his wrists. Wrongness and guilt wriggled under his skin. He forced his focus past the dead sentry to the golden lights of the Lion's camp. *Feel nothing.* He had a mission. He had a Draco Sang baby to find. He had a country to conquer. Petty remorse had no place in it.

Ferth stalked past the dead human. He killed two more guards with cold calm. They reached the camp perimeter. No alarms sounded. His heart thrashed against his ribs. His first time in Elysium. They darted past tents, clinging to the blackest dark, following the map the scouts had drawn for him. Dawn was in three hours. He'd be home in less than one. Silence reigned. The fire pits were cold. The camp slept in peace.

His blood sang through his veins, steady and strong. When the baby's tent came into view, uncertainty struck. He could not make a mistake. The neatly ordered tents all looked the same. Then he saw the tiny shirts hanging out front.

Ferth pointed, and Thirro returned a solemn nod. He retied the bow and quiver between Thirro's wings. After a deep inhale, Ferth drew a long knife and gave the signal.

No guard or lock barred their entry. They slipped into the tent without resistance. A man and woman slept on a wide bed. Ferth swiped the baby from a nearby basket, marveling at the ease of it all. He turned toward the door and found a sleek panther crouched in his path. The cat growled, deep and deadly.

Ferth balked. He'd heard about the abomination, but nothing could have prepared him for this. Power and intelligence radiated from dark eyes. How could something so disgraceful send fear and awe down his spine? He held the baby in front of his chest as a shield. The woman bolted upright in bed. Silver flashed, and the cat stumbled with a hiss. Thirro's knife clattered to the floor next to it. Ferth leapt past the panther and thrust the baby into Thirro's arms.

"Fly." The word was raw with adrenaline.

Thirro whirled toward the tent door. Ferth blocked the lunging panther as Thirro took off into the night sky, the baby tight in his arms.

The scream that sailed from the woman's lips rent Ferth's heart. She unsheathed a sword that lay on a chair next to her bed and charged. Muscle and training took over as he blocked her wild attacks. Canines sank into Ferth's calf as the woman slashed across his shoulder. The human and her pet fought as if connected, striking in rhythm. A man nearly the size of Laconius edged forward, trying to get a lane into the fight. The cramped tent was suddenly Ferth's greatest ally. He fought desperately to keep them from landing a killing blow, her sword reach longer than his knife. He did not want to die, and to his dismay, he did not want to kill them. Not after this shocking display of loyalty and courage. Did this not prove that they in some way still shared his Draco heritage?

Blood dripped off the panther's foreleg, and Ferth aimed a few hard strikes to that side, forcing the woman to protect her pet. When the cat stumbled, Ferth whirled and sprinted out of the tent.

Horns sounded. Blood gushed from his calf and shoulder as he pounded through camp. Hot breath clouded the frozen air as he hurled away. By the time the sleepy soldiers recognized him as the enemy, he'd flown past. Adrenaline sent his pain to the far reaches of his soul as he charged around tents and passed low buildings. He didn't slow at the delta. Cold water stung his wounds and slashed up his legs. He dove right and then left as the whistle of arrows cut the night. Nearly to the northern banks, he slammed face-first into the shallows as agony tore across his side. The arrow embedded in the river bottom, the fletching quivering above the water surface. Standing, he clutched his knife in one hand and pressed his other against his ribs where the iron had slashed his flesh, mere inches from bringing death. He ran.

"Commander," a watchman yelled when Ferth hit Skotar. "Do you need help?"

Yes. He needed a lot of it. How much blood could the guard see in the darkness? "Don't leave your post," Ferth yelled, his voice wheezy. "Be alert for an attack."

"Yes, sir."

Ferth shuffled along the thin trail, cursing his foolishness.

He should have had someone at the banks waiting for his return. The guard couldn't leave his post at a vulnerable time like this. Ferth's wounds hadn't surpassed his pride enough to use his horn and wake the entire camp to come to his aid. He'd make it home. To Shale. And he'd do it in pain rather than shame.

Weak and shaking from shock and blood loss, he stumbled the last mile. Red handprints along the trees marked his progress. He fell. Hands trembling, he cut through the lacing on his leather vest. It flopped to the dirt. His right arm locked against the gouge in his side. He ripped an uneven strip off his shirt and wrapped it weakly around the weeping wound. Panting, he pinched his eyes shut.

Four tiny white shirts hung neatly in a row. The image was bright and clear, as if he stood again in front of the tent. The drying swaddle blanket was embroidered with gold and purple thread, as if the baby were a princess. *She was to that mother.* Ferth forced his eyes open, but the vision didn't clear. Those clothes would be there tomorrow with no baby to adorn. Had his mother fought to keep him too? Had she been left with only lovingly crafted scraps of fabric? Had she wanted to keep him? Had his mother cried with the same anguish that mother had tonight? Fought with such ferocity? As the hope blossomed, Ferth knew it was a dangerous one. And with it came guilt and regret for what he'd done this night. Could his mother have loved him that much?

Ferth shoved the thoughts away. They hurt, and he was in too much pain already. And it didn't matter. He'd never know his mother. She'd have been happy to be rid of him now. She was probably dead anyway. He was a leader of Skotar. The baby would become a powerful Draco Sang. As he was. She was better off with her own kind.

If only he truly believed that.

With a howl, Ferth lurched to his feet. Spots clouded his

vision. Dawn dispelled the darkness as he wobbled toward camp.

Shale waited at the edge of the tents. Her face bleached when she saw him. She ran for him as he staggered across the grass.

He squinted, sure he hallucinated the worry on her face. She slipped under his arm and braced him up with a strong hand around his waist. Blood smeared across her shift.

He'd died.

He'd died, and this vision was his reward.

"I will take care of the baby," she said.

He looked down at her through dotted vision. She was so beautiful. The dream enhanced the size of her lips, the bright green of her eyes, the luster of her skin. *You love me too?* He almost said it.

"You must insist that the care of the baby be given to me." Her voice was hard and insistent.

"I'm not dead?"

She scowled and dragged him forward.

As they neared command, Captain Jobu and a group rushed outside. Thirro, whole and healthy, beamed at Jobu's side.

Thanks for coming back to help me.

Ferth nearly crumpled, but Shale steeled his spine with her own.

Jobu held the baby awkwardly from his body as she screamed. The high pitch reverberated off Ferth's teeth and down his bones.

"Well done, commander," Jobu said. "Victory."

Ferth nodded, his thoughts muddled and distant. The howling shredded the remains of his sanity.

"Tend to your wounds," Jobu yelled over the angry infant. "I will be waiting for a full report."

Ferth turned away. Shale yanked a clump of fur on his

back. He jerked in surprise. Wide green eyes pressed into his thoughts, pleading.

"My slave will care for the baby," Ferth said.

Jobu looked her up and down and thrust the bundle forward. Shale let go of Ferth, leaving him teetering on wobbly knees. She tenderly drew the baby to her chest. The wailing stopped. She stroked the tiny head and swayed.

"Protect her well," Jobu said to Ferth. "She is Uictoria. And she is my daughter now. She does not leave your tent." Jobu faced the gathering crowd. "Where's my breakfast?"

Two slaves darted away. Jobu returned to his tent.

"I'm glad you made it back, commander," Thirro said.

Too tired to care that Thirro was a liar, Ferth said, "Tell Keal he's running this morning's training. Send the healer and breakfast to my tent."

Thirro's jaw tightened at the string of commands. "Yes, sir."

Ferth's muscles had seized while he stood there. The full pain of his wounds nearly knocked him out when he sought to walk. Baby at her chest, Shale sidled up. Ferth gripped her shoulder as he stumbled forward. He hissed in agony as he tumbled onto his bed. He wavered on the edge of consciousness as the healer stitched and cleaned. The healer's face morphed into Keturah's. She kept saying *I love you* and *never mistake humanness for weakness.*

In the deep recesses of his mind, he admitted that the panther and her master were not weak or disgraceful. They'd radiated honor and prowess and vitality. He'd felt the devotion they had for each other. The thoughts ricocheted around his skull, wounding the scaffolding of his world and weakening the roots of his ambitions.

Feverish flames licked at his body as the healer stood up. He twisted his face to see the woman.

"Clean him," she said. "I'll be back tonight with new dressings."

"Yes," Shale said, not looking up from the baby tucked in her wing. She dipped cloth into a pot of milk and held it to the baby's lips. She brushed her lips along the baby's brow. Tiny sucking sounds filtered over.

Beautiful.

Ferth closed his eyes on his desires and let the shadows have him.

He woke, naked, to Shale dabbing a warm cloth over the circle of bare skin on his chest. She didn't acknowledge his waking, her face grim as she scrubbed at sweat and dried blood. His throat burned. He croaked out a moan. She dutifully brought a cup to his lips. Warm broth coated his insides. Her hands roved over his body, but he was too tired and injured to enjoy it. Defenseless as a lamb, he closed his eyes and slept.

FORTY-TWO - PARADISE
CAL

"We can't fit in there," Uriah said.

Cal squinted at the narrow cleft in the rock. "I can see why they call this the birth canal."

"My ma said I barely made it out of the *first* birth canal."

Cal chuckled, but underneath frustration boiled. He flung his pack to the ground and sat on a rock near the canyon entrance. They'd been hiking through swamps and thorns for nearly a week, and their goal supposedly lay just beyond the narrow passage. The too-narrow passage. And there was no light at the other end, beckoning him forward. They'd walked the cliffs for miles, failing to find another entrance.

"Asvig said others have fit through," Cal said.

"A small child. Maybe."

As they studied the crack, a raven soared out of the darkness. Cal wheeled back as the glossy black bird dove at his head. The bird circled up, eyeing them suspiciously before wheeling around and darting back into the canyon.

"Raven," Cal yelled. "Wait." The bird did not return. "I guess this is the right place."

"*See you on the other side.*" Lyko ducked into the opening.

"No. You'll follow me. Who knows what this opens into?"

Lyko took another step, and Cal pressed his will onto the hewan. Lyko growled his annoyance as he finally reversed. Cal took a large swig of water and hung his pack in a tree. His sword too. He'd be going in blind, with only his bone-handled knife. He turned to Uriah. "You can be glad you've hardly eaten for weeks."

Uriah rolled his eyes.

Cal's heart hammered against the cold stone as he squeezed into the rock. The canyon widened slightly at the bottom, where Lyko crawled near the dirt. Seconds ticked by like hours as they shuffled sideways, scratching along the walls. Uriah came up with new curses for every inch.

"I can see the end," Cal said as a sliver of light came into view. "But I think I am truly stuck this time." Panic rolled up his spine as his chest wedged tight. Short, shallow breaths puffed against the frost.

"Suck in or die," Uriah said.

Cal breathed out his last drop of air and shoved forward. His head banged against the side, and a trickle of warmth dripped down his cheek. It itched, but he couldn't move to wipe it. As he slid forward, the mountain gave way, opening to sunlight.

He blinked at the expansive inner mountain sanctuary. Hidden paradise. Air warmed by the deep mountain kissed his face. Water trickled down the back wall, running along the right side of the cavern before disappearing underground. Lavender moss carpeted the ground. Small animals ran around the cluster of trees. Birds sang. Floral fragrances fiddled with his senses.

Next to a tidy garden, an old woman sat on a stump. Scarred milky eyes stared blankly in his direction. The raven perched on her shoulder, its glossy face trained on the three trespassers.

"Hello, Pelussa." Cal's voice rang through the cavern, echoing off the walls. The chirping died.

"No need to shout, boy. I'm blind, not deaf. And you wasted your time and your blood coming here." Her voice was a deep croak.

Cal's hand flew to his face. Red smeared his fingers.

"Can we have a drink?" Uriah asked.

"You interrupt my solitude and now you want to dirty my stream?"

"Yes, please, ma'am."

The woman and her raven cocked their heads in disturbing synchronization. "Where's your hewan?"

Uriah blanched.

"Heartbreaking. Truly heartbreaking," she said in a *tsk-tsk* tone. "The Draco Sang bring nothing but sorrow and death."

A chill ran down Cal's bones. Uriah looked as if he'd been paralyzed.

"That's why we must fight. Keep them out of Elysium," Cal said.

"Fool!"

Cal reeled as if slapped.

"King Andras is a fool too, and so is Captain Titus. If you want my help, destroy the canals. Let the river do her job. Let her fight. Only she can win this war."

Cal scrambled for words. The river would be impossible to turn back now. "Kiptos needs the water. The Rugit stopped the drought. Kiptos sends food to all of Elysium."

Pelussa laughed, a shrill sound. "You're a good little soldier. Following orders and repeating what you're told."

Heat rolled over Cal's face.

"I'm blind, and I see better than you. Kiptos is already dead. Elysium is lost."

Cal's toes curled in his boots. He'd fought Dracos. Tasted of their violence. Was she right? Fear tapped against his ribs.

"I'm not heartless. You can stay here with me. If you do your share of the work. Your big friend is especially welcome. He may share in my peace."

Worry wormed through Cal as Uriah studied the woman, his gaze panning the idyllic surrounding with longing in his eyes.

"It's beets and rutabaga for dinner. Wash up at the *bottom* of the stream. Make sure your wolf doesn't trample my flowers as he's chasing the squirrels."

"Is she serious? Does she take me for a weasel?"

"A blind woman would care about her flowers," Cal said.

"Titus hates us."

"I might agree with you."

The river ran clear and cool, the best water Cal had tasted. He sat near the edge.

Pelussa's gravelly voice cut across the clearing. "Careful near the bacaroot. It can kill you."

Cal looked around; he couldn't see Uriah.

"Yes, I'm talking to you, boy."

Cal glanced over his shoulder. The wrinkled bronze face and white eyes tilted his direction.

"You're sitting on it."

He looked down at the fleshy round leaves, hating that she made him feel like a blind fool.

"It's the purple tubers you don't want in your mouth." Pelussa turned back to the bean pods in her lap.

"Why do you keep it here if it's poisonous?"

"To make poison. Of course."

Cal rolled his eyes as he turned away and spoke to Lyko, *"She's even worse than they said."*

Lyko padded up to Cal. His nostrils flared. *"It stinks."*

"Very helpful, thanks." Avoiding the bruise-colored tubers scattered around his legs, he stood. He cleared his annoyance with a walk around the grotto's perimeter before joining

Pelussa and Uriah.

With effort, he kept his hands clasped behind his back as Pelussa tended a small fire and roasted skewered vegetables. He had a feeling his help would be more than unwelcome. As they ate, the raven perched across from Cal. Its beady eyes bore holes into Cal, who shifted under the scrutiny. The raven studied Uriah next.

"What's her name?" Uriah asked.

The bird let out an indignant caw.

"*His* name is Ipsum."

"Nice to meet you, Ipsum," Uriah said.

The insulted raven ignored the greeting.

"Captain Titus speaks highly of you. Says you've spent a lot of time in Skotar," Cal said.

Embers popped in the fire.

"Were you born there?"

Creamy eyes tilted up. "A question for a question. From each of you."

Cal's gut tightened. "Fine."

Uriah nodded.

"Yes," she said. "I was."

"Where?" Cal asked.

"Uh-uh. My turn. Who are your parents?"

For the first time ever, Cal was grateful he didn't have a name for his father. "My mother's name is Mira. I don't know my father." He could answer as shortly as she did.

Uriah's sad eyes studied the faltering flames. His voice floated soft and tender over their secret haven. "I was born in Skotar as well."

Cal nearly fell off his log. Uriah had never spoken of his past. The woman's thin lips tightened into a thousand wrinkles.

Uriah's eyes turned glossy, reflecting the dying coals. "My mother was a slave. The favorite of the Lord of Gristlecove. He was a hyena Draco. Cold and mean. He could shred your soul with a look. I was four when my ma bore another child for him. A sister. Twelve years ago, when Suzaena was five and I was nine, Ma decided we would escape to Elysium." Uriah took a breath. "We nearly made it."

His deep voice seemed to cast a spell over the clearing, binding Cal's limbs to the ground. Each word punctured a new hole in his chest. Her face stricken, Pelussa shooed and snatched at the air as if fishing for flies, or fighting invisible demons.

"We were five miles from the river delta when Ma heard them coming. She grabbed me, kissed me, and told me to never look back. Then, she shoved me down a gully. I stayed in the pit, caught in the brambles, a long time after the sound of the Dracos whipping her and dragging her away had faded. I only remember black grief after that. It was late fall, and somehow I made it across the delta alive. A family in Kiptos saved me from starvation. I found Titus a year later. Or truthfully, *he* was the one who found *me*."

Cal couldn't breathe. Uriah's pain pulled the night over them like a cage. Uriah stood; he trudged to a flat section of thick moss and stretched out across it. Heaviness pressed on Cal's shoulders as he followed.

"I'm sorry," Cal whispered to the space between them.

"I wonder," Uriah said. "If I saw my sister again, would I be able to recognize her? I might fight her. Kill her in this war. And never know it."

"Yes. I know." Heavy emotion strangled the quiet words. "I had a brother there too." *Had.* It was easier to think of it as a past thing. There would be no future with his twin.

Uriah's head snapped up.

"But I've never met him. Or my father. I can't imagine how terrible it would have been for you to lose the ones you knew and loved like that." Heat rose to Cal's eyes as he voiced his own frail hope. "Maybe your sister defeated her beast."

"That's not how things work there. That's not what happens." He rolled away. "I'm sorry about your brother."

"I wouldn't trade him for the brother I already have."

Uriah didn't answer, but the tension in his body loosened.

For they *were* brothers—fathered by hate and mothered by love. And they shared blood with the enemy invaders.

Despite his heartache, the mountain sanctuary swaddled him in sleep. Cal woke to soft sunlight and the music of nature. Possibly he could stay here forever. Forget the war, forget the Draco Sang, forget Zemira. Endless peace—

"Good. You're finally awake. Let's go," Lyko said, jerking Cal out of his fantasy. *"I'm one glare away from pulling that pretentious raven's wings off."*

"I'm not awake," Cal said, wishing the beast couldn't speak to his mind whenever he wanted. He groaned and rubbed his stubbly chin. His injured back hurt more after sleeping on the ground. After a long drink in the clear stream, he found Uriah near the waterfall, sitting on a ledge high up the mountain.

How could he drag Uriah back to war if this was the healing he needed? Cal left him to his solitude. Uriah finally came down when Pelussa passed around berries and torn lettuce.

"Thank you for your hospitality," Cal said.

Lyko sulked away from the group. *"No thanks from me. I don't want leaves and berries for breakfast. Ever."*

Cal's lip twitched before he turned serious and spoke again to the frowning old woman. "I'm sorry I can't convince you to return with us. I see that you would be a great value to our efforts."

"You've got to work on your lying skills." Lyko lapped at the river.

Pelussa huffed at Cal as if insulted. She turned to Uriah, knowing exactly where he stood. Bony fingers gripped his forearm. His brows rose.

"You've given your sacrifice. You've paid too high a price. Don't let them destroy you. Stay here. Stay in paradise. Rest. Here you will find peace."

Miserable brown eyes flickered to Cal.

"Stay." Cal stood and walked toward the canyon, trying to reach the shadows before the ache of leaving his brother broke him. As he put a hand on the cold granite, Uriah's voice sliced the air.

"I have seen Skotar—the viciousness, the brutality, the greed. The Draco Sang will not have Elysium. Freedom is worth fighting for. Poe knew that. He knew better than anyone. He gave his life to save another. I do him no honor staying here. I will fight for my people."

My people. The humans. No matter their blood, they belonged here. In Elysium, where freedom and fairness reigned.

"I will glorify Poe's name and his legacy," Uriah said.

"Rawh." Pelussa waved a dismissive hand and turned her hunched back on them.

"We are camped at the Rugit. I hope you change your mind," Uriah said.

Pelussa didn't respond.

Uriah strode to Cal. "Let's get out of here." Uriah led the way into the canyon, the fire of determination blazing in his eyes.

Heaviness lay over camp when Cal, Uriah, and Lyko returned. Silent, solemn soldiers watched them walk by. Cal's pulse quickened. Had there been an attack? How many had been killed? Uriah's jaw clenched, as if he too felt the ill wind. They picked up speed as they wove toward command.

Cal tore open the tent door. "What's happened?"

Titus and Asvig jerked up from their meal. Relief washed Titus's face as he leapt from his chair.

"Come. Eat," Titus said.

"Who died?" Cal asked, not moving from where he stood near the door with Uriah, both poised to fight.

Titus exhaled, his blue eyes hard. "Zemira's baby was kidnapped by the Draco and taken to Skotar."

Air didn't come. Blood drained from Cal's face, his heart. The room swirled. Uriah pitched forward, clutching the back of a chair.

"Two Draco snuck into camp five nights ago. Killed four sentries. The flyer took the baby and flew across the river. The other fought his way across the delta."

Fury boiled in Cal's blood. "And I wasn't here. I left Callie unprotected."

Asvig spoke from his seat across the table. "She had an army around her. You didn't fail her. We did."

"Go see Zemira and Shem," Titus said. "Report tomorrow."

Uriah ducked out of the tent, his face pallid.

"There is no report," Cal said, bitterness coating his tongue. "Pelussa isn't coming. The trip was a fool's errand. The *delightful* woman did have a message for you, though." He made a piss-poor effort to rein in his rage. "She says we're all staring across the delta at our own death. Destroy the canals or die."

Asvig and Titus stared, certainly debating whether to punish his coarseness and disrespect.

Cal didn't give them the chance. "I'm sneaking across the delta tonight. I'm getting our baby back." His tone was steel and his gaze glacial.

"I've already denied Zemira that," Titus said.

"Good."

"Why would I allow you to go?"

"I'm not asking permission. You'll have to lock me in a cage to stop me."

"And me."

"Lyko too."

Titus sighed and glanced at Asvig, who threw up his hands in defeat. "We desperately need intel on their camp," Asvig said.

"It's too dangerous," Titus said.

"I'll report back in the morning," Cal said, his insides in knots.

"Sit," Titus said. "Eat. Before you rush breakneck into enemy camp, you stop and think. Keep your head. We'll plan this together."

Cal sat, his stomach in his throat, and prepared to go to Skotar.

Ferth picked at his plate of eggs and brown bread as Shale hummed softly to Uictoria. His slave swaddled the baby and tucked her in the basket that lay next to Shale's bedroll. Ferth hadn't slept well since Shale and Uictoria had moved in. The baby cried all hours of the night —cried for her mother. Shale's scent swirled through his senses, and pain itched across his injuries.

Shale slipped out of the tent, and the tether that chained him loosened. He should be training with his unit, not lying in bed, wounded. He growled in frustration and picked up twin daggers. Standing in the middle of his tent, his head nearly brushing the ceiling, he performed basic moves and thrusts. The stitches on his ribs, shoulder, and calf protested, but he ignored the pain. He danced in a violent rhythm. His blood sang out the moves, guiding the blades through invisible enemies. He jabbed hard and fell forward as fire lanced his side wound. His knives clattered to the floor.

He jerked at a sharp intake of breath. Shale rushed to his side, gentle fingers reaching for his ribs.

"You shouldn't be doing that," she scolded. "Let me see it."

She tugged his shirt up and hissed at the trickle of blood. Concern traced her intelligent green eyes.

She was too close.

His racing blood changed tune as her fingers felt along his side. *Don't touch me.* The wolf sealed his lips. A powerful need heated his limbs. His pounding pulse drowned out all thought. Her scent washed into his chest—potent, vigorous, and *fertile.*

Ferth pushed her back, shoving her onto his bed. Knees on either side of her waist, clawed hands pinned her shoulders. But she didn't fight back. Her beautiful face, framed in rich brown hair, stared at him in shock and horror. The blade he found strapped to her creamy thigh inflamed his lust. He left it there. Silky flesh yielded beneath his fingers. Her shift tore as he pulled it up. Pleasure thrummed through him. The wolf raced through his heart, wild for dominance, eager to be free of his foolish self-made restraints.

"Ferth." His name came quietly, softly, but it struck him like an anvil. For a flicker, he saw her pain, and he faltered. He did not want her eyes to look like that, marred by fear and misery.

He cared what she felt.

Instead of slicing her clothing clean off, he sank his claws into his bedding. Flames engulfed him. "Go." His voice was raw and grainy. "Run."

He tore at his mattress as she scrambled to her feet.

And he let her slip away.

When his bed lay in a heap of feathers and thread, his blood still howled. Passion fogged his thoughts. His shirt matted to his weeping wounds. Wild, Ferth tore out of his tent and towards the training ground.

"Keal!"

Ferth panted as the gorilla loped away from the gathered troops. A grin grew on his goofy face. "Welcome, Commander. Come to check on our progress? It's not the same without you, but they've been working hard."

Ferth picked up a practice sword and threw another one to Keal, who caught it with a look of confusion but followed his commander to the training squares.

"Don't stop until I pass out," Ferth said.

"Sir?" His gaze focused on the blood seeping through Ferth's clothes.

"Then carry me to my tent and call the healer. That's an order." Ferth attacked, and the gorilla's sword slashed forward to block.

FORTY-FOUR - VENGEANCE
CAL

Cal rested by the Rugit, three miles west of camp. Moonlight kissed the Seraf Mountains with silver light. He studied the river. A third of a mile wide. Near freezing temperatures. And he'd come east of the canals to avoid patrols near the delta. The waist-deep current would fight him hard. He tied a rope around Lyko's flank and lashed it around his own waist. He secured his knives and checked the buckle over his dagger.

"Let's go."

Water penetrated his boots like ice picks. He sucked in and plowed forward. He gripped Lyko's side, holding them together as they marched deeper. The water lifted Lyko, forcing the wolf to swim. Cal's limbs fought him with every step. Halfway across, the numbing water had reached his chest.

"Flyer," Lyko said.

"Go under." Cal inhaled and slid down. Ice slapped his face, and the river ripped at him, thrusting Lyko against the side of his neck. He planted his feet and pushed back. He counted to twenty. *"Clear your face and tell me what you see."* Cal's

frozen eyes stung as he watched the wolf strain upwards through the murk.

"It turned back."

Cal lunged, his head breaking free as he gulped down the welcome air. He battled his frigid feet. Skotar seemed impossibly far away. Skin burned. *"Come on."* He grabbed Lyko with numb hands and powered forward. He lessened his drive against the current, saving his waning strength. They slipped farther and farther east.

Once more they hid from the flyer, and Cal nearly hadn't been able to bury his head in the watery coffin again. As they trudged up the enemy banks, Cal reached a snowy hand to grip a boulder, but his fingers didn't bend. He tumbled into a thicket. He needed to keep moving. He couldn't feel his fingers, and his body trembled. His thoughts turned to a warm fire, a clean dry bed, roasted dinner.

He didn't deserve those things, not when he'd failed in his mission. Freezing was nothing.

"That was refreshing." The wolf shook his thick coat and stood at the ready, eyes alert.

"How delightful for you." Cal dumped the water out of his boots, his fingers struggling with the laces. He checked his knives and shook out his sodden coat, then he balanced on stiff legs and followed Lyko. Adrenaline roused his muscles. He was in Skotar. He walked on the land of his blood, his father's land. The enemy's land. Was his brother here?

They ran for a mile. Heat pumped through Cal's veins, fighting back the chill.

"Two Dracos to the North." Lyko veered south into thick forest. He slowed, leading them away from sentries or exposed areas.

Fatigue tugged at Cal's senses as the Draco Sang camp came into view. A guard walked the perimeter, flashing in and out of view. Cal counted about two hundred tents.

"*Such a small army,*" Cal said. "*What do you think? No more than five or six hundred Dracos?*"

"*Maybe we can convince Titus to attack before more arrive.*"

"*We're attacking now.*"

Lyko flashed his canines.

"*That's got to be command.*" Cal indicated a tent larger than all but the kitchens. "*Let's start there.*" Titus had thought they might be brash enough to keep her there as a trophy. But would they find a sleeping chief instead? Titus had described his father as a buffalo with curling horns and a massive frame. Would Cal recognize him? It wasn't just his damp clothes chilling him as they waited in the shadows. He decided right then and there that, if he did meet the bull, he wouldn't hesitate to kill him, fulfill his vow and avenge his ma. He unsheathed his Dracosteel dagger. "*What's the most important thing?*"

"*Stay hidden.*"

"*We're caught, and we're dead.*"

"*What are we waiting for?*"

Cal rubbed the wolf's ears and crept out of the trees.

The camp reeked. Sweat, sewage, and animal filth assaulted Cal's senses. His eyes watered, and his stomach contracted. He swallowed the need to cough as they slipped into camp behind the sentry's back. Putrid waste lined the walks and tents.

Heart racing, they stalked in silence. Cal's eyes darted as they crept toward the center. Five Dracos sat around a campfire twenty yards to the left. They didn't look up. A Draco guarded the door to the command tent as they slunk around back.

"*We'll have to kill it,*" Lyko said.

Every second seemed an eon, their risk of detection increasing. "*I'm going in. You sniff around camp. And, Lyko...*" Fear rose in Cal like a tidal wave.

Lyko pressed a cold nose to Cal's brow and strolled into the filthy shadows. His chest caved at the sight.

He adjusted the blade in his palm and inched forward. The back of the guard's head came into view. *They killed Poe. They raped your mother. They kidnapped Callie. They're here to destroy Elysium.* He attacked. She gasped when he grabbed her, the last sound she'd ever make. He slit her throat and leaned her upright against the tent. Dripping blade angled up, he slipped inside. He closed the flap behind him, ending the hint of moonlight and the puff of fresher wind. The fleshy air inside clogged his lungs. He fought off the prodding cough that rose and held his sleeve over his mouth and nose.

The empty front room had a dark table marked with scratches and stains. Mismatched chairs surrounded it haphazardly. Farther in, past a second partition, he found a wide bed. A badger Draco slept between two naked women. *Human slaves.* Anger boiled like magma. Blood and filth smeared the gray sheets. Nasty odors festered. Embers glowed in a pit to the side.

He held his breath and slid his boots along the dusty floor. He put a knee on the bed and froze as one of the women shifted. He had no desire to slit slave throats. The Draco lay on his stomach. Cal lifted his knife, and with conviction, plunged it into the Draco's back, straight through his heart. The Draco bubbled a groan as Cal jerked his dagger out.

"No baby," Cal said as he left the room. *"But there are humans here that need saving too."* His nerves hummed. *"I killed some sort of commanding Draco. He was sleeping."*

"No baby on the west side," Lyko said. *"But, well done. Don't stop there."*

Cal could have killed Dracos all night. *"I'm headed east."* Cal stalked out of the tent. Blood dripped off his knife and splattered in the dirt. Moving from shadow to shadow, he weaved between the lines of tents.

A woman stepped into his path. Her breath hitched. Color drained from her pale cheeks. He lunged, his dirty blade glistening as he drove it forward. It froze in the air, inches from her heaving heart.

She was no Draco Sang. A slave. He looked into piercing green eyes, and the surrounding universe hazed into oblivion. A current, almost tangible, lashed across the shallow space. She sucked the air out of his lungs. Even in the darkness, her radiance struck him.

"Something smells wrong. Strange. Inviting," Lyko's voice crashed into Cal's mind, tearing him from the woman's entrapment. *"The scent is driving me mad. I need to find out what it is."*

Cal inhaled. How long had he stood paralyzed? He broke the gaze of the female now branded across his soul. He sprinted past, leaving her a statue, clutching her chest.

"A woman saw me. We need to get out."

"Why didn't you kill her?"

An image hovered in his thoughts. Emerald eyes. High cheekbones. Tall. Strong shoulders. Rich brown hair. Full lips, parted slightly in fright. *"I couldn't. I won't."*

A fraction of Cal's feelings must have traveled to Lyko because the wolf sent a seductive growl through Cal's head. *"Shall I wait in the woods whilst you mate the enemy?"*

Cal's thoughts chased after the beautiful woman. *"She isn't Draco Sang. She's human."* And she belonged in Elysium with him. He would save her. He would save them all—he would think on that later. He'd so far failed to find even the one he'd come for.

"She's no doubt sounding the alarm as we speak."

"Meet me at the southwest corner. We're crossing at the delta."

"*Follow him.*" Shale's heart flipped and fluttered.

"*I already am.*" The hawk soared out of the forest in pursuit of the handsome stranger. "*He joined a white wolf. He's like us!*"

A riot of hope and yearning exploded in Shale's chest. "*I want to know the exact path they take. Tell me if a sentry picks them up.*" Shale took a moment to suffocate her excitement before she ducked into Ferth's tent.

He slept like the dead. At first, when Keal had brought in the limp body drenched in sweat and blood, she'd thought him dead. She surprised herself by being horrified. After Ferth's attack, she should have wanted him destroyed. Should have wanted to kill him herself. Instead, she'd been immensely relieved when his chest heaved up and down. She chided her foolishness. Ferth was dangerous. He'd proven today that she'd lived in false security for too long.

She turned to the baby and, though she slept, Shale picked her up and rocked her to her chest. The man's face lit up her thoughts. Something familiar about him tugged at her memories. Perhaps he was the baby's father, and she recognized the resemblance. Perhaps she would see him again. It was a foolish dream, but it gave her hope wings. Softly, she sang her mother's lullaby to the infant at her neck.

> *Starshine, starbright, my little light.*
> *You come trailing paradise.*
> *Don't cry; you'll see you bring it with you.*
> *Sleep in peace, my starshine, my starbright.*

Hope blossomed in her chest as she swayed in the darkness.

"They're crossing at the delta. He took down a sentry with a throwing knife, but at least one other has spotted them. Guard is prepping to fire." Xandra's words shredded Shale's bright thoughts.

"Can you stop him?"

Shale closed her eyes and focused so she could watch through Xandra's eyes as her brave hawk flew straight at the Draco sentry's head. He wheeled back as claws slashed his face. He roared and swung, but Xandra was gone, flying at full speed into the trees.

"Thank you, Xandra."

"I can't follow the wolf and his man across the river now."

"I know. Come home." Shale eyed the wolf-man in her tent, a heap of darkness. If they could call this place that.

FORTY-SIX - CAPTAIN FERTH

Ferth peeled his eyes open as shouts of alarm cut through his sleep. His body groaned in one giant ache. The tent door flung open, and Dara barreled in.

"Jobu's been murdered!" Yellow eyes popped out of her head.

Her words wormed through the fog. As they registered, he jerked forward. "What?"

"Stabbed in the back as he slept."

"Who?"

"Don't know. Some say the slaves did it. There were two in his bed. Didn't think they had it in them."

Ferth rolled to his feet, his head dizzy. Pain flared across his wounds. He'd been an imbecile yesterday. Shale lay on her pallet against the wall, the babe tucked against her neck. Green eyes blinked at him as he marched by. Regret and uncertainty festered in his chest whenever he looked at the little orphan, so far from her mother.

As he stepped out of his tent, a new scent punched him in the face. He breathed deeply, mulling over the rare scent of wolf. It hardly made sense that a wolf would pass through camp. Wild animals wisely avoided this area. But he recognized the familiar scent of his own kind.

Dawn lit the chaos reigning over camp, and Ferth pushed the thoughts away as he joined the throng in front of Jobu's tent.

Pearl and another slave huddled together near the door. A soldier hovered over them, his sword flashing before their bloodless faces.

Ferth ducked into the command tent where the three other unit commanders gathered. The fire blazed in the bedroom, illuminating the deep gash in Jobu's back. The wolf scent lingered over the scene. But how? Ferth's mind raced as he stared down at his dead captain, now leaving a power vacuum he needed to fill.

"What happened?" Ferth asked the other commanders.

"We haven't found a weapon," Emil said. "But the slave women were in bed with him."

"You don't think they did it?"

"He is not liked among the slaves," Mina said.

"Who is?" Ferth's voice snapped more than he intended. "But they are just slave women, especially weak from what I saw." That wasn't exactly true; he'd seen the iron in Pearl's eyes, as hard and sharp as tempered Dracosteel.

"The guard is also dead. Throat slit clean open," Emil said.

"So, it wasn't the slaves. What other important details are you leaving out?"

Emil and Mira recoiled. Disgust and anger at his insolence painted their faces. Commander Dynacuss sat on a chair and watched.

At the sound of a scream and the snap of a whip, Ferth bolted outside. The slave girls knelt in the mud as the lash came down again on their backs. The thin fabric of Pearl's shift split open, revealing a bloody spine.

Anger seethed under Ferth's fur. He lunged forward,

ignoring his healing stitches, and jerked the strap from the young soldier's hand. Fire raced along Ferth's shoulders as he whipped it across the Draco Sang's legs. The guard fell to his knees with a howl.

"You forget your place," Ferth yelled, delivering a second lashing to the soldier's back. The same number he'd inflicted on the innocent slaves.

"They killed our captain," the Draco cried, his face distorted in pain and shock.

"I'll be the judge of that. And they're not capable of killing our captain." Ferth turned to the cowering slaves. Pearl's gray eyes held his for a moment.

She only wished she had done it. Ferth's voice softened. "Go."

The slaves clutched at each other as the crowd parted, letting them through.

"I am your new captain now," Ferth said, his voice cutting across camp.

Mina stepped forward as if to challenge him.

A sentry broke through the crowd. He bent forward, panting. Blood dripped from lacerations on his hoggish face. "An enemy soldier escaped. A man and a wolf."

Adrenaline thrashed Ferth's veins as he stood rooted to the spot. A fallen Draco did this.

An abomination had slipped into camp and murdered their captain while they all slept. And the soldier had been another son of Attor. A wolf brother. But *fallen*. What was he like? How had one capable of murder not been worthy of his blood? The hog sentry's mouth moved, and Ferth fought through his earth-shattering thoughts to hear.

"Killed Rosco with a throwing knife through the lung."

"Did you kill him?" Ferth said, his voice rising.

"I sent arrows after him as he crossed the delta, but did not see him go down." Fear flickered across the sentry's face.

"Kneel," Ferth said.

The crack of his whip sent a hawk startling out of a nearby tree. Three lashes, and Ferth's stomach turned. He could no longer bear to raise it again.

"Go find the healer," Ferth said to the sentry. "Thirro!"

The bald eagle took a tentative step out of the crowd.

"Fly north to Laconius. Hopefully he's already through the Danbe Canyon. Tell him of Jobu's murder. Tell him Captain Ferth awaits his arrival. Find out when that will be."

"Yes, captain," Thirro said before spreading brown wings and taking to the sky.

"Mina, double the sentries over the delta and along the river." This was her chance to put up a fight. Black eyes studied his, flicking over his bloody whip and seeping wounds. He towered over her.

Her lips thinned, and she nodded curtly. Emil's shoulders slumped.

Good. Ferth didn't know how much longer he could stay standing, let alone intimidate the troops. "Back to work!"

Dracos scattered.

In the privacy of his tent, Ferth fell forward on the bed Shale had replaced after he'd torn his to shreds. Exhaustion washed up his back, and pain laced through his head as his body relaxed.

"Would the *captain* like a healer?" Shale said.

"News travels fast."

"You were very loud."

He didn't think he'd been that loud. "And breakfast."

After a visit from the healer, some food, and a good washing, his mind cleared, and his muscles warmed. He set up council in the command tent to discuss events over dinner. Ferth looked up in surprise when Laconius walked in, Thirro trailing behind.

"Father." Ferth rose. "You're here. Where are your troops?"

"Two weeks behind. I pushed ahead with a small group, and when Thirro found us, we finished the journey together. There is much to discuss." Laconius thudded into the chair. "A captain, and still only half a Draco?"

"Bring meat and wine," Ferth said to an attending slave as heat flushed through his veins. He wasn't *half* a Draco. Maybe the fur was never going to grow over his face. Maybe his plight would be a life spent fighting the dragon for the last shred of his heart. But Ferth had gone from underling to captain within months. His father had no right to cut him down for a bald spot in his fur. Ferth sat, his face placid, but underneath, his temper thrummed.

Laconius drained the glass set at his place. The slave turned away, and Laconius gripped his forearm and jerked him around to face the glass. "Keep it full."

"Yes, sir," the man said. He poured the wine with trembling hands.

The tent door flew back, and Shale's eyes jerked open. She'd nodded off again while mending one of Ferth's shirts. Over the last weeks her sleep had been constantly interrupted by a hungry baby or Ferth-filled nightmares.

Ferth led Laconius into the room, heading straight for the baby. Laconius picked up the tiny girl. He sniffed her and smiled. Shale's heart turned to lead.

"Tasty little thing. You did well with her."

"Thank you, Father."

"She can't stay here. We must get her to Shi Castle. Get her a proper nursemaid, away from battle."

The gold eyes of the wolf flicked to Shale briefly, and for a heartbeat she thought she might have seen sorrow and regret there, but it was gone in a blink. A fantasy.

Ferth's face was stone when he said, "Thirro can make the journey in a day."

"We'll have Ore take her tomorrow night when he reports." Laconius turned black eyes on Shale, and her insides withered. "Have the baby well-fed and wrapped by sundown tomorrow. Have a skin of milk for Ore to feed her through the journey."

"Yes, sir." She dipped her head. Laconius's eyes bore into her, roving over her body, studying her. Ice formed over her skin. Ferth would not be able to protect her from him.

Laconius handed her the baby, and the males left the tent. A heavy breath hitched out of Shale. She turned to prepare, but not to send the baby north. No. They were going south. Tonight. She was done suffering under the hands of the corrupt Draco Sang. She'd die before she let the baby she'd grown to love so dearly go. *And I might.*

FORTY-EIGHT - JACKAL
FERTH

Ferth left Laconius in the command tent. After reporting to the hard-to-please chief, Ferth's nerves buzzed, and his head hurt. He was hungry again, but he couldn't face Shale, not when he could practically still smell his father drooling over the slave—*Ferth's* slave. Another problem to add to his list.

He headed toward the food tent. He was rounding a corner when he saw a familiar figure step out of one of the tents for the common soldiers. He knew that petite frame, the light gait. It was the amber fur coating her skull and the pointy gray ears that had him blinking and squinting.

"Jade?"

She whirled at the sound of his voice.

He halted. Her delicate nose and mouth were slightly elongated, her cheekbones sharper, her brows darker and bushier. Black lined her round eyes as if she wore kohl, making the violet hue pop. But there was no fur on her golden face, an attractive quality for any Draco Sang. Except when it was half a face—then it was a shame.

Jade's rosebud lips curled up. She strode forward, her

elbow up and her fist over her heart. He returned the greeting. The moment he dropped his elbow, she punched him, her sharp knuckles drilling into his Draco brand. The scent of female jackal whooshed over his face.

He leaned back, feigning injury. "Right in the heart."

"I have good aim."

Awkwardness hit at her serious tone. Ferth scrambled to think of something safe to say.

Jade shook off the tension with a smile. "Didn't take you long to become captain."

"Didn't take you long to transform. When was the last time a twelve-year-old grew fur? Oh, wait. How old are you pretending to be today?"

"I'm still fifteen." The way she said it, like she no longer cared if he believed her. It made him wonder. Was she telling the truth? With her sharp eyes and jackal features, she looked older now too. "But as far as the rest of them know, they think I'm one of the youngest transformed Draco Sang on record."

"Congratulations."

She flashed canines. "Congratulations on gaining such a stalwart warrior in your half company." She polished her claws on her leather vest. "I hear you need a new commander."

He laughed—truly laughed. He hardly recognized the low rumble that relaxed his whole body.

She frowned, her eyes darkening like stormy skies.

He howled—it felt so good.

She pounced. Her wiry thighs wrapping his waist, her claws digging into his shoulders.

His amusement died as his injuries protested her playful attack. "I'm glad you're here," he whispered. He might regret admitting that later, but she was his friend, and it was the truth.

She relaxed, resting her soft cheek on his shoulder. She inhaled. He scowled when her hand found the back of his neck. He wasn't ready to give her what she wanted, even if he might be starting to believe she was old enough. Gently he set her back on her feet and took a step back.

"So, you think you want to challenge Thirro for a commander position?"

A devious grin spread, her face hardening into lethal lines. "I thought you'd never ask."

Ferth chuckled, having no doubt this little jackal could take down Thirro. But would it be wise to put them in the ring together?

FORTY-NINE - PLANS
SHALE

*B*aby tight in her arms, Shale shuffled through camp to the slave quarters. She found a healer tending to Pearl's back. The rest of the closely packed beds were empty, the slaves busy around camp. Shale muttered a string of obscenities as she crouched at Pearl's side.

"That was colorful." Pearl sat up so the healer could wrap linen around her torso. "Thank you," Pearl said as the old woman helped her into a clean shift.

"I'll bring you something to eat," the healer said.

Shale waited until the older woman left before speaking again. "I brought you something too." She held out the baby, and Pearl took her with a squeal.

She kissed the baby's cheeks. "Good morning, tiny queen."

"And this." Shale held out a cup, Ferth's cup, containing his whiskey. And it was only the beginning of the day's crimes.

Pearl opened her mouth.

"Don't ask. Just drink."

Pearl chugged it. She grimaced as she handed the cup back. "Oh, yes." Her voice was hoarse. "Burn it all away."

"To Jobu's death," Shale said. "And the handsome man who killed him."

"You saw him?"

"As he was leaving." Shale couldn't help the sly grin spreading over her cheeks.

"May he come back for the rest of them," Pearl said.

Shale was done waiting on false dreams. She was going to get it done herself. "Do you still have any Lussa?"

Pearl's eyes slitted as she studied Shale.

"Please."

It was a miserable, painstaking process to stripe the baca-root of its telltale anise-flavored skin, then distill the poisonous polyps into a clear, odorless liquid. A slave woman, Pelussa, had discovered it years ago. King Icor found out, but even after torturing her blind, she never told him anything about it. She was most likely dead now—but not forgotten by the slaves. They had named their weapon after her.

Pearl often came to breakfast with dark circles under her eyes and the purply black dye from the bacaroot skins under her nails. Shale wondered where she kept her precious hoard.

"Why?" Pearl asked.

"Laconius has ordered her taken to Shi." Shale's gaze dropped lovingly to the sleeping babe. "I won't let that happen."

"And how's poison going to save her?"

"I have a plan."

Pearl's pale eyes went wide as dinner plates.

"And I won't burden you with it. But I promise at least one dead Draco." Shale knew Pearl would never leave Kenji. And Shale would never forgive herself if she led her friend into death.

Pearl didn't speak for a long time, just drank in the smell and feel of the baby. It was those wide, innocent eyes that seemed to decide it for Pearl. Her face had turned as cold and hard as her name when she looked up at Shale. "I will get you a dose. Protect this baby. Stay alive." Pearl kissed Shale's face. She handed back the baby and stood. She walked out of the tent with her spine straight and her head high, despite the wounds hidden beneath her shift.

That night, Shale waited impatiently for Ferth to return from the command tent. Her anxiety rose the longer he took, and the longer the Draco Sang had to realize twin short swords and a bottle of whiskey had been stolen.

Ferth stumbled in, drunk. She feigned sleep as he lurched over the baby's basket. She watched through slits in her lashes and held her breath as a meaty paw reached out. He stroked the baby's head and touched her cheek with shocking tenderness. He drew his hand back and growled softly, shaking himself. He pulled away from the crib and flung his muscled body over his bed. His breathing slowed and steadied.

Chest tight, Shale counted out nine minutes before she shifted herself to her feet. Hands trembling, she strapped the milk and poisoned whiskey to her shoulder and the stolen short swords and weapon belt to her waist. She tied the sleeping baby to her chest with a long strip of linen. One of Ferth's blankets made a cloak for her and the baby.

"*Clear,*" Xandra said.

Goodbye, Ferth.

Shale stepped out of the tent. She glided through camp, following the hawk's lead. It would be safer for her to move west and cross where the river deepened and the patrols were scarce. But still deadly. Two slaves attempting escape had been shot down last week. However, she had to cross at the shallow delta so the baby could stay warm and dry on her chest. The sentries shifted in less than an hour. She needed to be across the river by then.

"They don't watch their backs well," Xandra said. *"The two with eyes on the delta are sitting at the stations. Flyer roving east and west along the banks."*

As soon as the flyer made his circle and headed west again, Shale stepped onto the thin trail the sentries used.

She'd given the baby a drop of alcohol, but still she silently pleaded for her to stay asleep. She checked to make sure blankets hid the infant, then took the poisoned whiskey in her hands.

"Sirs," Shale said.

Two arrows cocked her direction as the sentries whirled around. The guards each stood on boulders watching the delta, one to her right and one to her left.

She realized too late she should have divided the whiskey into two bottles. "I bring a gift. Chief Laconius arrived, and he's pleased with the work." She forced a laugh. "Or more likely it's just that he's drunk."

The left arrow lowered slightly.

"He sends whiskey for the sentries." She held it higher and glanced around. "I thought there were three?"

"No, just two," the beetle Draco said. Moonlight flickered on his iridescent skin.

"Laconius wouldn't send us whiskey on shift."

Her pulse sped. "Must have miscalculated. Thought your shift was ending." She turned. "I'll take it back and tell him what good soldiers he's got."

"Bring it here, slave."

Arms straight in front, hiding her bulge, Shale marched up to the Draco on the right and handed him the bottle.

"That's for the both of us," the vermin on the left said, striding over from his station.

The beetle pulled the stopper and drank deeply. The rat grabbed for the skin, and the last of the drink gushed to the ground. Panic pounced on Shale's ribs as the rat punched the beetle in the face. The sentry crumpled to the ground.

Shale stepped back. "I'll go for more. I'll be right back."

"Oh, no." The guard gripped her wrist, jerking her forward. "You won't be reporting this."

The blanket slipped open, and the guard stared down in confusion at the sleeping baby. Her training, from long ago but not forgotten, came back in a rush. Shale pulled a stolen sword free and sliced across the sentry's gut before he drew his own blade. He stumbled back, and Shale silenced his roar with a thrust across his throat.

The baby woke, crying in short bursts as she sheathed her soiled sword and ran. Icy water cut into her shins as she splashed into the delta. The High Sea whirled in the moonlight on her left.

Elysium and freedom spread before her when Xandra spoke. *"Flyer is almost back. He'll see you in moments."*

Shale picked up her frozen feet, sprinting through the muddy water. Halfway there. Two hundred yards. Elysium beckoned. One hundred yards.

"Spotted," Xandra said. *"It's headed your way."*

The flapping of wings filled her ears. Her heart sank. She tilted her eyes toward the sky, and her heart stopped. Like an arrow, the gray bird dove at her. A blade glistened in its outstretched claws. Shale reached for her swords. A familiar whistle pierced the night. An arrow shot through the bird's wing, and it careened to the side, shrieking as it narrowly missed the shallow river. Shale's head whipped to the dark banks where the shot had issued, but she saw nothing. The bird flapped weakly north, retreating. She sheathed her swords and pulled the makeshift cloak back, exposing the baby. Panting and fearful, with her hands above her head, she stomped south through the numbing river. The baby's cry sailed across the water. She dragged her shaking legs up the muddy bank and past the first row of sharp timber fencing.

A soldier stood five paces away, her bow drawn and leveled at Shale. She whistled three notes. "Drop your weapons."

Shale set her sword belt in the dirt but didn't dig around for the knife on her thigh. She rocked the whining baby and shook out her frozen feet as she waited.

Another soldier broke into the clearing, his sword flashing.

"Who are you, and why did you cross the river?" the woman demanded.

"Shale. I'm an escaped slave from the Skotar camp. I come with information and to return this stolen baby."

The sentry spoke to the other soldier. "She drew the flyer within range. I hit him in the wing."

The man picked up Shale's swords and gripped her elbow. "Come with me."

Her heart slammed against her ribs as he led her through the forest. *I made it. I'm here!* Despite the clamp on her arm, she was free.

Shale's eyes widened as she entered camp. Joy swelled at the tents lined up in precise rows. No garbage littered the walks.

"Not as many rats to hunt," Xandra said as she circled high above, out of sight.

Shale reeled as a wolf popped out from behind a tent and blocked their path.

The guard's grip tightened on Shale's arm as if in fear.

The wolf's golden eyes locked on Shale. *Ferth!* She froze for a heartbeat. Slowly her breath returned. This wolf wasn't Ferth. She was free from him forever.

The white predator slunk forward and sniffed at the

blanket hiding her treasure from the cold and wind. He growled, and the hairs on her spine stood up.

A figure appeared behind the wolf, and she gasped at the gorgeous man still hovering in her thoughts. Honeyed eyes locked on hers, and he jolted when the recognition hit.

"She crossed from Skotar at the delta," the guard said. "Claims to be an escaped slave. I'm taking her to Titus."

The man never took his eyes off her. "Thank you, Erak. I'll handle this. Return to your post."

His voice rang through her bones. Where had he haunted her dreams? Where had he come from? How did he feel so familiar?

"Yes, Cal." Erak turned to leave.

The baby cried and Shale pulled back the cloak. Cal's whole face changed. Starlight glittered over the moisture growing in his eyes.

"Callie," he whispered.

Callie. After this man—her father. The name settled like a warm bath. Shale had been unwilling to call her Uictoria. She began to untie Callie to hand her to her father, but Cal held out a forestalling hand.

"No. You must be the one to return her to her mother. You can't imagine how ... I can't ..." Words failed the man, and he turned his face away, hiding emotion. "Come."

He reached an arm out to support her back, but retracted it without touching her. He guided her to another large tent, grabbing a torch from a campfire along the way. The wolf yapped once before Cal threw back the flap. "Zemira! Shem!"

A feline growl greeted them. Shale hesitated on the threshold.

Cal threw his torch at the waiting logs. The fire crackled to life, illuminating two sleeping bodies and a panther.

There are so many more like me.

"What is it, Cal? Can't it wait until day?" the woman asked, her voice sleepy and annoyed.

The baby chose that moment to cry out, and the woman shot up. A large bare-chested man jerked up next to her.

"She's here," Cal said, his voice giddy.

Shale's chest swelled with joy when the woman's eyes landed on the babe in her arms.

"My Callie?"

Shale reverently held her out as she glided forward. A heart-melting cry escaped the mother. She took her baby and held her against her face. Tears rolled down her cheeks. The woman's bliss was palpable in the room. The mother turned the baby toward the man. Streams streaked his round features as well.

"My girl," he said as he kissed the tiny face. He pulled back the linens, and the mother laughed as he kissed the tiny arms and chest.

As their tears bathed the baby, Shale felt as if she watched something not meant for her. Something too sacred, too beautiful for her to witness.

As she stepped toward the door, the woman caught her eye. She extended a hand. "Come."

Shale reached forward, and the woman's wiry hands gripped her fingers.

"What's your name?"

"Shale."

"You took care of her."

It wasn't a question. Shale wondered if they could see just how much she loved Callie. She nodded.

"Thank you, Shale," Zemira said.

The man's deep voice cut in. "Zemira and I owe you our lives."

"No," Shale said. "You owe me nothing. She gave me the courage to escape. I owe her. You."

"Tell us everything," Zemira said.

Shale's knees buckled at the thought.

Concern flashed across Zemira, and her dark eyes took in Shale's wet shift. She gave Cal a chiding look.

"She needs help."

Cal wiped at his eyes and stepped forward. "I know." He leaned in and kissed the baby's cheek. "Uncle Cal's sure glad you're home," he whispered.

Zemira beamed at Cal, and a pang of jealousy ran through Shale at their closeness. She longed to have a family like this. She used to have a family. But they had been torn from her.

Cal's eyes found Shale. He was not the father. Hope made her feel wild and unfettered. Maybe her dream was not dead. A blissful smile lit up her face.

Seemingly frozen, he stared at her. Stared at her eyes, her mouth. After a charged moment, he broke her heavy gaze and led her out of the tent.

"Better take you to Captain Titus," Cal said.

The weight of the baby lifted from her chest, the blanket of freedom lay heavy on her shoulders. Shale sagged, then stumbled.

The wolf darted out. Thick fur caught her as she fell. Ferth's musky smell hit her as she folded over its back.

Could she never fully escape him?

Cal's hands gripped her waist, sending lightning along her nerves. Warmth spread through her sides as he helped her off the muscled animal and to her feet.

"Thanks," she mumbled, her face hot.

"Titus can wait. Sleep first." Cal held out an elbow, and gratefully she latched onto the muscled forearm like a lifeline.

Back in the privacy of his tent, Cal glanced around awkwardly. "I should have borrowed clothes from Zemira."

He dug in his trunk and set folded fabric on his bed. "You can use mine if you want until I can get you a better set." He pointed to a basin. "The water is cold, but it's fresh." He ran a nervous hand through chestnut hair. "We'll leave you to rest. I'll come back in a couple hours with breakfast."

"Where are you going?"

He shifted on his feet. "I'll be just outside."

"Standing guard." Her voice held an edge of challenge.

The side of his lip turned up—just enough to hint how handsome his smile would be. She wanted to see it. Something for her to look forward to. So many bright lights now illuminated a future of great possibilities.

"Holler if you need anything," he said. The wolf followed him out.

She sighed, a deep releasing exhale. She and the baby—no, *Callie*—had made it to Elysium alive. And now she was in Cal's tent. His bed. And she was not afraid.

Bliss bubbled in her chest. She grinned as she fingered the clean clothes folded neatly on the fresh bed. She threw off her dirty rags, her slave uniform. *Never again.* Bare skin prickled against the cold and the thought of Cal on the other side of the canvas.

She scrubbed at sweat and grime. The night air of the spacious tent nipped at her tender skin. She shivered, feeling vulnerable without the protection of other bathing slave women surrounding her. Hiding her. She looked down at her chest, at the Draco Sang brand she'd hidden for three years. She scratched at the layer of grayish marl she'd spread over it. It wasn't a perfect solution, but she kept her long hair over the spot when she bathed or changed around other slaves. She'd managed to keep her secret safe, keep Xandra safe. There were other slaves with Draco brands, but their animals had been killed. It was better they didn't think the same had happened to her. It was better to hide the truth.

She was done hiding.

She dunked the rough cloth into the soapy water and scoured at the delicate skin above her left breast. Chalky rivulets ran down her body. Her brand shone white against pink skin.

GS10285.

Exposed. Her mouth curved up in a bow. No. *Liberated.*

Glee galloped through her chest. She threw the towel into the bucket with a splash and held out her arms. The slave brand on her forearm glistened in the low firelight.

Her brands were her badges—of pride, of strength, and now, of freedom. Her cackling laughter rolled like thunder, wild and exuberant. She twirled, her arms outstretched, her eyes closed, and her head tilted up. Unbound hair tickled her back.

"You alright—"

Her eyes popped open as Cal's voice cut off. She jerked into a huddled crouch.

Cal's mouth hung limply, as did the drawn dagger in his hand. "I heard …" His brow furrowed in confusion as he glanced around the tent. He looked at his boots.

"I'm fine," she said with a snap.

"Alright then." He whipped around and darted back out of the tent.

She sucked in calming breaths. He had simply left. No remarks. No advances. He seemed as flustered as she.

Her joy returned, however less feral now. Elysium was all she had dreamed of. And she had a lifetime to enjoy it. Gloriously clean, she strapped her knife back to her thigh and snuggled into the large pants and shirt.

Cal's clothes, she thought with a thrill.

She fell into bed wondering why she still smelled Ferth. His half-human face filtered across her vision. She hoped his punishment for her escape wasn't too severe.

FIFTY - STRIPPED
FERTH

"You may choose," Laconius said through an icy smile. Black hair coiled down from curling horns. The queen's chief made the pretense of relaxing in a large chair, but his shoulders cinched tight. Rage tinged his beady eyes.

Ferth swallowed, trying to dislodge the dread clotting in his throat. He'd woken, with a sinking feeling, to an empty tent. She'd gone. Taken the baby and left. Escaped. He'd yet to sift through his shockingly complex feelings about it. He missed her. He hated her. He hoped she was safe. He wished her back in chains. He was irate at himself and at her.

He stood before his father. Condemned. *A failure.*

Laconius's square jaw rippled. The other officers in the command tent blurred out of focus.

"Be stripped of your rank, your place, your name. *Or,* be stripped of the skin on your back."

"I'll take the lashes." His voice was flat and solid, but his still-healing wounds sang out in warning.

Laconius nodded his approval, his body relaxing. "Ovis, bring me the crop."

A chair shrieked as the Draco rushed to obey. Laconius stood and thumped an encouraging hand on Ferth's shoulder before leading the group outside. The sun seemed to stall its rising as they walked the chilly path to the training yard. The gathering crowd grew.

To enjoy Ferth's shame. They thought seeing him beaten would make them feel better. *No.* Watching him not break would quell them.

"Do you wish to be tied?" Laconius asked.

Ferth spit on the ground.

His father's lip twitched up on one side.

Ferth ripped his shirt over his head and dropped it in the dirt. The breeze ran chilling fingers down the red gash along his ribs and shoulder. The rope, braided with steel thorns, dangled from Laconius's paw. Ferth gripped the leather straps hanging from the high training bar. Arms stretched above his head, human patch of skin on his chest bare to the world, he waited. Good thing he'd already peed.

Heavy feet shuffled. The fur on his back stood on end.

Don't scream.

Speeding leather whistled. Searing pain lashed his back and spread through his limbs. He grunted and smashed his teeth together. The whip landed again. Inches lower this time. He arched and clenched the leather with slippery fingers. He would not fall. He would not scream.

Laconius wasn't going soft on his son.

Whip. *Three.*

Ferth didn't expect him to.

Whip. *Four.*

Blood dripped down his burning back and into his pants. *Five.*

The agony was everywhere. It consumed him. *Six.*

Ferth searched the crowd. Thirro's eyes danced in glee.

Seven.

Distress painted Jade's delicate features. He wished she didn't have to see this.

Eight.

Dara and Mina stood together with twin expressions of rapt attention, taking pleasure in watching Ferth taken down a notch, or—

Nine.

He was on fire. In hell. His head couldn't keep up with the overwhelming pain. His skull throbbed. Black and red spots flickered in his vision. His fingers slipped in the leathers.

No. Don't let go. Do not fall.

Ten.

Pearl stood at the back of the crowd, unnoticed by the Dracos. Gray eyes latched on his.

Come to watch. Get her revenge.

Eleven.

But her lips didn't mock. Her face didn't revel. Her intent eyes held him up. She lifted her chin in defiance, as if inviting him to do the same.

Twelve.

Skinny and cold and all alone in the crowd, she fed him courage, comfort, and compassion.

Thirteen.

His gaze didn't break from Pearl's, and she held it. Anchored him. She stayed there as stone. For him.

Fourteen.

I am stone.

Fifteen.

I'm wrong about humans.

Sixteen.

Pearl's eyes blurred into a vision of Shale.

Seventeen.

Shale left me.

Eighteen.
She left me.
Nineteen.
She left me.
Twenty.
Goodbye, Shale. I wish you well.
Twenty-one.

FIFTY-ONE - SHALE
CAL

As the sun rose, bringing life to the camp, word of Callie's return and the escaped slave spread. A few brave soldiers approached Cal as he sat guarding the door of his own tent, but he had little information, and they soon left him alone with his festering thoughts.

The vision of Shale's unfettered dance clung to him. Dark hair cascaded down, a silky covering over rough scars. So many scars. What stories did they tell? What kind of hell had she suffered? And yet her smile had lit up the world.

Despite her strength, her soft silhouette was utterly feminine, so different than wiry Zemira. Shale would free him from those chains. And trap him in new ones.

Thirty yards down, Shem emerged from his tent bearing treasure. He held Callie up to the waiting crowd, and a rolling cheer washed across camp.

Happiness warmed Cal as he wormed his fingers into Lyko's fur. *"Don't let anyone in. I'll be back with breakfast."*

"Yup."

Uriah intercepted him. "I heard you already got the girl in your tent." Dark brows wiggled.

"She *did* sleep in my bed."

Uriah chuckled. "Without you."

"Give me time," Cal said, his voice teasing.

"I'd say you've got about until she meets me."

Cal pursed his lips.

"The truth hurts, brother. You just can't compete with this." Uriah stroked his wide jaw.

Cal punched Uriah on the arm.

"Ow. *That* hurts." Uriah rubbed his shoulder. "Touchy this morning. Already fallen in love, I see."

Cal laughed out loud. "I seriously think I might have. She's perfect."

Uriah snorted. "A soft wind could knock you over, you fall so easily."

Cal inhaled the fresh morning air. "It's the best way to live."

Uriah rolled his eyes, his voice deadpan. "Yes. I can see how well that's been going for you so far."

"Oh, yeah? And where's your girlfriend?"

"That's fair."

They were almost to the mess tent. "You coming to breakfast?"

"In a minute. I've got a message for Commander Asvig. Oh." Uriah dug into his pocket. "And I snagged this for you." Uriah handed over a letter before striding toward the armory. Cal watched him go, wondering if Uriah would ever look right without his bear, and knowing he would not. Pushing away the sudden grief, Cal turned to the paper in his palm and read as he walked.

Dear Callidon,
Your grandpapi and I are well and remain at Elssa's house in
Mitera. Papi's found he's now got the energy to play all day with
grandchildren. I've found work as a housekeeper at the city home of

Raja Darius—Titus's doing. They treat me well, and the house is exquisite. How far we've come from Siccum!

Of course I wish you could have stayed here with us, but I know you and Lyko are where you should be. I am so proud of you. So grateful you are my son. You've taken what many could have seen as a curse and turned it into a strength, a weapon of service for others.

I love you.

Ma

Write to me!

Cal glowed as he tucked the letter into his uniform. He conjured his mother's beaming face when he'd greeted her in Mitera and introduced her to Lyko. She'd seemed years younger. Radiant and alive—how she should have always been, but the savage Draco had stolen that from her. Now, his family was happy. And he would make sure they stayed that way.

He picked up breakfast plates and returned to his tent to find Lyko, teeth bared and ears up, pacing in front of the door, blocking Titus.

"Doesn't he know who's in command here?" Titus asked.

"Yes, he does." Cal tossed the wolf a roast chicken. "Nicely done, Lyko."

"Insubordination." But Titus's lips curved up.

"Shale is the slave I saw when I infiltrated their camp."

Titus's eyes turned serious. "The scouts haven't seen pursuers coming after her, and the Skotar sentries still watch the delta. Why did she risk her life to return a baby to people she doesn't know?"

"Let's go find out."

Titus pulled out a long knife and held it forward as he wrenched the tent open. The precaution was unneeded. The woman didn't shift a hair from her prostrate position.

Cal's blood warmed to see her spread over his bed. *His* shirt draped around her curves. The curves he tried in vain not to picture. She looked so peaceful, so young and unburdened in sleep. He set the plate of potatoes, pig, and pears on the table and pulled open the window flaps, letting in the sun.

"Excuse me, miss," Titus said.

The girl's green eyes popped open. She lurched to a sitting position. Her hands flew to her chest, clutching the loose clothes.

"I'm Captain Titus. Welcome to Elysium, Shale. It's a pleasure to meet you."

Her eyes drifted from Titus to Cal to the plate on the table. Cal carried it to her, and her fingers leapt to the dish. He put a mug in her hand. She brought it to her lips and moaned.

He bit back a smile, thinking of the first tavo he'd had. To share the creamy-spiced goodness with her was even more of a pleasure. Her calloused hands gripped the cup like treasure.

Titus studied her in silence as she dug into the food. Every few bites, she looked up, and red dusted her cheeks before she shoveled more in.

"How many soldiers are at the camp?" Titus asked.

He doesn't waste time.

She didn't flinch. Didn't look up from her meal. "Five hundred and three. You took out seven this winter, but ten more arrived yesterday. Ferth is now Captain after you killed Jobu." Eyes flicked to Cal. "There are three unit commanders under Ferth. He'll appoint two more soon. Queen Mavras's second, Chief Laconius, arrived yesterday. Two thousand troops are expected in six days. They intend to attack immediately. They'll struggle to feed the troops beyond midsummer. They'll need to hold Elysium before snowfall, for the food as well as for the victory."

Titus glanced at Cal, his face betraying his delight, before turning back. "Where's your hewan?"

Cal reeled.

"Didn't I mention that?" Lyko said.

He hated when Lyko kept secrets.

Shale looked as if she'd been turned to ice.

"Your animal," Titus said.

She studied the captain for long silent seconds.

Titus didn't change his calm demeanor. "They call me the collector for a reason. You can't hide it from me. I am very good at picking out Dracos."

"If you lose your heritage in Skotar, they kill your animal."

Cal swallowed sadness, but Titus's calm demeanor didn't change. "Yes. A terrible practice. Fortunately, that's not what happened to you."

Shale blinked in surprise.

"Your hewan is safe here," Titus said. "What's more, she is welcome and wanted."

Silent seconds ticked by as Shale studied Titus as if reading him.

Cal jolted as a hawk soared into the tent and landed gracefully next to her on the bed.

He stared. She'd defeated her beast while living among dragons.

"That's better." Titus nodded. "Impressive hawk."

"Xandra."

"Welcome to our army," Titus said.

The bird cawed.

Eio padded into the tent, and Shale nearly dropped her plate.

"Let me introduce my hewan. This is Eio."

"The Lion," Shale said, her voice shaky. Fear pinched her face. "Chief Laconius hunts you. Many have sworn to bring him your head."

Cal's blood frosted, but Titus's face remained impassive. "Yes. There is no love lost between us."

Shale set the empty plate aside, and her eyes glazed briefly.

"Sleep," Titus said. "We'll visit more later. You've already earned our praise, gratitude, and respect. You're a brave soldier, and we'll gladly have you join us. But you've earned the right to move south and never return, if you choose."

Green eyes lit up her whole face as his words hit home.

Please don't leave. Cal exited the tent after Titus, taking one last look at the girl curled up on his bed before he closed the flap.

"I'm going after Laconius," Cal said as they strode toward command.

Titus halted, and what looked like grief swept across his face. He put a hand on Cal's shoulder and steered him back the other way. Cal marched along in confusion, willing Titus to explain, but the man had turned to iron.

When they arrived at Titus's tent, Eio stood guard out front instead of joining them inside as usual. Cal's brows pinched together as Titus stopped near the cold fire pit. He again put a hand on Cal's shoulder.

"Laconius is your father."

Cal's mind folded over on itself, and then a volcano of thoughts erupted. Laconius. Second to the queen. Leader of the enemy. He raped his ma. He stole his brother. He destroyed their family. "I'm going to kill him." Hatred blossomed in Cal's chest.

"You'll get the chance soon enough. I've wanted him dead for eighteen years."

"And yet he lives." And was leading an army into their land.

"He isn't so easy to kill." Titus's voice took on a warning

tone. "Do not underestimate him. For now, we prepare for battle."

They'd be more prepared for battle with the enemy's head cut off. "If it's all right with you, I'd like to have you as my father."

Titus's eyes glistened. "Son." He lifted sinewy arms, and Cal leaned forward into the embrace. Home.

Ferth couldn't move. The healer had gone an hour earlier, and still he lay prostrate across his bed. The balms and herbs plastered to his back had soothed the sharpness from the pain, but his skin and muscle pulled tight and stiff. Laconius was skilled with the crop—it came with experience. And Ferth had no permanent damage or deep injuries, unless he counted the new scars. He did not.

But he was tired. So tired.

Get up. Get up and stand before your troops. Show them you are above the pain. You are above it all.

His face didn't come off the sheets, but his gaze shifted to the door as feet shuffled outside. A slave entered, a sturdy woman with crimpy hair and hard-set eyes.

"Captain, sir, how may I assist you?" Her voice was placid.

No. She would not do. "Go get Pearl."

Her brow furrowed, her only sign of disapproval, before she left. An eternity later, Pearl slipped into the tent. She stood a foot from the door, her hands clasped in front of her shift dress, her face blank.

"Come here," Ferth said, his voice harder than he intended. His back hurt.

She glided to his side.

"Help me up." He held out his arm.

She gripped it with calloused, wiry hands and pulled up. He howled. She flinched.

Panting and grimacing, but sitting upright, he said, "Bring me a drink."

"Yes, captain."

He sucked down air, pushing his pain into a dark corner of his mind. When she reappeared, he'd gained some control. The drink was strong. *Thank you, Pearl.* The burning in his throat and belly a welcome distraction, he pointed to his trunk, and she darted over to retrieve his clothes. Wordlessly she helped him into his shirt. Lifting his arms was torture. Palms braced on her shoulders, he stood and untied his pants, bloody and sweaty from the whipping. They dropped to the floor. Pearl helped him into a clean pair. Finished, she turned away, but he gripped her thin shoulders, stopping her. She kept her face tilted down.

"Pearl," he said.

She turned at the tenderness in his voice. Silver eyes found his.

"Thank you," he said.

She balked.

"You strengthened me this morning. You got me through it. You kept me up. Holding on." He took his hands off her shoulders. "I will find a way to repay the favor."

Her mouth hung open. He left his tent with a smug smirk. It fell when he saw Laconius approaching.

"Captain." Dark eyes glowed with pride. Yes, Ferth had taken his beating well. "My son."

Laconius's gaze flicked over Ferth's shoulder, and Ferth

turned to see Pearl exit his tent. She looked up, and her posture shifted. She hobbled over, and her face turned away.

"You there. Come here," Laconius said.

She ignored him, pretending she didn't know he spoke to her.

"Slave girl." His voice hardened.

Pearl looked up, her eyes beseeching Ferth before she focused on the chief.

"Come with me." He turned his head to Ferth. "We'll push the command meeting back an hour."

"No," Ferth said. Why did every second of his life feel like a battle? He wanted to rest. He was so tired.

Laconius looked at him, incredulous.

"She's in no position to satisfy you currently." Ferth's voice exuded cockiness.

His father's brows nearly reached his horns. He chuckled. "Fine. Keep your plaything. My gift to you. Although you lost the baby, you made me proud today." He thumped Ferth on the back in derisive compliment.

Ferth's claws dug into his palms, clenching against the wave of anger and flare of pain. He fantasized slamming his father in his wide snout. Maybe knocking out a few of those big teeth. His fists remained at his sides. "Thank you, Father," Ferth said through a locked jaw.

Pearl darted back into his tent.

His debt was paid.

FIFTY-THREE - DISTRACTED
SHALE

Shale's heart beat faster when Cal came into his tent, her focus homing in on the young man.

"You're up," Cal said when he spied her sitting near the fire.

"And fed again." She'd wanted to see him smile. He didn't. He strode to his trunk and rummaged around, brows drawn.

"They issued me a tent," Shale said.

He shifted a pile of neatly folded shirts.

"My own tent."

"What?" His chin tilted her direction, but his eyes stayed at his work. "Stay here as long as you like."

Shale frowned.

He pulled out a stiff leather vest and thick pants, then set them aside.

She unfolded her legs and slid from the chair. She padded close and laid a hand on his corded forearm, below his rolled-up sleeves. He dropped the knives he held and looked at her in surprise, as if just realizing she was there. His golden gaze focused on her face. Those eyes. She knew those eyes.

"I'm going to my own quarters," she said. "I wanted to say thank you for taking me in when I arrived. I am not used to such kindness or care." She didn't expect the emotion that expanded in her chest—hope and gratitude, and something deeper in her belly. Her voice thickened. "You're a good man." She wanted to run her fingers up his arm, feel the warm muscles. She forced her hand away from his skin. *Don't rush it.* She was free now, with all the time in the world.

One corner of his lip tilted up. Almost a smile. "You just don't know me well enough yet."

The wicked dance in his eyes hit her like a memory. His familiarity itched at her sanity. Had she known him as an underling? When she smiled, his gaze traveled to her mouth, and her blood awoke.

"I'm a good judge. You'll see," she said, tilting closer, aching to be held, kissed.

"You're comparing me to Draco Sang. You're in Elysium now. You'll soon learn." He didn't close the gap. Didn't put those strong hands on her waist and draw her in. He turned back to his knives.

Disappointment sank through her like a stone through water. "Well then, I'm off to scout." She made the words float out in a teasing tone.

He chuckled, but didn't look up, distracted once more by his preparations. *For what?* Her mood darkened when he didn't seem to notice her leave. Or care. The camp didn't feel quite as welcoming anymore.

A visit to baby Callie and some dinner perked her up, but she had a hard time falling asleep in her tent. The air was too clean; the tent was too quiet; the bed was too soft.

"Cal snuck out of camp," Xandra said.

Shale bolted upright, rubbing at the sleep clinging to her face. *"What time is it?"*

"Midnight. I've been watching him for an hour. He reminds me of master Ferth."

So her eyes weren't playing tricks on her. An eerie wave of recognition washed over Shale as she sat in bed, blankets clutched to her breast. When Cal had tilted his face, it could have almost been Ferth, turning his human features towards her. They shared the same heart-piercing golden gaze, as did Lyko. How could it be?

Xandra broke through Shale's churning thoughts. *"He's been careful not to be seen by his own sentries. He's going west along the river with his wolf."*

"Skotar. He's going back." Cold fingers squeezed Shale's heart. The brave fool. Luck and Xandra had saved him the first time. But a second time?

She'd sworn to never return to Skotar. And she swore it again to her empty tent. *Never again.* She almost relented, almost accepted the freedom and safety of staying in her warm bed surrounded by Elysium soldiers. Almost.

"I'm up. I'm getting dressed."

"Hurry," Xandra said. *"He's nearly to the river."*

FIFTY-FOUR - MEETING
FERTH

Ferth's eyes flew open as wolf scent shot up his nose. He jumped off his bed, the stripes on his back flaring. He glanced at Shale's empty pallet, a reminder of why he'd been whipped. And what he had lost. He stalked forward, nostrils flared.

The scent was stronger than before, wild and familiar. It itched at his brain and chafed at his chest. His grip tightened on his sword. In the short hours before the dawn, silence reigned over camp. Sentries patrolled the outskirts, partially visible through the tents as they made their rounds.

Jobu's dead body flicked through Ferth's mind. His heart sped, and his limbs steadied as he crept toward command. The abomination would not succeed this time. His fall would be Ferth's redemption, his glory.

Nerves on fire, Ferth pulled back the tent flap and slipped into the dark command room. The scent suffocated his thoughts as he inched toward the bedroom. The divider lay ajar and, through it, a figure stood over Laconius.

In the man's hand, a blade made from Dracosteel glistened. He held it out, frozen over the chief.

Ferth's muscles coiled to attack. Protect his father. Kill the invader. A white wolf appeared, blocking his path. Ferth recoiled at the golden stare. The familiar eyes devoured the air from his lungs, binding him in confusion.

The blade in the killer's hand hitched a fraction higher over his father.

"No," Ferth yelled as the knife plunged down. He lunged, slamming the wolf back, knocking him into the man.

The blade sank deep into Laconius's chest. It landed wide, missing his father's heart. The wolf's paws crashed into Ferth's chest, shoving him to the floor. The killer ripped his blade free as Laconius's roar shook the tent. Laconius jerked forward. As the human thrust his knife down again, Laconius thrashed his head, hooking a horn into the man's side, tearing through flesh.

The human gasped and crumpled over his knees. The golden-eyed wolf whirled with a distraught whine. The assassin held out shaking hands and gripped white fur.

Ferth jerked to his feet, his wounded back barking. The wolf and his man ran from the tent. Blood dripped along the floor in their wake.

"Kill him, son," Laconius gurgled as he flopped back on his bed, a hand clutching at the hole in his chest.

Ferth tore at a strip of bedding and tied it furiously around Laconius's weeping wound.

"Go," he wheezed. "Get them."

Ferth tightened the knot, willing his father to live, then flew from the tent. He found a guard pursuing the wolf and his man.

"Go to Laconius. He needs a healer. I'll bring in the enemy."

The guard grunted and turned back.

A tinge of worry struck Ferth as he left camp and entered

the trees. Could the killer have help? Could he have escaped? The fresh blood on the trail told him no.

A quarter-mile into the woods, he spotted his prey. The full moon lit up the scene. The man stumbled as he ran, an arm pressed over his stomach. The wolf turned his cursed eyes—Ferth's eyes—back on Ferth, staying behind the wounded man like a guard.

Ferth barreled forward, closing the gap. He swung his sword. The wolf lunged. Sharp canines sank into Ferth's forearm. The sword in his right hand fell to the dirt, but his left fist connected with the man's wounded side. The man dropped to the ground and rolled onto his back.

The wolf stood over the human, his bloody fangs bared and threatening. Ferth pulled a knife from his belt. To end this. Kill the man who'd murdered Jobu and nearly ended his father.

The human groaned, and blood gurgled in his throat. "Brother," the man said. "My brother." The man tilted his face, and Ferth's world shattered. Ferth's human face stared back at him. "I found you." A sad smile spread.

Thoughts churned in a confused whirl. The only thing stopping Ferth's strike was the man's face. Proof. His face. His twin. His blood.

No. This was the enemy.

But—

My brother.

He had a brother.

Ferth gasped, willing air into paralyzed lungs.

The wolf crouched in front of Ferth with his familiar scent, stirring Ferth's insides and awakened old longings for home. He needed to kill this man, needed to avenge the wrong, but he could not move. Could not strike out at that face. *My face.* Yearning struck deep and fast. The blade slipped from Ferth's hand, and his legs buckled. His thoughts jammed into place as his knees rammed in the ground.

He had a brother. A blood brother. And he wanted to keep him. Know him. "Brother," Ferth said, the word delicious and powerful on his tongue.

His twin lifted an ashen face. "Cal."

"Ferth." Amber eyes locked on their matching pair and a tentative connection formed, new, yet deeper than any loyalty he had ever known.

A branch broke. Fast footsteps heralded someone's approach from the south. Ferth's training failed him, and he stayed inert at Cal's side as Shale burst through the trees. She wore the clothes of an Elysium soldier.

He'd gone mad. Seeing visions. What new trickery was this? These faces couldn't be real. But her scent, like juniper and desire, palpable and strong, slapped his brain.

She held out a knife. He could disarm her within seconds. Kill her in a beat. Her green eyes pierced Ferth's for a moment, heating his heart. Her focus darted to Cal. Her face drained as she studied the wound.

"I won't stop you," Ferth said. "I won't hurt you."

She dropped to Cal's side and sliced through the leather vest that had done little to stop Laconius's horn. She ripped at his undershirt, exposing a deep jagged gash. She whimpered as she tore at the linens.

The white wolf's eyes never left Ferth.

Ferth jerked his head at shouting in the trees. His soldiers were coming. Coming to kill his brother. Coming to do what he should have already done. His thoughts warred. *Traitor* pulsed in his mind. He could not kill his brother, but his soldiers could. He stood. He would sneak back to camp.

A blood-stained palm wrapped around his wrist, and he turned his face to Shale's pleading eyes. He missed her. Ached for her. *Loved—*

He choked.

"Ferth." His name on her tongue trapped him. "Please help me. He'll die."

She would die. He should execute her. Her gaze broke him, remade him. He was hers to command. He wanted to follow her.

He found his sword and wordlessly got up, finally giving in to the human voice that had plagued him all his life. He stood, *treasonous fool,* ready to forfeit all he'd accomplished, all he'd worked for, his *life.* For what?

For his brother.

For Shale.

For the spark inside that lit this path forward.

Three Dracos broke into view. Ferth attacked, catching them by surprise. He killed the first in one stroke. The white wolf appeared at his side. Together they fought against the other two.

Ferth expected to feel like a traitor, like a coward. But as he fought to protect Shale and Cal, his chest expanded and his limbs strengthened. Unexpected wholeness filled up the deep void in his soul. The last Draco fell.

Panting and invigorated, Ferth whirled back to Shale.

"I can't stop the bleeding," Shale said, terror grinding out her words.

The wolf paced in a maniacal circle.

Ferth knelt. "Live, brother. Live!" *Live.*

He gripped Cal's palm. Belonging rushed through the touch. Tears flowed down Ferth's cheeks as love exploded through his heart. He gasped as fire shot along his spine and through his veins. Shifting shadows swirled around his eyes. He swayed and gagged. He blinked out the fog, and a gray wolf with golden eyes blinked back. Ferth glanced down in shock at his bare skin and wholly human features. *Unworthy of your blood. An abomination.* His father's voice faded into

Keturah's. *Your mother gave you courage and honor. You were made for greatness.*

His eyes flicked up at Shale's sharp inhale. She gaped at him, frozen and white-faced.

Cal wheezed. He needed a healer. Ferth crawled forward, adjusting to his new form. He picked up Cal's bloody bone-handled knife from the dirt and stuck it into his belt. Gingerly, he lifted his brother's fevered body into his arms, surprised by his own strength. *Never mistake humanness for weakness.*

Ferth ran. Power coursed through human veins.

Please follow, he thought to the animal he'd just created. He couldn't process it, but he knew deep in his soul that he didn't want to lose this new wolf. This part of himself that now wasn't. He nearly tripped when he heard a returning voice in his head.

"I will."

With a new burst of energy and hope, Ferth charged through the forest. He would outrun death.

"Brother," Cal said, pain lacing the word.

"I'll get you home." The burning in Ferth's arms and back hardly registered as he pressed on in a fearful frenzy. "You're going to be fine."

"No." The severity in Cal's tone halted Ferth's feet.

Cal's face was too pale, his breath too shallow, his pulse too weak.

Ferth laid Cal in a bed of ferns as Shale caught up. If he could just tighten the bandages …

"Brother." Cal smiled as he took in Ferth's matching features.

"Stay with me," Ferth pleaded. He pressed a hand to Cal's sticky side, willing the life to stay inside. He needed more time. He needed a lifetime.

Sorrow crossed Cal's eyes, and anguish painted his face.

"Our mother?" Ferth couldn't stop the question that he'd harbored forever.

"Mira. She lives."

Mira.

"Ma is …" Words seemed to fail him, but the look in his eyes told Ferth that she was all the goodness he'd ever dreamed of. "Find her. She is with Grandpapi and Aunt Elssa in Mitera. Take care of her. Tell her I love her. Tell her it was worth it to bring you back."

Joy swept through Ferth despite the exquisite pain cracking his heart. His vision blurred. "You will tell her. You *will.*"

"And tell Titus …" Cal coughed.

"You will tell them everything." Ferth wanted Cal to live more than he'd ever wanted anything before. Above gritted teeth, tears poured down his cheeks, falling on his brother's ashen forehead.

"Tell Titus that he was always my true father. He will welcome you. He has watched for you."

Ferth's limbs lay heavy, overwhelmed.

"It is enough to know that I found you. I didn't dare to hope that I would ever meet you. That I could feel so much." The brightness in Cal's eyes cut through the agony on his face. "But I am satisfied. And you will go home. You will protect our family."

"With my life," Ferth said. "With every breath and ounce of my strength and skill. I swear it."

Cal looked to Shale. She knelt close by his side and took his hand. "I saw your scars," he said. "And they are beautiful. I wanted you to know that."

She leaned over and pressed her lips to his, a soft, sad kiss. Her tears slipped onto his cheeks as she drew back.

And then Cal smiled, full and glowing.

She touched his curving lips. "You're smiling." She sobbed

as her fingers danced over his face. "And it's beautiful." She kissed him again.

Feelings overwhelmed Ferth as the pain in his chest intensified. He couldn't process what was happening between the woman he loved and his brother.

Cal reached a bloody hand out and rested it on the white muzzle on his chest. "Lyko. Protect our brother. He is your master now. He is your home."

A heart-wrenching wail escaped the wolf. Lyko licked Cal's face. He nuzzled his master's neck. His long spine shuddered. With a whimper, he turned stricken eyes up to Ferth.

"Brother," Lyko said in Ferth's mind. The voice was Cal's, with the same southern accent and rich tones. Ferth twitched in shock. *"Little brother,"* Lyko said to the gray wolf, but Ferth heard it in his mind too.

Ferth's gray wolf, slightly smaller than Lyko, lowered his head to Lyko.

Cal's eyes glazed over, and his pulse silenced. His hand slipped off Lyko's head and settled on the ground.

Shale's pale lips curled back. "No."

"May the Dragon keep you …" The words cut over Ferth's tongue like razors. The Draco Sang death rites were poison in his mouth, but they were all he knew. He didn't continue. His world was dissolving into agony and confusion. What was he supposed to say? To do?

"I believe we will see him again," Shale said.

How many had she lost? She laid a comforting hand on his thigh. He latched onto her hope. It kept him from drowning. He had to keep breathing. He had to keep thinking.

Lyko howled. He howled as if he could destroy the world with his pain. The song of sorrow rumbled through Ferth's bones and pierced his raw heart.

"Shh, Lyko," Shale pleaded as the torment rang through the forest.

Ferth rested a palm on the wolf's head, and Lyko's grief silenced. But the pain still howled through Shale's heart. The brothers had seen each other truly, like mirror images, but Ferth's face was sharper under a thick beard, and his hair hung in a wild mane. His Draco uniform draped loosely around his shoulders. Ferth, the fearsome Draco Sang who tore through her dreams, now knelt before her in all his human glory—striking and vibrant.

The brothers had come together for one bright moment before they were ripped apart. Would she ever experience that same joy? She had already experienced that pain.

The joy that spread over Cal's face when he'd seen Ferth, *saved* Ferth, had lit up the night. Beauty more exquisite than any darkness.

Her soul shattered for the brothers, two halves that could never be whole.

"Four more Dracos incoming," Xandra said in Shale's mind. *"And the raven is back."*

The raven hewan had followed them across the river, keeping back, but watching with keen eyes. "We need to go," Shale said.

Blood trickled down Lyko's bite marks on Ferth's arm as he scooped up his brother's lifeless body. With the white wolf in front and the gray wolf behind, Ferth and Shale fled Skotar. As they passed the slumped sentries she'd killed at the delta, the raven swooped over. It let out a beckoning caw before flapping south, guiding them home.

ACKNOWLEDGMENTS

Thank you to Monster Ivy Publishing, to Mary Gray, Cammie Larsen, and the entire team for believing in my book. Thank you to Rich Storrs for his insightful edits and for his hard work in polishing and elevating this manuscript. Thank you to my awesome family, especially my mom, Bonnie Jean, and my sister, Katherine, for reading my early drafts and giving me much needed encouragement. Thank you for my husband, Doug, and our kids for all the times you let me lock myself in the office to write. Thank you to Rebekah Romney for sharing your expertise, both as an attorney and a writer. Thank you to my Texas writer's group: Jen Looft, Jen Johnson, Lisa Lewis, Debbie Ochoa, Stacy Wells, Priya Ardis, and Nuha Said. Thank you to my California writer's group: Jen White, Autumn McAlpin, and Cara Cragun. And most importantly, thanks to God for inspiring me to start writing fiction, for gifting me the perseverance to keep going, and the creativity to spin a compelling story.

Mary Beesley believes humans are born to create, and promotes creativity in all its beautiful forms. She's learning calligraphy and watercolor. She loves exploring our magnificent planet and finding all the best places to eat around the world. But nothing beats coming home and sharing a pot of slow-simmered spaghetti Bolognese and homemade sourdough with  friends and family. If she's not in her writing chair, you'll probably find her hiking in the Utah mountains with her husband and four children. Find Mary at her website www.-marybeesley.com and on Instagram or Twitter @maryr-beesley.

www.ingramcontent.com/pod-product-compliance
Lightning Source LLC
Chambersburg PA
CBHW070746190726
48292CB00002B/430